Dead Reckoning

by

Su García

Copyright

Dead Reckoning

Map of Symi

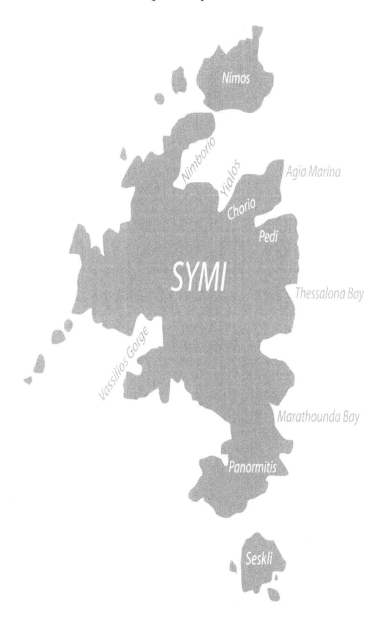

Dead Reckoning

In the midst of this chopping sea of civilized life, such are the clouds and storms and quicksands and thousand-and-one items to be allowed for, that a man has to live, if he would not founder and go to the bottom and not make his port at all, by dead reckoning, and he must be a great calculator indeed who succeeds.

(Henry David Thoreau)

Prologue
1992

As the music reached a crescendo, Marta Fabrini, in full view of thousands, threw herself off the St. Angelo Castle battlements and disappeared from view. All who saw this violent act held their breath. Seconds later, a spontaneous thunderclap erupted in La Scala Opera House in Milan as the audience, rising en-masse, paid homage to this forty-two-year-old Italian soprano. When the curtains re-opened, Marta Fabrini walked forward into a sound wave of frenzied approbation and slowly bowed as single stemmed roses landed at her feet. She should have been revelling in the well-earned applause but her mind was elsewhere. Both her husband and son were about to face important challenges in their own lives and they needed her at home to give them encouragement and support.

Antonio Romano, Marta's husband, was Milan's chief prosecution counsellor and about to prosecute a corrupt Italian Minister in a high profile case which required his constant police protection; while Paolo, her ten-year-old son, had a trial for his school's junior football team which, for him, was far more important.

As Marta took her third curtain call she wondered why she persisted in juggling a demanding solo career with her roles as wife and mother. Her Greek mother-in-law always remained tight-lipped on the subject, showing her displeasure with raised eyebrows whenever Marta failed to put her family first. Well, thought Marta, as the curtain closed for the final time, Signora Romano would have no grounds for complaint this time. The Milan Opera house was only minutes from her home in Via Manzoni.

Via Manzoni, Milan - (07.30 hrs)
Antonio Romano walked into the kitchen, his tense, handsome
face clean shaven, his dark designer suit well cut, a Latin
mixture of pure testosterone and sound values. A man at the
height of his career.
  He hadn't slept. He had tried, but the tangled mess of his bed
linen attested to his lack of success. At four in the morning he
had given up, left his wife sleeping soundly and walked into the
lounge, a huge expanse of modern glass, chrome and cream
leather, his naked torso reflected in the mirrored surfaces as he'd
moved through the empty space. Within a few hours he would,
like his wife, give his own polished performance, but his stage
would be Milan's imposing courthouse and his audience, three
senior Italian judges, whom he had to persuade to send Carlo
Cantotti to jail for life. There would be no single stemmed roses
at his feet, no resounding applause from the gallery, only quiet
gratitude from the many who had suffered at the hands of this
crooked Government Minister.
  As he poured himself some fresh orange juice, he felt like a
man on death row rather than Milan's public prosecutor. The
slight shake of his hand as he spilt juice on the work surface was
not lost on Marta as she stood by the open door, her hair
dishevelled, her towelling robe hiding her nakedness beneath.
After years of pre-performance nerves she knew what a
churning stomach, dry mouth and sweaty palms felt like and
sympathised with her husband. She had no doubt that Carlo
Cantotti's defence would be ripped apart by her husband's
skilful cross-examination techniques, but, right now, Antonio
needed her to convince him of that fact.
  She walked up behind him and placed her arms around his
waist in a tender embrace. 'I love you,' she whispered, 'and I'm
so proud of you.'

Antonio stroked her hands and she felt some of the tension ease from his taut muscles. 'I just wish this case was over and we could get back to some normality, all this constant police protection is doing Paolo no good at all.' He sighed audibly. 'Our son told me yesterday that he felt like a freak at school and wanted to know why his class mates were avoiding him.'

Marta's heart sank. 'What did you say?'

'What could I say? How do you explain to a ten-year-old that evil men like Carlo Cantotti will stop at nothing to get their own way, including kidnapping a child.'

Marta hated their situation as much as her husband but she knew someone had to prosecute Italy's criminal faction and if police protection was the only way to achieve this, then that was a price worth paying. She turned him round and placed her arms around his neck. 'Antonio, it won't be forever. Once this case is over we can take Paolo back to Symi for the holidays where he can be as free as a bird, just like you were as a child.' She reached up on tiptoe and brushed her lips across his mouth. 'One day, Counsellor, your son will be old enough to understand and will idolise you for standing up to such men.'

'Speaking of which, where is our future provider?' he asked, looking at his watch over her shoulder.

'Sleeping the sleep of the innocent, no doubt,' replied Marta, pealing herself from his chest and heading for Paolo's bedroom.

'Tell him I'm leaving in ten minutes and if he doesn't want to miss his football trial he'd better be ready.'

Marta entered Paolo's bedroom and looked down on a dishevelled head of dark-brown curls half buried under a Batman design duvet. She threw the cover back exposing Snoopy pyjamas, two empty crisp packets and the latest Nintendo toy.

'Wakey, wakey, Paolo. Your father said if you're not ready in ten minutes he's going to leave without you.'

'But what about my football trail?' wailed Paolo as he jumped out of bed and rushed to the bathroom still half asleep, his pyjama bottoms at half-mast.

Marta shook her head and placed the empty crisp packets in her pocket. Her eyes scanned the bedroom like a CCTV camera and paused at Paolo's bulging school rucksack lying on the floor, his football strip, boots, socks and shin guards crammed inside, filling every square inch. She assumed Paolo's nanny had packed it the previous evening while she was at the theatre and felt a twinge of guilt for not being there to do it herself.

She picked up the photograph frame sitting on her son's bedside table and looked at the picture taken off the Dodecanese island of Symi the previous summer. Antonio, Marta and Paolo were sitting in the cockpit of their classic yacht, *Arabesque*, looking tanned, wind-blown and happy. A family without a care in the world.

'I'm counting to ten, Paolo,' she shouted through the bathroom door, a glint of mischief in her eyes. 'Your father and I will be very upset if you miss your football trial because you were playing Nintendo games long into the night and then overslept.' She placed the frame back on the bedside table and picked up the rucksack before walking towards the hall. 'One, two, three...'

At eight fifteen, Antonio opened the apartment door and nodded to the Italian police officer who was standing guard outside.

'*Buongiorno*, Officer.'

'Counsellor. Allow me to take your baggage.'

They moved towards the lift, Paolo struggling into his blazer and hopping on one leg as he pulled his socks up, Marta

8

ramming his school cap on to his head as he shot by. 'Where's my rucksack?' he yelled down the hall.

'The police officer has it, Paolo, now hurry up,' said his father, holding the lift door open.

'Don't I get a hug?' called Marta.

'Oh, Mamma,' complained Paolo as he rushed back into her arms before disentangling himself from her embrace and dashing back along the corridor.

'Good luck with the trial,' she shouted as the lift doors closed swallowing up her words.

She walked back into the lounge, her mind returning to the thorny question of her career. The demands on her time as an opera soprano were pulling her further and further away from her role as a wife and mother. Paolo is growing up so quickly, she thought, and I'm missing so much of it. She sighed as she opened the balcony doors knowing that she had only one choice. If she was to enjoy her son's childhood, her career would have to be put on hold.

She peered over the balustrade as Antonio's Maserati appeared from the underground garage and moved out onto Via Manzoni, police outriders at the front and back, blue lights flashing and sirens wailing. She could see Paolo's little face smiling up at her from the back seat, his hand waving madly. With a broad grin on her face she waved back, her heart full of love for the two most important men in her life.

Moments later an explosion shattered shop windows, glass flying everywhere as the Maserati left the road in a ball of fire, the car bomb turning it into a tangled mass of charred metal and torn body parts. Marta's screams pierced the morning air as debris rained down on Via Manzoni.

Chapter One
The Aegean - 1995

Saturday (pre-dawn)

Only a few goats witnessed the Emerald Star as she approached the Dodecanese island of Symi in the dead of night and let go her anchor off the enclosed bay of Ayia Marina. There were no navigation lights, no sound from within the one-hundred-ton vessel, only the outline of a rusty blue hull barely visible in the starlit night.

Ghostly figures took to small craft and glided across the inlet in silence, the plaintive wail of a baby quickly muffled by his mother's breast. When the crew returned, the Emerald Star slowly reversed into deeper water and evaporated into the night leaving no footprint, her mission complete.

Panayiotis Stanis leant his elbows on the coach roof of *Phoebe II* and helmed the tiller with his right foot. He had been out all night, casting trammel nets into the Aegean Sea off the south coast of Symi, hauling red snapper, sea bream, bass, mackerel and little fishes, all destined for the homes and restaurants around Yialos harbour and in Ano Symi, the island's main village situated high on the hill above the quay which the locals referred to as the Chorio. Like his father and grandfather before him, Panayiotis loved fishing and had no wish ever to leave the island of his birth.

Phoebe II was his pride and joy, named after his daughter who was born only weeks before he completed building the boat. With the help of skilled craftsmen he had followed an age-old Symiot boat building tradition, finally launching the vessel from the slipway in Pedi Bay, the reflection of her white-painted hull, royal-blue cuddy and trim shimmering in the aquamarine clear water.

She was still immaculate even though she had plied the waters around Symi for eighteen years, her tripod of metal rollers standing proudly on the starboard bow, always ready to haul-in the yellow and orange nets. She had protected Panayiotis through fair winds and foul and, like a homing pigeon, she could find her own way home.

He rounded the Kouloundros Rock light at the south-east corner of Symi and pointed the bow north, feeling the warm breeze move across the back of his neck as he changed direction. It was a moonless night, the sky a pincushion of stars, the sparkling water alive with phosphorescence from the boat's bow wave, his mind far away on the other side of the island where he imagined Marta Romano sleeping soundly in her villa. The thought gave him a warm feeling inside.

Two dolphins raced along his starboard gunwale, their passing marked by a fluorescent silver flash. Panayiotis smiled and raised his hand in salute; like him, the dolphins had fished these waters for years. In reply, they leapt out of the sea, arcing through the night air before diving back below *Phoebe II's* hull and circling once more, playing in the turbulence of the boat's wake before moving north-east into Symi Channel to feed.

Panayiotis watched them go, remembering his daughter swimming amongst these gentle mammals years before in Thessalona Bay, while he hauled up his fishing pots at dawn. She was only seven then but already a confident swimmer, a tiny mermaid whose giggles echoed off the bay's sheer cliffs as the dolphins' snouts tickled her legs and arms.

What would she be dreaming of now, he wondered, in that fancy apartment in Athens where her mother had taken her when she was eight years old? Did she dream of Symi and the dolphins or had the bright lights of the city turned her head in

11

the years since she'd left her island home? He wished he could share this night with her and whispered a prayer for her dreams. The rhythmic throb of a multi-cylinder diesel engine punctured his thoughts, his ear immediately cocked to the sound. Panayiotis stared ahead expecting to see the navigation lights of a larger vessel but nothing pierced the darkness. He frowned and cut the engine. His ears were not playing tricks on him, something was out there and it was a lot bigger than Phoebe II. He tracked the sound as it crossed his horizon, moving in a south-easterly direction and slowly fading. Panayiotis placed his broad hand on the tiller, his muscles flexed. Minutes later the boat rocked from side to side taking each wave broadside as the wash from the invisible ship rippled across the water's surface towards Symi's limestone crags before crashing against its rocky shoreline. Lashing the helm, he walked into the cuddy and picked up his VHF radio handset and selected Channel 16.

'All ships, all ships, all ships. This is a navigation warning from the fishing vessel *Phoebe II, Phoebe II, Phoebe II*. My position is, three-six degrees, three-five minutes North and two-seven degrees, five-three minutes East. A large motor vessel steaming without lights is travelling in a south-easterly direction from the Symi Channel into the Rodos Sea and is a danger to shipping. End of navigation warning. *Phoebe II*, out.'

He replaced the handset in its housing on the cuddy wall. Any vessel cruising at night without lights was not only a hazard to shipping but probably up to no good. Panayiotis was intrigued.

Chapter Two

Marta shot up in bed, woken by her own screams bouncing off the bedroom walls, sweat pouring down her face, her heart pumping against her chest.

She had been standing on a deserted stage looking out on an empty auditorium. The conductor had tapped his batten on his music stand and raised his arms. As the opening bars of 'O Mio Babbino Caro' filled the theatre, Marta saw Antonio and Paolo appear in the aisle and slowly walk towards her, her son's face wreathed in smiles.

She knelt at the footlights, her arms outstretched, longing to hold him, but the orchestra pit was too wide.

'Mamma,' cried Paolo as his father lifted him over the heads of the string section. 'Mamma.'

She tried to grab his tiny hands but before their fingers could intertwine the auditorium exploded, the elegant architecture erupting into a million red and gold fragments, Paolo's small body flying through the debris, his limbs twisted and torn, trapped between broken violin strings and ragged pages of sheet music. 'NO,' she screamed, 'NO! NO!'

Marta lay back against her pillows and began to breathe deeply trying to calm her racing heart. Her eyes stared into the darkness refusing to close while-ever the nightmare persisted in filling her retina. She felt exhausted and profoundly sad and, in the silence of the night, knew she would not get back to sleep.

It had been months since the nightmare had plagued her dreams and she wondered, as she moved around the kitchen making a hot drink, what had triggered its return. Over the years she had tried everything to combat post-traumatic grief, but just when she thought she was winning the battle, it grabbed hold of her once more and refused to let go.

Holding a mug of freshly-filtered coffee, she wandered out into the balmy Mediterranean night, the perfume of jasmine filling her senses from the bushes growing in profusion around the garden. She crossed the lawn and made her way along a gravel path to the octagonal stone and glass building perched on top of a craggy outcrop of rocks. This was Marta's music room where, years before, she had spent many happy hours studying opera scores and playing the piano while Antonio and Paolo kicked a football around in the garden or swam in the warm, aquamarine waters at the foot of the Vassilios Gorge far below. This room had now become her refuge from the world, a place where she could lick her wounds and try to overcome the pain of her loss. It had been three long years and the black void somewhere within her solar plexus refused to heal.

Through the plate-glass window Venus sparkled in the western sky, its silver light flickering across the rippling waters of the Aegean Sea. She sank onto the piano stool and stared out across the black liquid expanse and tried to still her mind, the violent images gradually fading, leaving her spent.

Lights from a small boat crossed her horizon reminding her that *Phoebe II* was somewhere out on the east of the island, her skipper returning home with his catch after a night's fishing. She wondered if Panayiotis was thinking of her, the thought acting as a balm to her troubled mind.

Panayiotis Stanis and Antonio Romano had known each other since childhood, as boys, swimming off the rocks or fishing with Panayiotis's father during many long, hot summer vacations. Antonio's mother was a Symiot and the family's house sat regally above Yialos Harbour commanding magnificent views across the bay.

14

Marta had known that the island held a very special place in Antonio's heart and was delighted when, years later, he'd suggested building a villa on the island's west coast where they could both escape the pressures of Milan life. In her honour he had named their island home Villa Fabrini, and, since his death, the villa had become her sanctuary. A place where she could find peace and try to mend.

Panayiotis had been her rock, always there to pick up the pieces whenever her world disintegrated around her. He had stood by her side as she buried her husband and son in the Cimitero Monumentale, in Milan and, when Antonio's mother died of a broken heart three months later, he was there once more providing much needed support at the old lady's graveside in Symi.

Finally, when Marta had collapsed on stage during a performance of Tosca, it was Panayiotis who had persuaded her to leave Milan and make Symi her permanent home. She could recall standing in the apartment on Via Manzoni wringing her hands.

'How can I, Panayiotis? What about my life here? My career?''

'You need to find peace, Marta.' His hands had closed around hers, feeling strong and comforting. 'There's a good bereavement counsellor on Rhodes, only an hour away by ferry. And Milan is a short flight from Athens when you need to return.'

It had all made perfect sense.

Many times since that day he had been there as her grief threatened to engulf her, his presence giving her the strength to carry on, her anchor in a turbulent sea. Marta adored him and always would. She sipped her coffee and closed her eyes.

15

There was only one problem. Panayiotis made her feel guilty. She was well aware that he loved her but she was incapable of returning that love, preferring to hold onto her past like a talisman, keeping Antonio and Paolo close and refusing to contemplate a future without them.

Marta lifted the lid of the piano and ran her fingers gently over the keys, the random notes forming into a lullaby, one of Paolo's favourites. The melody tore at her scars, the masochistic action only adding melancholy to her pain.

Licking tears from the side of her mouth she played on, her eyes following the lights of the small boat as it disappeared from view, her mind willing Panayiotis to release her from her guilt and find a new life with someone who deserved him and would make him happy.

Her inner voice immediately countered that wish. 'It's impossible, Marta, and you know it. Panayiotis cannot walk away from you anymore than you can move on.'

Chapter Three

In the east, a ridge of mountains broke free of the night, their stark outline visible in the dawn light as *Phoebe II* chugged passed the deep inlet of Pedi, the village waterfront and pier still deep in shadow at the far end of the bay. Panayiotis stretched his well-muscled arms above his head and cracked his fingers to ease the stiffness left after a night's fishing. Wooden boxes lay at his feet full of the night's catch, silvered scales catching the light of the sun's first rays.

It would take another thirty minutes to reach his mooring in Yialos harbour where he would mend his nets and sell his catch to Symiot housewives and restaurateurs before climbing the Kali Strata steps to the Chorio high above where Symiots had lived for centuries, protected from invading pirates by their strong castle.

It had become his daily ritual to breakfast at the Jazz Café, two-thirds of the way up the ancient stone staircase, then continue on to his mother's house beside Syllogos Square for a shower and a well-earned rest.

He walked to the bow enjoying the sight of flying fish fanning out ahead of the prow and gliding low over the sea's surface for many metres before crashing back into the sea. As he watched this flying display his eye caught a flash of light on the hillside above the small bay of Ayia Marina.

Normally the sun's reflection on a shard of glass or a quartz stone would have passed unchallenged, but intuition kept Panayiotis's eyes glued to the lower ridge. He slowly scanned the slope, devoid of vegetation except for the clumps of maquis which clung to the rocks like limpets. He saw nothing at first then backtracked to a particularly gnarled bush, his eyes adjusting to the shadows. Something was out of place; a patch of red, conspicuous amongst the coarse green foliage. It moved.

Grabbing his binoculars off the peg beside the radio, he pointed the lenses at the gnarled tree and brought the scrap of red into focus. By the bush sat an African woman in a red shawl. By her feet a small boy threw stones at a tin can and to her left three men lay on the ground. Gradually he picked out other groups scattered across the hillside, some with head-in-hands, others watching his fishing boat as it motored past before disappearing from view.

Panayiotis slowly lowered the binoculars onto the cuddy roof. It didn't take a genius to recognise illegal immigrants littering the Symi skyline nor to associate them with a vessel creeping about Greek waters without lights.

The information made him feel sick. Panayiotis was a humanitarian at heart and he knew that these refugees had no home, no prospects and no money. They had been dumped on a small Greek island, just five miles from the Turkish coast by crooks who made their living from human trafficking. This dishevelled group were now in European territory but they probably believed that the land beneath their feet was the Greek mainland. That lay two hundred miles to the northwest across the Aegean Sea so these displaced people had been duped and their life savings were now in the hands of criminals. Panayiotis knew he had no choice but to bring their dreams of a better life to a premature end.

The VHF handset rested in his right palm, his thumb hovering above the PTT (press to transmit) button. He paused, delaying the moment when his words would shatter the ideals of these simple people. He knew that many of them would be dehydrated, possibly starving, and that the elderly and very young would be incapable of further progress. He also knew that his daughter would never forgive him for what he was about to do; nevertheless, he depressed the button illuminating the TX sign on the VHF handset and his voice went out across the airwaves.

'Hellenic Coastguard. Hellenic Coastguard. Hellenic Coastguard. This is the fishing vessel *Phoebe II* . . .'

Nishan Amato dragged his body along a ditch keeping in the shadows of the low shrubs and wild-pink oleander bushes. His khaki shirt was badly torn, his brown trousers stained with goat droppings and amber coloured dust. Bloodied scratches perforated his African skin, his wiry hair impregnated with burrs. Only his dark-brown eyes could be seen staring out through the undergrowth, a hunted animal, increasingly dehydrated and far from home.

Having turned his back on the beach he had moved, alone, over the low hills, cutting behind the silent buildings of the waterfront before turning inland. High above him on an elevated ridge a large, white village, washed in morning sunlight, dominated the valley, the eastern slopes below becoming ever more visible to human scrutiny as the night-shadows retreated towards the sea.

Intent on staying as far from civilisation as possible he followed a dry-stone wall as it crossed rough ground, keeping close and bending low. A revving engine cut the silence. Nishan peered over the wall and saw a car speed down the winding road from the upper village and park by the water's edge. Three uniformed officers and two large dogs emerged from the vehicle and set off along the bay's coastline heading for Nishan's original landing site. Out at sea, a gunmetal motor boat raced south, white spume flying from its stern, a blue and white diagonal flash on its bow, then, failing to find what it was looking for, it had made a 'U' turn and sped back north.

19

Nishan knew it was essential to keep on the move and to locate an isolated homestead somewhere inland where he could find water, maybe some fruit or nuts from the cultivated trees and good shelter, before the burning sun leeched any remaining energy from his joints.

His eyes searched for an escape route. To his left, high above a gulley cutting between two hills he could see a small, white church perched on a ledge, stark against the sterile earth. A tall stone wall spanned its base and a cluster of dark-green trees stood like sentinels at its rear. The church was isolated from anything else in the valley, ideal for his needs and where there were trees, he thought, there might be water.

To reach the gulley he needed to cross open ground and had to move fast before the sunlight exposed his position. Checking behind and seeing no human activity he crouched ever lower and ran, hoping his dust-covered clothing would act as camouflage, never stopping until he was again in cover amongst the undergrowth. His lungs were burning, the vein in his temple pumping hard. Perhaps, he thought, beyond the next hill there will be a major road leading to the interior and the anonymity of a large city.

Nishan began to climb, scrambling over rocky boulders, their jagged edges stabbing at his skin and slicing across his joints. Spiked bushes tore at his hair and clothing while loose stones hampered his passage, the smallest wedging themselves inside his cracked plastic shoes.

Pausing for breath he looked up, dust particles clogging his nose and mouth. He tried to focus but his eyes were staring through a haze, his eyeballs pitted with dirt and the gulley was now getting steeper. He began to claw his way over the rocks scrambling ever closer to the tall stone wall.

A few metres from the top his hand grabbed at a rock and he felt it move. Seconds later the boulder crashed down the gulley smashing into his left ankle as it bounced away over the uneven surface. He bit his tongue trying to stop himself screaming from the intense pain. Nishan was at the bottom of his reserves, willpower alone pushing him on.

The solid wall towered above him, too high to scale so he hobbled around its curved perimeter until he reached a heavily padlocked wooden door. Resting his back against the solid frame he looked up, unsure if he could go on, his morale fading fast. Then his brain registered the sound of running water.

He mounted some steps to his right and hovered at a wrought-iron gate checking for danger, fighting the urge to rush forward to the source of the sound. All seemed deserted. The gate grated on its hinges but he didn't care. His eyes flicked from side-to-side as he staggered across a flat, stone terrace separating the church from a locked and shuttered house and paused above a sunken yard. Embedded in the chapel wall was an alcove, at its centre, a tap. Stumbling down the three steps he fell on his knees and turned it on.

Nothing happened. He twisted the top of the tap back and forth willing water to gush out but the spout remained stubbornly dry. Desperately looking for the source of the sound he crawled on and found a concrete cistern tucked between the rocks, its metal inspection plate heavily padlocked, running water evident within. In sheer frustration he slammed the lid with the edge of his clenched fist knowing his action was futile, the tinkling sound of driving him crazy.

Returning to the terrace he peered over the edge and couldn't believe his eyes. There, locked within the circular wall was an irrigated garden. Tomatoes, melons, green peppers, aubergines and salad leaves were growing in regimented lines between trees of apricots, almonds, figs and lemons.

He felt his stomach clench, the sight too much to bear. Staggering backwards, his eyes blinded by the sun, he pushed open the chapel door and collapsed inside on the cool, tiled floor, all hope gone. The Madonna and Child looked down on him from a wooden screen; Mary, cradling her son to her neck, her expression one of compassion and love. He looked up into those limpid eyes and asked her for a miracle before handing his destiny into her tender care and drifting into oblivion.

Chapter Four

Marta twisted the throttle of her Piaggio motor-scooter and engaged first gear. She was running late. The wheels bit into the hard-packed surface of the drive and powered forward, away from Villa Fabrini.

The morning air felt fresh on her face as she accelerated onto the main road, her dark hair streaming out behind, still damp from the shower and held away from her face by a cream and white silk headband. She was not pretty but her full lips, wide cheek bones, long straight nose, and high forehead harmonised perfectly with her deep-set soft-brown eyes below sculptured dark eyebrows. Hers was an imposing face, a face full of character.

Snaking around the hillside she approached the Chorio and threaded her way through the winding back lanes of the village calling a cheery hello to shopkeepers and the elderly as she went by.

When she reached the road above Yialos she paused and looked down. The sight never failed to raise her spirits. There, far below, Yialos harbour was spread out at her feet, a gem of the Mediterranean. The cluster of gabled villas painted in pale ochres, yellows, blues, greens and paprika seemed to hover above the harbour like a mirage. A grey and white clock tower stood at the point of the quay backed by a two-storey building which housed Symi's Hellenic Police Station painted in Greek colours, the national flag flapping in the breeze. Yialos's shops, cafés and restaurants were hidden from view under cream canvas awnings while a mixture of fishing boats, yachts and motor boats lined the edge of the quay, the whole picture shimmering in the early morning light. She revved the throttle and sped down the long straight to the hairpin bend overlooking

23

the outer basin then turned and headed towards the lower village.

The quayside was quiet at this time of the morning, a brief respite before the day's complement of foreign tourists arrived by ferry from Rhodes to enjoy the ambience of this well-known ancient port. Driving parallel with the water, she imagined the shop-keepers setting out their wares in the distance; a cornucopia of local crafts, sponges and holiday trinkets to entice visitors to spend their drachmas. Veering left she turned uphill, knowing *Phoebe II* would be at the head of the harbour gently rocking against the harbour wall. Marta smiled knowing that Panayiotis would be waiting for his breakfast at the Jazz Café.

Negotiating the ever narrowing lanes which meandered behind the villas on the south side of Yialos, she finally drew to a stop by a crumbling stone wall a few feet below Casa Romano.

Antonio's family home stood majestically on a corner of the Kali Strata where the ancient steps took a sharp right turn towards the upper village. Panayiotis was sitting by the front door as she came into view, a cool bag by his side and a brown cardboard box at his feet. She thought how handsome he was in a rugged sort of way.

'*Kalimera*, Marta. You seem to be running a little late this morning.'

'Yes. I overslept.'

Panayiotis frowned. 'Marco delivered these about ten minutes ago.' He tapped the brown box with his foot. 'I told him you'd pay him later.'

'Thanks.' Marta opened the box, the aroma of freshly baked bread playing havoc with her rumbling stomach. She picked it up, unlocked the front door, and disappeared into the cool dark interior. Panayiotis followed and began moving tables and chairs from the interior out onto the terrace while Marta started up the coffee machine. It was eight forty-five and the Jazz Café was about to open for business.

Casa Romano had taken on a new lease of life in the last year. The ground floor had been re-modelled into a bijou cocktail-bar café; another of Panayiotis's ideas. Marta's mother-in-law had grown up in this house, only leaving it when she had met Antonio's Italian father. For years it had been used as a family holiday home but no one was now alive to enjoy it.

'It would be perfect,' Panayiotis had said one wet Thursday afternoon eighteen months earlier as he followed Marta into the entrance hall at Villa Fabrini carrying some furniture. 'Casa Romano is ideally situated for all those exhausted tourists who make the climb up the four hundred Kali Strata steps. What could be better than to sit beside the historic thoroughfare looking out on one of the best views in the Mediterranean, having a morning coffee or an evening cocktail?'

'What do I know about running a bar café, Panayiotis?' Marta assumed he was joking. 'You can't make cocktails with the drinking song from La Traviata.'

'No one is asking you too.' He paused, appearing to tread very carefully. 'I just thought the project would do you good, take your mind off things.'

'Yes, but . . .'

'No buts, Marta. Think of it as therapy. I'm not suggesting you run it. Get a manager in to do the work or lease the business to someone else.' He hesitated. 'I know Antonio would have liked the idea. He may have been a lawyer but he had a commercial head on his shoulders and would not have wanted to see his family's home left to rot.'

Marta slumped onto an antique chaise-longue in the hall, her knees shaking, her face crumbling at the mention of Antonio's name. 'Don't you think I have enough on my plate right now

25

completing on the sale of the apartment in Milan and tying up Antonio's estate?'

She could feel his strong hands grip her shoulders, lifting her back onto her feet and pinning her there until she felt strong enough to take her own weight. 'All I'm asking is that you think about it.'

'OK. OK. I'll think about it,' she whispered, resting her head on his chest.

'Look, you wouldn't be doing it alone, I'll be here.' He leant his chin on her crown, the aroma of gardenias from her hair invading his senses. 'You could make the upstairs into an apartment for guests or stay there yourself some nights rather than drive back here.'

Marta shook her head.

'It would be a sound investment, Marta, and on the basis your mother-in-law would disapprove, I assumed you would you find the idea appealing, and a good way to spend some of her inheritance.'

Marta's fist came out looking for human contact. He ducked and walked into her kitchen. 'That's more like the Marta I know,' he chuckled. 'Coffee?'

The Romanos' wealth had never bothered Panayiotis. Marta knew that jealousy was not in his DNA. Antonio had always said that the fisherman wouldn't have known what to do with wealth even if he'd had it. However, it hadn't stopped Marta's husband from suggesting numerous ways for his friend to make money out of tourism to improve his financial situation, but Panayiotis had just shrugged his shoulders and carried on fishing. Funny, thought Marta, as she stood at the kitchen door watching him operating the coffee machine, he was now trying to do the same to her.

Despite Marta's immediate rejection, the seed was sewn and steadily took root. A month later, returning from a flying visit to Milan to speak to the Italian police detective about the unsolved murders, she had stood on the quayside watching Panayiotis mending his nets.

'Jazz Café,' she announced.

'What?' Panayiotis looked up from *Phoebe II's* cockpit.

'Jazz Café. I thought I'd call Casa Romano the Jazz Café. Even a soprano knows a thing or two about jazz.'

Within weeks, the conversion was complete and on the day the new sign was fixed to the wall the whole village had come out to celebrate, the local priest adding his blessing as he downed a large glass of Ouzo.

The only person who did not seem enamoured by the opening was Panayiotis's mother. Anastasia Stanis, dressed in black, her grey wispy hair tied back in a bun at the nape of her neck, had remained in the background, accepting Marta's hospitality out of duty rather than joy.

The venture was a complete success, just as Panayiotis had predicted, and Marta found that she was enjoying herself for the first time since turning her back on Milan. The Jazz Café had become her hobby, giving her a purpose in life and a reason to get out of bed in a morning.

'Did you have a good night?' she asked as she appeared on the terrace and placed two cups of espresso coffee, a basket of freshly cut bread, some soft feta cheese and a jar of local thyme honey on the marble topped table, two knives wrapped in Jazz Café serviettes appearing from her skirt pocket.

'Not bad,' said Panayiotis, sampling the coffee and nodding towards a feral kitten playing with a stone further down the Kali

Strata steps. 'I've brought you some sea bass.' He pointed to his cool bag sitting on the bar counter. 'What about you?'

Their eyes locked. Marta's hands dropped to her lap as she looked away. 'I...had another nightmare.'

'But I thought you said they'd stopped,' he countered, trying to sound unconcerned and failing.

'I did. Maybe it's the time of year that's brought them back.'

Panayiotis pressed his fingers into his forehead, the third anniversary of the murders instantly relevant. 'I hate thinking of you all alone at Villa Fabrini, especially at this time.'

Marta bit her lip wondering if he was going to say something that they would both regret. She held her breath.

'You should get yourself a pet,' he announced, throwing the feral kitten a piece of bread.

Marta exhaled slowly and watched the small black ball-of-fluff pounce on the offering and felt her stomach clench, remembering how Paolo had often pestered her for a kitten and had been refused. The disappointment on her son's face had been palpable. She looked at Panayiotis and shook her head. 'Having a kitten around the house would be a constant reminder of Paolo and I couldn't cope with that, yet.'

'Just a thought,' said Panayiotis, pouring more coffee. 'Just think about it.'

She couldn't help smiling. 'How many times have I heard you say that?'

He leant across the table and wiped a crumb from her cheek. 'You have to learn to love again someday, Marta. Maybe loving a pet would be a good start.' Marta drummed her fingers on the table top. He lowered his hand and quickly changed the subject. 'Now, what were you asking me?'

Marta brushed her cheek with a napkin, thankful that he wasn't going to press her further. 'I was asking you about fishing.'

For a split-second neither spoke then Panayiotis leant back in his chair and began to recount what had happened to him since four o'clock that morning. '. . . I was passing Thessalona Bay in the dark when a large freighter crossed my path going the other way without navigation lights . . .' Marta sat transfixed, her eyes gradually widening in disbelief. '. . . Right now,' he finished, 'the police are bringing the immigrants in piecemeal and dumping them by the harbour in Kambos Square.'

'How many are there?' asked Marta, horrified.

'I don't know. I asked Sergeant Nicolaides when I was making a statement at the police station earlier. He thought there were over fifty.'

'What about the ship that brought them here?'

'Probably tucked away safe and sound in a Turkish port by now. That's where it was heading when I lost track of it, but then I don't have radar on *Phoebe II* so maybe some other vessel was able to follow her movements after my "all ships" radio call on VHF.'

'What will happen to them, Panayiotis?' In her mind, Marta was already making up emergency food packs and supplying fresh clothes.

Panayiotis looked down at his fingernails and went very quiet.

'Panayiotis. What will happen to them?'

'They'll be taken to Rhodes by ferry, processed there, then shipped onto Athens where they will be incarcerated in the Lavrios Detention Centre until the Greek Government decides what to do with them.' He wasn't enjoying this one little bit.

'But you said there were women, children and babies in the group. What will happen to them?'

Panayiotis looked at Marta, his expression pained. 'I don't know, Marta. I really don't know.'

Chapter Five

Saturday (mid-morning)

Nishan Amato awoke with a start. He had no idea how long he had been asleep but the sun would have lasered his forehead had it not be for the tall fir trees providing some shade. He ached all over, the skin around his ankle resembling an inflated balloon, throbbing in unison with his pulse.

Earlier, his sub-conscious mind had registered female voices, far off, but getting closer. He blinked fatigue from his eyes and crawled to the chapel door, cracked it open and peered out. Three women were walking along a narrow track towards him carrying wicker baskets and talking animatedly. Sliding through the door, closing it quietly behind him, he had crabbed his way to steps at the rear of the terrace leading out onto the hillside and found cover in the rock-strewn undergrowth of a fir copse.

He now listened but there was no sound coming from the buildings below so he assumed the women had gone. From the corner of his vision, however, he saw movement to his right. He waited, not daring to move a muscle. A nanny goat stepped forward into the edge of his vision, her kid standing a few feet behind, the mother's slit eyes watching him closely.

Nishan closed his eyes and silently thanked the Virgin Mary for answering his prayers and softly began to hum. The goat moved her head from side-to-side listening to the melody and very gradually stepped towards the source of the sound. Nishan had done this many times before in his homeland and knew that his voice calmed and mesmerised the animals making them easier to handle.

Ignoring his sore throat, he continued to hum. Gradually the gap between them narrowed until the nanny goat's whiskers brushed Nishan's nose. He slowly removed his right shoe and pushed it beneath her as sweat dripped into his eyes from his hairline. The nanny goat stood perfectly still and allowed his right hand to stroke her left flank, his shoulder gently easing her into position, his voice continuing to fill her ears with a lilting refrain.

Sliding his hand down her abdomen, his fingers located one of her teats. He paused. A muscle rippled down her body and settled. Nishan began massaging one teat with a gentle downward action, aiming jets of warm milk into his shoe, only ceasing to hum when the milk slid down the back of his throat, the velvet liquid soothing his larynx and quenching his thirst. Lying back against the tree trunk he watched the goat step away, her kid nuzzling the teat from the other side and taking its fill, its action flooding Nishan's brain with memories, making him homesick for his own goats and his old way of life.

Attempting to get his bearings he stood, clinging to the Cypress tree for support and trying not to put weight on his left foot. He could see the well-trodden track leading away from the chapel and decided to follow it, hobbling forward, keeping hidden whenever possible, determined to continue west to some European city and anonymity.

The pain was excruciating as he dragged his left foot behind him. There was no shade now, only blinding sunlight. Even the slight breeze of the morning had abandoned him and he sank to his knees, sweat running in rivulets down his face. He heard dogs barking in the vicinity, looked from left to right trying to get a fix on their position, then hobbled forward towards the top of a rise hoping to find shelter on the other side. What he found was a man holding a shotgun, the barrel pointing directly at his head.

31

Panayiotis yawned as a couple with a teenage daughter approached the Jazz Café and sat down at a table on the upper terrace.

'Right, I'm off to bed. It's been a long night.' He waved as he disappeared around the right-hand bend, striding out with his cool bag over his shoulder heading up the final one hundred steps to his mother's house beside Syllogos Square.

The new arrivals ordered two lattes, one espresso and three croissants, pointing proudly to their yacht tied to the harbour wall far below.

Marta enjoyed mixing with the yachting community. They had become regular visitors to the Jazz Café, attracted to Marta's establishment by recommendations from fellow cruisers on their daily radio net. From April to November, skippers, crews and guests would make the long climb to the old village to visit the castle and museum or for a meal in Syllogos Square and break there climb at the bar cafe for a well-earned coffee or cocktail, while they enjoyed the stunning view of Symi Bay and their own vessels moored in the busy harbour. Marta loved sailing and had a real empathy with these people. She was about to engage this family in conversation when she noticed her other customer.

Police Chief Kakos was sitting with his back to her resting his feet, one on top of the other, on the low retaining wall before him. His left arm hung loosely by his side, a lit cigarette casually held between forefinger and thumb. Marta could see his captain's rank clearly visible on the epaulettes of his uniform shirt, his dark blue trousers tucked neatly into a pair of heavy duty black boots and his jet black hair, streaked with natural grey highlights, lifting in the morning breeze below a pair of Armani sunglasses which rested on the top of his head. Marta felt a shiver travel down her spine and had no idea why she reacted in this way whenever she saw him. Krios Kakos had always been very civil to her, but something in the way he looked at her made her wary. She felt the same way about snakes.

The Jazz Café was the perfect breakfast stop for Chief Kakos between his substantial villa in the Chorio and his office in Yialos, but Marta had noticed that if Panayiotis was still there when he arrived, he would pass by with only a nod of the head. She had suspected for some time that he had an ulterior motive in choosing to remain only when she was alone and the thought made her skin crawl.

'*Kalimera*, Marta.'

She nodded. 'Chief Kakos.' She kept her voice low and chilled. 'What would you like this morning?'

He looked her up and down, undressing her with his anthracite-grey eyes. 'Just a coffee,' he replied. 'I need to be in Yialos shortly to deal with some illegal immigrants, so I don't have time for breakfast. Perhaps you would join me.' He placed his sunglasses back on his nose and pulled out a chair.

Marta could feel anger bubbling up inside and wasn't sure if it was because Krios Kakos was arrogant or the fact that he was a police officer.

Police uniforms often triggered a hostile reaction in her since becoming a widow and she had no intention of socialising with this particular policeman, whatever his rank. 'I don't think so, Captain. Like you, I am also rather busy.' Marta pushed the chair back under the table and returned to the bar, sensing his irritation and hoping her rebuttal would not impact negatively on the refugees in Kambos Square.

Panayiotis walked into the kitchen and found his mother wiping some pots at the sink.

Anastasia Stanis turned her head. 'I suppose you've had breakfast already.' Her implied criticism was not lost on her son. 'What have you brought for dinner?'

'Some squid. I sold all the fish to customers earlier.' He opened the cool bag and emptied the contents onto the kitchen table.

'And what did Marta Romano get for her trouble?' Anastasia slammed one pot upon another.

Panayiotis ignored her, opened the large old fridge standing by the door and took out a bottle of water. 'I'm off to bed, Mama.'

Anastasia gripped the edge of the sink and watched him depart, knowing her jealousy was pushing her son away but unable to help herself. She had never liked Marta Romano since her arrival on Symi. Whilst she was married, her summer visits to the island were a minor inconvenience, Panayiotis spending more time at Casa Romano than with his own family. But since the death of Antonio and his son, Panayiotis had taken on the role of protector to his close friend's wife without realising that the widow would drop him like a stone once she found a suitable substitute. Anastasia had tried to point this out to her son many times but he refused to listen, insisting that he was only doing what any friend of the family would do in the circumstances, and pointing out that if the situation were reversed, Antonio would have done the same for him.

If only his father, Eduardo, hadn't died in the storm of eighty-six, she thought. The Coastguard had never found her husband's body, undercurrents in the Rodos Sea used as an excuse for their failure to locate him, even though others who perished that night were washed up onto the shoreline around Panormitis Bay. If he'd survived, she argued inwardly, maybe my daughter-in-law, Leonora, would not have left Panayiotis for that Athenian city banker, and my granddaughter would now be eating wholesome food fresh from the Mediterranean with her parents and grandparents, instead of consuming all that junk food they advertised on the TV from fast-food chains in cities like Athens.

She placed the squid in the sink, running cold water over the black-mottled bodies and took her anger out on the tentacles and guts as she tore them away from the body of each squid before pulling out the quill and removing the wings and outer skin. Laying each squid on the chopping board, she crossed to the kitchen table and slumped onto a wooden chair, picked up a razor-sharp knife and slit the pure white flesh, laying it out flat before scoring the soft inner surface.

Anastasia had become a bitter old woman since becoming a widow, her fears of a lonely old age poisoning any rational thought. She believed that Marta Romano was usurping any influence she had over her son and had become the main focus of Anastasia's venom. She prayed for the day when Symi became free of the Italian widow.

Krios Kakos descended the Kali Strata steps and walked out onto the quayside, his mind full of Marta Fabrini. She was only three years his junior, but the fact that she was Antonio Romano's widow, had a curvaceous body, and had no interest in his status or good looks made her a challenge which his ego refused to ignore. He was used to having any woman he wanted and the more Marta ignored his advances the more he desired her. The conquest of this Italian soprano was now infiltrating his dreams and occupying his waking hours. She's probably playing hard to get, he decided. What I need is a reason to apply some gentle persuasion.

Yialos harbour was full of tripper boats, private yachts, motorboats and small fishing craft all packed closely together, their bows held at right-angles to the quay by anchor chain or rope and their sterns tied to bollards and rings embedded in the harbour wall. The Police Chief nodded to various shop-keepers as he walked towards Kambos Square where two of his officers stood guarding a large group of Middle Eastern and African immigrants, corralled together, their eyes downcast, their clothes shoddy and unwashed, in sharp contrast to the tourists who passed by in a constant stream, photographing them to show friends back home.

'Sergeant, how many have you arrested now?' demanded Krios.

Christos Nicolaides jumped to attention. 'Fifty-two, Sir. I understand there are six more being brought in who were hiding in the one of the derelict windmills on the ridge. What do you want me to do with them?'

'Do?' replied Kakos. 'What do you think we should do? Put them up in the Nireus Hotel, compliments of the Greek taxpayer?'

The sergeant turned puce from the neck up.

'They are vermin, man, and will be treated accordingly. No one asked them to come here, and the sooner they are shipped out of Symi the better. What time does the ferry leave for Rhodes?'

'Four-thirty, Sir.'

'Then make sure they're on it. I will hold you personally responsible for any who are still on this island tonight, is that clear?'

'Yes, Sir.'

Christos watched the Police Chief walk towards the Town Hall and felt the bitter taste of bile burn at his throat. He had been in the Hellenic Police Force for thirty-two years, working on various islands around the Aegean. Never, had he come across a police officer who was so sadistic and couldn't understand why the man refused to show any compassion. He

36

loathed Krios Kakos and knew that by leaving the immigrants without shade or water, the department was contravening police procedure. He could not afford to cross his boss however; his police pension and his daughter's job at the Town Hall were too important.

Danielle Nicolaides was sitting at her desk typing a report on her word-processor when her boss walked through the door. Her stomach muscles twitched at the sight of Krios Kakos, his dominant Greek features making her go weak at the knees. She followed him into the inner office, a large square room on the second floor, its high-beamed ceiling cobwebbed and cracked from years of neglect.

'Close the door, Danielle.' Krios walked to the window overlooking Kambos Square and watched a young African woman suckle her baby, her black nipple fleetingly exposed as she moved the child's head to one side. Danielle watched him adjust his dress as he turned. 'So, what do I need to deal with this morning?'

Danielle pushed the door closed with her foot and walked over to the oak desk, her hips swaying and her red body-hugging dress leaving little to the imagination. 'Your counterpart in Rhodes wants more information about the illegal immigrants arriving there this afternoon. I told him to ring back in fifteen minutes.'

Krios nodded impatiently.

'And, your wife rang. She wants . . .'

'I'm not interested in what my wife wants.' Krios moved back to his desk, his hand stroking Danielle's well-proportioned buttocks as he passed by. Her body flexed like a cat. 'I would like to examine all the documentation on the Jazz Café.'

'That's held by the major's office and he's away in Athens at the moment,' said Danielle, leaning her right hip on the edge of the Police Chief's desk.

'Then I assume you won't have any difficulty extracting it from his filing cabinet while his secretary is at lunch.' He rubbed his forefinger across her left knee and along her inner thigh until he reached the hem of her dress. He stopped and massaged the skin. 'I'm sure I can rely on you, Danielle.'

Danielle's nerve endings rippled with expectation, her nipples hardening in response. 'Yes, Chief. I'll make sure it's on your desk by two o'clock.'

Krios squeezed her thigh, burying his fingers in her soft flesh. 'Excellent, Danielle. Excellent. I'll be at the police station if you need me.' He rose from his chair and walked out of the room leaving his young secretary in a state of sexual arousal.

Chapter Six

Kambos Square was heaving when Marta arrived on the scene. She had rushed down the Kali Strata steps and out onto the harbour, squeezing through the crowds at the corner by the old Customs House and had run smack into Christos Nicolaides.

'Whoa,' cried Christos, peeling her off his chest. 'Where are you going in such a hurry, Miss Fabrini?'

Marta looked about her, dark faces filling the square, the sun beating down on their heads. 'I've come to try and help the immigrants, Sergeant Nicolaides. How long have they been here?'

'That depends, Miss Fabrini.'

Marta frowned. 'I'm sorry, I don't understand.'

Christos shuffled on the spot. Marta had heard from Panayiotis that the sergeant was passionate about opera and one of her most loyal fans. 'It depends on when they were arrested,' he stuttered. 'Some have been here for three hours, some for less.' His eyes met hers and quickly looked away.

'Have they had any water? What is happening about providing some shade? Surely you can't leave them in Kambos Square without protection from the sun, especially the women and children.' Marta's questions tripped over each other. 'And why are all these tourists being allowed to gawp at them as if they were animals in a zoo?'

Christos bit into his top lip trying to remember which question to answer first. 'Miss Fabrini, I have my orders from Chief Kakos. I'm to keep the illegal immigrants in the square until they are put on the Rhodes Ferry and taken there for processing.'

'But, Sergeant, that's not until later this afternoon.' Marta voice was beginning to rise. 'Has the Hellenic Police Department no compassion? These people,' she described an arc with her right arm, 'have lost their homes, their families and their livelihoods due to warfare or famine or some other Third World disaster. You can't leave them all day in the burning sun without food or water.'

Christos shrugged his shoulders and shuffled some more. Marta realised that she had echoed his own thoughts on the subject.

'Please, Sergeant, do something. We can't stand by and watch them suffer like this.' She looked around the crowd for Krios. 'Where is Chief Kakos, anyway?'

Marta knew her words had placed Christos in a difficult position and could sense his indecision. 'Why don't I go and buy some bottles of drinking water from the supermarket while you gather together the most vulnerable in the group and put them across the road in the shade of the old fish market.' Without waiting for an answer she walked through the crowds to a group of women trying to shield their children from the sun's rays and noticed that some had open sores on their legs. 'We should also get a medic down here to tend to their wounds.'

Marta was inwardly screaming at the injustice of it all but knew it would do nothing for her cause if she lost her temper. Thankfully her suggestions had galvanised the sergeant into action and as she crossed to the alley leading to the supermarket, tourists were already being shepherded away from the square and a young police officer was helping an old lady to her feet and assisting her across the road towards the covered market.

'You bastard, Kakos,' Marta whispered under her breath as she made her way through the crowds. 'These poor people should be given their basic human rights and if you're not prepared to do it, then I am.' She entered the supermarket pulling her purse out of her bag feeling energised for the first time in years.

In no time Marta was moving amongst the throng of immigrants, distributing bottles of water and looking into the gaunt eyes of those who had nothing more to give.

Commandeering the help of some of the local women, she brought milk, bread and cheese to the needy, feeding those who were too exhausted to feed themselves. Finally, when she was satisfied all that could be done had been, she climbed the Kali Strata steps to the Jazz Café and sat on the apartment balcony looking out across Symi Bay wondering what the future held for those in Kambos Square. The sight of one child holding out his hands to her, his huge brown eyes full of hope and trust had cut into her like a hacksaw blade. Without thinking, she had gathered him in her arms, her own loss compounded by the warmth of his small body, her heart aching for the chance to turn the clock back and cuddle her own son.

Nishan was staring down the barrel of a gun. He raised his hands in subjugation and remained statue still. The Symiot called to someone close by, never taking his eyes of the huge African, and motioned with his rifle for Nishan to kneel down. A young boy appeared, nodded at some instructions and ran off down the track towards the village. Nishan cursed under his breath.

Twenty minutes later he was roughly escorted into an open-backed truck by a young police officer and driven to Yialos harbour. Here, he was off-loaded in Kambos Square to join the rest of the illegal immigrants.

An older police officer, who appeared to be in charge, was busy moving tourists away from the area and didn't see Nishan arrive. He quietly slipped to the back of the square and sat down behind a group of refugees sitting cross-legged on the concrete floor. One turned and offered him a half-empty bottle of water. He took it, nodding his head, and drank the contents in one gulp. The empty plastic bottle slipped from his hand as he slid into a semi-prone position and dozed.

The sound of the group being herded into line ready to be moved woke him. He raised his aching limbs into an upright position holding onto the trunk of a tree for support and suddenly felt exposed, being a head and shoulders taller than the men around him. A large Roll-on/Roll-off ferry was docked, stern to the quay, at the outer end of the harbour, lorries and cars bouncing across its metal ramp as they embarked and disappeared into the bowels of the ship. Nishan scanned the houses on both sides of the harbour, stacked like pastel-coloured playing cards one above the other, and noticed that some were derelict. If the immigrants were to be loaded onto the ferry as foot passengers they would have to pass below these derelict buildings. He wiped the stinging sweat from his eyes with the edge of his shirt and slowly made his way to the back of the line, a plan formulating in his mind.

The older police officer had gone ahead leaving the young officer to chaperone the group from the square. They followed his lead, shuffling round the end of the harbour and past the many shops and cafés lining their route. Nishan appeared to be dropping behind, limping badly and in obvious distress. The officer looked back on several occasions but Nishan kept himself out of the policeman's line of sight, tucked well in to the right side of the road, his head down, eyes scrutinizing each building and alleyway as he passed until he found what he was looking for.

A set of concrete steps formed an arch as it curled up to a first floor door. Beneath it, a narrow alley led to a low crumbling wall bordering an overgrown piece of land at the rear.

Nishan didn't hesitate. Slipping under the arch, he hobbled through the deserted passage and scrambled over the wall, landing in a bed of thistles, adrenalin pumping through his muscles. He lay with his back to the wall and waited, holding his breath. Nothing happened. Minutes went by but no one seemed to be searching for him. Taking a few deep breaths, he slithered on his stomach, his elbows pulling his body mass through the undergrowth until he reached the derelict house at the back of the plot, its roof open to the elements, the walls fractured and leaning inwards in places. He hid at the rear, his ears alert to every sound, listening for signs of pursuit. All was still.

Taking stock of his situation he crawled out of the rear of the house and moved ever higher, away from the harbour and possible discovery. Settling into another derelict house he peered through a gap in the front wall which gave him sight of the harbour, now some distance below. Down on the ferry he could pick out his fellow immigrants standing or sitting in groups on the foredeck, their dejected posture in stark contrast to the passengers further back, who leant over the ships rails waving to onlookers ashore or relaxing on bench seating chatting with animated hand gestures. A loud blast from the ferry's horn rent the air and the ship slowly moved away from the dock, turned into the channel and steamed away into the bay beyond.

Nishan tracked its progress until all that was left was its wake then collapsed back into his hideout and fell into a deep sleep.

Krios Kakos was speaking into his office phone as the ferry rounded Koutsoumba Point and moved into the Symi Channel.

'Yes, it just left. There were fifty-eight in total. The captain put them on the foredeck away from the paying customers.' He paused as the person on the other end of the line made some comment. 'No, Angelo, there aren't any more. I'm assured by my sergeant that fifty-eight landed here this morning and fifty-eight are now heading to you in Rhodes. All I can say is "good riddance". My report will be coming across to you on tomorrow's hydrofoil. Let's hope the Hellenic Coastguard do a better job in the future and pick them up at sea. Flea-infested illegals sitting around Kambos Square all day do nothing for the tourist trade around here.' He paused again. 'OK, Angelo. Bye.' He placed the phone back on its cradle and opened a file lying on his desk, marked JAZZ CAFÉ.

Danielle could be heard tapping away on her word processor and Krios wondered, not for the first time, why most women were so easy to manipulate. Christos Nicolaides thought his daughter had been given the job as secretary to the Police Chief because of her secretarial skills. Krios sneered to himself. Christos Nicolaides couldn't have been further from the truth, and the truth would probably kill him. Danielle Nicolaides was, in Krios Kakos's opinion, nothing but a useful tool in his overall plan.

Chapter Seven

Saturday (p.m.)

As night fell across the Chorio Panayiotis sat on the terrace of his mother's house drinking coffee. A general buzz filled the air from the restaurants and bars which were full of visitors in their summer finery enjoying Symi by night.

He felt replete. Anastasia had cooked their squid to perfection, flash frying it in local olive oil, fresh lemon juice, crushed garlic and parsley until the flesh curled and the natural sugars caramelised along the grid pattern created by her knife. Accompanied by stuffed aubergines and rocket salad, all produced locally, Panayiotis thought the meal surpassed any offered in the local restaurants.

It was Saturday and *Phoebe II* would remain snatching at her mooring lines while Panayiotis joined some of the old men of the village for a few beers and a game of backgammon in the bar by Syllogos Square. He enjoyed listening to them reminiscing about the old days, stories he had heard many times before.

Petros Vasilakis, the oldest in the group, had been a sponge diver, working for months at a time off the Egyptian coast, risking his life to harvest sponges from the seabed. Some of his friends had died from nitrogen in their blood-stream from too rapid an ascent or been killed by sharks off Venizelos Island near Benghazi. Petros had escaped death but had lost his right foot to gangrene.

Then there was Dareious Halkis who suffered from claustrophobia and couldn't cope with working under water. He became a human pack-horse, working for EFLA, the Union for Harbour Stevedores and Boatmen, spending his life earning a pittance climbing the Kali Strata steps to the Chorio day after

45

day, carrying heavy loads on his back from the holds of the visiting cargo ships in Yialos harbour. Dareious had no idea how many times he had made that journey but for forty-three years he had plied his trade until his crumbling knee joints finally ended his daily toil. He now walked with two sticks.

Finally, there was Giorgos Constantinou from Crete, who arrived in Symi as a young police recruit in the Horoflaki Police Force, enforcing law and order in the villages and countryside. He often recounted his weekly treks on foot from Yialos in the north to Panormos Bay in the south following the well-trodden dirt track leading to the Holy Monastery of Panormitis, returning at weekends to spend time with his pals. It had been a four-hour slog each way with little shade.

He joked about the old priest from Ayios Ioannis church who, during confession, had heard Giorgos admit to strong feelings for a young Symiot girl. Some days later he was horrified to learn that the young lady and half of Yialos were also aware of his feelings.

'So much for the sanctity of the bloody confessional,' quipped Giorgos, ordering another beer.

He had eventually married his beautiful Symiot girl and transferred to Rhodes to work. Forty years later when he and his family returned to Symi, a great deal had changed. European money had funded a smart new road along the length of the island and the local police department were sporting their first police car, a second-hand and rather rusty old Fiat. It wasn't the best form of transport he'd seen but he had to admit it was definitely an improvement on shanks's pony. As for the old priest, he had long gone to his sanctuary in the sky, 'and good riddance,' said Giorgos, flicking his worry beads back and forth across the back of his hand and returning to his favourite tipple.

To Panayiotis these men were the backbone of the island, like his father, who should have been sitting in the same bar recounting his own tales of misadventures at sea. Sadly, unlike the others, he had never made it home.

His thoughts turned to Marta and the recurrence of her nightmare. Panayiotis didn't want her to be alone over the coming weeks and tried to think of a way to get someone into Villa Fabrini without Marta realising he had anything to do with it. Paolo's nanny, Rosa Necchi, was the obvious choice. She had worked for Marta for years and adored her. When Marta left for Symi, Rosa remained in Milan, not wanting to uproot herself so late in life so Marta had bought her an apartment in the city and kept in touch on a regular basis to ensure Rosa needed for nothing. Panayiotis knew that if he could persuade her to come to Symi for a holiday, Marta would be delighted and he could relax knowing that she had someone to lean on.

There was only one problem. Panayiotis didn't speak Italian and Rosa didn't speak Greek. He was still pondering his problem when the house phone rang. He got to his feet to answer it but Anastasia got there first.

'Anastasia Stanis.'

Panayiotis could hear his daughter on the other end of the phone.

'What?' Anastasia was partially deaf in both ears and had a natural aversion to the telephone, holding the ear-piece at the end of her outstretched arm.

'Phoebe, Grandma. Phoebe, in Athens.'

'It's OK, Mama, I'll take it.' Anastasia nodded and handed the phone over to her son, sitting once more on her hard-backed kitchen chair where she had been dozing.

'Dad, it's me, Phoebe.'

A warm smile crossed Panayiotis's face. '*Yiasou, Koreetsi mou.*'

Anastasia's head shot up at the sound of her granddaughter's pet name, her eyes staring intently at her son as she smoothed her hair into a semblance of order.

'She can't see you, Mama,' whispered Panayiotis watching her across the kitchen table. 'Well, that's great Phoebe. How long will you be staying?'

Anastasia was now on her feet her hand stretched out flapping around Panayiotis's ear demanding the return of the phone. Panayiotis ignored her.

'Super. Your grandmother and I will be at the ferry to meet you. By the way, *Koreetsi mou*, how's your Italian these days?' A broad smile crossed his lips at his daughter's positive response. He looked at his mother who was now dancing about with frustration. 'I think your Gran would like a word. I'll ring you back tomorrow as I have something I need you to do for me. See you at the end of the week. Bye.'

He left the house, his mother's voice bouncing off the walls as she shouted down the phone to her granddaughter. Walking across the square he made a mental note to clean-up his own property down on the waterfront in Pedi. Phoebe would want the privacy of her own bedroom during her three week stay on the island, he thought, rather than stay at her grandmother's house. She was now eighteen and had a small scooter stored in the shed behind his own home and could visit his mother whenever she wanted. He decided to make a start on the cleaning the following day while his daughter telephoned Rosa Necchi in Milan.

Anastasia put down the phone and walked over to the window as Panayiotis disappeared into the bar. Her anger was beginning to push him away and she didn't know how to stop it or deal with his lack of faith.

On Symi, as in all of Greece, Sundays were days for prayer and family communion but for too long Anastasia had walked from her home to Ayios Lefteris church alone, her son conspicuous by his absence. After his wife rejected him, Panayiotis turned his back on the Greek Orthodox Church. His agnostic views were then reinforced when his closest friend and Godson were murdered in Milan. To Panayiotis religion had become an irrelevance. Anastasia had spoken to Father Voulgaris about it but Panayiotis had steadfastly ignored his ministrations, preferring to work on his boat or remain at his house on Sundays while the local population paid homage to their maker.

Maybe, she thought, Phoebe could be persuaded to make her father see sense. She decided to talk to her granddaughter about his lack of faith and his infatuation with Marta Romano during her visit. Panayiotis might listen to his daughter and mend his ways. After all, she thought, a son's duty was to look after his mother, especially when she was widowed.

The evening was well advanced as Krios sat in the dark, only the street lights around Kambos Square cutting through the shadows of his office. He was alone. A mobile phone vibrated in his trouser pocket. Lifting it out, he sat it on the desk. The ringing stopped and he waited, knowing it would ring again. Thirty seconds later he picked it up and placed it to his right ear.

'Kakos.'

'We have a green light,' confirmed a familiar voice on the other end of the line. 'Tuesday the eighteenth. Name, Poseidon. Seventy-five foot motor-boat registered in Delaware. Captain's name, Kostas. Last port, Iskenderun.'

Krios wrote the instructions down. 'Cargo?'

'The usual,' said the voice. 'Forty kilos.'

Krios smiled. 'Tell Captain Kostas I'll be waiting.' He closed the phone and unlocked the lower left-hand drawer of his desk and pulled it open. His fingers found the small black ledger sitting below several buff-coloured files. Pulling it out, he turned the pages and noted the details from the phone-call then returned it to the safety of the locked drawer.

Leaning back in his chair he clasped his hands behind his head, his chin pushed forward, lips closed, and allowed a memory of his father to surface.

It was 1992 and at the time Krios was heading the Hellenic Police Force Narcotics Division, a position given to him by his father, Police Colonel Kakos, in a clear case of nepotism. That day, the Colonel had been shaking with barely contained rage as his son stood before the large polished desk in full uniform, an expression of nonchalant insolence written across his face.

'This is the last straw, Krios.' The Colonel pointed to a report lying open on his desk. 'I've bailed you out many times during your police career, but tampering with evidence and using physical force to obtain a confession is cause for immediate suspension and removal from the division.'

'The lad was as guilty as sin and you know it,' countered Krios, looking bored. 'He just took some persuading to admit it.'

'He happens to be the son of a senior politician who is now demanding a police enquiry, convinced that the drugs were planted on his son before his arrest and wanting answers as to why the boy has three cracked ribs and a ruptured spleen.'

Krios shrugged his shoulders. 'I'm sure you can paper over the cracks, Father. After all, the Kakos name is at stake.'

For a short, overweight, sixty-five year old man, the Police Colonel moved around the desk with lightning speed and slapped his son across the face. 'Don't you talk to me like that, you piece of shit. I've put up with your arrogance and womanizing for years. You're a disgrace to the force and an embarrassment to the family. Your brother agrees with me; Athens would be a much better place without you.'

Krios clenched his fists, his thumb knuckles digging into his thighs, curbing the impulse to throttle his father.

The Colonel returned to his desk and pulled out a sheet of paper from the file. 'Your days in Narcotics are over, Krios. You're being transferred to the Aegean island of Symi where you can shuffle papers all day long and help old ladies cross the street. The current police chief is retiring and you are to take his place. Be thankful that you go as a police captain and not some low-ranking officer.'

'And, if I refuse?' Krios's lip curled as he looked at his father with contempt.

'Then you'll remain in Athens and face the music. This time the family name won't save you. Now, get out of my sight.'

Krios could still feel the cold steel band crushing his chest as he strode out of the building, eyes staring directly ahead, shoulders erect, chin held high, chiselled Athenian features devoid of expression. He was seething inside but to his associates he appeared cool, controlled and focused.

In the silence of the Town Hall, Krios's words were clipped and dripping with venom. 'Well, father, you may have thought Symi was a backwater but you couldn't have been further from the truth. The cartel simply moved their drug operations to Symi, with *me*.' He picked up his keys from the desk and walked to the door. 'It's a shame you didn't know that before you died.'

Chapter Eight

Krios laughed to himself as he stepped out of the Town Hall and slowly strolled along the quayside noting the national ensigns of the yachts lining the harbour wall, the predominantly European flags hanging limply in the still evening air.

On large motor-yachts glamorous men and women, dressed in the latest fashions had gathered on the rear decks drinking and chatting quietly, their uniformed crews circling with trays of champagne and cocktails, all illuminated by down lights from the hard canopy above.

Krios reached the clock-tower at the end of the harbour and turned to look up at the police station balcony, its peeling façade contrasting sharply with the glittering opulence opposite. No doubt, he mused, Evadne would be drumming her delicate fingers on the dining table at their villa as she waited stoically for her husband to come home. He crossed the road and mounted the stairs two at a time, checking his watch as he walked along the balcony.

The Police Chief's appearance in the main office went unnoticed. Alex Laskaris, the on-duty officer, was asleep in his chair, his feet resting on the top of the desk.

'What in God's name do you think you're doing?' shouted Krios.

The young man cracked his shins on the edge of the desk as he sprang to his feet and stood to attention.

'I need a lift home. Now.' Alex watched the door swinging violently to and fro in the Police Chief's wake.

He rushed around the desk, grabbed some keys from a hook on the wall and leapt down the stairs. Chief Kakos sat rigidly in the police car's passenger seat staring straight ahead, the ominous silence pre-empting trouble. As the car wound up the hill to the Chorio Alex became more and more agitated. Finally his boss spoke as the car glided to a halt by the rear of his villa.

'A report of this incident will be placed on your file, Officer Laskaris. Perhaps that will help you concentrate your mind.' With that, the car door slammed and he was gone.

Alex clenched his fist and hit the steering wheel. It had been a very long day. He had started his shift at five o'clock that morning when news of the illegal immigrants had been passed on from the Hellenic Coastguard and, apart from a short break for lunch, he had been on the go ever since. He started the engine and reversed back down the road wishing he had never become a police officer.

Evadne was pacing the hall floor as her husband walked through the door.

'What time do you call this, Krios? Any longer and I would have lost my appetite.'

Krios ignored his wife and walked into the cloakroom to wash his hands. 'You could always have started without me, Evadne.'

'And, for once, Krios, you could have been on time.' Evadne stood her ground, an elegant middle-aged woman with shoulder-length fair hair tied in a chignon, her midnight blue shift dress accentuating her slim figure and blue eyes, her matching linen pumps edged in gold. 'What earth shattering event kept you in Yialos today?'

Krios placed the hand towel on the rail and walked back across the hall to the large oak dresser. 'Fifty-eight illegal immigrants, actually. They were dumped on Symi at dawn. My staff have been running around the island with tracker dogs all day ferreting them out of their hiding places and arresting them. They were despatched to Rhodes by ferry this afternoon and the police there now have the dubious pleasure of processing them.

Rest assured, Evadne, I will make it clear in my report that the incident has severely delayed your dinner and that it must not be allowed to happen again.'

Evadne ignored his sarcastic comment. Having been married to him for twenty-three years she was immune to his barbed words.

As Krios glanced through the day's post, Evadne went to inform their cook, Sybil, that dinner could now be served. Minutes later, she walked out onto the terrace where a table had been set for two and looked over Symi Bay. Even the beauty of the vista couldn't ease her frustration.

Evadne Kakos had never expected to make Symi her home. As a socialite, Athens had been her playground and she had assumed that her husband would rise through the ranks of the capital's police force and provide her with a sophisticated lifestyle, rubbing shoulders with the great and good of Athens society. Sadly, her husband's limited intelligence, inflated ego, pure avarice and an over-active libido had put paid to his glittering career.

Evadne could only watch in horrified silence as her father-in-law exiled him to a Greek backwater rather than suffer the ignominy of a criminal investigation and family scandal in Athens. She felt trapped in a world where she didn't belong and with a man she had grown to despise.

She had tried to integrate into island life but her Symiot neighbours were suspicious of strangers, especially those from the big city and did nothing to make her feel welcome. Evadne needed to find a way to escape her isolation but in the Krios family divorce was not an option.

The smooth strains of a tenor saxophone eased Nishan back into the real world, now lit only by stars. He took time recalling where he was and why. Easing himself into an upright position he checked for damage, every muscle complaining as he moved, the pain from his ankle gripping his leg in a vice. Voices came and went but none seemed to come close. The music was like a magnet, its lilting refrain calming his taut nerves. He decided to follow the sound in the hope of finding food so moved to his right and squeezed through a gap in the stonework.

Staying in deep cover he struggled on across rough ground, the sound of the saxophone luring him upwards until he could go no further. A dark alley now blocked his path. He could hear human chatter and glasses clinking above the sound of the music, the scraping of chairs as people moved around above him. Unable to make progress without being seen he lay out of sight and waited.

Evadne couldn't sleep. The atmosphere at dinner had been strained and she now had a headache. Krios had been restless for hours, either moaning or snoring as he lay by her side, his constant movement disturbing her peace. She got out of bed and crossed to the bathroom intending to find some aspirin. Walking past the window she looked down at the harbour. Yialos was now quiet, the bars and restaurants along the water's edge closing for the night. She watched as lights went out in various establishments, the sound of scooters fading into the distance as the locals headed home.

Returning with a glass of water and two tablets she looked across at her husband lying naked on the bed, hands twitching, eyes firmly closed, the sheet draped across his groin. She slumped onto the side of the bed and recalled the first time she had seen him naked.

It had been on their wedding night at the Cipriani Hotel in Venice, a present from her parents. Krios had walked from the bathroom, his dishevelled hair wet from the shower, his body exposed. She felt instantly embarrassed. Being a virgin bride she had little knowledge of men or their physiques, having grown up with two sisters and a very puritanical father.

Intercourse had proved to be painful and her husband's lack of finesse demoralising. Her father-in-law had been a very domineering figure who expected Kakos women to bear their problems in silence and with dignity. Evadne was no exception, so she had gritted her teeth and suffered the indignity of the nightly sexual attacks without complaint.

She tried to talk to Krios about it but he refused to listen, convinced of his own sexual prowess, telling her openly that his other women never complained. His infidelities had cut her to the quick, adding to her woes, yet to Krios, these extra-marital affairs were meaningless, his approach to women chauvinistic and transient. For her, they were a constant torment and any love she had felt for her husband had been stamped on so often that it was now crushed beyond repair. All she felt was disgust for the man who shared her life.

Krios began to breathe heavily, his eyes restless beneath his eyelids. Evadne placed the glass on the bedside table and put her head in her hands, recognising the signs of another erotic dream. Then he moaned. She squeezed her temples with her fingers trying to override her pain, wondering where it would all end. Suddenly her husband gave out a low guttural cry, shattering the silence.

'Marta,' he growled. 'Oh, Marta, yes!'

Chapter Nine

Sunday (early hours)

By two o'clock on Sunday morning all was quiet on the hillside above Yialos harbour. In the shadows, a figure crept across the Kali Strata steps and into an alley alongside the Jazz Café then began rummaging through the dustbins looking for food. The figure paused. Someone inside the bar could be heard moving about. The scavenger wedged himself behind the refuse bins, out of sight, and chewed on the night's leftovers.

Marta locked the Jazz Café's main door. Phillipe, her manager, had left with the last of the customers so Marta was alone. She always enjoyed this hour of the day, a throwback from her nights at the opera, and she moved about the bar enjoying the sounds of the Buena Vista Social Club playing Latin jazz.

My life has changed beyond all recognition, she thought, flicking the switch on the dishwasher. How could I have gone from the grandeur of the opera stage to owning a bijou bar in a small island like Symi? It doesn't seem possible. She ached for her late husband, longing for the tenderness of his touch.

Her spinal cord quivered as a panic attack threatened to overwhelm her. 'Stop it, Marta. Stop it, now!' Her voice was tense, intent on fighting the turmoil in her head. 'Concentrate on the here and now.'

She walked over to the fridge to check the contents and noticed the carton of milk. The feral kitten she had seen playing on the Kali Strata steps came to mind along with Panayiotis's words. She hesitated, unsure of herself, then took the carton out and poured some milk into a shallow dish, opened the side door to the bar and placed it by the step. To her surprise the kitten was standing at the entrance to the alley hissing as it stared at the café's dustbins, its body arched, its black fur standing erect along its spine. She assumed other cats were raiding the bins and was about to shoo them away when a shaft of light from the bar illuminated the ground to her left and she saw a heavily swollen dark foot poking out from beside one of the bins.

Marta slowly went into reverse, feeling for the door frame with her spare hand, her heart racing. Once inside, she stood in the middle of the café trying to think what to do next. Images of the illegal immigrants in Kambos Square rotated through her mind, Panayiotis's explanation of their fate ringing in her ears. She didn't want to get involved but some need, deep inside, drove her on.

Walking around the bar, she switched off the CD, grabbed a loaf of bread, some cheese and the carton of milk and steeled herself to reopen the door. Maybe whoever it was would have gone, she thought, as she slowly turned the door handle. She paused, listening for any movement, conscious that she was leaving herself wide open to attack.

Gritting her teeth, she eased the door open. The kitten had disappeared and all seemed quiet, maybe too quiet. It was hard to see if the foot was still there but she didn't wait, quickly placing the items on the outside step and retreating into the safety of the café, leaving the door fractionally open.

I need a weapon, she thought and grabbed a bread knife off the rack, pulled a chair close to the bar and sat, waiting, watching the gap for movement.

Minutes passed. Marta continued to breathe deeply, trying to still her rapid pulse as she tapped her fingers against the knife, counting down the minutes until impatience got the better of her.

'This is ridiculous,' she whispered, standing up. 'He's probably long gone.'

At that second, the loaf of bread slowly moved out of the shaft of light followed by the cheese and milk. Marta's left hand went to her mouth. She didn't know whether to laugh or cry so she held her breath and sat back down. Finally, the empty milk carton reappeared, dark fingers steadying the item then gently pulling away.

Marta counted to ten then moved across to the door, opened it a little wider, picked the carton off the ground and backed towards the bar, her hand shaking violently. She flicked the switch on the CD player and chose a Miles Davis track. '*Summertime*' filled the room.

Nishan hovered by the step, his heart racing, milk staining his chin. Was this a trap? He didn't know what to do. A muted trumpet sounded through the crack in the door, the soft refrain steadying his nerves. Gently he pushed the door with his fingers, the light moving across his arm as the gap widened. He could see her sitting in the middle of the room, her hands holding onto the edge of her seat, a knife resting in her lap, her eyes transfixed on the gap. He wiped his chin on his sleeve and bit his lip. Easing his body into the pool of the light he sat on the ground, his knees brushing his chin, his hands raised above his head and his face contorted in pain.

Marta saw the agony in the foreigner's eyes and beckoned him inside having no idea what she was going to do next.

He seemed to take forever to pluck up the courage to move but finally he struggled across the threshold and crawled towards the bar, resting his back against the hard wooden surface. Marta noticed again that his left foot and ankle were badly swollen and he was covered in cuts and bruises. The stranger leant his head back and closed his eyes, his pulse throbbing wildly at his neck. Marta walked around the prone figure and eased the side door closed with the tips of her fingers, laying the bread knife back on the counter, all fear gone.

The next two hours raced by as Marta tended to the stranger's wounds, tying packs of ice in tea-towels around his swollen ankle, feeding him scrambled eggs for his hunger and Ibuprofen and Paracetamol to ease the swelling and dull his pain. He was filthy, his black curly hair matted and full of burrs, his fingernails ripped and bleeding and he smelt foul. She knew she had to move him away from the Jazz Café if he was to be safe from prying eyes.

Thank goodness my car is close by, she thought, trying to think of a way to explain her plan to the immigrant. Using pen and paper from the bar she made a childlike drawing of her car. He followed every sweep of the pen, constantly rubbing his bloodshot eyes.

As she drew the wheels she saw the stranger clench his fists and rotate his hands describing an arc. 'Yes,' she exclaimed, nodding furiously and pointed again at the drawing. 'Yes, we have to go.' Her eyes travelled up to the wall clock above the bar. It was four fifteen, only an hour or so before dawn.

With the immigrant lying in the back seat covered in blankets, Marta drove slowly away from the Jazz Café thankful that she kept Sundays free. She now had twenty-four hours to plan what to do next.

As they pulled into the drive of Villa Fabrini she could hear heavy breathing emanating from the back seat. She left him there while she organised somewhere for her invalid to sleep, her mind in a quandary.

I can't let him sleep in the house, she thought, it's too risky. On the other hand, leaving him outside on the terrace doesn't seem right either. She tapped her teeth together trying to think of a solution then looked at the garage. He'll just have to sleep in there.

Nishan felt himself being shaken and opened his eyes, pulling the blanket below his chin. The fragrance of flowers filled his nostrils, fresh country air reaching into his lungs. He tried to sit up but his limbs refused to work. Hands gently held his calves and eased his legs over the door sill until he felt solid ground below his feet. Pushing his body out with his arms he staggered into an upright position, the cool metal of the vehicle pressing against his shoulder blades.

Two wooden walking sticks were pushed towards him, each one tapping the back of his hands until he held them in his palms. As he adjusted his weight and raised his bandaged foot off the floor, the woman pointed to a single-storey building to his right and beckoned him to follow.

Bracing himself against the building's door frame, he scanned the interior lit by a single bulb hanging from the rafters. An old mattress lay on the oil-stained concrete floor with pillows and blankets scattered on top. Alongside, a rickety metal table held a plastic bowl full of water, soap, towel, disposable razor and a crazed hand mirror. On a rustic hook, a dark cotton wrap hung to the floor above a coil of garden hose attached to a water tap by the entrance. The woman lifted the hose holding onto the spray gun, pressed the toggle and aimed a jet of water out onto the drive. Closing the toggle she held the hose above her head and looked at him, her eyebrows raised, her lips puckered. Nishan sniffed his armpit and wrinkled his nose. She nodded, her lips creasing into an enormous smile.

As a shaft of daylight found a crack in the door frame she handed him an old rusty key then placed the palms of her hands together and raised them to her left ear, feigning sleep and walked off into the dawn. Nishan watched her go, picturing his mother doing the very same thing when he was a child and suddenly felt very sad.

Marta locked her kitchen door and slowly climbed the stairs, mental and physical exhaustion taking over as her adrenalin levels dropped. She jammed the back of her bedroom chair under the door handle, undressed and climbed into bed. It had been one hell of a day, but she felt a strange sense of wellbeing and drifted into an undisturbed deep sleep as birdsong from Villa Fabrini's dawn chorus welcomed the morning.

Chapter Ten

Sunday (11.00 hrs.)

Sunday was well advanced when Marta awoke. For some minutes she lay where she was recalling the events of the previous night and having second thoughts about what she had done. In the cold light of day, the reality of her situation hit home and she felt panicked by the potential consequences of her actions. After all, she thought, who was this man who had crawled into the Jazz Café from nowhere? How was she going to help him anyway on a small island in the middle of the Aegean, and wasn't it madness for her to be harbouring an illegal immigrant? There was nothing for it, she decided, but to notify the authorities and leave them to deal with him. Once that decision was made she felt more in control, her churning stomach steadying as she headed for the shower.

Once dressed she walked out onto her bedroom veranda and saw the stranger sitting on a bench outside her music room staring out to sea, his filthy clothes discarded, the dark cotton wrap now expertly tied around his lower body, leaving his black muscular back exposed to the morning sun. Marta bit her inner cheek, the sight weakening her resolve. She was torn between the logic of not getting involved and the need to help someone less fortunate than herself.

Refusing to think further, she pulled her hair into a clasp at the nape of her neck and went out into the garden, pocketing a pad and pen as she passed the study.

Her lodger looked deep in thought as she approached so she coughed loudly. '*Kalimera*. My name is Marta.'

He stared up at her with unblinking eyes.

This is not going to be easy, thought Marta. She pulled the pad and pen from her pocket and drew a stick figure with long

63

hair dressed in a skirt and blouse, below which she wrote the word MARTA in large letters.

'Me,' she said prodding her chest with her index finger. 'MARTA.' She pointed to the drawing, then back to herself. 'My name is MARTA.'

He shook his head, his forehead creased.

Try another tack, Marta. She clasped her hair then her skirt and handed him the pad. 'MARTA,' she repeated pointing to herself.

The pause seemed endless but his lips slowly parted as confusion gave way to understanding, a broad smile lighting up his whole face. 'MAR-TA,' he announced, emphasising both syllables equally. 'MAR- TA.'

She dropped the pen in her excitement. 'Yes, MAR-TA. Here.' She retrieved it from the gravel and thrust pen and pad at him. 'Now, you draw.' Her fingers nudged his hand and pointed at his chest.

The tip of his pink tongue crossed his lower lip as his head dropped and slow lines appeared on the blank sheet. A stick figure appeared in trousers and curly hair, the word NISHAN printed below. Returning the pad, he pointed to his chest. 'NISHAN.'

Marta rolled the word around her mouth. 'NISH-AN.' She repeated it, as his head bobbed up and down. She smiled and stretched out her right hand. '*Kalimera*, Nish-an.'

The immigrant reached for a walking stick and pulled himself into a standing position, towering over her small frame. Placing his right hand over his heart he bowed from the waist. '*Selam*, Mar-ta.'

'Well,' said Marta's inner voice, 'that was excruciating, but at least we are now on first name terms.' She looked down at his swollen ankle, convinced herself it was broken and pointed to the pergola terrace, beckoning him to follow.

While he settled onto a chair below the bignonia clad canopy, Marta grabbed the filthy clothes lying in a pile on the garage floor and threw them into a bucket of warm soapy water liberally laced with disinfectant and placed them behind the garage. She then began to redress his ankle, her mind racing, covering several topics at once.

All thoughts of reporting him to the police had been abandoned with his first smile. It was clear Nishan needed help and her natural instinct was to do whatever she could to assist, irrespective of logic. However, that was easier said than done. He needed new clothes and shoes but anyone seeing her buying these in Symi would immediately be suspicious. A doctor ought to examine his ankle but that was out of the question and she desperately needed to find out where he was from and where he was going before she could plan the next step.

First things, first, she thought as she cleared away the old bandages and went to organise a late breakfast. Walking from the kitchen with a jug of iced orange juice, some bread, cheese and honey, she had an idea.

From the bookshelf in her study she pulled out her old World Atlas. As it landed on the pergola table a cloud of dust rose from the binding. Marta coughed, rubbed the leather cover with a napkin and sat down.

'Nishan,' she said, turning the first page. 'Where is your home?'

Nishan pushed the pen and pad across the table to her. 'Your home,' she said drawing a house, then found the page in the Atlas showing the chain of Dodecanese Islands and pointed to Symi. 'My home,' she announced, tapping the table with the flat of her hand and pointing at the drawing. 'My home.'

Nishan examined the page rubbing his ear. He placed his finger on Symi, looked at the villa then at Marta.

'That's right, Nishan. My home.'

Nishan began turning the pages one by one and Marta could tell that he was searching for something. Land mass after land mass passed by, each coloured in soft hues of pink, green and yellow. He finally stopped and examined a chart in great detail then smiled. Leaning back in his chair he closed his eyes. When he opened them again Marta was holding her breath. He leant over the page placing his index finger in the top right hand quadrant. 'Nishan,' he said, looking into Marta's eyes. 'Nishan.'

Marta slowly pushed his finger away and read the word printed across a patch of green on the chart - E T H I O P I A. She was stunned. 'Ethiopia. Nishan, you're from Ethiopia?'

'Etiopia,' repeated Nishan, nodding. 'Addis Ababa. Haile Selassie.' He looked at her, trying to make her understand.

It was now Marta's turn to close her eyes. 'Ethiopia,' she whispered, overcome with the knowledge. The African sitting at her pergola table was a very long way from his home, and the question was, why? The phone's ringing tone put paid to further thought. Nishan immediately looked scared but Marta shook her head and walked into the house trying to recall what she knew of Ethiopia.

'Hello. Who's calling?'

'Marta, its Captain Silvano. Louis Silvano.'

Marta immediately reverted to her mother tongue.

'*Buongiorno*, Captain Silvano, how are you?'

'I'm fine, and you?'

'Oh, you know, taking one day at a time.'

'That's why I'm ringing, Marta. Are you alone?'

Marta didn't want to admit that she had an Ethiopian illegal immigrant sitting outside, so she lied. 'Yes, why?'

The Captain paused, his silence ominous. 'I've received a call in the office from someone who wanted to remain anonymous. He said he had information about the car bomb.'

Marta gripped the edge of her desk, her knees feeling weak, all thoughts of her immigrant gone.

'Are you there, Marta?'

Her words were barely a whisper. 'Yes, I'm here.'

'He mentioned Paolo's school rucksack and said a copy was made in Turkey, packed with Semtex then swopped for Paolo's as he got into the car.'

'No, that's impossible.' Marta shook her head. 'Paolo loved that rucksack, he took it everywhere with him, it never left his . . .' As the sentence died on her lips she grasped the significance of the captain's words and lowered herself into the swivel chair. 'Do you think he was telling the truth?'

'I don't know, Marta. Anything is possible.'

'Did he sound Italian?'

'No. We are having his accent analysed now but the suggestion is that he's Greek.'

'Greek?' Marta stared out across the Aegean trying to make sense of it all. 'What happens now?'

'Now, we wait. Whatever information this man has he will hope to trade it for cash. As you know, I've always suspected that the bomb was either in Paolo's rucksack or Antonio's legal case but I haven't had any evidence to prove it.'

An exploding Maserati filled Marta's mind and her body went into spasm. 'Will you pay if he rings back?'

'I will do whatever it takes to find the murderers, Marta, you know that, and if the Turkish connection is true, Interpol will be getting involved. In the meantime, do you remember anything, no matter how small, about Paolo's rucksack that might help us discover what happened that morning.'

Marta's jaw dropped. 'Captain Silvano, it was three years ago. Paolo's nanny and I gave you all the information we had at the time. How can I possibly remember anything else after so long?'

'I know, Marta. I know, but think about it, please.'

Marta pinched the top of her nose. Captain Silvano sounded just like Panayiotis. She clutched her ribcage trying to stop the ache inside. 'I will, I promise, and thank you for keeping me informed.'

'You deserve nothing less, Marta. I only wish I could tell you that I've found the men who killed your husband and son but I can't, that's why I need your help. Just ring me, Marta, if you think of anything at all.'

'I will.' Marta hesitated before going on. 'Did you find out anything about Police Chief Kakos here in Symi?'

'Yes, and it's quite interesting. Through contacts in Rome I've learnt that his father was the Hellenic Police Colonel around the time Krios Kakos arrived in Symi. In 1992 a politician's son was arrested in Athens on drugs charges and had to be hospitalised after interrogation. I can't find out if Krios Kakos was involved, but he was definitely the senior captain in the narcotics division at the time.'

Marta dragged her mind into the present. 'And the head of the Hellenic Police Force wouldn't want the Kakos name dragged through the dirt if his son was involved, would he?'

'All I can say is, you don't get moved from the headquarters in Athens to a small island in the Dodecanese without good reason. I've had a newspaper article about the arrest translated into Italian. It's pure conjecture, of course, but the implication was that the drugs were planted on the boy in order to put pressure on his father. If I were you I would stay well away from Police Chief Kakos.'

Too late, thought Marta, as her stomach muscles clenched again. 'Thank you, I'll try, and good luck with your enquiries. Arrivederci.'

Marta put down the phone, her mind in Milan, her eyes staring aimlessly out at the panoramic view through the window.

'Mar-ta, you speak Italian,' said the immigrant from the study door.

'Yes, Nish-an. I am Ital . . .' Marta froze. She slowly turned around and looked across the room at her lodger. 'What did you say?'

Chapter Eleven

Sunday (p.m.)

The afternoon at Villa Fabrini was surreal. Nishan slowly revealed his life story, faltering in broken Italian and using her atlas as a guide. She couldn't get her head around the fact that she was sitting in her own villa, on a tiny Aegean island, conversing with an Ethiopian illegal immigrant in her native tongue and understanding every word he said. What she learnt left her speechless.

Nishan's full name was Nishan Amato. He had been born in Addis Ababa in 1966 and was now twenty-nine years old. His mother, Nuria, was Ethiopian but his father, Amato, was half-Italian, sired by Luigi Amato, a young Italian soldier stationed in Addis Ababa between 1939 and 1942 when Italy controlled that part of the Horn of Africa.

Nishan's grandmother had been left abandoned when the Italians pulled out of Ethiopia, Luigi neither knowing that she was pregnant with his child nor keeping to his promise to return to her one day.

She had gone back to her village and brought up her son alone, dying of dysentery when Amato was fifteen years old. An Italian Catholic priest had taken the young boy back to the city and taught him everything he knew of his father's culture and language. Amato grew to love all things Italian and when he married Nuria and had a son of his own he passed on this love.

Nishan recalled as a small boy sitting on his father's knee listening to stories of the Roman Empire, and falling asleep as Amato sang Italian lullabies in a deep baritone voice.

In 1974 the communist Derg threatened to overthrow Haile Selassie, the Lion of Judah. Amato left his wife and child and went to fight for his King and was killed in action. His body was never found but Nuria was told sometime later that he had been captured by the guerrillas in an ambush and summarily executed. Nishan's mother was now alone and vulnerable. As Haile Selassie escaped to England, she moved her son far from the political upheaval in Addis Ababa and lived out her days on the lower slopes of the Ahmar Mountains tending her goats and living off the land.

Nishan grew into a strapping youth who, like his father, continued the passion for all things Italian. He would ask the nuns at the nearby mission to give him what information they had of his grandfather's homeland and one, Sister Francis, would talk to him in Italian as he helped out in the mission gardens.

In 1992 his mother died in his arms from tuberculosis and Nishan could see no future for himself in a country dogged with conflict and drought. He buried his mother on a hillside near their home, sold his goats and went to find work in the local town until he had saved enough money for his journey, then handed the proceeds into the safe care of Sister Francis and went in search of Luigi Amato and a better life.

His journey had taken him eighteen months, crossing the Red Sea from Djibouti to Yemen at night, then onwards by foot, train or truck through Saudi Arabia, Syria and Turkey, hiding from corrupt border police, fighting off Somali and Yemeni robbers and enduring discrimination, harassment and extortion from human smugglers as he moved from country to country.

He was arrested in Syria and spent weeks in a cockroach infested Damascus jail before being released with no explanation and left to fend for himself. In Turkey he was attacked trying to help a young Iraqi girl from being gang raped, the six youths leaving him bruised and battered in a gutter.

71

Finally, in the Turkish port of Iskenderun he learned of a coastal freighter taking illegal immigrants to Europe. He was destitute and couldn't raise the extra one thousand dollars to pay for the passage but Sister Francis found the money for him and sent it to Turkey by means of the ancient Hawala payment system based solely on trust, telling him he could pay it back once he reached Italy.

In a cramped, dark, airless hold of the Emerald Star, with no food or water, he travelled along the Turkish south-coast with fifty-eight other men, women and children, each hoping for a better life in Europe. Exhausted and dehydrated he arrived in Symi and, after escaping arrest, crawled up the hillside of Yialos to the Jazz Café and found Marta.

'Why didn't you go to the Italian Embassy in Addis Ababa and tell them your story?' asked Marta.

'I try,' said Nishan in broken Italian, 'but no one listen.'

'Couldn't the priest have helped, after all he knew your father?'

'He not alive.'

Marta dug her fingernails into the palms of her hands trying to stop herself screaming with anger at the injustice of it all.

'Where is it?' he asked tapping the table as the sun waned.

Marta knew her answer would bring Nishan to his knees. 'You're technically in Europe, Nishan, but you're on the island of Symi. The mainland of Greece is two hundred miles away to the northwest, across the Aegean Sea.' She traced the distance on the Atlas with her finger.

'And Italy?'

'A few hundred more.' Marta remembered Paolo asking her if he could make it into the school football team, his pleading eyes mirrored in this African's face. The memory tore her scars wide open. She crossed her fingers and spoke again. 'I need proof that your grandfather was Italian. Do you have anything that belonged to him. Anything at all?'

Nishan leant on his sticks and hobbled out to the garage. When he returned he was holding a small leather pouch, stiff with sweat and grubby from constant use. He dropped it into Marta's lap and moved to the window.

Marta untied the leather thongs that kept the flap secure and placed her hand inside. She eased the contents out onto the palm of her hand and felt a shudder go down her spine. She was staring at a metal dog tag on a thin chain alongside a tiny silver locket encasing a plait of black and grey hair. Accompanying these was a sepia photograph of a young man in army uniform leaning against a war torn building smoking a cigarette, his cap at a jaunty angle. 'Is this Luigi Amato?'

Nishan nodded.

'Whose hair is in this locket?'

'My grandmother and my father, his baby hair. It is good luck in my country. The locket, it was a gift from my grandfather before he leave Etiopia.'

'Do you know where your grandfather came from in Italy?' The raw emotion on Nishan's face was something she would never forget. He shook his head, a forlorn hope in his eyes.

Marta closed the atlas and looked into those deep brown eyes. 'Finding Luigi Amato is not going to be easy after all these years, Nishan, he might already be dead.' She sensed her words were cutting him to the core and weighed up her next words carefully. 'Do you believe in fate, Nishan?'

He cocked his head in surprise.

'I do, and I believe fate brought you to the Jazz Café last night. I have no idea how I can help you but, God willing, I will try.'

Chapter Twelve

Monday

After a second night with little sleep Marta felt jaded. She picked up the cardboard box by the steps of the Jazz Café and unlocked the door. Nishan had remained at Villa Fabrini with strict instructions to stay out of sight.

Casting a careful eye around the bar for any incriminating signs of Saturday night, she tried to look nonchalant as Panayiotis walked through the door.

'Morning, Marta. How was your weekend?'

Marta kept her back to Panayiotis as she concentrated on the Gaggia coffee machine, her pulse racing. 'Fine, Panayiotis, and you?'

'Oh, the usual Saturday night banter with Petros and his cronies in Syllogos Square.' He started moving tables and chairs outside. 'I spent yesterday spring cleaning my house down in Pedi.'

Marta looked at him over her shoulder as the coffee machine hissed and steam rose from a jug she was holding. 'Why' she called out.

'Because Phoebe's arriving on Friday.'

Marta came around the bar with two coffee cups. 'That's wonderful news, Panayiotis. How long will my goddaughter be here?' She set the cups down at their usual table and returned for the rest of their breakfast.

'Three weeks.' Panayiotis was beaming from ear to ear. 'She'll be too cramped in my mother's small box room at her age, so I rolled up my sleeves and set to with the bucket and mop. I nearly called you to come and help.'

Marta cut through the fresh loaf trying hard to avoid his gaze and quickly changed the subject. 'Captain Silvano rang yesterday afternoon with a new lead.'

Panayiotis's eyes shot up from his breakfast. 'What did he say?'

Marta told him about the rucksack and the background on Krios Kakos. 'It would appear our Police Chief has form.'

Panayiotis's retort was cut short at the sight of Krios appearing around the corner of the Kali Strata. Their eyes met, their mutual dislike clouding the bright morning. Marta froze; she could see the Chief's image reflected in Panayiotis's cold stare and hoped he hadn't heard her last comment.

Krios continued down the steps nodding briefly to Marta as he went by, his intention to breakfast at the Jazz Café obviously curtailed by the presence of the fisherman. He paused, turned and retraced his steps. 'Kyría Romano, I need you to come down to my office sometime today. There seems to be a complication over the Jazz Café's licence.'

His intimidating manner was not lost on Marta. 'Surely that is dealt with by the Mayor.' She met his gaze head on showing nothing of the turmoil going on inside.

'He has asked me to deal with it in his absence. What time can I expect you?'

'I can get away around eleven o'clock if that's convenient?'

He blinked agreement then continued on his way, Marta's stare boring a hole in his spine until he disappeared from view. 'That man gives me the creeps.' She shivered, releasing the tension in her shoulders.

Panayiotis placed his hand on hers. 'Do you want me to come with you?'

As always, his touch felt warm and reassuring. 'No, Panayiotis, you've been up all night. You need to get some sleep. I'm sure this is all a misunderstanding.' Panayiotis looked sceptical. 'Don't worry, if I have a problem I'll let you know.'

'Be careful, Marta, remember what Captain Silvano said.'

Problems with the Jazz Café are the least of my worries, thought Marta, pushing her breakfast plate away, her appetite gone. She refused to dwell on it and returned to the matter of Phoebe. 'How would you feel if I offered Phoebe some work experience here at the Jazz Café? She could practise her language skills on our foreign customers.'

'Good idea,' agreed Panayiotis. 'Do you think Phillipe would object?'

'Object?' The idea of her manager objecting brought a smile to Marta's face. 'He'd love it. He could spend his evening's ogling all the young men who came to chat up our resident Aphrodite.' Marta's teasing struck home.

'Perhaps, it's not such a good idea after all.' Panayiotis could vividly remember what he and Antonio had been like when they were young.

Marta chuckled. 'She's eighteen, Panayiotis and quite capable of looking after herself. You don't need to wrap her in cotton wool.'

'That's easy for you to say, you don't have a daughter.' Marta's face drained of all colour. 'God, I'm sorry, Marta, I didn't mean . . .'

Marta raised her hand in the air pretending it didn't matter, but her liquid eyes told another story. He ran his hands through his thick wavy hair, his faux pas hanging between them like a bad smell.

'Morning, Boss.' Phillipe's buoyant words broke the tension as he stood by the terrace steps, his buff leather satchel slung over his left shoulder, his cream linen trousers and loose cheese-cloth shirt a counterpoint to his vivid green and white bandana and matching espadrilles.

'Good morning, Phillipe, you're early.' Marta walked into the bar and loaded the coffee machine once more.

'My alarm clock's faulty. It woke us up an hour early and Jean-Claude's been like a bear with a sore head ever since. I decided to get out of the way.'

'Well, I need your help. I'm trying to persuade Panayiotis to allow Phoebe to come and work at the Jazz Café during her three-week vacation on Symi.'

'That's a great idea,' agreed Phillipe. He turned to Panayiotis. 'Your gorgeous daughter would bring a certain *je ne sais quoi* to the establishment, and think of the extra trade she would generate.' He winked at Marta as he threw his satchel on the floor and pulled out a bar stool.

Panayiotis grunted from the end of the bar.

'As you can see, her father is not impressed with the idea.' Marta slid a cup of espresso coffee towards Phillipe.

'Well, what father would be, my dear?' countered Phillipe, adding sugar to the cup. 'The girl's ravishing. With looks like that I'd lock her up in a tower and throw away the key. I really can't think who she resembles in the Stanis family.'

Panayiotis raised his eyes to the ceiling, picked up his cool bag and headed for the exit. 'I can see I'll get nothing but grief from you two today so I'm off home where I can get some peace and quiet.'

Phillipe and Marta looked at each other, the image of Anastasia Stanis hovering between them etched on their expressions.

'And, don't say it,' he shouted as he made his way outside, 'I know exactly what you're thinking.'

Phillip raised their hands, palms out, and began crooning Al Jolson's *'Mammy'* at the top of his voice, the refrain nipping at Panayiotis's ankles as he climbed to the Chorio.

The harbour clock struck eleven as Marta walked into the Town Hall and took the stairs two at a time. The empty corridor echoed to her footsteps as she approached the Police Chief's office. Here she stopped and took a deep breath. oblivious to the cracked and peeling surface of the door or the tapping of fingers on a keyboard within. It was imperative that the licence for the Jazz Café remained in force but Marta was not a Symiot and only one complaint from a neighbour could put that licence at risk. If Captain Silvano was correct, she wouldn't put it past Krios Kakos to manufacture such a complaint if he wished to manipulate the situation to his advantage. Well, let battle commence, she thought as she gritted her teeth and pushed the door aside.

'*Yiasou*, Danielle. I'm here to see Chief Kakos. He's expecting me.'

'Of course, Miss Fabrini. Please take a seat. I'll tell the Chief you're here.'

'I prefer to stand, thank you.'

Danielle nodded and picked up the phone as Marta walked to the window and stared out over Kambos Square. Krios could be heard answering from within his office.

'Miss Fabrini is here for her appointment,' announced Danielle formally. Mumbled words escaped through the gap in the Chief's door-frame but Marta couldn't decipher what was said. She waited patiently as Danielle chewed the end of her pencil. Finally the secretary placed the phone on its hook and looked across at Marta.

'I'm sorry, Chief Kakos is busy at the moment. He asks you to wait and hopes to be available shortly.' Danielle lowered her eyes to the desk, her colour rising.

Marta gritted her teeth, angry at the Police Chief's head games. 'We're all busy, Danielle. Please inform your boss that I'll try to return at midday or, better still,' she paused, expanding her lungs for greater volume, 'I'll contact the authorities in Rhodes and deal directly with them regarding the Jazz Café's licence.' She didn't wait for Danielle to respond but took her leave with a backward wave and was out in the corridor when she heard the shrill tones of the secretary's phone.

'Miss Fabrini,' shouted Danielle as Marta reached the top of the stairs, 'Chief Kakos is free now.'

Marta smiled to herself, licked her index finger and painted a figure one on the air. She returned to the office, walked straight past Danielle and entered the inner sanctum without knocking.

Kakos was seated at his desk and looked up as she entered. 'Marta, you're very prompt.'

Marta didn't answer. Krios moved around his desk and held out a leather chair for his visitor. 'Please, take a seat.'

As she settled onto the proffered chair she could smell his subtle aftershave and felt his hand running along the back of her chair, his thumb scribing a line across her blouse. Marta chose not to react.

Shuffling some papers lying on his desk, he finally spoke. 'Now, about your licence.' His eyes met hers and his rhetorical question brought an immediate response.

'What about my licence?' asked Marta, 'and, why can't it wait until the Mayor gets back?'

Krios smiled. 'All in good time, Marta, all in good time.' He shuffled the papers once more. 'There appear to be some discrepancies which need to be examined.'

Marta feigned surprise. 'Surely not?'

Krios pulled a blue file from the middle of the stack. 'I've discovered that on the original application, certain documents were overlooked.'

Marta leant forward placing her arms on the desk, giving Krios ample opportunity to view her décolletage. 'I'm sorry?'

Krios relaxed back into his chair savouring the moment. 'It would appear that Casa Romano was registered in your mother-in-law's name. I realise that the untimely death of your husband followed shortly afterwards by that of his mother complicated matters for you here in Symi, but there is nothing on this file to state that you are the rightful owner of Casa Romano or the Jazz Café.' Krios shrugged his shoulders looking smug and continued. 'In short, Marta, you appear to have been trading illegally.'

Marta decided to played the innocent and see where it would lead. Her forehead puckered, a look of panic spreading across her face. 'I . . . I don't understand. Are you sure?'

He nodded, licking his lips.

'But, this is terrible. Have you . . .can you suggest any way to solve the problem?'

'Well.' Krios rested his arms on the desk and fiddled with his wedding ring. 'The law is the law, Marta, but as Symi's Police Chief I do have some influence here in the island. I'm sure you don't want to see the Jazz Café closed down, but to guarantee the licence I would need to rectify the discrepancy. Do you understand what I'm saying?'

Marta placed her hands together on the desk and nodded. Krios immediately covered them with his own sending shock waves through her arms.

'I would be doing you a very big favour, Marta, and would need to know that any action I took on your behalf would be . . . appreciated.'

'Chief Kakos . . .'

'Krios, please.'

'. . . Krios, in what way would you want me to show such appreciation?' Marta leant back releasing her hands from under her opponents grasp. 'Are you suggesting some financial payment or are we talking of something more . . . tactile?'

Krios appeared to be unaware that he was rubbing his hands as his eyes devoured her. 'I find money so degrading, don't you?' He stood and strolled around the desk, resting his left buttock on the desktop, his knee pressing against her thigh. If I'm to bend the rules, especially for someone with your looks and experience, I would much prefer payment in kind.' He took a strand of her hair and wound it through his fingers. 'Need I say more?'

No, thought Marta as she stood up and pulled her linen handbag along the desk top where it had been lying, all signs of innocence evaporating from her granite features. 'Krios, please don't bend any rules on my account.' She raised the flap on the bag's outer pocket and placed her hand inside. 'I'm confident that my law firm in Athens would never have overlooked such a fundamental point. A simple phone call to them or the Notary in Rhodes will produce a copy of the title deeds showing that I have legally owned Casa Romano for three years.' Her hand reappeared holding something solid. 'I can only assume that the relevant document, here in Symi, has been lost or deliberately removed.' Marta's inference was obvious as she opened the palm of her hand and exposed a portable voice recorder, the recording light glowing red. 'My husband never went anywhere without his Dictaphone recorder. It avoids any misunderstanding later.'

Krios's right eyelid began to twitch. Marta switched off the voice recorder and placed it back in her bag before walking to the door. 'I will be happy to erase this conversation from the tape once I receive a signed letter from you confirming that the Jazz Café's licence is in order. Shall we say by close of business tonight?'

Krios began to clap, slowly. 'May I congratulate you on a first class performance, Marta. You seem to have me at a disadvantage. Danielle will deliver the letter to the Jazz Café this evening.'

Marta knew this was a Pyrrhic victory and now feared for herself and Nishan, but she refused to be intimidated. 'It was a pleasure doing business with you, Chief Kakos. *Kalimera.*'

The restaurants around Kambos Square were alive with tourists as Marta left the Town Hall, her head held high. She knew it was now imperative to keep Nishan's presence at Villa Fabrini a secret until she could find a way of getting him off the island, and part of her wished she had never set eyes on the Ethiopian.

The pharmacy window jolted her out of her reverie, the drugs displayed behind the glass reminding her that she needed more pain killers, antiseptic cream and support bandages. She knew no one would question those purchases so she rummaged in her handbag for her wallet and went inside.

Evadne stood hidden in the shade of the trees at Kambos Square and watched Marta Romano walk out of the Town Hall, oblivious to her surroundings and deep in thought. At a second floor window Krios stood watching her disappear into the crowd of tourists, and arrogant smirk across his mouth.

Evadne clutched her chest and felt her emotional shield buckle under the pressure of suspicion. 'Not again,' she whispered, 'please, God, not another affair.'

She turned away, tears stinging her eyes and escaped to the solace of Ayios Ioannis church where she dropped to her knees and prayed for release from the pain and humiliation of this latest assignation. Symi wasn't Athens, she thought, everyone knew everyone else's business in this small community and Marta Romano wasn't some cheap slut, but the island's resident celebrity. Word was bound to get out and when it did Evadne's position in Symi would be untenable.

She squeezed her eyes shut and tried to get her head into some semblance of order, trying to find peace amongst the church icons and silver offerings from past souls in torment. She failed. Her heart had been attacked too often and was in danger of going into terminal decline. She picked herself up off the floor and shook her head at the Madonna and child. This time she couldn't turn the other cheek.

As Marta opened the door of the pharmacy Anastasia Stanis could be heard waxing lyrical about her jaundiced views on tourists to an audience of three Symiot ladies and the shop assistant.

'. . . just look at the way these young girls dress. I saw one this morning showing off more than she had covered. It's disgusting. If I had my way, they'd all be packed off to Rhodes on the ferry.'

The doorbell announced Marta's arrival and suddenly she found herself the centre of attention. Subconsciously she checked the top button of her blouse, then realising what she'd done, snatched her hand away from her cleavage and smiled. 'Good morning.'

Anastasia's thin lips remained firmly closed, her back rigid as she sat on a wooden chair while the others returned Marta's greeting. Marta was in no mood to be ignored and walked over to Anastasia determined to engage her in conversation. 'Good morning, Anastasia, I understand Phoebe is shortly coming to Symi. You must be delighted.'

Anastasia mumbled something inaudible and fiddled with her handkerchief.

'I was discussing it with Panayiotis earlier,' continued Marta, undeterred, 'and I suggested that Phoebe might like to

83

work with Phillipe at the Jazz Café during her stay so that she can practise her languages on the tourists and make some new friends.'

Anastasia had gone puce at this news. She physically vibrated as she replied. 'Did you? Did you indeed? Well, I'm sure my son made it very clear to you that my granddaughter is coming home to spend time with her family, not provide the Jazz Café with cheap labour.'

The pharmacist appeared from the back of the shop at this juncture and witnessed a collective intake of breath from her customers. 'Kyría Stanis.'

Anastasia turned to see the pharmacist holding a small white package.

'Your prescription is ready.'

'About time too,' grumbled Anastasia, struggling to her feet. She took the package and walked out of the shop without a backward glance as Marta finished their conversation alone.

'Actually, he thought it was a great idea.'

The pharmacist looked at those remaining, a frown crossing her brow. 'Who's next?'

Chapter Thirteen

Monday (midday)

Phillipe was serving some customers on the lower terrace when Evadne came into view walking up the Kali Strata steps. She stumbled, catching her toe on the uneven surface and fell forwards, breaking her fall with her hands. Phillipe covered the twenty yards in seconds, helping her to her feet and checking for cuts and bruises.

'Please,' insisted Evadne, embarrassed by all the attention, 'I'm fine. Really.' She released her hand from Phillipe's arm intent on continuing alone but her knees felt like jelly and her right hand was badly grazed. As she wobbled onto the next step Phillipe again came to her rescue and insisted she rest at the Jazz Café while he made her a strong coffee laced with brandy.

'You should have that hand looked at,' he suggested, bringing the coffee tray onto the terrace and placing it in front of Evadne who was dabbing the grazed area with a blood stained handkerchief.

'You're very kind. I'm afraid my mind was elsewhere and I wasn't looking where I was going.'

'I'll get our first aid kit. Would you like me to ring your husband?'

Evadne's head shot up. 'NO! I mean . . . No, thank you. Once I've had my coffee and rested a few moments I'm sure I can make it home in one piece.' Her coffee cup rattled in its saucer as she picked it up, the strong smell of brandy reaching her nostrils as the contents touched her lips. 'This is very good,' she said, pink blotches appearing across her cheek bones in an otherwise pasty face.

'Take your time, there's no rush,' soothed Phillipe, fussing round her like a mother hen. 'When you're ready, I'll walk you to your door. We can't have people saying we don't know how to look after our customers, now can we?'

Evadne tried a smile warming to the care being shown to her, care she had lacked for so many years. 'I'm sorry, I don't even know your name.'

'Phillipe. Phillipe Dupont. I own the art gallery across the harbour and manage the Jazz Café for Marta Fabrini.'

The smile was gone in an instant replaced by a stone mask as Evadne grabbed her cup with both hands desperately trying to stop it shaking. She gulped down the contents playing for time fighting back the sexual images corrupting her mind. 'Of course, Phi . . . Phillipe. Do forgive me. For a moment I'd forgotten where I was.'

'My dear, don't mention it. Now, you just relax while I finish dealing with the other customers. Its closing time in ten minutes so I'll only be a jiffy, then we can get you home.'

The brandy had certainly done its job and Evadne reached her front door with no further mishap. Phillipe declined an invitation to take a glass of wine at the Kakos residence handing his charge into the capable hands of the cook and took his leave. Returning down the Kali Strata steps he came face to face with Marta steaming up the other way.

'Whoa! Which cat has got your tail?'

Marta looked up at Phillipe, shook her head and headed for the café entrance, fumbling with her keys. Phillipe followed her through the door experiencing a touch of *déjà vu*.

'What is the matter with that woman?'

'Who? Evadne Kakos?'

Marta was now behind the bar ramming dirty glasses into the dishwasher and looked up in surprise. 'Evadne Kakos? No, of course not.'

Phillipe frowned, now totally confused.

'Anastasia Stanis, that's who.'

Phillipe was none the wiser and looked it. He pulled Marta from behind the bar and sat her on a bar stool. 'Boss, what are you talking about?'

She filled her lungs and deflated them like a pressure valve before recounting what had happened with Anastasia in the pharmacy. 'The woman is impossible, Phillipe. How Panayiotis puts up with her I'll never know. The whole of Yialos now thinks we want to use Phoebe as cheap labour!' Marta was off her stool and pacing the bar room floor.

'Calm down, Marta. No one in their right mind would think that. People adore you here in Symi and they also know Anastasia Stanis. Most of them have been on the wrong end of her sharp tongue at one time or another.'

'Maybe you're right.' Marta sat down again and sighed once more. 'I don't know what's wrong with me, Phillipe, I seem to lose my temper at the least provocation these days.'

'Here,' said Phillipe, pouring her a small Metaxa brandy. 'Drink this. It will help, and forget about Anastasia Stanis. If Phoebe wants to work here, nothing her grandmother or her father thinks will make one iota of difference.'

Marta sipped the brandy, the rich fumes acting as a balm to her pent-up emotions. 'I know, I just see red whenever that woman has a go at me. By the way, why did you assume it was Evadne Kakos?'

'Oh, nothing. Forget it. I've put two and two together and made six.' Marta was all ears.

Phillipe explained what had happened to him while she was in Yialos. 'It just seemed coincidental that she seemed highly stressed out and you resembled Cleopatra with PMT.'

Marta imagined Evadne Kakos had probably felt the backlash from her husband's temper that morning, however, she couldn't verbalise this to Phillipe or he would want to know why

Krios was so cross. 'How strange.' she said, twiddling the stem of the glass between her fingers. 'Perhaps I should pop by later and see if she's alright.'

Phillipe looked at his watch. 'I'd leave well alone if I were you.' His advice seemed to hold hidden meaning. 'I must dash, Jean-Claude will be wondering where I've got to.'

'OK. See you tonight. I'll be here early as I'm expecting a letter from the Town Hall.'

Marta watched him go and decided she should head home as well. She had an illegal immigrant waiting to be fed!

The grating sound of truck gears broke the silence above Vassilios Gorge. Nishan was instantly alert. He hobbled from the pergola terrace to the garage and locked himself in as the shadow of the truck cut across a crack in the door. Minutes later a scooter bumped over the uneven surface, stopped by the garage and fell silent, Marta's voice rising as the 250cc engine died.

'Hi, Takis. You're late today.'

The short, wiry Greek jumped down from the truck's cab. 'The water tanker from Rhodes was late arriving in the port, Marta. That's put everyone back half a day. Still we shouldn't complain, back in the seventies folks could only rely on rainwater to fill their cisterns.' He moved to the side of the truck and unwound a large flexible tube and dragged it across the gravel.

'I'll leave you to it,' shouted Marta as she entered the house, her fingers crossed hoping Nishan was nowhere to be seen.

Trying to concentrate was impossible; her hands were shaking like a leaf so she gave up and flopped onto a kitchen chair and waited for Takis to finish. Finally, she heard him close the cistern lid out on the terrace. Time to pay, she thought, as she grabbed her wallet and a Mythos beer from the fridge then wandered out to the truck. 'Here you go, Takis. Something to quench your thirst.'

Takis took the beer and the cash and wrote out a receipt on a scrappy piece of paper. 'Thanks, Marta.' His smile lit up his cragged, sunburnt face as he climbed back into his cab.

'If you're passing the Jazz Café,' she shouted, 'pop in for a coffee and a brandy, on me.'

Takis waved and reversed the truck up to the garage door, engaged first gear and crunched his way up the drive, the metal end of the tube banging against the chassis as the truck rocked from side to side. Marta sighed with relief and knocked on the garage door. 'All clear, Nishan, you can come out now.'

Nishan propped himself against the door jam, his eyes scanning the drive for strangers.

'It's OK,' said Marta, seeing his concern. 'That was Takis who delivers fresh water to the farmhouses in the area. We're in the countryside so we're not connected to a mains water supply.'

Nishan's look spoke volumes. What would Nishan know of a mains water supply, she thought, he probably thinks I collect my water from a well. 'Were there any other visitors this morning?'

Nishan shook his head.

'Good. Let's look at that ankle again. Is it very painful?'

Nishan hopped along behind her and entered the kitchen, resting his sticks by the island console. 'No bad.'

'Here,' Marta threw him a box of Ibuprofen. Take two of these while I get another ice pack.'

While Marta cracked ice into a tea towel she began to formulate a plan to legalise Nishan's presence in Greece without Krios Kakos finding him first. If she could talk to the Italian Ambassador and show him the items which Nishan had brought from Ethiopia he might agree to provide sanctuary while the Italian authorities investigated Nishan's claim. Her problem was that the nearest Embassy was in Athens. As she pondered her predicament the phone rang.

'Hello.'

'Marta, is that you?' The voice sounded so very familiar.

'Rosa! What a wonderful surprise. Where are you?'

'At home.'

'How are things in Milan?'

'Empty, without you.'

Paolo's nanny catapulted him into the forefront of Marta's mind trailing pain in his wake. She felt nostalgia tug at her heart strings and tried to keep her voice steady. 'It's wonderful to hear your voice, Rosa. I've missed you so much.'

'Me too, so I thought I would come and see you, if that's allright?'

'Oh, Rosa, I would love it. How quickly can you get here?' All Marta's troubles seemed to evaporate in an instant.

'Would this Friday be OK? I know it's short notice but I'd rather not be on my own right now.'

Marta knew Rosa was still pining for Paolo and completely understood. 'Of course it's OK. I'll be at the dock to meet you.' She turned and saw Nishan standing in the doorway looking oddly out of place in his tattered, stained clothing against the soft pastel warmth of the lounge décor. She handed him the dripping ice pack and made a decision. 'Can you do me a favour, Rosa?'

'If I can?'

Marta hesitated. 'I need some clothes. Do you have a fax machine?'

'No,' replied Rosa, sounding surprised.

Marta realised how ridiculous her request was. 'No, of course you don't. Is there anyone close by who does?'

She waited. The phone appeared to be dead. 'Are you there, Rosa?'

'Yes, sorry, I was thinking. Dr Navarre has a fax. I've heard it working when I've been sitting in the waiting room.'

'Dr Navarre? Surely he died years ago.'

'No, not the father. This is the son. He took over his father's practice.'

'Excellent. If you can get me his fax number, I'll send you some instructions.'

Rosa sounded unsure. 'Marta, what do I know about buying clothes for you?'

'They're not for me.' Marta paused, 'they're for a . . . friend, in need.'

'I'll ring Dr Navarre straight away and ring you back.'

'Grazie, Rosa, you're an angel, and I can't wait to see you. *Ciao.*'

Marta walk towards Nishan beaming from ear to ear.

'Now, young man, we need to get you measured for a new set of clothes. Come into the study.'

Nishan didn't argue and followed her like a lamb. Moving around him with a tape measure she noted figures on a writing pad. 'Have you any idea how big your feet are?'

Nishan shrugged his shoulders. 'I remember I take rubber shoes from dead body in desert but they small for me.'

'Never mind,' said Marta swallowing hard. 'Sit down and put your good foot on my lap.'

She was printing out the fact sheet when Rosa rang back. 'Don't worry about funds, Rosa, I still have my account with La Rinascente. I'll ring the manager and tell him to expect you. The fax is on its way to the surgery right now.'

'OK. See you on Friday, Marta. *Ciao.*'

With Rosa Necchi's voice ringing in her ears Marta disappeared into the kitchen to prepare some food, leaving Nishan standing in the hall looking vacant. Ten minutes later she paused, mid-chopping, curious about Rosa's sudden decision to

91

visit Symi. Why do I think Panayiotis has something to do with this? she thought, and carried on chopping. How could he, she concluded, the man doesn't even speak Italian.

Chapter Fourteen

Monday (evening)

Anastasia slammed the bowl down in front of Panayiotis and went back to the cooker. She spooned the rest of the thick fish soup into a second bowl and carried it to the kitchen table before settling herself in a chair.

'Mama, what's the matter?' Panayiotis put down his soup spoon and stared across at her.

Anastasia ignored him and began to eat.

'For goodness sake, Mother, say what's on your mind, the atmosphere in here is as thick as the soup.'

Anastasia placed her spoon in the bowl then sat back with her arms folded across her chest. 'You are.'

'Me. Why?' queried Panayiotis, mirroring her posture.

'Because I'm sick of you and your big mouth. I was in the pharmacy this morning when your floosy walked through the door and announced to the world that Phoebe is to work at the Jazz Café.'

'Firstly, Mother, I don't have a floosy and secondly, Phoebe will be the one to decide if she wants to work at the Jazz Café. Right now, she hasn't even been asked.' The timbre of Panayiotis's voice was dropping like a stone.

'Oh, really?' replied Anastasia, equally guttural. 'And, when do you propose to put this idea to your daughter, as you drop her off at Casa Romano?'

'Don't be ridiculous, I'll be speaking to her tomorrow and will let her know what Marta has suggested. Personally, I think she will love the idea, but she knows her own mind and will decide for herself.'

'May I remind you that my granddaughter is here to spend time with us, not act as a cheap skivvy to some toffee-nosed tourists who frequent that woman's bar? And as for that Phillipe fellow, his disgusting habits go against the teachings of our church. Phoebe is far too young to be mixing in such dreadful company.'

Panayiotis stabbed his soup with a chunk of bread. 'Your granddaughter is eighteen years of age, has probably got a boyfriend of her own and spends most of her weekends frequenting the bars and low-life discos of Athens in the company of heterosexuals and homosexuals. Given the choice of working at an upmarket bar café gaining useful work experience or getting bored sitting around Syllogos Square listening to a load of old biddies talking about the price of tomatoes, I imagine she'll opt for the café.'

Anastasia rose to her feet and leant across the table, the pocket of her pinafore soaking up the soup. 'How dare you speak to me like that? If your father was alive he would have you out of this house before your feet touched the ground.'

'If my father was alive,' countered Panayiotis, waving his spoon under her nose, 'I wouldn't even be living here and you wouldn't be able to interfere in mine or Phoebe's lives because you wouldn't know anything about them.'

Anastasia dug her fingernails into the pine table edge. 'Everyone in Symi knows about your life. Believe me, I hear the gossip. Instead of running after a woman twice your age, you should be setting a good example to your daughter. What sort of signal are you sending her when you won't even go to church to confess your sins?'

'Leave God out of this. As for Marta Romano, if she was twice my age she'd be eighty-six. You insist on believing village gossip instead of the truth and I'm glad my father is not here to see it.' Panayiotis picked up his soup bowl, pushed past his mother and emptied the contents down the sink drain.

'At least I kept my husband for thirty-six years,' yelled Anastasia twisting to face her son, her finger now prodding his chest. 'You failed to keep your wife for twelve, and if your daughter is allowed to fraternise with drunken tourists and mincing perverts you'll be losing her as well.'

Panayiotis pushed his mother's hand aside, his eyes blazing, his mother's venom reaching deep inside him. He wanted to slap her across the face and the very thought rocked him back on his feet. He grabbed the sink for support and stared at Anastasia as if seeing her for the first time.

'You have a vicious tongue, Mama, and your jealousy is spreading through you like cancer. This time you've gone too far.' Panayiotis walked out of the kitchen, packed his belongings into two large holdalls and dumped them in the hall. 'Now we're even,' he shouted as he opened the front door. 'You've just lost your one and only son. I hope you're satisfied.'

White anger prevented Anastasia from doing anything to stop him; she just stood in the waning light and allowed her life to unravel.

Danielle was seated at the bar when Marta arrived at the Jazz Café that evening. She was holding a glass of rosé wine and perched seductively on the edge of a stool tapping her foot to the sounds of Billy Holiday at the Cotton Club, her short black and gold leggings and skimpy voile top hiding very little of her shapely curves.

'I'm sorry, Danielle, have you been waiting long?'

'No, I've just arrived. Phillipe kindly offered me a glass of wine and told me you were on your way.'

'That's good.' Marta walked around the bar and poured herself a gin and tonic. 'I assume you have the letter for me.'

'Yes. Krios . . . I mean, Chief Kakos, asked me to deliver it personally and assures you that all is in order.' Danielle pulled an envelope from her gold tasselled bag and placed it on the bar. Marta picked it up and carefully read through the contents. 'Excellent. Please thank Chief Kakos for his prompt attention to this matter and thank you, Danielle, for acting as post-mistress.'

'Oh, that's alright. It's great to get away from the office early and spend time enjoying this,' she gathered in the whole bar with a sweep of her arm, 'instead of being stuck at my desk typing letters.' She noticed a middle-aged man eyeing her from a table by the door and uncrossed and re-crossed her legs.

Marta came back around the bar and pulled up a stool next to Danielle. 'Cheers,' she said as they clinked glasses. 'Here's to the Jazz Café.'

'I'll drink to that,' replied Danielle sipping her wine. 'It must be wonderful to own this bar. You get to meet so many rich and famous people . . .' Her face turned pink as she realised what she'd said. 'I mean . . . other rich and famous people.'

Marta waved her hand in the air, dismissing the correction.

'I'd love to be part of your exciting world. All I ever do is watch from the side-lines.'

'It's not all it's cracked up to be, Danielle.' Marta looked at her expensively clad customers sitting on the terrace sipping cocktails, their designer jewellery twinkling in the candle light. 'Sure, it's nice to have beautiful things, but material wealth will not guarantee health or happiness.' She suddenly thought of Nishan, the comparison so stark. 'To someone held in a refugee camp in Athens, Danielle, your life here on Symi is in the stratosphere.'

'Oh, I know, but I can't change the world and from where I'm sitting. Symi is just a dull, attractive island with nothing to offer a young person like me. Is it wrong to want what these people have?' She nodded to the customers.

Marta studied Danielle and understood her inner frustration. Wealthy tourists passed through the island like a summer tornado, unsettling the younger Symiots and leaving them feeling abandoned and irrelevant. 'Be careful what you wish for, Danielle. All that glistens is not gold. Don't be hoodwinked into believing it is.' Marta finished her drink and stood up. 'Now, you'll have to excuse me. I need to massage the egos of my illustrious customers.' She winked at the young secretary. 'That's one of the disadvantages of being well-known.'

'Darling,' enthused some theatrical female on the lower terrace as Marta appeared in the doorway. 'Do come over and say hello to Jinny and Michael. They're dying to meet you.'

Chapter Fifteen

Tuesday (mid-morning)

Captain Kostas manoeuvred the 75ft motor boat, *Poseidon*, into the centre of Yialos harbour and engaged reverse gear. He slowly increased power on both engines forcing the water below the stern to churn like a riptide causing the adjoining yachts to snatch at their mooring lines. As the heavy anchor sliced through the surface of the water and dropped like a stone the vessel motored backwards, the gap between the stern-platform and the quayside gradually reducing until the crew were able to throw both stern ropes ashore to Spiros, the harbourmaster. With practised ease he slipped these through metal rings on the quay and made fast. As the crew took up the slack he nodded to the captain high above him on the flying bridge who was speaking into a two-way radio. Seconds later the captain cut the engines.

Krios stood on the balcony of the police station and watched *Poseidon's* American ensign flap in the breeze. Captain Kostas looked across and for a split second their eyes met and held. Krios's nod was hardly discernible but the captain's thin smile acknowledged the gesture before turning away.

Sergeant Nicolaides was seated at his desk when Krios walked through the door.

'Sergeant, who's on duty this morning?'

Christos stood to attention. 'Alex is down on the harbour dealing with some new arrivals and Galen is having a late breakfast break.'

'Right.' Krios waved his hand indicating that Christos should be seated, then walked to the notice board pretending to show an interest in the notices pinned there, his face turned away from his Sergeant. 'Expecting any problems today?'

'No, none.' Christos frowned.

'Good.' He scratched his neck. 'I seem to be surplus to requirements in the Town Hall this morning. Your daughter runs my office like a well-oiled machine.'

The sergeant's face creased with delight. 'I'm pleased she's giving satisfaction.'

Krios turned and leaned against the wall. 'Oh, she's certainly doing that.' He paused. 'What time did you come on duty today?'

'Six-thirty.'

'Umm.' The Chief's eyes travelled upwards to the fluorescent light in the centre of the nicotine stained ceiling, its tube flickering due to old age. 'Well, there's no point in us both being bored. Pop off and have your coffee break, I'll watch the store. It's not often I get the chance to help out at the sharp end, and I'm sure Danielle will be grateful for getting me out from under her feet.'

Christos didn't need asking twice. 'Well, if you're sure.'

Krios nodded and tipped his head towards the door. 'Go on, before I change my mind.' His smile was infectious.

'Right, I'll be on my way then.' Christos grabbed his cigarettes and lighter from his desk and departed, chuckling to himself.

Seconds later Captain Costas mounted the police station steps and entered the building. The Police Chief was standing by the counter waiting for him.

'Your passports please,' demanded Krios, officially.

Captain Kostas handed over the passports and his crew list without saying a word.

'What was your last port of call?'

'Iskenderun, Turkey.'

'And, where are you headed?'

'Kos, to pick up passengers, then onto Athens.'

'Do you have any fire arms, illegal immigrants or drugs on board?' Krios continued checking the passports, not bothering to look up.

'No,' muttered the skipper, his hand shaking.

Krios stamped the crew-list and gathered the passports together. 'Excellent. These all seem to be in order.' He handed the documents back to the captain. 'You will need to show your Greek Transit Log, ship's papers and this crew list to the Port Authority on the other side of the harbour and pay your harbour dues but that is all merely a formality.' He extended his hand across the counter. 'Have an enjoyable stay here in Symi, Captain,' their palms met in a handshake, 'and a profitable onward passage to Athens.'

Captain Kostas dropped the passports and crew list into his canvas bag, nodded and left, pushing his uniform hat to the back of his head in a jaunty manner as he made his way around the harbour to the Port Authority office.

Krios watched him go, mentally ticking the entry in his black ledger.

Panayiotis kicked the door of his pick-up truck shut with his foot, carried a box of supplies onto the porch and dropped them on a sun-bleached pine table. He stretched his back and stared out at Pedi Bay watching the yachts and small fishing boats bobbing up and down in the breeze that funnelled down the valley and out onto open water.

His house sat amongst others skirting the bay, the beach just yards away from his front door. He had bought it in 1974 from a retired fisherman whose wife had died of cancer; at the time he and Leonora were just married. He had steadily extended it as the years went by, adding a second storey, a second bathroom and a garage when funds allowed. As a child, Phoebe had always loved climbing out of bed and running straight into the sea, splashing about naked in the shallows as her mother prepared breakfast. With little or no traffic along Pedi's waterfront, life for a child was unfettered.

He picked up the box and carried it into the kitchen, clearing a space on the worktop with one hand as he balanced the box against the edge of the unit. Once the groceries were stowed he climbed the oak staircase to the first floor, tossed his working clothes in the corner of his bedroom and stepped into the shower. From the bathroom window he could see the hillside rising behind the house, the goats meandering through the scrub chewing at anything edible, their bells tinkling as they moved. He had forgotten how pleasant it was to be away from the bustle of the Chorio with its church bells and scooter horns cutting through the constant ambient noise of human conversation. Here in Pedi all was still, only the lapping of the waves on the shingle beach and the sounds of the goats' bells breaking the silence.

He should have felt tired after a night's fishing. Instead, he felt invigorated; free from his mother's constant criticism. Once showered he returned to the kitchen, opened the pine-dresser and pulled out a bottle of Ouzo. Grabbing a straight glass from a shelf and a bottle of mineral water from the fridge he walked out onto the porch and sat, drink in hand, watching the flight of the swifts as they soared and dived between the roof tops. He lifted his glass to the sun, the milky liquid glinting in the light and toasted his surroundings.

'To Pedi,' he said, and drank deeply. 'It feels good to be home.'

As he lowered his glass his eyes fell on the boathouse further round the bay, its stone walls and pantile roof enticing him to come closer. Minutes passed in indecision. Finally, leaving his empty glass on the porch table, he lifted a rusty key from a hook on the kitchen wall and slowly wandered along the edge of the beach. It had been too long since he had been inside the boathouse, too many raw memories barring him from crossing the threshold. He chewed his inner lip as the building drew closer. Could he do this without Antonio? He had no idea, but now he was back in Pedi, he knew he had to try.

The key ground in the salt-encrusted lock, refusing to turn. Panayiotis swore and returned to the house, grabbing a can of WD40 from the garage shelf. Back at the boathouse he sprayed the lock and key liberally with the lubricant and twisted the key backwards and forwards until he felt the lock mechanism give way. Sweat was beading on his brow, his heart beating like a jack hammer against his chest. He clasped the chafed wooden knob and rotated it, easing the door away from its frame, the corroded hinges objecting like arthritic joints. The sunlight squeezed around him and bounced off a stainless steel pushpit poking out from under its winter cover, the gold lettering of *Arabesque* clearly visible on the stern below. Panayiotis leant his head against the yacht's hull, his hands flat against the teak rail and closed his eyes.

Within the privacy of the boathouse emotion swept over him like a tsunami, years of pent-up grief flooding out in gut-wrenching sobs which echoed around the interior walls, rising on a tide then gradually abating until he was spent. He lowered his hands and lifting the bottom of his shirt wiped his stained face and swollen eyes with the soft cotton fabric then stepped back and rested his buttocks on one of the three cradles horizontally supporting the yacht's mast, its standing rigging wound loosely around the metal casing.

He had no idea how long he sat there. Images of Antonio and himself decommissioning *Arabesque* on that October day all ran through his mind; removing the mast, moving her into her winter quarters, winterising the engine and outboard and covering the topsides in yards of canvas. He could taste the beers they drank that last evening to celebrate the end of another sailing season, Antonio laughing at one of the barman's jokes as he ordered another round. Months later Antonio was dead.

Panayiotis hadn't returned to the boathouse since that day even though *Arabesque* was now his, willed to him by his closest friend.

He walked to the bow, his hand gently caressing the yacht like a lover. He could hear Paolo's infectious laughter radiating from the cockpit followed by the joyful sound of Marta singing to the wind, her hair flying free in the spray. His eye's watered once more. So many memories, he thought. So many ghosts.

'Well, old friend, maybe it's time we became re-acquainted.' His words misted the dark blue gelcoat as he began to untie the straps holding the winter cover in place. Gingerly at first, Panayiotis released the canvass from its constraints, his actions gaining speed as his need to see *Arabesque* became more and more urgent. When the last strap parted he climbed onto the bow via a pair of wooden steps and began rolling the cover over and over, each rotation exposing the graceful lines of the yacht's classic design.

With dust motes clouding the air Panayiotis lifted the canvass roll off the deck like an elongated sausage and threw it over the stern. His tears were now tears of joy as he searched in vain for signs of deterioration. *Arabesque* appeared to be fine. He stepped into the cockpit and placed his hands on the helm feeling Antonio's presence at his right shoulder, nudging him to get a move on. Panayiotis laughed out loud.

'Arabesque, I think it's time we went sailing.'

Marta sat at Villa Fabrini considering Nishan's future. 'Do you have any idea where your grandfather's family might be in Italy?' This was the third time Marta had asked Nishan that question, and for the third time Nishan shook his head.

'I have to find a way of proving that you have Italian blood in your veins, and, as you don't have a passport, we must locate your grandfather.'

'But, I show you proof. You have dog tag and photo.'

'That's not enough in law, Nishan. You could have stolen them.' Marta's head shot round, her eyes boring into Nishan. 'You didn't, did you?'

'What?' asked Nishan, trying to understand her accusation.

'Steal them from someone else.'

He looked as if he'd been punched. 'No. No, I no steal.' He grabbed the family relics off the desk and clutched them to his chest as if his life depended on it.

'OK! OK! Forget I mentioned it.' Marta turned back to the computer. 'Now, let's try again with the Army website.' She tapped some key words into her search engine and they both waited for an Italian response.

Three hours later they were still at it when Panayiotis walked through the door.

'Oh, my God!' Marta leapt to her feet and tried to hide Nishan using her five-foot-four-inch high frame. It didn't work.

Panayiotis stood with his mouth open, trying to take in the scene before him. No one spoke. Nishan had no idea who the stranger was and subconsciously placed his hands on Marta's shoulders to protect her. All Panayiotis saw was a huge black man in tattered clothing about to strangle the woman he loved and he reacted accordingly.

Marta watched in horror as the two men crashed into each other, papers flying everywhere, the furniture creaking under the strain of two opposing stags locking horns in the rutting season.

'STOP IT! STOP IT, NOW!' yelled Marta as the men rolled around the floor trying to kill each other. Her words fell on deaf ears so she screamed, the power of her vocal cords piercing the chaos like a thunder clap. Both men froze, their eardrums bursting from the decibels.

Having gained their attention Marta cut the scream mid-breath and took command. 'Panayiotis, GET UP!' She switched to Italian. 'Nishan, ENOUGH!' She kicked them apart and stood with her feet splayed, hands on hips staring down at the bloodied figures. Her brain was working overtime. Greek first, she thought. 'Panayiotis, meet Nishan Amato.' She pointed to her lodger her eyes never leaving Panayiotis's face. 'Nishan, meet Panayiotis Stanis.' She repeated the gesture holding Nishan's gaze.

It was obvious neither combatant could quite take it in. Nishan spoke first, wiping blood from his lip. 'Is he friend?'

Marta nodded. 'Yes, Nishan. Panayiotis is a very dear friend.'

'Will he tell police?'

'Not if I have anything to do with it. However, now he knows you're here, he must be told everything.'

Panayiotis lost patience. 'Marta, for Christ sake, stop speaking Italian and tell me who the hell this is.' He staggered to his feet and collapsed onto the settee rubbing the knuckles on his right hand.

Marta took a deep breath. 'Panayiotis, this, as you can see, is one of your illegal immigrants. He's travelled all the way from Ethiopia to get here and is trying to reach Italy to find his Italian grandfather.'

Panayiotis's eyebrows reached his hairline.

Marta tried again. 'He understands Italian and, as a fellow countryman, I intend to help him reach his goal.' Her arms were now folded across her chest in defiance.

'But, what happens if . . .'

Marta raised her hand blocking his words. 'He won't. Now stop dripping blood onto my sofa and go pour yourself a drink. I'll explain everything'

'But . . . '

'No buts, Panayiotis. Just do as I say.' She led Nishan through to the kitchen and settled him in a chair. 'Nishan, Panayiotis doesn't speak Italian so you can't tell him your story. However, I can. Trust me, you're in no danger. In fact, this man is your best hope of getting off this island.'

The wrinkles above Nishan's nose creased like crumpled paper as he tried to understand what Marta was saying.

She knelt in front of him and rested her arms on his knees. 'Nishan, Panayiotis is a fisherman. He has his own fishing boat. He can take you to the Greek mainland. Do you understand me?'

Nishan looked across at Panayiotis standing in the doorway and slowly nodded. Panayiotis nodded by reflex even though he hadn't understood a word.

Marta pushed herself upright with her hands and turned to Panayiotis. 'Are you going to get that drink or do you propose to stand there all night looking vacant?'

Panayiotis raised his hands in submission, walked across the kitchen and poured himself a stiff brandy from the drinks cabinet. Marta produced a tissue and dabbed Nishan's now swollen lip.

She smiled. 'Will I ever get you better?'

Her patient looked at his bandaged ankle feeling the pain searing up his leg and shook his head. 'I need tablets.'

The ebony pigment around his lips had turned a muddy grey by the time Marta handed him the Paracetamol and water. 'Would you like some coffee?' she asked, looking concerned.

'No. You tell friend my story.' They watched Panayiotis standing by the sink, his disapproving stare chilling the air between them.

Marta tapped Nishan reassuringly on the shoulder, settled herself on a stool by the breakfast bar and attempted to thaw relationships. 'Right, Panayiotis, this is what I know.'

Panayiotis pulled out a dining chair, leant his arm on the heavy oak dining table and crossed his legs. 'I'm all ears,' he announced, sarcastically.

Marta pressed her lips together and straightened her skirt. 'Well, perhaps I should start at the beginning. In 1939 Ethiopia was under Italian control and Italian troops were stationed throughout that country. Nishan's grandfather, Luigi Amato, was nineteen when he arrived with his regiment in Addis Ababa and, like many other young soldiers, fell in love with a local girl and got her pregnant . . .'

The sun was setting by the time Marta reached the end of her story, '. . . I couldn't leave Nishan at the Jazz Café for obvious reasons so I brought him here and have done what I can to make him comfortable while I try to trace his Italian relations.'

Panayiotis turned the army dog-tag over in his fingers and carefully examined the sepia photograph. When he finally spoke his words cut to the bone. 'I'll repeat what I tried to say before, Marta. What happens if Krios Kakos finds him first?'

She wriggled on the end of Panayiotis's hook. 'He'll be arrested, I suppose.'

'Marta. I'm not worried about Nishan, he can handle himself. Christ, he's made it this far. I'm talking about you. Aiding and abetting an illegal immigrant is a criminal offence as you well know and Kakos would make damn sure you paid in full for your mistakes.'

Marta felt the solid floor turn to quicksand as Panayiotis drove home his point.

'At the very least you would be deported from Greece. More likely, you could find yourself serving a prison sentence in some godforsaken jail on the mainland.'

Marta's hands felt like ice. She had conveniently forgotten her own position in all of this and knew that Panayiotis was right. She recalled her meeting with Kakos the previous day and her bowels turned to water. 'Then, I'd better make sure he never finds out.' Her statement hung in the air like a guillotine, its presence pervading the room with menace.

Nishan rose from his chair and went over to Marta. 'Your friend. He no believe?'

Marta was jolted from her despair by Nishan's words. 'No, Nishan. I mean . . . no, its not you Panayiotis is questioning. It's me.'

'Why?'

'Because by helping you I could be arrested and thrown into prison.'

Nishan hobbled to the door and peered into the dusk seeing nothing. 'Your friend. He right. Better I leave. I stay is dangerous for you.'

Irrational panic coursed through her body and she shook her head violently. 'You have nowhere else to go, Nishan, so listen to me, and listen carefully.' With every word her resolve stiffened. 'You'll stay at Villa Fabrini while I find your grandfather, then I'll get you off this island to safety. I promise.' She translated the sentence for Panayiotis, brooking no argument.

Nishan looked at Panayiotis from the other side of the room, his questioning gaze self-evident. The decision would be for the older man to make. Silence descended like a lull before a storm. No one spoke.

Panayiotis sat deep in thought examining the evidence in his hands. The minutes ticked by. Finally he looked up. 'Marta, I think this whole idea is crazy but, if you're determined to go ahead with it, you'd better leave me to get Nishan off this island. My daughter would expect nothing less of me.'

Marta was across the room before he could finish the sentence, hugging him so tightly he could hardly breathe. Nishan looked on smiling in a lopsided manner, a translation unnecessary.

'I'm famished,' she announced releasing Panayiotis, 'and, as I'm the only one who can speak both Greek and Italian around here I suggest we continue to talk while I cook dinner.'

Over warmed spinach and feta pie with sautéed garlic potatoes and a Greek salad the three conspirators considered their options, Panayiotis systematically taking control.

'Where are you sleeping, Nishan?'

'Where do you think? Marta's voice had risen an octave. 'In the garage.'

'You'd better show me.' He helped Nishan struggle to his feet and the two men wandered out, leaving Marta to clear away the dishes.

'I'll bring up a single bed from Pedi tomorrow along with some of my old clothes,' announced Panayiotis as they reappeared. 'You'll need to adapt them as best you can. For now, we need to call it a day. I have some fish to catch.' He gave Marta a peck on both cheeks and shook Nishan's hand. He was about to depart when Marta stopped him with a question.

'Panayiotis, why did you call here today?'

He fumbled with his car keys trying to find the right words. 'I had some news for you.' He looked up and saw his reflection in Marta's eyes. 'I wanted you to be the first to know. I'm launching *Arabesque* next week and I'm hoping you'll be there when I do.'

Marta didn't know what to say. Like Panayiotis, *Arabesque* held so many memories for her and she felt suddenly scared. Could she handle seeing the family yacht after so long without falling apart? Her eyes searched Panayiotis's face for guidance. He squeezed her hand knowing the trauma she was going through and waited. 'Of course I'll be there,' she said, trying to be brave. 'Try keeping me away.'

Panayiotis was too choked to get any words out so he simply nodded, and walked out.

Marta lowered herself onto a dining chair and poured herself another drink. 'You know, Nishan,' she said, raising her glass, 'this could be your lucky day.'

Chapter Sixteen

Friday (am)

The dockside was packed with lorries, cars, motor bikes, foot passengers and well-wishers as Evadne pushed her way through the crowd and waited to embark. The Rhodes ferry had already arrived and was berthed stern-to the dock with an assortment of vehicles, their engines running, poised to disembark. It would be a few minutes before Evadne and her fellow passengers would be allowed onto the ship so she reached in her handbag for her mobile phone and dialled Athens.

'*Kalimera*. My name is Evadne Kakos. I have an appointment with Dr Stavros tomorrow at eleven o'clock. I was asked to ring the day before to confirm the appointment.'

'One minute please.'

Evadne covered her nose and mouth as the trucks driving past belched exhaust fumes.

'That's fine,' acknowledged the secretary, 'Dr Stavros will be waiting for you. Please ask the receptionist to call me on your arrival and I'll come down to meet you.'

'Very well,' replied Evadne through her fingers. 'Who should I ask for?'

'Selene. Selene Vangelis.'

'Thank you, Selene. I'll see you tomorrow.'

The ship's foot passengers were now pouring off the vessel, each jostling with his or her neighbour trying to make headway. Evadne felt someone push into her and turned to find Marta Fabrini standing at her side. Evadne saw red.

'Do you mind,' she demanded, a thunderous expression on her face.

Marta's eyebrows crossed. 'I'm very sorry. I'm afraid I couldn't help it. I'm being pushed from behind.' She paused, recognition dawning across her face. 'Aren't you Evadne Kakos?' Marta felt an elbow dig into her back and winced.

'As if you didn't know. I'm amazed you have the audacity to come anywhere near me, under the circumstances.'

Marta's jaw dropped to the floor. 'I beg your pardon?'

'Please don't play the innocent with me, Miss Fabrini. I would have thought a woman of your status would have shown greater discretion. Now if you'll excuse me, I have a ferry to catch.' Evadne grabbed the handle of her weekend case and dragged it across the concrete slipway, merging with the crowd boarding the ship.

'Marta. Marta! Over here.' Paolo's nanny stood balancing two large cases against her legs, her handbag slung around her neck and a pashmina over her arm, waving madly. Marta followed the familiar voice until she spotted Rosa Necchi creating a roundabout amongst a throng of moving humanity.

With Evadne Kakos's sharp words still ringing in her ears Marta pushed her way through the melee and pulled Rosa and her luggage to the back of the quay, the blast of a truck driver's horn spurring them on.

'Would you ladies like some help,' enquired Panayiotis, coming to their aid.

'I thought you'd never ask,' retorted Marta, breathing heavily. 'Where's Phoebe?'

'In the truck. Rosa, welcome to Symi.' Panayiotis kissed her on both cheeks.

'*Buongiorno,* Panayiotis.' Rosa pulled her handbag from around her neck and wiped her throat with a hankie. 'Oh dear, Marta, it's so hot here.'

Marta could have sworn that Rosa winked at Panayiotis as she pulled away from his embrace, but both were innocence personified as they looked her way.

112

Panayiotis picked up Rosa's cases and ushered them along the harbour. 'Where's your car, Marta?' he shouted over his shoulder.

'Up top.' She pointed at the Romanesque houses on the hillside. 'I've a taxi waiting to take us up there. It seemed more sensible than trying to park down here on the harbour.'

'Right then, I suggest we all adjourn to the Jazz Café for a well-deserved cold beer. Why don't you take Rosa in the taxi and I'll bring the cases in the truck with Phoebe?' Panayiotis was now powering ahead parting the crowds like an ice-breaker.

Marta nodded and took Rosa's elbow, guiding her along the crowded quayside until they reached the taxi rank. 'I'm sorry, Rosa, in all this chaos I haven't even had time to say hello.' She hugged her guest warmly, opened the car door and helped her old friend inside. 'Jazz Café, please,' she called to the driver.

The rotund, dishevelled Symiot ground his cigarette butt into the broken concrete then eased himself with difficulty into the front seat and gunned the engine. A welcomed blast of cool air immediately fanned the women and they collapsed back into their seats their hands firmly clasped together.

'Well,' Marta looked at Rosa's damp complexion and noticed the grey hairs streaking her short brown hair. 'You're finally here.' She squeezed Rosa's hand tightly. 'How long is it since you've seen Symi?'

Rosa watched the harbour dropping away as they progressed upwards. 'Five years.' She swallowed hard, pain creasing her face. 'I'd forgotten how beautiful it was and it hasn't changed a bit.'

'No, it hasn't,' agreed Marta, 'apart from Casa Romano. You'll get quite a shock when you see what I've done to our old family home.'

Rosa's eyes wandered back to the panoramic view of the harbour glimpsed between the houses as the taxi wound its way around the narrow bends leading to the lane below the Jazz Café, and soaked up Symi's splendour.

Phillipe was chatting away to Rosa in Italian when Panayiotis and Phoebe finally appeared around the corner of the Kali Strata. Phoebe squealed and ran down the steps into Marta's arms nearly knocking her flying. 'Aunt Marta, do you really mean it. Can I work here at the Jazz Café?'

Marta hugged her goddaughter then held her at arm's length. 'My, oh, my! Where did my little imp with scabbed knees go? You look positively stunning, Phoebe. You could give Claudia Cardinale a run for her money.'

Under a golden tan Phoebe's cheeks took on a rosy hue. 'Rubbish,' she said wrinkling her nose, her tom-boyish traits only skin deep. 'The scabs are still there you just can't see them through my leggings.' The others laughed at her improbable statement.

'Believe me, dear,' quipped Philippe, staring at her trim figure, 'the guys around here will not be interested in your knees.'

Panayiotis coughed loudly and changed the subject. 'How about some drinks, Phillipe, before we all die of thirst.'

The manager took the hint. 'Beers all round?' His audience nodded in unison.

'You haven't answered my question Aunt Marta. Can I really work here?' Phoebe's enthusiasm was infectious.

'That's the general plan, Phoebe, if you're agreeable. I thought it would give you some work experience and as you're studying languages and journalism this is the perfect place to practise.'

'When can I start?'

Marta looked at Panayiotis over her sunglasses seeing him tense. 'That has to be a family decision, Phoebe. Why don't you have a couple of days to settle in at home then come and talk to Phillipe? He's the one in charge around here, not me, though I don't want you working late into the evening. The road back to Pedi at night is a death trap, particularly on a rusty old scooter.'

'It's not rusty or old,' objected Panayiotis, taking a beer from Phillipe.

'It is too,' countered Phoebe. 'The handlebars squeak and the seat is all split.'

Marta smiled into her beer and translated for Rosa.

'Well, young lady,' said her father leaning forwards, 'with your pay from the Jazz Café you can trade it in for a new one, can't you?'

Phillipe raised his eyes to the heavens and crossed to the other side of the terrace where some customers were waiting.

Rosa placed her hand on Phoebe's shoulder in a motherly way and whispered in her ear. 'I imagine your tips will be so high, Phoebe, you'll be able to buy yourself a car.'

'What did she say?' asked Panayiotis nodding in Rosa's direction.

Phoebe repeated the comment in Greek causing Marta to choke on her beer.

'Why do I get the impression I'm out of my depth here?'

'Woman power, Dad,' exclaimed Phoebe, raising both fists in the air, then blowing her father a kiss.

Rosa chuckled as she repeatedly slapped Marta on the back in an attempt to stop her choking. 'Phoebe, quit while you're ahead.'

As Marta's car approached the entrance to Villa Fabrini she pulled into the verge and cut the engine. 'I need to tell you something before we get to the house, Rosa. I have someone else staying here right now . . .'

Ten minutes later they turned into Villa Fabrini and Marta pipped the horn three times to tell Nishan she was home. The car ground to a halt outside the garage and she unfastened her seatbelt.

Paolo's nanny stretched inside the rear of the car and was struggling to pull one of the cases from the back seat when a large ebony hand reached across her shoulder and lifted it out with ease. She turned expecting to see a lanky teenage youth. Instead, she found herself staring at a tall, muscular, mature African leaning on a stick, his left foot heavily bandaged.

Marta came to stand at his side. 'Rosa, this is Nishan Amato.'

Rosa's eyes travelled up his immense torso, taking in his slim waist, broad chest and wide shoulders, feeling her neck creaking as she reached his forehead. '*Buongiorno*, Nishan. My name's Rosa Necchi and I'm here to look after you.' Her words were like music to Marta's ears.

Nishan looked down at this short, rotund lady with her soft Italian voice. '*Buongiorno*, Signora Necchi.' His smile was warm and welcoming.

'Please call me Rosa.'

Nishan looked at Marta, who nodded. He dropped the case on the floor and placed his right hand over his heart. '*Selam nesh way*, Rosa.'

'That's an Ethiopian welcome,' whispered Marta.

'*Grazie*, Nishan. *Grazie*. Now, what have you done to your foot?'

Marta tucked her arm through Rosa's and waltzed her off to the house, leaving Nishan and the cases behind. 'That's a long story which I'll tell you over lunch. Let's get you settled first.'

The guest bedroom resembled a men's outfitters as Rosa stood surrounded by clothes, the empty case discarded to one side. Marta looked on with amusement as her ex-employee attempted to check the items off against a list in her hand.

'Four pairs of underpants, four men's handkerchiefs, four pairs of socks, four white cotton tee-shirts . . .'

'Enough,' announced Marta grabbing the list from Rosa's hand. 'What's the damage?'

Rosa went to her handbag and pulled out a long receipt. 'It's all here.' She handed it over. 'Oh, except the electric razor. I got that at Milan airport.'

Marta pocketed the receipt and scratched her head. 'Well, I guess we'd better get this lot down to the garage for Nishan to try on.' She began gathering up the items of clothing in her arms until only her forehead was visible.

'Here, let me help you.' Rosa grabbed half the pile and followed Marta down the stairs. 'Now I understand why everything had to be extra-large!'

Marta and Rosa were halfway to the garage when they were stopped in their tracks by a deep, rich baritone voice singing *"La Donna è Mobile"* from Verdi's opera, *Rigoletto.* Marta couldn't believe her ears and looked across at Rosa who returned her dazed expression, seemingly equally dumbfounded.

Nishan, oblivious to his audience, brushed dust out of the garage door with a long-handled broom, each sweep of the head moving in time to the melody.

When the final notes evaporated on the air, Rosa dropped everything on the floor and clapped furiously. Nishan's head slowly appeared around the garage door, looking for all the world like a puppy caught raiding the rubbish bin. Marta was so stunned she didn't know what to say and continued to stare at Nishan in disbelief.

'Where-ever did you learn that?' she asked, finally.

'My father. He sing Italian songs to me, many times. It is bad?'

'No, Nishan. It is very good. Tell, me, who trained your voice?'

'Sister Francis. She give me lessons at the Catholic Mission after Mass. She very kind.'

Marta handed her pile of clothes to Rosa and walked up to her lodger, took the broom from his hand and dropped it on the ground. 'Nishan Amato, come with me.'

He hobbled after her to the music room closely followed by Rosa, his new clothes abandoned on his bed. Marta plonked her rear onto the piano stool and indicated with a nod of her head for Nishan to stand at the window, then began playing the opening bars of "La Donna è Mobile" from memory. She looked up, her eyes alive with excitement. 'Now, Nishan, sing it again please.'

'Why?' asked Nishan, looking nervous.

'Because . . .,' Marta burst out laughing. 'Never mind, Nishan, just sing.'

As the sun reached its zenith over Villa Fabrini, Nishan sat on Panayiotis's single bed in the garage and looked at the blue jeans covering his legs. He tried to remember a previous time when he'd worn new clothes, but failed. His only memory was of third-hand cast offs from Africa Aid or some other charity. Carefully picking up the sandals from a cardboard box, he smelt the aroma of freshly tanned leather. The right one slipped onto his foot with ease, the cushioned insole caressing his rough skin like silk. This can't be happening, he thought, pulling a pure white tee-shirt over his head. I'll wake up in a minute and be back in the bowels of the Emerald Star smelling of sweat, or vomit, or worse. He stood in front of the wall mirror and viewed his reflection. The young man looking back at him from the other side of the glass was a complete stranger.

Chapter Seventeen

Friday (midday)

Phoebe dripped her way across the pebbles and grabbed her beach towel off the concrete slipway alongside the road. The water had been like liquid velvet on her skin as she'd dived and surfaced repeatedly; a human dolphin at play. The place was deserted, apart from tourists lunching at a waterside taverna. A single decker bus descended the hill from the Chorio, turned the corner and drove along the waterfront to the south side of Pedi Bay where it stopped and disgorged its passengers. Phoebe sat on an upturned wooden dinghy and flicked seawater from her hair, watching the fishermen on a small trawler berthed alongside Pedi's mole mending their nets in the midday sun. She waved as they looked up, their hands flashing across the yellow nets with practised ease. How different from Athens, she mused.

Symi was always a great joy to her, especially Pedi where all her childhood memories had originated. She looked over her shoulder and saw her father watching from his bedroom window. He pointed to his watch. It was lunchtime and he was hungry.

Rising from the wall she sauntered across the road leaving wet footprints on the porch tiles as she entered the house. Her bedroom was on the ground floor at the rear with its own en-suite bathroom. She stripped off and stood under a cold shower feeling her suntanned skin tingle with the sudden drop in temperature. Her stomach was rumbling when she reappeared draped in a cerise sarong, her thick, dark hair piled high on her head, held in place by a tortoiseshell clasp.

'Are you ready, *Koreetsi mou*?' asked her father, rattling his house keys.

'Yep. I can smell the restaurant's grilled sardines from here.' She came up behind him and wrapped her arms around his waist. 'Dad, when are you going to tell me why gran wasn't at the ferry dock this morning?'

Panayiotis held onto his daughter's arms feeling the warmth of her body through his shirt. 'What can I say, Phoebe. Your grandmother and I simply don't see eye to eye on anything these days.'

Phoebe pressed her cheek against his shoulder blades and hugged him tightly. 'I guessed as much when you said we were staying in Pedi.' She released him from her grasp and pulled him out of the house. Let's go eat. This subject will probably be more palatable on a full stomach.'

They walked arm-in-arm along the sea shore, father and daughter in total harmony. Wolf whistles from the fishermen on the mole were answered with a finger salute from their fellow seadog, a wry smile on his face.

The taverna was full when they arrived. Mateus rushed out wiping his hands on a teacloth tucked into his expansive waistband and rearranged his customers to make room for Panayiotis and Phoebe who both ordered grilled sardines, Phoebe requesting sparkling water and Panayiotis a beer. While the pair waited for their food and drinks to arrive the conversation continued.

'What was the cause of the argument this time?' Phoebe picked up a bread roll and tore it apart.

'You,'

'Me? What have I done to upset gran?'

'Nothing. Well, that's not strictly true.' Panayiotis inhaled deeply and snorted like a bull. 'Your grandmother is convinced that I've persuaded you to act as cheap labour at the Jazz Café because, and I quote, "Marta Romano is my floosy".'

'That's ridiculous.' Phoebe sat back in her chair and ticked off points on her fingers. 'For a start, I'm eighteen and can make up my own mind. Secondly, it isn't your decision and thirdly, Aunt Marta is not your floosy.' She paused. 'Is she?'

Panayiotis shook his head.

'And, fourthly, I would have thought the advantages of me working at the Jazz Café far outweighed the disadvantages irrespective of how much I'll earn.'

'Ah, but your grandmother doesn't see it that way. In her eyes, you're here to spend time with us, not tourists, and . . .'

'Dad, I love gran, but if she thinks I'm going to spend three weeks sitting with a group of old women getting bored senseless while you're off fishing, she can think again.'

'That's exactly what I told her. It didn't go down at all well.'

'Perhaps if I explain she'll understand.'

'I doubt it. The cause of your grandmother's anger isn't you, Phoebe, it's me. Apparently, I'm a bad example for you because I refuse to go to church and because I bring shame on the Stanis name by fraternising with, and I quote again, "a woman who is twice my age".'

Phoebe nearly fell off her chair. 'What?'

Panayiotis raised his hands, palms forwards.

'Is she completely senile? Your agnostic views are nothing to do with her, and, frankly, with Mama genuflecting every five minutes around Athens I would say I'm getting a very balanced viewpoint on religion.' She stopped talking while Mateus placed water and beer in front of them before moving on. 'As for Aunt Marta, can I assume gran is riddled with female jealousy?'

Panayiotis ran his thumb down the condensation on the outside of his glass. 'Perhaps, Phoebe, but deep down your grandmother is a very lonely, embittered old lady who pines for your grandfather and misses you like crazy.' He looked at his daughter from under his eyelashes. 'There was a time when she was a loving, caring individual but these days nothing seems to please her. I've tried, believe me, but always being the butt of her criticism has worn me down until I finally decided to move back to Pedi. Maybe you can make a difference. Take my advice, Phoebe, give her lots of hugs and make her feel very special. You never know, she might listen to you.'

Phoebe studied her father noticing how the troubles of the past decade had etched themselves into the furrows of his face. 'Do you love Aunt Marta, Dad?'

The question came out of the blue and hit Panayiotis smack between the eyes. He was about to refute it but stopped himself and looked out to sea. His words, when they came, were so soft they were almost a whisper. 'I suppose I've loved her since the first day I saw her, Phoebe, but in those days she was my best friend's wife and a budding opera star. Whatever has happened since, Marta is still a well-respected soprano and will only ever have two real loves in her life, Antonio and Paolo. All I can do is watch over her and be there when she needs me.' He turned his attention back to his daughter. 'Does that answer your question?'

'Yes, Dad, it does.' She placed her hand over his. 'For the record, I'm really sorry life has been so shitty for you.'

Panayiotis burst out laughing. 'I suggest you curb your language young lady or you'll also be out of the family will.'

The sardines were oozing olive oil and crushed garlic when they arrived, curtailing further conversation. Over coffee Panayiotis changed the subject.

'I've a surprise for you, Phoebe.'

'Don't tell me, you've bought me a new scooter.'

Panayiotis clenched his teeth and frowned. 'Phoebe Stanis, you're impossible. Now, do you want to know what I have to say or shall I keep it to myself?'

122

Phoebe fluttered her eyelashes provocatively, melting her father's heart.

'I've spent the last week re-commissioning *Arabesque*. I intend to sail her for the rest of the summer.'

'When are you launching her?' Phoebe was all ears.

'Sunday. I need to get the mast put back on but the locals will help me providing I buy the beers.'

'Right,' said Phoebe rising to her feet and saluting her father. '*Arabesque's* cabin boy reporting for duty, sir!'

'Perhaps you should check with your grandmother first. She has enough hang-ups about the sea without her one and only granddaughter growing flippers.'

'No problem,' shouted Phoebe as she eased her way through the tables and out onto the road. 'I'll go see her now.'

'I take it you're not paying for lunch, then?' called Panayiotis, placing his wallet on the table and signalling for the bill as his daughter disappeared along the waterfront.

The Chorio dozed in a post lunch stupor as Phoebe parked her scooter at Syllogos Square and walked over to her grandmother's house. A feeling of apprehension butterflied in her stomach as she fumbled with the wrought-iron gate and stepped across to the front door, knocking twice. Taking a deep breath, she opened the door and called out. 'Gran, it's me, Phoebe, hello.' Her call echoed around the empty hallway. She wandered through to the kitchen and tried again. 'Hello. Gran, are you there?' Silence. She walked back onto the front terrace and leant over the wall hoping to see her grandmother in the lane. It was deserted. Intent on leaving a note she returned to the hall and found her grandmother standing by the bedroom door, hair dishevelled, defiance written all over her face.

'Hello, gran. I'm sorry, were you resting?'

Anastasia pushed her wispy hair into some semblance of order and held out her arms. 'My dear girl, the sight of you is all the rest I need. I haven't seen you for months.'

Phoebe went into her grandmother's embrace smelling onions and oregano on her flowered apron strings. They remained in this position for some seconds before Anastasia patted her granddaughter on the back, suggested some coffee and walked through to the kitchen.

Phoebe sat at the wooden table feeling like a UN peace-keeper in the presence of an intransigent dictator and searched for a suitable opening line. Anastasia beat her to it going straight for the jugular.

'I understand you're working at that bar on the Kali Strata?'

Phoebe felt her hackles rise, swallowed hard and kept her voice low. 'Nothing is decided yet. I have to talk to Phillipe in a couple of days' time.' She decided to be diplomatic. 'What do you think to the idea, gran?'

Anastasia raised her eyebrows and pulled her chin into her neck. 'Why would you be interested in my opinion, Phoebe? From what your father tells me, you have a mind of your own these days.'

Phoebe walked around the kitchen table and wrapped her arms around her grandmother's neck. 'Because I value your opinion.' She felt Anastasia's rigid shoulders begin to relax and kissed her on the top of her head.

'Well, child, I can't say I'm happy about it. You're only here for three weeks and I'm sure you have ample opportunity in Athens to mix with foreigners.'

Her xenophobic emphasis on the last word was not lost on Phoebe. 'You're right on both counts, gran.' Anastasia's spirits rose. 'But with dad off fishing most nights and sleeping most days I won't be seeing a lot of him anyway and I'm sure you won't want me under your feet all the time.' She waited for her words to sink in. 'Let's be honest, I don't have a lot in common with the elderly ladies here in the village.'

Anastasia grunted. 'Yes, but . . .'

Phoebe was on a roll. 'I thought I would come here for breakfast and then help Phillipe from, say, ten till one. Go back to Pedi for lunch with Dad, have the afternoon to myself and return here for dinner with you before starting the evening shift. How does that sound?'

Anastasia wanted to argue but couldn't find a suitable way to counter Phoebe's plan. She changed tack. 'I hope they're going to pay you a decent wage. Marta Romano is certainly not short of a drachma or two. Why she wanted to turn Casa Romano into a bar in the first place is beyond me.'

'Gran, I'm sure Aunt Marta will pay the going rate for an eighteen-year-old with no experience so don't worry about that. The Jazz Café is becoming very famous, you know. I read a review on it in the Athens press only last week. Working there will be great for my CV. My friends will be green with envy when they find out.'

Anastasia leant her head on Phoebe's arm appearing to accept defeat. 'Well, if you're sure, but I don't want you mixing with those foreign boys who roam about Yialos harbour with too much money and no sense.'

Phoebe smiled behind Anastasia's head then rearranged her facial features and returned to her seat. 'Are you going to ask how dad is?'

Anastasia tensed immediately. Undeterred, Phoebe continued.

'He's decided to put *Arabesque* back into the water so I'll be sailing on Sundays.' Phoebe could see her grandmother's eyes narrowing. 'He so loves that yacht, doesn't he?'

'Oh, yes.' Anastasia's mouth turned down at the corners. 'He loves anything to do with the Romano family.' Phoebe

125

pretended to ignore her grandmother's acrimony. 'After spending his whole life fishing, you would think that sailing would be the last thing he'd want to do.'

The doorbell rang curtailing Phoebe's trite reply.

'Answer that, will you, dear. It's probably Father Voulgaris.'

You devious old biddy, thought Phoebe, as she opened the door and stared into the cold grey eyes of one of Symi's spiritual leaders. '*Kalimera*, Father Voulgaris. Do come in. My grandmother is expecting you.' She stepped back noting the flecks of dandruff on his black cassock, his greasy rat's tail of hair tied back with a black band beneath his hat. Greek Orthodoxy didn't seem to encompass personal hygiene, decided Phoebe, breathing in stale sweat as the authoritative figure brushed past her and walked into the kitchen.

'I see your prodigal granddaughter has returned to the fold, Anastasia.'

Anastasia kissed the back of the priest's hand, pulled out a chair for him and directed Phoebe to pour more coffee. 'It's wonderful to have her back home, Father, believe me.'

'Will we be seeing you in church on Sunday, Phoebe?' He smiled, stained teeth protruding from a mass of grey facial hair.

Phoebe gritted her teeth as she picked up the coffee percolator, unsure how to reply.

'Of course she will, won't you, child?' said Anastasia, asserting her authority. 'Phoebe?'

Phoebe handed the priest his coffee. 'My grandmother would be disappointed if I didn't attend, Father, so I'm sure you'll see me there.' She smiled sweetly at her grandmother conceding defeat. Anastasia nodded regally and turned her attention back to the priest.

'Gran,' said Phoebe, in a rush, 'I think I'll leave now. I'm sure you and Father Voulgaris have things to discuss and I need to get back to Pedi. As soon as I've spoken to Phillipe I'll let you know what's happening at the Jazz Café.' She pecked her grandmother on the cheek and picked up her keys.

Phoebe was not to be let off the hook quite so easily. Anastasia gripped her shorts and turned to the priest. 'Father, my granddaughter and I would value your opinion on whether she should work at Marta Romano's bar during her vacation.' Phoebe's heart sank. 'Do you think it's a suitable place for an eighteen-year-old?'

The priest sucked on a wooden tooth pick playing for time. 'In normal circumstances I would say not.' Phoebe could have killed him. 'But Phoebe lives in Athens which, as you know, my dear, is a den of iniquity. If she can survive living there, I'm sure she'll survive working at the Jazz Café.'

Phoebe wanted to kiss him, but looked as his grizzled beard and decided against it. 'There you are, gran. If Father Voulgaris believes it's OK who am I to argue?' She peered at her grandmother sideways. Game, set and match to me, she thought as she eased her shorts from her grandmother's grasp. 'Now, if you'll both excuse me, I'll be on my way.' She was out of the door before her grandmother could think up any other hurdles for her to jump over and sighed with relief.

That was close, she thought as she straddled her scooter and gunned the engine leaving a trail of blue smoke from the exhaust as she accelerated out of the village.

Panayiotis was gutting a barracuda when Phoebe arrived home. 'How did it go?'

Phoebe opened the fridge and took out a can of Coke. 'On a scale of ten; four and a half!' She flicked the ring with her thumb and drank straight from the can. 'I was doing fine until Father Voulgaris arrived, then it went a bit downhill . . .'

She gave her father a brief explanation of events, the odd expletive peppering her prose. '. . . Still, he came good in the end. What's for dinner?'

'Barracuda. Do me a favour and chop some garlic, onions and tomatoes and pop them in the pan.' He pointed his knife at the cast-iron frying pan on the stove. 'So, you're off to church on Sunday?'

Phoebe wrinkled her nose and nodded.

'Well, at least your mother will be pleased. I suggest you stay with your grandmother for lunch then come and join me at the boatyard. By then we should have *Arabesque's* mast up and the rigging sorted.'

Phoebe was attacking the onions with grave intent. 'OK. I'll try and see Phillipe after church then I'll know what I'm doing on Monday.' She dropped the onions into the hot oil.

'Marta will be in Pedi to see the yacht launched so you can let her know your plans when you get back.'

Phoebe moved the onions around with the wooden spoon and added the garlic and tomatoes. 'Where do you want these when they're cooked?'

'Lay them in the bottom of the roasting dish with the potatoes, carrots and parsnips. I'll char the fish and stick it on top with a bit of stock and some oregano and we can leave it all to cook slowly in the oven while we have a swim.' He winked at his daughter as he peppered the fish.

Phoebe beamed. 'Now, that's what I call good planning, Dad.' She turned back to the stove licking her top lip, already tasting the salt water.

Chapter Eighteen

Sunday (mid-morning)

Sunday had dawned bright and clear; a perfect day to launch *Arabesque*. Marta and Rosa drove across the island to Pedi, excitement and apprehension battling for control. The classic yacht lay in her slings above the dock casting a shadow over all who stood below her. Marta moved forwards, her hands clasped tightly together trying to control her emotions. The others watched her, no one invading her privacy as she paused by the jetty, her heart thumping against her ribcage as she followed the familiar dark blue hull describe an arc in the air as the derrick turned towards the water and gently lowered its precious cargo towards the cobalt sea. The yacht's wine red keel kissed the water and disappeared as her crew cast off her restraints and the Hinckley Bermuda 40 rested, port-side to the dock, her fenders protecting the hull from damage. She looked forlorn without her mast but her gleaming gelcoat and sparkling chrome stanchions made up for this temporary disfigurement.

Panayiotis nodded to his crew and ropes, recently coiled on the teak deck, appeared to take flight, unravelling as they travelled towards the wharf. Other strong hands plucked them from the air and whipped them around secure metal rings in the concrete quay before returning them to the yacht's own stainless steel cleats. *Arabesque* was finally launched and berthed securely beside the derrick, only hours away from feeling the wind in her sails.

Panayiotis stepped ashore, his concentration never wavering from Marta's face as he came forward, then wrapped his arm around her slight frame and walked her across the jetty. There wasn't a dry eye in the yard.

'Hello old friend,' she said, brushing away a tear. She placed both hands on the yacht's guardrail and pulled herself aboard then leant towards the coach-roof and placed her lips against the warm varnished surface. *Arabesque* whispered a welcome as only sailing boats can.

The pungent smell of fresh varnish and engine oil pervaded the cabin as Marta descended the companionway steps, bringing back a myriad of memories. She settled herself at the chart-table and let her eyes scan the yacht's familiar interior, settling on the framed photograph of Paolo at eight-years-old, standing on the stern-deck with his fishing rod in one hand and a large sea bass in the other, his face, a picture of pride and amazement. Marta brushed two fingers across her lips and gently pressed them against her son's face, recalling every detail of that day, the pain of the memory clawing at her heart. Spontaneously she lifted the chart-table lid to examine the contents inside and came across Paolo's sunglasses hiding between sets of Admiralty charts and heard herself whimper as she clutched them to her chest, hearing her son's voice complaining that he couldn't find them. She rested her head in her hands and closed her eyes. Paolo had driven her to distraction over losing things. He was constantly chided by his parents for being such a scatter brain.

Marta stopped breathing, her head came up and she stared straight ahead remembering the day Paolo lost his rucksack.

'ROSA!' Marta was up the companionway steps and out of the cockpit in a flash, heading towards the foredeck and Paolo's nanny. 'Rosa, can you remember the day Paolo lost his rucksack at school?'

Rosa scratched her head. 'Yes. Yes, I can. He came home in tears saying he'd left it in the school locker room but when he went back for it, it wasn't there. He was terrified you and Antonio would be angry. Why?'

'When was that exactly?'

'Oh, goodness.' She looked at her deck shoes for inspiration. 'I think you were away. Yes, that's right, you were at the Teatro dell'Opera in Rome, because you rang home just before the performance to say goodnight to Paolo and he was too nervous to speak to you.'

'OK, OK. Now, am I right that the headmaster found it the following morning on a peg in the corridor?'

'Yes,' answered Rosa, now with perfect recall. 'We didn't think anything of it at the time. Paolo was always forgetting where he'd put things.'

Marta turned to Panayiotis. 'Can I use your phone?'

Panayiotis hadn't understood one word. 'Sure. What's the problem?'

'I'll tell you on the way to the house. I need to ring Milan, urgently.'

Minutes later Captain Silvano was taking down the details. 'Can you be precise on when this happened, Marta?'

'No, not right now, but the date is in my work diary at Villa Fabrini. I can tell you later this afternoon.' She paused. 'Captain Silvano, could someone have taken the rucksack to make a copy then returned it to the school the following day?'

'Maybe. With luck the headmaster will have a record of everyone working at the school that day which might give us a clue.'

'There's something else.' Marta felt empowered. 'On the morning of the murders, Antonio was already in the lift with the police guard waiting for Paolo. As my son ran out of the apartment he shouted to his father asking where his rucksack was and Antonio said that the policeman had it and to hurry up.' She paused. 'Did the police guard take it deliberately so he could swap it for the bomb once they reached the garage?'

131

'Can you remember if you'd seen the police officer before that day?'

Marta closed her eyes and forced herself to concentrate. 'No . . . No, I'm sure he was different from the usual guard. The regular policeman was taller and older.' Marta's legs went to jelly. 'Oh, my God. Was he the murderer?' Her blood pressure rocketed.

'We don't know that, Marta, not yet, but my gut reaction is that we're getting close. If you can send me a faxed description of the man you saw, I will circulate it to the other officers. One of them may remember him.'

'I'll do it as soon as I get home.' She was shaking like a leaf. Another thought formed into a question. 'I know this sounds crazy, but can you recommend a private detective?'

Captain Silvano swallowed air. The last thing he needed was Marta getting involved with the investigation. 'Why?'

'I've promised someone here in Symi that I would help locate an old Italian soldier from the Second World War and, so far, I've drawn a blank.'

The captain coughed to hide his relief. 'I have just the man. Alberto Zappa. He worked with me here in Milan before retiring and now does the odd private investigation. I'll get him to give you a ring.'

Marta put down the phone and leant against the kitchen wall, her haunted face drained of all colour.

'What is it, Marta?' demanded Panayiotis, searching her expression for clues.

She looked across at him and continued to shake. 'This is going to sound crazy, Panayiotis, but I think I've seen Antonio's murderer.'

132

Chapter Nineteen

Monday (a.m.)

It seemed odd eating breakfast alone in the Jazz Café. Marta sat at the bar toying with her croissant thinking of Panayiotis and Phoebe together in Pedi and suddenly felt left out. She poured milk into a dish and went into the alley hoping to see the kitten but it wasn't there. 'Even the cat has abandoned me,' she complained, walking back inside, an image of Nishan and Rosa enjoying each other's company at Villa Fabrini adding to her misery. She flicked the switch on the music centre. 'That's enough, Marta Fabrini. You're not a victim, so stop acting like one.'

Seconds later Dave Brubeck's classic *'Take Five'* filled the void and Marta's mood lightened. As the Jazz Café's clock chimed the half hour, Marta picked up her coffee cup and walked out onto the Kali Strata which was bathed in a warm morning glow. It was empty. Below her and, as yet out of view, the hooves of a mule pack clattered on the steps, the sound echoing off the buildings. She waited for the leading mule to appear around the lower corner, it's back heavily laden with building supplies for some house renovation higher up the hillside, its head down, ears twitching as it slowly ascended, a journey it had done hundreds of times before. Nose to tail, a crocodile line of other equine low-loaders steadily came into view, climbing sure-footedly towards the Jazz Café where they paused for a loving pat on the neck from Marta before continuing on their way. The sight of these docile animals undertaking a journey which their forebears had trodden for centuries always made her smile. She nodded to the old Symiot driver bringing up the rear, his bowed legs and knobbly knees tanned to nut-brown from years exposed to the Mediterranean sun, his gnarled hands, nicotine stained and riddled with arthritis gently tapping the hind-quarters of the last mule with a short stick and clicking his tongue against his teeth in an attempt to hurry his charges along.

Marta's smile was wiped off her face when Krios Kakos appeared around the bend, standing back against the dry-stone wall as the mule train passed by. His eyes met hers across the conga-line and Marta froze.

Seconds later, he mounted the steps to the bar, crossing the threshold recently vacated by Marta and went inside. She stood behind the counter placing it between them like a barrier and busied herself clearing away her breakfast things.

'Good morning, Marta. Did you receive my letter from Danielle?'

Marta nodded making no comment.

'I do hope our little contretemps the other day has not affected our ability to be civil to each other.' He looked so smug to Marta.

She stopped what she was doing and raised her head, her expression, glacial. You bastard, she thought as she formulated a response, you're so thick skinned you ought to be tanned. The silence between them crackled with static. 'In this business, Chief Kakos, we learn to be civil to all our customers.'

He leant against the counter, his chest resting on his arms, his eyes boring a hole in her forehead. 'I'm surprised you're not flattered by my interest, Marta. In my experience, most women of your age are very grateful for any male attention they can get.'

Marta found his comment offensive but was determined not to rise to the bait. 'Then I'm sorry to disappoint you, but I appear to have more admirers than the women who welcome your advances.'

Krios didn't flinch. 'I must assume from that comment that you are propositioned regularly, Marta.'

'No, Chief Kakos, most other men keep their affections for their wives.' She needed to change the subject before her temper got the better of her. 'Now, can I get you a coffee or are you passing through?'

When he spoke again his words were pure acid. 'Would it have helped my case if I had smelled of fish?'

Marta's reaction was instantaneous; her right palm shot out and made contact with his left cheek.

Phoebe stood in the doorway, eyes like doorstops. Krios sensed that someone else was in the bar and slowly turned, a red wheel mark clearly visible across his face.

'I'm sorry,' mumbled Phoebe riddled with embarrassment. 'I didn't mean to intrude.'

Marta shot round the bar, white-hot anger clearing from her vision. 'You haven't, Phoebe. The Police Chief was just leaving.' She took Phoebe by the arm and propelled her across the Kali Strata terrace and sat her on a wrought-iron chair facing away from the Jazz Café. 'Now, young lady, let me explain how we run things around here.'

By the time Phillipe arrived Phoebe was fully conversant with the layout of the Jazz Café and trying her hand at operating the coffee machine. Marta had made no mention of the scene with Krios Kakos and Phoebe began to believe she'd imagined it. Phillipe, oblivious to events, opened his mouth and stepped straight in.

'I've just seen the Police Chief on the harbour. He looks as if he's run into a wall.'

Phoebe concentrated on making coffee while Marta watched from behind. 'I'm glad you noticed, Phillipe, as it was my hand that caused it. The man's insufferable and deserved all he got.'

Phillipe's jaw dropped to his chest.

'Aunt Marta, how long do I steam the milk for?'

Marta's head was pounding. 'You tell her, Phillipe, and close your mouth, you're causing a draught.'

She sat on the apartment balcony remonstrating with herself for being so stupid and watched Krios Kakos talking to Sergeant Nicolaides by the clock-tower, apparently wearing his reddened cheek like a badge of honour. Evadne Kakos's sharp words and strange behaviour down at the ferry dock sprang to mind and Marta had a sudden premonition that things were not right in the Kakos household and that she was somehow implicated. Still smarting from Krios's insult, and before reason could take hold, Marta left the Jazz Café and walked up to the Kakos villa. She had no idea if Evadne Kakos would see her but she was determined to get to the bottom of the problem, one way or the other.

Indignation carried her up the steps to the main door. She rang the bell and waited. The cook finally answered and invited Marta into the hall while she went to find her mistress. Marta paced the ceramic tiled floor admiring the antique dresser and gilt-framed paintings as she passed by. Someone has good taste, she thought, doubting it was Krios. She was on her third circuit when Evadne finally appeared at the top of the stairs and regally descended, her cream linen trousers and burnt-orange silk blouse exuding quality.

'I understand from Cook that you wish to see me.' There was no pleasure in her voice.

Marta turned. 'That's correct. I came to enquire if you were feeling better?'

Evadne frowned. 'I'm sorry?'

'My manager at the Jazz Café told me that you were feeling faint the other day and needed his help.'

'Thank you for your concern but it was nothing. Perhaps too much sun.' A pink blush appeared above Evadne's collar. 'Shall we go into the morning-room?' She indicated a door on her right and took the lead.

The room was light, airy and welcoming. Pale yellow walls bordered a pastel ceramic tiled floor, mostly hidden by a large circular white rug. White and lemon linen drapes wafted in the breeze from the two huge windows framing the outer Bay of Symi in all its magnificence. Impressionist watercolours decked the walls, the whole drawn together by a tall gilt Rococo mirror suspended above an imposing white marble fireplace. Evadne sat at one of two cream settees expecting Marta to do the same. Marta chose to remain standing.

'So, Kyría Romano, what can I do for you?'

'Perhaps we can begin by you calling me Marta.'

Evadne played with her wedding ring, twisting it around her finger.

'May I call you Evadne?'

A pregnant pause ensued, Evadne seemingly vacillating between a desire to reject the request and the need to be polite. Her nod, when it came was barely visible.

'Thank you. Now, Evadne, have I done something to upset you?'

Evadne's hands gripped the edge of her seat cushion, eyes moving erratically around the room.

'Obviously I have.' Marta walked to the empty settee and sat opposite the Police Chief's wife, leaning her elbow against the upholstered arm. 'Your reaction to me at the ferry dock on Friday was far from friendly. However, I'm afraid I have no idea what I've done wrong. Goodness, we hardly know each other.'

Evadne raised her chin in defiance and tried to take the high ground. 'I have reason to believe, Kyría Ro . . . Marta, that your relationship with my husband is far from platonic.'

137

Marta blew a fuse. 'If you're suggesting what I think you're suggesting, Kyría Kakos, you've got the wrong woman. I wouldn't touch your husband if he was the last man standing. His attitude to women is Neanderthal, his ego taller than the Eiffel Tower and his professional conduct questionable in the extreme. What you or any other woman finds attractive about this man is beyond my comprehension and frankly, I'm insulted by your accusation.' She ejected herself from the settee and towered over her accuser like a Gorgon. 'Correction, I have touched your precious husband. I smacked him across the face less than two hours ago for being downright insolent.' She crossed to the door and grabbed the handle before continuing. 'Whatever you think of me, you're wrong and I'd appreciate it if you didn't spread these malicious rumours around Symi. It happens to be a very small community and, unlike you, I have to live in it without the condescending protection of this island's Police Chief.' The door bounced on its hinges as Marta pulled it open revealing the flustered cook holding a silver tray of delicate china cups and saucers and a pot of steaming coffee.

'KYRÍA ROMANO. WAIT!'

The cook backed away from the door and carried her tray into the rear of the house, leaving Marta frozen in time. The oppressive silence appeared to be manacling her to the spot and she was drowning in a sea of injustice and rage. Evadne's words surfaced through a tide of emotion.

'Kyría Romano, I was out of order and obviously under some misapprehension. I am in your debt. I've wanted to slap my husband for years but I've never had the courage to do so. I hope you hurt him.'

Marta raised her eyes to the top of the door frame and cleared her throat. 'I imagine his left cheek will be wearing the imprint of my hand for the rest of the day.'

Evadne walked to the window and wrapped her arms around her chest as Symi Bay swam before her eyes. 'Please accept my apology. Accusing you of being one of my husband's loose women has been a terrible mistake. I have no excuse, of course, but when I saw you coming out of the Town Hall last Tuesday looking very pleased with yourself and then caught sight of my husband's supercilious expression as he stood at his office window watching you walk across Kambos Square, I'm afraid I assumed the worst.'

Marta shook her head in disbelief trying to persuade herself that this was for real and not some tragic Italian opera. 'Is this why you tripped outside the Jazz Café and needed Philippe's help to get home?'

Evadne hesitated. 'Yes, and I'm very grateful for your manager's concern.'

Marta rummaged inside her bag for the Dictaphone tape then turned and looked directly at her accuser. 'I promised your husband I would wipe this tape but I think you should hear it first. You won't like what you hear but it will explain my apparent happiness last Tuesday.' She crossed the morning-room and placed it in Evadne's hand.

'Is this incriminating evidence against my husband?' A flash of pure malice crossed Evadne's face.'

'Yes.'

Evadne gripped the tape like a sword and appeared to Marta to be strangely liberated. She looked up, her proud demeanour back in place. 'I will return it, Kyría Romano. You have my word.'

A telescopic passerelle emerged from the silver-grey stern of *Intermezzo* and juddered its way towards the quay, coming to rest inches above Krios Kakos's feet. He stepped aboard ignoring the captain and crew and took the rear stairs two at a time to the upper deck where the owner, Fabio Grigio, waited in silence. Moving into the plush saloon Krios embraced a short, rotund, balding Italian, his thick neck and double chin merging into one, his heavily-lidded green eyes magnified behind thick lensed spectacles.

'*Buongiorno,* Krios. How are things in Symi?'

Krios knew what Fabio was referring to, raised his eyebrows and nodded while Miriam, the uniformed stewardess, hovered, within ear shot, ready to provide drinks on demand. Krios had never seen her before and assumed she was new.

On the quay, passers-by gawped at the one hundred-and twenty-foot motor-yacht, taking photographs to show the neighbours back home or standing, hoping to catch a glimpse of some well-known celebrity or two. Krios walked over to the black-tinted windows and looked down on the crowd feeling superior, revelling in the knowledge that the onlookers would be disappointed. This owner preferred his anonymity, remaining under the radar whenever possible. Fabio Grigio had never courted fame but was nevertheless infamous.

'I plan to leave on our little jaunt around eight o'clock tonight. Is everything arranged?' asked Fabio picking up his coffee cup. He waved the stewardess away with the flick of his hand, impatient for her absence.

Krios answered without turning round. 'Of course.' He waited until the stewardess had departed. 'I assume she will be staying ashore tonight.'

'Naturally. Miriam is looking forward to sampling the delights of Symi at my expense. Perhaps you could get one of your officers to act as her escort.'

Krios noticed Alex Laskaris talking to one of the crew by the passerelle. 'That won't be a problem.' He paused, running the tip of his tongue across his upper lip. 'I thought I'd bring a guest.' He looked back over his shoulder at his host expecting agreement and wasn't disappointed. 'The shipment from Turkey will meet us in Thessalona Bay . . .'

An hour later Fabio Grigio placed his hand on the Police Chief's back and walked him out onto the upper deck. 'I'll see you later then, Krios.' They parted at the top step, the Italian unwilling to go further. When Krios stepped ashore he beckoned Alex over to his side, gave some instruction to the young officer and left.

Alex looked from his superior's departing back to the stern of Intermezzo unsure whether to laugh or cry. He had hoped to spend his free evening playing basketball with his mates followed by a few beers. No chance of that now, he mused, scratching his head.

Danielle was tidying her desk ready to go for lunch when Krios returned to the Town Hall.

'Come into my office, Danielle.'

She followed him, annoyed that he might detain her from leaving. She checked her watch praying that the boutique behind Skala Square wouldn't close before she got there to try on the figure-hugging dress displayed in the window.

'I've just come from *Intermezzo*.' That grabbed Danielle's attention.

'I had no idea she was coming in today. Is she still here?' Danielle was now torn between buying that little black number or wandering provocatively past the magnificent motor-yacht in the hope of attracting the crew's attention.

'Yes, she's still here. In fact, tonight I'm invited to a cocktail party on board and can take a guest.'

Danielle stopped breathing.

'I wondered if you'd like to join me.'

Danielle's cry of delight could be heard on the other side of Kambos Square. She really did need that dress now. She rushed out of the office and dashed across the square on four inch mules, her buttocks playing catch up beneath her leopard skin leggings, much to the delight of male onlookers.

Krios sat at his desk cleaning his nails with the blade of his Swiss army knife pondering on the evening ahead, the anticipation giving him an erection. As for his wife, she would be spending another night dining alone.

Chapter Twenty

Monday (evening)

Alex Laskaris wanted to impress *Intermezzo's* stewardess so chose a table on the upper terrace of the Jazz Café.

'This is a great spot, Alex.' Miriam looked over the heads of the other customers to the twinkling lights across the harbour.

'That's why it's so popular,' replied Alex. 'Plus Marta Fabrini, of course.'

'Of course,' said Miriam, and changed tack. 'How about a cocktail?'

Alex turned and raised his hand to Phoebe serving at another table. He was beginning to enjoy himself being seen out and about with a good looking female. Phoebe arrived at his shoulder.

'Hi, Alex, are you going to introduce me to your friend?'

'Phoebe, meet Miriam from *Intermezzo*.' He pointed to the motor-yacht dwarfing everything else in the harbour. 'Miriam, this is Phoebe, heavily disguised as a Jazz Café waitress but, in reality, a budding journalist studying at Uni in Athens. Be careful what you say, it could appear in print any time soon.'

Phoebe clipped him around the ear and shook Miriam's hand. 'Now, what can I get you? I can recommend "Sex on the Beach".'

Alex resembled a beetroot and dived into his cocktail list. Miriam, amused by his embarrassment, winked at Phoebe and ordered a daiquiri.

'Make that two,' he spluttered trying to gain composure as Phoebe turned away. 'Miriam, have you worked on *Intermezzo* long?'

'No. I've only been on board a couple of months and most of that was spent crossing the Atlantic from the Caribbean. Fabio Grigio owns an island off Grenada.'

Having never crossed an ocean, Alex was impressed. 'At least you get to see the world. I spend my days shuffling paperwork and chasing illegal immigrants around the local hillside.'

'What illegal immigrants?' asked Phoebe returning with their drinks.

'Haven't you heard?'

Phoebe shook her head.

'We had fifty-eight illegal immigrants land on Symi last week. They were dumped on the beach at Ayia Marina by some ship in the middle of the night. It was your dad who found them climbing the hill as he returned from fishing at dawn. He reported the sighting to the Coastguard on the VHF. I'm surprised he didn't tell you.'

'What happened to them?' asked Miriam.

'We gathered them together in Kambos Square, put them on the ferry to Rhodes and sent them packing.' Alex failed to notice Phoebe clenching her teeth. 'I imagine they are now cooped up in Lavrios Detention Centre near Athens while the Government decides what to do with them.'

'Phoebe, dear, some customers want their bill.'

Phoebe turned to Marta, guilt spreading across her face. 'I'm sorry, Aunt Marta, I'm on my way. Alex, introduce Aunt Marta to Miriam.'

'Alex,' chided Marta imitating a school mistress, 'I can't have you monopolising all the good looking girls at my establishment.' Her expression relaxed into a broad smile. 'Although I must say, you have excellent taste.' She walked around to Miriam and stretched out her hand. 'Hello, Miriam, welcome to the Jazz Café. Is this your first visit?'

'Good evening, Miss Fabrini.' They shook hands. 'Yes. Alex has kindly agreed to forfeit his night off to chaperone me around Symi.'

Marta frowned so Alex explained. 'Miriam is the stewardess on *Intermezzo* down there. She's been given the night off.'

Marta gave the ship her full attention. 'Isn't that an Italian ensign at the stern?'

'Yes,' said Miriam, 'the owner is Italian.'

'Really, would I know him?' Marta caught sight of Krios Kakos walking along the quay, Danielle tripping along beside him in five inch heels and a black dress that would better be described as a belt. Alex noticed too.

'I'm not sure, Miss Fabrini. My boss is Fabio Grigio, the Italian property tycoon.'

Marta's eyes followed Krios and Danielle as they boarded the ship. 'Really?' She turned away from the harbour. 'How about another cocktail?'

'No thanks,' said Alex. 'Once we've finished our drinks we have a dinner reservation at the Syllogos Restaurant.'

'Well, Miriam, it was nice meeting you. Do come again.'

'I will,' said Miriam draining her daiquiri. 'Goodnight.'

Marta stood and watched *Intermezzo* move away from the quay and hoped Evadne Kakos hadn't seen what she had just witnessed. Crossing to clients who had been trying to gain her attention, she had a niggling suspicion that Fabio Grigio's name was important but couldn't think why. Captain Silvano will know, she thought, and made a mental note to question him about the Italian property tycoon when they next spoke.

In the dark of the terrace Evadne watched *Intermezzo* leave her berth and move into the bay, the bright lights of her rear deck illuminating the passengers from above. To get a more detailed view she raised her binoculars and focused them on her husband and felt the ice-cold blade of a knife slice into her chest. She saw him take two glasses of champagne from the steward and hand one to Danielle who leant provocatively into his arm, her tight fitting black dress exposing too much flesh, her dark-brown hair cascading over her shoulders in loose curls. 'Dear God, Krios, is that what you've come to.' She took the tape-recorder out of her pocket and placed the earpiece in her ear. As *Intermezzo* floated off into the night, Evadne listened again to her husband's foiled attempt at manipulating Marta Romano for sex and mentally hammered the final nail into the lid of her marriage.

Chapter Twenty One

Intermezzo moved serenely out of Symi Bay and, staying close inshore, cruised south along Symi's eastern shore under a canopy of stars. The frothing white wake from the ship imitated the bubbles in Danielle's glass of Cristal champagne and she leaned out over the rail feeling the breeze lifting her hair and cooling her alcohol-flushed cheeks. She rose on her toes to get a better look at the waterline and enjoyed the freedom of feeling bare feet on teak, her high-heeled shoes abandoned at the ship's stern on arrival.

'Don't fall over, Danielle?' Fabio Grigio stood beside her, his delicate aftershave tempering the ozone aroma of the sea.

'I'm sorry?' Daniele focused on her host's face, his skin peppered with indentations from the boils and pimples of his youth, his big lips giving an impression of an elderly wrasse.

'You appeared to be mesmerised by the water.'

Danielle wasn't sure how to respond. She was certainly feeling out of her depth but didn't want Fabio Grigio to know that. On the other hand, her limited database of social chit-chat didn't give her much scope for conversation. She decided to compliment her host instead. 'I feel very privileged to be invited here this evening, Sir.'

Fabio smiled into his champagne glass. 'There's no need to be so formal, Danielle. Please called me Fabio, and don't thank me, thank Krios. He felt you would make a very pleasant addition to our small gathering, and I have to say, I agree with him.' His eyes wandered over her plunging neckline as he clicked his thumb and forefinger at an invisible steward. Like magic, the steward appeared from nowhere holding a bottle of chilled champagne and refreshed her glass. 'Have you been introduced to the rest of the party?'

Danielle looked across the deck at two small groups of middle-aged men, each expensively but casually dressed, all in serious discussion. 'I think so.' She moved away from the rail willing Krios to come and rescue her and sipped her drink playing for time.

'We're expecting others to join the party when we arrive in Thessalona Bay. Enjoy the short passage and do help yourself to the canapés. I'm assured by my chef that they are the best in Greece.'

A tray of bite-sized delicacies was wafted under Danielle's nose and, not recognising any, she picked the nearest one to her. The seared scallop encased in a warm fusion of wild mushroom, asparagus and lemon mousse melted in her mouth.

'If you'll forgive me, I need to speak with Ernesto Ferruchini. Business first, pleasure later.' He winked, lowered his eyes to her black shrink-wrapped nipples and backed away.

Danielle wasn't sure she'd heard him correctly as he left her, something about not needing a swimsuit, but she couldn't be sure and anyway, Krios was approaching from the saloon so she forgot all about it.

The anchor splashed into Thessalona Bay and *Intermezzo* reversed towards a sheer cliff, coming to rest lying parallel to the shore some fifty yards away. The second officer, balanced precariously in the ship's tender, attached a stern-line to the rocks, the slack being taken up by an electric winch.

The bright lights illuminating the stern deck ruined Danielle's night vision so she walked to the bow and allowed her pupils to adjust to the darkness. Gradually she was able to pick out the shallow beach and the small white church of Ayios Giorgos nestling in the shadows. *Intermezzo* appeared to have the narrow bay to herself and high above Danielle's head the top of the cliffs eclipsed part of the Milky Way as it curved around the skyline like the edge of a caldera. The silence was interrupted by small bells tinkling on the breeze from goats rummaging around the undergrowth at the base of the cliff. Danielle thought it was all magical.

She felt a little tipsy and was having difficulty focusing. Lunch had been forfeited to retail therapy as she rushed around Yialos buying her outfit, but she knew she looked sexy and longed for Krios to run his strong hands over her curvaceous body.

Way off on the Turkish side of the Symi Channel Danielle noticed a light moving steadily towards the bay, but she was distracted by Krios resting his hands on her shoulders and kissing the nape of her neck.

'Happy, Danielle?'

Her hips provided the answer. Circling her head to allow greater access for her boss's lips she again caught sight of the light, now split into three; green, white and red. 'What's that?' she whispered.

'My cock.'

'Not that. That.' She pointed to the lights closing on Thessalona Bay.

Krios lifted his head off her right shoulder and peered out to sea. 'Probably our visitors.'

Danielle was intrigued. 'Are they coming from Turkey?'

'Umm, that's right.' Krios's words were smothered in her long hair.

'Do the authorities know?'

'I am the authorities, Danielle, now, let's go back and join the others.' He gently pulled her away from the prow and followed the contours of the ship back to the bright lights of the stern. 'Hungry?'

'Starving. I could eat a horse.'

He pulled her hand into his groin. 'All in good time Danielle. All in good time.'

A powerboat dropped its anchor in Thessalona Bay and dowsed its lights. *Intermezzo's* second officer jumped into the tender and steered away from the ship's transom then arced towards the smaller boat. Dark figures moved around in the starlight as the tender bobbed up and down, the second officer handing his cargo carefully into the dinghy with muffled instructions. Minutes later he was back and more crew stepped onto the swim-platform and helped bring the tender's load aboard.

Danielle was oblivious to any of this as she enjoyed the sumptuous meal with Fabio's guests, revelling in their attention. The glass doors slid open and a steward entered walking up to Krios and speaking privately into his right ear. Krios, in turn, nodded to Fabio and excused himself from the group. Danielle, sitting between them, hardly noticed his departure, her head floating on a surfeit of excellent food and expensive wines, her eyes glazed. Fabio's gorgonzola charged breath fogged her cheap gilt earring as he whispered in her ear.

'If you would like to freshen up a little, the steward will show you to the bathroom.'

She wasn't sure if her host's left armpit or her perspiring skin caused the sour body odour floating around them but when a trickle of sweat slid down her cleavage she headed towards the waiting steward.

The state room door opened onto a huge circular bed taking centre stage. Danielle entered, hearing the door brushing the deep-pile carpet as it closed behind her. She sank onto the satin sheets and giggled. 'I feel like Marilyn Monroe,' she announced taking in the sumptuous décor. Looking up she put her tongue out at her image in the mirrored ceiling and hiccupped.

'Oops, Danielle,' she whispered covering her mouth with her hand and staggered to the bathroom where a jug of iced water sat next to two crystal glasses with the initials FG engraved on the side. She drank deeply leaning against the door for support then lifted her dress, dropped onto the toilet seat and emptied her bladder, watching her reflexion through walls of tinted glass.

The toilet flush seemed to work automatically as she stood up taking her by surprise and she giggled again pulling her tight dress over her naked crutch. Her hand flicked hair away from her face as she pouted at her reflection in the wash-hand basin mirror and applied lip gloss with practised ease across her fire-engine red mouth. Swishing her head from side-to-side to create greater volume in her dark curls, she turned sideways and admired her shapely body, improving the overall look by plucking at her nipples to make them stand out. Peering closer to the mirror she noticed a red mark on her neck where Krios had been earlier. 'Naughty, naughty,' she chided, wagging her finger at the mirror, 'Father Voulgaris wouldn't like that, now would he?' Her reflection stuck two fingers in the air and turned away, ramming the lip brush into a black sequinned bag.

The steward was waiting patiently on the other side of the cabin door. 'This way, Miss,' he said, taking the lead.

Danielle was mesmerised by his taught muscled backside as he preceded her along the lavish wood-panelled corridor and up the chrome and glass staircase. Nice butt, she thought as he stepped aside and she glided into the saloon like a fashion model, ten pairs of male eyes undressing her as she crossed to Krios sitting in a mahogany-leather, wing-backed chair, a crystal brandy balloon in one hand, a Cohiba cigar in the other. She rested her left hip on the arm of the chair and let her left thigh straggle the curve as she inhaled the pungent aroma of burning Cuban leaf.

Ernesto Ferruchini, reclining on a brocade settee on the opposite side of the saloon, leered at her exposed Brazilian crutch.

Suddenly the room lights went out and spot lights above the sundeck illuminated a mud floored wrestling pit, while the quadraphonic sound system blasted out Tina Turner's '*Simply the Best*' at one hundred decibels.

Danielle watched the men rise as one and jostle to be the first through the sliding glass doors and into the cool night air. From either staircase, two bronzed muscular women, naked bar a G-string, walked to the pit, mounted the ropes and began massaging their bodies with oil.

Danielle didn't have a clue what was happening so stood on a chair to get a better view as the well-endowed Amazons smashed into each other, grey mud flying everywhere. Fabio started the betting by backing the blonde in the blue corner which triggered a frenzy of gambling amongst his guests. Within minutes, thousands of drachmas had changed hands as pairs of mud-spattered women pulverised each other in an attempt to gain superiority, male supporters screaming encouragement, testosterone levels soaring as designer polo-shirts and chinos took on a muddy hue.

Danielle was mesmerised by it all and when the women finally dived into the sea, followed closely behind by their now naked supporters, Danielle was game for anything. She slid out of her little black number, ran down the starboard staircase to the swim platform and jumped into the water squealing like a banshee for Krios to come and get her. When she surfaced, it was Fabio Grigio's face filling her vision, his eyes alight with desire, his fingers massaging her clitoris.

High on a cocktail of drug-laced booze Danielle didn't care. She closed her eyes, leant her head back, opened her legs and felt the unique sensation of cold saltwater surge into her vagina ahead of a hot throbbing penis. Stainless steel bars pressed into her shoulder blades. She grabbed the rungs of a step ladder and clung on like a limpet, her toes locked behind a rotund torso, her hips balancing on fleshy knees as one thrust after another ground into her groin.

Danielle thought she was levitating as her body rose from the water and seemed to float down a wood panelled corridor then flop onto soft silky cushions, her hair dripping saltwater into her eyes, misting her reflection in a mirror above her head. She blinked and watched herself stretch out across a huge bed, her arms and legs spread wide. This is the life, she thought, feeling like a film star. Minutes later her dream turned into a nightmare.

Champagne bubbles fizzed along her inner thighs as the cold hard edge of something solid split her vulva and rammed into her uterus. She screamed for Krios but her cry was cut off by a penis ramming into her mouth, a thick salty discharge coating her tonsils and sliding down her throat making her gag. As she came up for air her brain was in turmoil trying to make sense of masculine hands bruising her skin, teeth biting into her neck and stale breath invading her lungs. She tried to escape but strong hands pulled her back, turning her onto her knees, the sensation of both her vagina and anus being stretched beyond endurance sending shockwaves through her body.

Her throat burned, her lower orifices throbbed in excruciating pain and her muscles begged for release. She fell off the bed and crawled to the door, her progress stalled by another human piston hammering into the depths of her lower bowel as she rocked on all fours. When it finally fell away she opened the door and crawled out into the corridor, every muscle in her lower body trembling.

Her eyes focused on two pairs of upright hairy legs so she raised her head. Krios was standing in the corridor in the throes of his own carnal desire, shafting the taught backside of the young steward who was bent forward, his hands and left cheek pressed against the wood panelling, his face contorted, grunting with each stroke. Danielle lost her grip on reality, felt her world implode and blacked out.

On Nimborio Beach, Miriam and Alex lay peacefully on a small jetty looking up at the stars, their toes lapping the still waters of the bay. Behind the beach a tamarisk tree stood guard over a pile of clothes laid casually across the seat of a motor scooter.

Alex's professional curiosity finally got the better of him.

'Miriam, why weren't you needed on *Intermezzo* tonight?'

She sighed and rested her head in the crook of his arm.

'Fabio Grigio was having a 'boys only' night out with his cronies. I was surplus to requirements.'

Alex thought Miriam's reply was rather strange considering Danielle had been one of the guests but he didn't want to ruin the best evening of his life so didn't push the point.

Miriam blinked saltwater from her eyelashes and ran her hand along Alex's arm. 'I wish I could do this every night.'

'So do I,' agreed Alex, brushing his lips against her temple.

Miriam chuckled. 'Oh come on, I bet you bring girls here all the time.'

Alex didn't know whether to lie and appear experienced or tell the truth and appear pathetic. 'No comment,' he muttered, finally.

'Well, lucky the girl who gets to be here with you next time,' said Miriam, looking at Alex sideways. 'By this time tomorrow I'll be in Cyprus.'

Alex felt depressed. 'I suggest we make the most of the time we have left then.' He raised himself onto his elbow and lowered his mouth gently onto hers, closing off further conversation. They slipped back into the water; entwined in a romantic embrace as the warm Mediterranean Sea rippled to the motion of their two bodies swaying in perfect harmony.

Chapter Twenty Two

Tuesday (04.00 hrs.)
Intermezzo lay at anchor off the Nireus Hotel in Symi Bay, all evidence of the night's activities scrubbed away by her crew. The visiting powerboat had long since returned to the Turkish mainland under the cover of darkness, her female wrestlers generously compensated for their contribution to the evening, her illegal cargo of drugs now safely hidden inside the bowels of the ship.

Danielle had no idea how she'd come to be in the tender, fully dressed, her shoes and bag clasped in her hand. She felt two crew members lift her gently onto the quay and help her across to the hotel entrance where a night porter waited with a room key. She didn't argue. On reaching the bedroom she lay on the bed curled into a foetus position beneath the covers, cowering like a damaged animal licking its wounds. As she lay with her pain, trying to understand her predicament, one thought dominated all else. Krios Kakos had used her and abused her for the benefit of his friends.

Marta Fabrini's words in the Jazz Café came to mind. *"All that glistens is not gold."* Somewhere in the dark recesses of Danielle's mind a seed of hatred began to germinate, fed by a growing need for retribution. As sleep erased her pain Danielle dreamt of getting even.

The sun was high by the time Panayiotis drove into Pedi Bay with the balance of his night's catch and parked his pickup truck by the house. Phoebe was waiting inside. He only had to look at his daughter's face to know he was in trouble. Taking the path of least resistance, he backed out again, quickly.

'Where do you think you're going, dad?'

'I've left something in the truck.'

'Like hell you have. What's all this about some illegal immigrants who you reported to the authorities.'

Panayiotis's heart sank and he peered around the doorframe biting the inside of his cheek. 'Who told you?'

'Never mind who told me. Is it true?'

Panayiotis scratched his neck, irritated at feeling guilty without cause. 'Look, Phoebe, it isn't that simple.'

'Oh, really, dad.' She crossed her arms and glared at her father. 'How complicated does it get to pick up a VHF transmitter and inform the Hellenic Coastguard that fifty-eight terrified and homeless people are crawling up Pedi's hillside. With humanitarian friends like you none of us need enemies.'

'Damn' it, Phoebe, what was I supposed to do. They would have been caught anyway. This is a small island for Christ's sake. Tell me, where were they going to go? Where would they find food and shelter?' He pulled a limp octopus out of the box balanced under his arm and threw it in the sink, angry at his own complicity in the matter.

'I can tell you where they've gone,' shouted Phoebe. 'They're banged up in Lavrios Detention Centre in Athens probably overrun with cockroaches and suffering from dysentery, with no bloody hope of reprieve. I hope that hangs heavily on your conscience, father. Being your daughter certainly hangs heavily on mine.' She grabbed her sarong off the back of the kitchen chair and stormed out of the house.

'Oh, that's right. Vent your spleen then bugger off. You're just like your mother. She never saw things from my perspective either.'

Phoebe stopped in her tracks. She shot round and stormed back into the kitchen. 'OK, let's hear it from your side, and it better be good.'

157

Panayiotis looked at his daughter in utter amazement never expecting her to call his bluff. She'd got him by the balls and they both knew it. He paused then slowly smiled. 'I'll do better than that, Phoebe Stanis. Get dressed. I'm going to show you something.'

He drove like a maniac through the back streets of the Chorio and along the Panormitis road with Phoebe clinging on for dear life.

'For goodness sake, dad, slow down, you'll kill the pair of us. What would gran do then?'

Panayiotis looked at her from the corner of his eye as he negotiated a bend. 'Probably join a nunnery or climb into bed with Father Voulgaris.'

Phoebe burst out laughing. Her father took his foot off the gas and tried to keep a straight face. 'Well, maybe that's a bit far-fetched, but you get my drift.' His attempt at sobriety failed miserably as a belly laugh escaped from deep within his diaphragm, the tension between them dissipating with each guffaw.

They continued on in silence. 'Where are we going, dad?'

'Wait and see.'

Marta was in the garden of Villa Fabrini when the truck turned into the drive. For a split second she wanted to delay its approach to allow Nishan time to hide, then realised it was Panayiotis. Phoebe sat in the passenger seat of the truck, curiosity painted across her features.

'Hi, you two. What's up?'

Panayiotis stepped out of the vehicle and leant against the roof. 'My daughter seems to think I haven't got a heart.'

'Well, she may have a point, look at the way you treat those poor fish.'

Phoebe chuckled and kissed Marta on both cheeks. 'Don't expect sympathy from Aunt Marta, father, she's known you for too long.'

'Now, what's this all about?' asked Marta.

Phoebe slammed the truck door and looked across at her father. 'Alex Laskaris told me all about the illegal immigrants, last night at the Jazz Café.'

'Oooh,' groaned Marta knowingly, 'and, I imagine, you're not impressed with your nearest and dearest.' She too looked at Panayiotis still propped against the bodywork, who answered for his daughter.

'You could say that. She told me what she thought of me and I accused her of being like her intransigent mother, which didn't go down very well.'

'I'm not surprised, Panayiotis. Leonora makes Golda Meier look like Tinkerbelle.'

'Thank you, Aunt Marta. Anyway, I've called his bluff and he doesn't know what to do, so he's brought me here hoping you'll get him out of a hole.' Phoebe puffed out her chest, bloated with moral virtue.

Marta held Panayiotis's attention across the head of her Goddaughter. He ran his tongue around the outside of his teeth, raised his eyebrows and slowly nodded towards the garage.

'Phoebe,' said Marta taking her arm, 'come with me.' When they reached the garage Marta raised her voice and spoke in Italian. Phoebe looked at her Godmother wondering who she was talking to. 'Open the door, Phoebe. Go on, it won't bite.'

Phoebe gently pulled at the door. As her eyes adjusted to the interior her hands smacked against her mouth.

'Nishan, meet my Goddaughter, Phoebe Stanis. She speaks Italian although she's Greek and she has some very passionate views on the plight of refugees. Please tell her what Panayiotis has done for you since you arrived at Villa Fabrini.'

159

Nishan walked into the sunlight and waved to the fisherman. He towered over Phoebe and looked into her wide Hellenic eyes then greeted her in Amharic. '*Selam nesh way*, Phoebe.'

She was too stunned to react. Marta placed her hands on her Goddaughter's shoulders and squeezed her skin. 'Your father and I are going to leave you and Nishan to get acquainted. When you're both ready, come and join us on the terrace. It's nearly time for lunch anyway and knowing Rosa, two more won't be a problem.'

As Panayiotis passed by his daughter, he couldn't resist having the last word. 'Gotcha, Phoebe!'

The five conspirators sat around the pergola table tucking into a warm green bean and crisply fried prosciutto salad with chicken and pea frittata, chatting at ten to the dozen, Phoebe demanding to know everything.

Over the conversation Marta heard the telephone ringing. 'I'll be back in a tick,' she said rising from the table. 'Help yourselves to more food. Panayiotis, do you want another beer?'

'I'll get it,' he said, squeezing past Phoebe, 'while my daughter thinks up an apology.'

They walked into the kitchen together. 'Have I done the right thing?'

'Definitely,' replied Marta, leaving him at the fridge, 'and, I'm sure Nishan isn't complaining either.'

Panayiotis plucked a can of beer from the cooler and returned to the terrace, taken aback by Marta's comment. She walked into the study and picked up the phone.

'Signora Romano, its Alberto Zappa, in Milan. I have some information on that old Italian soldier you asked me to investigate.'

Minutes later Marta came around the corner beaming from ear to ear. 'Nishan, we've found your grandfather and he's alive.'

It was dusk by the time Danielle opened her eyes in the Nireus Hotel. She looked around the hotel bedroom trying to reprogramme her brain but nothing seemed to make sense. She needed to pee and began to swing her legs towards the floor when long knives cut through her lower body bringing her to an emergency stop. She yelled out in pain then muzzled the sound in mid-flow, taking deep breaths as she eased her shattered body off the bed and made slow shuffling movements across to the bathroom. It took ten minutes for the stinging urine to leave her bladder, the clouded liquid marbled with traces of blood as it rotated in the toilet bowl. She carefully undressed, stepped into the shower and let the warm water cascade off her head, her knees giving way from under her as her body slid down the wall tiles and sank to the floor. She began to cry, her tears mixing with the soothing spray as it gurgled down the plughole taking with it any remaining vestiges of innocence.

She sobbed until her tear ducts had no more to give. Crawling out of the cubicle on her hands and knees she eased herself onto a white towelling bath mat and pulled a thick bath towel around her shoulders. Here she sat on her knees, hunched against the shower screen, rocking backwards and forwards in the fading light.

She knew that dealing with the previous night was going to be bad enough, but dealing with the present was even worse. She needed to get into some normal clothes and return to her studio flat, but, she thought, how was she going to achieve any of this when she could hardly walk?

With sheer determination she crept to the phone and dialled zero.

'Hello. This is room…' She didn't know where she was.
'Does the hotel have any Paracetamol?'

'Yes we do. I'll get a member of staff to bring them up to you shortly.'

Danielle knew she couldn't be seen, but getting back to the bathroom would only increase the pain that was already unbearable. She counted to ten, took a deep breath and began to move. A white envelope lying on the floor by the bedroom door caught her attention. She pulled herself along the carpet and reached for it noticing the *Intermezzo* logo on the bottom left corner. The message inside was short and to the point.

Danielle,
Your room is paid for until midday Wednesday.
Fabio Grigio sent the enclosed.
Enjoy!
KK

Twenty, crisp ten-thousand drachma notes burned into the palm of her hand. Danielle felt sick and crabbed her way to the bathroom to retch into the toilet pan, calling to the staff member to leave the tablets on the bed as she willed herself not to faint. With teeth ripping into her bottom lip she heaved herself onto her feet, filled a glass with water and staggered back to bed, grabbing and swallowing the tablets on the way. She prayed they would go to work on her nerve endings as she lay down, the drachmas scattered across the bathroom floor like confetti.

Marta and Rosa were in a state of euphoria over finding Nishan's grandfather as they watched Panayiotis and Phoebe depart.

Alberto Zappa had tracked Luigi Amato down to a small town in Calabria using army and medical records and local know how. Luigi was alive and well and living with his daughter and her family in Cosenza.

162

The situation was delicate because Nishan's grandfather had never divulged his affair in Addis Ababa to anyone in Italy. When the war ended he'd returned to his parent's house in Parma in the north of Italy, then met a local girl, fallen in love and married her, all thoughts of Ethiopia firmly locked in his brain's archive file.

In 1947 his daughter, Teresa, was born and as there was no work for Luigi in Parma he moved his young family to Milan where he got a job on the railways. His wife had died of a stroke years later leaving Luigi alone in the big city. Ageing and isolated, he was persuaded by Teresa to go south and live with her. She had married an accountant and had three children. Luigi agreed and had lived in Cosenza ever since.

When Luigi was told of Nishan's existence he turned ashen, headed for the local church and confessed his sins. After many Hail Marys he took his daughter to one side and told her the truth. Teresa's initial reaction was one of disbelief but Nishan's story was so moving she gradually warmed to the idea of her Ethiopian nephew, promising to help her father do all he could to assist his grandson reach Italy.

However, Nishan had to prove he was indeed Luigi's grandson, not some African imposter, and DNA testing was the only proof the Italian Immigration Department would accept. Alberto Zappa had been browsing the internet and thought he had found a possible solution.

DNA Laboratories of Ireland were offering immigration DNA testing by post. The test kit could be sent by mail, a swab taken from Nishan's mouth and the kit sent back. The same procedure would have to be undertaken by Luigi in Cosenza but once both samples arrived in Ireland the test would only take three to four days to complete and the results could be faxed directly to Marta and the Italian Immigration Authorities from their head office. Luckily, the hair from Nishan's grandmother and his father, platted together inside the tiny silver locket, could also be tested for added verification.

Marta wasn't worried about the cost but about the timing. Each extra day spent at Villa Fabrini increased Nishan's chances of discovery and hers of being arrested. She told Alberto Zappa to contact the laboratory immediately and set the wheels in motion. The DNA kits were to be couriered to Symi and Cosenza for speed. After making a note of Luigi's contact telephone number she went to give Nishan the good news.

Marta knew his Italian wouldn't stretch to the technicalities of DNA testing but Phoebe had been convinced that she was wrong.

'Look, I'll stay with Nishan all day Sunday while you go sailing. I'm sure I can explain it to him.'

Panayiotis's eyebrows reached his hairline. 'What about your gran, Phoebe? She's expecting you for lunch on Sunday.'

Phoebe had dismissed the comment with a flick of her wrist. 'Oh, I'll think of some excuse.'

'It better be good,' replied her father. 'If I know my mother, she will see right through you.' He had looked at his watch. 'Now, let's call it a day. I need some sleep.'

Christos Nicolaides was on the phone when Alex came on duty that evening and the sergeant didn't look happy. Alex could only hear one side of the conversation but it seemed that Danielle Nicolaides had gone missing and his wife was getting worried. The sergeant was trying to calm her down by pointing out that Danielle was over eighteen and had probably stayed with friends. This logic didn't seem to appease his wife and Alex thought it prudent to make himself scarce.

He sauntered outside and leant over the balcony balustrade reflecting on his own night at Nimborio beach.

It had been almost dawn when he and Miriam had arrived back at the Nireus Hotel, Miriam sneaking him into her room under the nose of the hotel porter. She had already requested room service so they enjoyed an early breakfast in bed before Miriam donned her uniform and left to join *Intermezzo*.

On his way out Alex had bumped into the night porter who was going off duty and they had walked together along the quay chatting about the goings on at the hotel in the middle of the night when Danielle Nicolaides arrived legless from *Intermezzo's* tender and had to be helped to her room.

Alex considered telling Christos Nicolaides that his daughter was alive and well and sleeping off a hangover at the Nireus Hotel after a party on board but then thought better of it. Danielle wouldn't thank him for giving away her secrets to her father and he was already in deep water with Police Chief Kakos, so trying to explain his own presence at the hotel would only make matters worse. He decided to remain silent.

Returning to the office he agreed with the sergeant that Danielle was probably fine and suggested Christos took his wife out for an evening cocktail at the Jazz Café instead, wondering privately if Danielle's mother was partial to sampling their "Sex on the Beach"!

Chapter Twenty Three

Wednesday (9.00 am)

Sleep and regular doses of Paracetamol helped reduce Danielle's pain. The hotel breakfast, when it came, filled the void in her stomach but nothing could fill the hole in her psyche. She glanced at the drachma notes and felt defiled and dirty. No amount of showering could remove the facts. Fabio Grigio had paid for her services and had left Symi with a clear conscience, unconcerned by the effect his action had had on her both physically and mentally. Her body screamed for revenge but Intermezzo was long gone. However, her boss was still in Symi. She picked up the phone and calmly dialled a telephone number which she knew by heart. It rang three times.

'Kyría Kakos, this is Danielle Nicolaides. I wonder if you have the time to meet me at the Nireus Hotel.'

Evadne walked through the hotel reception and straight up to the first floor where she knocked on a bedroom door and waited patiently not knowing what to expect.

'Who is it,' called Danielle.

'Evadne Kakos.'

The door slowly opened and Danielle stood like a cripple covered in a bed sheet, her face drained of all colour. Evadne was shocked at the change in the girl from the happy and flirtatious female she'd spied through her binoculars, hanging off her husband's arm, to the young woman standing before her now. Any animosity she felt quickly dissipated as she helped Danielle back to bed and locked the door against possible intruders.

'I'm not sure why you've brought me here, Danielle, but I can see that something dreadful has happened and you obviously need help. On the phone you said you had something to tell me and, looking at you, I imagine it will not be pleasant to hear, but I have broad shoulders and an open mind. Whatever you have to say, say it and don't spare my feelings.'

Danielle nodded but no words emerged. Evadne read her thoughts, sensing her dilemma and took the lead. 'Let me help you, Danielle. What I know is that two nights ago you were a happy, fun-loving young woman on your way to *Intermezzo*. I imagine my husband invited you on board and that is why I'm here. If it helps, I watched you go aboard with Krios and saw the ship leave port.'

The significance of Evadne's words seemed to floor Danielle. She looked into the older woman's eyes expecting contempt and anger but Evadne's expression was blank. Slowly Danielle began to describe her night on *Intermezzo,* facing her own demons in the process and leaving nothing to the imagination. When her monologue came to an end, the abused girl picked up the twenty freshly minted ten-thousand drachma notes and placed them in Evadne's lap.

'I can hardly walk, Kyría Kakos, and I feel dirty inside. I'm terrified of what my father might do if he ever finds out. I just don't know what to do to make any of it better.'

The feel of the money made Evadne's blood run cold. She placed it back on Danielle's bedside table then took the young girl into her arms. Danielle cried like a baby oblivious to her tears and saliva soaking Evadne's silk blouse. 'You need to see a doctor,' were the only words Evadne spoke.

Danielle went rigid at the suggestion but Evadne knew that sexually transmitted diseases or pregnancy were a possibility and Danielle had to be examined, and examined immediately. The doctor's records would also act as additional evidence against her husband. 'Don't fight me on this, Danielle. Doctors never divulge information about their patients. Trust me, your secret is safe.'

A muffled thank you was just audible amongst the sobs.

'Firstly, we need to get you out of here. What shall we do about your clothes?'

The clinic was empty when Danielle was ushered into the treatment room an hour later wearing a knee-length green kaftan and white espadrilles, bought by Evadne at the local dress shop on Yialos harbour. The doctor had been advised by Evadne of Danielle's injuries and understood the delicate nature of the situation. Evadne brooked no argument at being present during the examination and as the wife of the Police Chief she got her way.

The three were closeted together for over an hour with Evadne insisting on having the injuries photographed before treatment began. Danielle needed stitches to close the tears around both her vagina and anus in addition to antiseptic swabbing on all the other abrasions. The doctor administered antibiotics and pain-killers by injection and wrote out a prescription for more in tablet form. The STD results, he said, would take a few days as the tests had to be processed on the mainland, but in the meantime Danielle was to rest, take her course of antibiotics and pain-killers, and think seriously about counselling.

Evadne placed the roll of film in her handbag and took Danielle back to her studio flat, promising to return on a regular basis. They already had a story for Danielle to use with family, friends and work colleagues, so, with nothing further to do, Evadne left her to sleep. Feeling emotionally drained, she stood for a moment out on the street staring at the ornate belfry of Ayios Ioannis church. For some reason she recalled her wedding day and the vows that she and Krios had made all those years ago in the presence of God. The validity of those vows and her religious beliefs were now in question and she demanded answers. Crossing to the church she knelt before the iconostasis as if in prayer, but her communion with her maker was far from pious. God was being tested and he was found to be wanting.

Phoebe was also feeling abandoned. She sat on Pedi beach waiting for inspiration to use on her grandmother but she waited in vain. Her inspiration was out to lunch and no amount of concentration was going to bring it back. She kicked at the pebbles around her feet and picked one up, hurling it into the sea in her frustration. Within the hour she had to be up in the Chorio for dinner and if she didn't find a plausible excuse, her plans for Sunday would be high-jacked by Anastasia and the church, making a full day with Nishan impossible.

'Bugger it,' she yelled, frightening the seagulls standing close by hoping for scraps. 'What I do with my life is my business, not gran's or her priest.' Her outburst didn't help and she felt ever more guilty and frustrated.

By the time she arrived in the village square she'd settled on *Arabesque* as her reason for absence, telling herself that if her grandmother didn't like it then that was tough. Full of resolve, she breezed into the house with a cheery 'Hello, gran. Something smells good.'

Anastasia was busy at the cooker checking a goat casserole and called out over her shoulder. 'In here, dear. Come and set the table, dinner is about ready.'

'Gran,' said Phoebe, collecting crockery and cutlery from the dresser, 'about Sunday.'

'Oh, you've heard already?' interrupted Anastasia.

Phoebe stopped mid-task. 'Heard what, gran?'

'About our outing to Panormitis. Did you meet Father Voulgaris in the square?'

'Er, no.' Phoebe was on her guard. 'Why are you going all the way to the south of the island for Mass. Is it a religious holiday?'

Anastasia placed the large tureen in the centre of the table and returned for the bowls. 'No, dear. Once a year the Abbot at Panormitis Monastery invites our congregation to celebrate the Divine Liturgy with himself and the monks in the Katholikon. It's very moving. Afterwards we place a wreath at the monument to poor Abbott Chrysanthos Maroulakis who the Italians executed as a spy in 1944. You probably don't know anything about that.'

Phoebe shook her head. 'I take it you'll be away for most of the day then.' she said, crossing her fingers under the table.

'That's right, dear. Father Voulgaris has arranged for us to have lunch in the refectory with the monks so I doubt we'll be back before mid-afternoon. I'm so excited for you. It's a great opportunity for you to see the Monastery and its wonderful museums.'

Phoebe's heart sank. 'Uh, I don't think I'll be able to make it, gran.'

Anastasia's dentures slipped. 'Why ever not, Phoebe? What possible reason could you have to miss such an important event?'

Phoebe took a deep breath and ploughed on. 'I've promised dad I would help him sail *Arabesque* on Sunday. I can't go to Panormitis and get back to Pedi in time so I'm afraid I'll have to stay behind.'

Anastasia used the serving spoon to dismiss Phoebe's words. 'I don't think so, Phoebe. You can sail on that stupid boat anytime. Attending the Divine Liturgy at the Holy Monastery of Archangel Michael is a rare opportunity and I expect you to be there, with *me*.' The emphasis on the last word was like a slap in the face.

Phoebe was tight lipped. Panayiotis was right, she had her mother's intransigent nature and was about to prove it. 'I can pray to God wherever and whenever I like, gran, but I only get to see dad once or twice a year. If it's a toss-up between fathers, I'll put mine first every time. I'm sorry to disappoint you but I'm going sailing on Sunday and that's the end of the matter.' She picked up her fork and started eating.

Anastasia hummed with disbelief. Her bosom rose with her chin and her eyes squinted with anger. 'You impertinent child. Don't you dare compare the Almighty with your father. Panayiotis is a disgrace to this family and a disgrace to our church. If you were half the adult you think you are, you'd recognise the fact and see him for what he is.'

'And, what exactly is that?' demanded Phoebe, rising to the bait.

'Immoral, inept and impenitent,' hissed Anastasia waving the spoon in Phoebe's face. 'Your father has sold his soul to the devil and will certainly go to hell.'

Phoebe couldn't believe her grandmother's vitriol and was spitting bullets. 'Is that right? Then you won't be surprised to learn that he thinks you're bigoted and bitter and rues the day you allowed Father Voulgaris to turn you into a religious zealot.'

By now both females were beyond reason. 'That's rich coming from a man whose debauched behaviour is the talk of Symi. Everyone knows he pursues that Romano woman as if she was a bitch on heat and she's no better, encouraging him with her feminine wiles. It's disgusting.'

'And, it's humiliating watching my grandmother salivating over a greasy, sanctimonious, dried-up old prune of a priest with bad breath who gets his kicks massaging the spiritual libido of old women.'

171

'Wash your mouth out child. You're referring to a man of the cloth.' Anastasia crossed herself three times.

'If you were a real Christian, gran, you would pity Marta Romano, not castigate her. Not only is she struggling to come to terms with being prematurely widowed in horrendous circumstances, she's also caring and considerate and a true friend to this family. Similarly, if you had any understanding of my father's feelings you would defend him against the wicked gossip from the old women around here who have nothing better to do with their time.'

Anastasia slammed the serving spoon against the table top, stew flying everywhere. 'Then explain to me why we had no problems in this family until Marta Romano arrived in Symi? It's not my fault she lost her own family. What right does she have to come here and try to steal mine? The Italians have always terrorized the people of this island; look what they did to us in the war. We never wanted them here then, and we don't want them here now. That Italian witch should go back to where she came from and you and your father shouldn't be so gullible.'

Phoebe wiped stew off her nose with her sleeve and pushed the bowl away. 'Think what you like, gran. What I know is that dad lost his wife to the glitterati of Athens, his father to the Aegean Sea, his mother to the church and his best friend to a bomb. None of which was his fault. All he has left now is me and a promise he made to Antonio Romano to watch over his wife. I happen to love Aunt Marta and nothing you can say will alter that.'

'She's not your Aunt,' screamed Anastasia shaking from head to toe. 'I'm your family, not her and I deserve more respect and consideration.'

Phoebe bit hard on her clenched fist trying to control her temper, terrified her grandmother would have a heart attack. 'I'm going to leave now, gran. I'm sorry to have upset you but I will not feel guilty for wanting to be with my dad. If God doesn't understand that then religion is a sham. I'll be at the Jazz Café if you need me.'

Phoebe stormed down the Kali Strata steps, slumped into a chair outside the Jazz Café and waited for Philippe to arrive. Steam was coming out of her ears and she knew her father would be livid when he heard what had happened.

'All I want,' she said to the wrought-iron table, 'is to help Nishan Amato find his family. What's so terrible about that?' The table didn't reply so she kicked it and yelped when it kicked back.

Alex and Christos were sitting in their favourite watering hole on the harbour enjoying a beer while Christos waxed lyrical about the effect a couple of cocktails had had on his wife the night before at the Jazz Café.

'I told you it would work,' said Alex.

'Nevertheless, I have to thank you for keeping the peace in the Nicolaides household. It was all a false alarm as it happened. Danielle was fine.'

Alex was fascinated. 'That's good to know. What happened to her?'

'Oh, from what I can gather from her mother, she went over to Pedi for a party and ate some barbequed prawns. The next thing she knew she was spewing up all over the place and spent the next twenty-four hours communing with her friend's toilet. She's back in her flat now looking like death and surviving on mineral water and dry toast.'

Alex was having difficulty keeping a straight face. 'My gran always said you should never trust shellfish. Me, I avoid them like the plague.'

'Really?' said Christos, emptying his glass.

173

'Fancy another beer, sergeant?' asked Alex, rapidly changing the subject and moving towards the bar.

'If you're paying lad, yes please, and make it a large one.'

Chapter Twenty Four

Thursday (a.m.)

Krios walked past the guest bedroom and tried the handle. It was locked. He descended the staircase frowning and walked out onto the terrace followed by the cook carrying a jug of freshly squeezed orange juice. She nodded a greeting trying to avoid any eye contact with her employer.

'Have you seen my wife this morning?' he asked, filling his glass.

Sybil shook her head. 'No, Sir. Kyría Kakos left me a message to say that she didn't want to be disturbed. I believe she's feeling unwell.'

'I see. Well, perhaps you would tell her that I shall be in Kos from today until Saturday morning at a police conference.'

The cook nodded again and made herself scarce, leaving Krios to finish his breakfast in silence. He then collected his overnight bag from the hall and left.

Evadne heard the front door close and watched her husband take the villa steps two at a time then disappear down the lane leading onto the Kali Strata. Lifting her dressing-gown from the guest bed she went through to her bathroom where she soaked in a deep warm bath, the pine crystals easing the tension in her back and neck and reducing her headache.

'Good morning, Kyría Kakos. What would you like for breakfast?' asked the cook as Evadne appeared dressed and ready for the day.

'Good morning, Sibyl. Just coffee and a croissant, please. Has my husband left for work?'

'Yes, about half an hour ago. He told me to tell you that he will be in Kos until Saturday at some police conference.'

'Fine. Then it will be dinner for one as usual. I'll be out for lunch.' She smiled at her cook and picked up the morning paper, quickly becoming engrossed in the latest scandals around Athens.

At ten o'clock she left the villa, unlocked her Alfa Romeo and drove onto the port, parking behind Kambos Square. Danielle, still in her pyjamas, answered the door; her hair dishevelled and her colour still pasty.

'I've brought you some croissant and *Spanakopita* from the bakery. How are you feeling?' Evadne crossed the threshold and studied Danielle, who walked as if she'd spent hours riding a horse.

'Sore,' said Danielle, taking the paper bag from Evadne's hand and placing it on the breakfast bar. 'Did the doctor say if the stitches would dissolve naturally or do I have to go back to the clinic to have them out? I can't remember much about yesterday other than the pain.'

'I'm not surprised. No, apparently, they will dissolve naturally. Have you taken your antibiotics?'

Danielle opened a cupboard door and took out two blisters of tablets. 'I'm about to. I've only just woken up.' She filled a glass with mineral water, dropped two small pills into the palm of her hand and swallowed both. 'Going to the loo is horrendous and my thighs are black and blue from the bruising.' Her eyes met Evadne's across the bed. 'I want to destroy them, you know.'

Evadne nodded. 'The church would tell you to turn the other cheek.'

'Yes, I know, but the church is made up of withered old celibates who don't have vaginas so how could they possibly understand?'

Evadne cringed. 'Has your mother accepted your explanation of Monday night?'

176

'Yes, thank goodness. She's told me to drink lots of water and only eat dry toast.' Danielle scrunched up her face. 'Mum would never understand the world that Fabio Grigio moves in.'

'Nor did you until Monday night, Danielle.'

'No . . . no I didn't, but I do now.' She looked at Evadne with steel in her eyes. 'Kyría Kakos, did your husband leave his office keys at home when he left for Kos.'

It was past midnight when Danielle crossed Kambos Square and came to rest against the side wall of the Town Hall beaded in sweat, pure malice keeping her upright. She felt a warm, moist liquid soak into her cotton panties from beneath her dressing and ignored the sensation as she dug a set of keys out of her skirt pocket. Slowly climbing the concrete stairs, she fiddled with the rusty lock intent on gaining access to her place of work. The key turned. She moved inside, deactivating the burglar-alarm from memory using a pinpoint flash light.

Struggling up the second flight of stairs, grabbing the balustrade for support, Danielle moved blindly across to her office and rested against her desk, her muscles trembling, the pain searing through her lower abdomen.

She waited for the pain to subside then, like a laser beam homing in on its target, she moved towards the inner office desk illuminated by the street lights of Kambos Square. Turning, she closed the heavy wooden shutters on the inside of the window blocking out the light, the familiarity of her surroundings easing her passage in the darkness.

She was feeling faint and took the weight off her feet by gingerly lowering herself into her boss's chair. Pointing the mini flashlight at the desk, she stared at the bottom left-hand drawer. 'Right, you bastard, let's see what you're hiding.'

Her fingers gripped the set of brass keys handed to her earlier in the day by Evadne Kakos. The fourth key engaged the internal mechanism of the old lock, the click sounding like a mini explosion in the dead silence. Danielle's pulse was in overdrive but she was undeterred. Gently she pulled open the heavy oak drawer and rummaged inside. What she found was about to shatter lives forever.

Chapter Twenty Five

Friday (am)

The phone was ringing as Marta entered the Jazz Café at eight thirty. She dumped her bag on a stool and picked up the hand set.

'Jazz Café.'

'Kyría Romano, this is ACS courier services. We have a package for you.'

Marta immediately changed direction. Fifteen minutes later she drove along the quay and made an emergency stop alongside *Phoebe II*. Panayiotis looked up through the dust cloud and saw Marta jumping onto the harbour wall.

'Panayiotis, how long do you intend to be in Yialos?'

He rested his elbow on the cuddy roof. 'About another half-an-hour, why?'

Marta held up the package. 'The DNA kit. Can you get it to Phoebe in Pedi and tell her to drive over to Villa Fabrini and take the swabs from Nishan. I'd go myself but Phillipe is having the morning off.'

'Why can't I do it?' asked Panayiotis, frowning.

Marta climbed over the gunwhale. 'Because the instructions are in English.' She looked about her anxiously. 'How much fish do you have to sell?'

'A fair bit,' he said, kicking the wooden boxes with his right foot, 'although I shouldn't think it will take long to shift them. It's Friday and the restaurants will be expecting a full house.'

'OK. I'll ring Phoebe when I get back to the Jazz Café and tell her to hang on until you arrive. I don't want to say anything over the phone for obvious reasons, but hopefully she'll catch on.' Marta handed the jiffy bag to Panayiotis. 'She's to follow the instructions to the letter and bring the kit straight back to the

Jazz Café so I can get it off to Ireland today. And tell her not to forget to include some strands of hair from Nishan's silver locket.' With that she turned on her heels, jumped back into her car, did a three-point turn by the Customs House and sped away along the harbour.

Phoebe was about to depart when the phone rang. 'Hi, Aunt Marta. What's up?'

'Nothing, sweetheart. Just stay put until your father gets home then do what he says. OK?'

Phoebe loved intrigue and whistled to herself as she tried to work out what was afoot.

Within the hour Panayiotis pulled alongside the house and found his daughter blocking his entrance, vibrating like a taught violin string. 'Inside,' he ordered, his palm pushing her body backwards.

'But, Aunt Marta said . . .'

'I said, inside.' He squeezed past her and headed indoors, Phoebe tripping over his heels.

'Marta wants you to take this to Villa Fabrini.' He held up the package and Phoebe could see the logo of DNA Laboratories of Ireland in the bottom left hand corner. Panayiotis repeated Marta's instructions carefully and made Phoebe repeat them again before he would allow her out of the house.

The old scooter was pushed to the limit, blue smoke pouring out of the exhaust and delivered Phoebe to Villa Fabrini in record time. She grabbed the package from under her seat and walked into the kitchen. Nishan was sitting at the table about to eat his breakfast.

'Don't,' she shouted. Nishan dropped his spoon. Rosa walked through drying her hair on a towel as Phoebe held up the package. 'We need to take the DNA samples.' She opened the jiffy bag and extracting a long, concertinaed leaflet. 'Has Nishan had anything to drink this morning?'

'No,' said Rosa. 'We were late getting going this morning. Marta kept us awake till one o'clock giving Nishan a master-class in the music room.' Rosa pulled out a chair and sat down. 'It was wonderful to watch, Phoebe. She was so intent on getting Nishan's pitch right she joined in. After all these years of refusing to ever sing again, she finally broke free and we have Nishan to thank for that.'

'Wow! I wish I'd been here.' Phoebe put the pamphlet down. 'Quite a surprise for you, Nishan.'

His expression was euphoric. 'She make wonderful sound, Phoebe, wonderful.'

'And she'll make wonderful complaint if I don't get this DNA sample sorted.' She washed her hands, placed them in thin medical gloves then unpacked three clear tubes and laid them carefully on top of the cellophane wrapper. She then picked up a silver envelope and pulled it apart at the top exposing three small cotton wool buds, similar to those sold in pharmacy shops for cleaning small orifices.

'Open wide, Nishan.' Phoebe pushed his head back with her elbow and like a professional wiped the buds around the inside of Nishan's mouth placing them in separate tubes and pushing a stopper into the top of each one to seal it. 'Well, that was easy. Do you have a pair of tweezers, Rosa?'

Rosa went to the kitchen cupboard and pulled out the first aid kit. 'You'd better give Phoebe your silver locket, Nishan. It's in the study.'

He hobbled away and returned with it in his hand. Phoebe pulled two small plastic bags from the package, gently eased silver and black hair strands from the plait and dropped them inside.

'Right, all I need to do now is seal the envelope and get it back to Aunt Marta.'

'Do you have time for a coffee,' asked Rosa.

Phoebe looked at her watch, biting the inside of her lip. 'Yes please, Rosa. Ten minutes can't make that much of a difference.'

While Rosa made the coffee, Nishan and Phoebe walked over to the music-room and sat on the bench outside watching the choughs gliding high on a thermal above their heads.

'Marta, she think my voice very good,' said Nishan, turning to Phoebe. 'She think I win place in Italy singing school.'

'Would you like that, Nishan.'

'I like very much. You think she right?'

'I don't know, Nishan, I'm not a singer, but if Aunt Marta believes it is possible, then it is.'

Rosa arrived and handed a mug to each of them. 'Marta is hoping to get him a scholarship at the Conservatorio di Verona where she studied as a student.'

Phoebe words caught in her throat. 'Oh, Nishan . . . I wish your parents could see you now. They would be so proud.' She pulled a tissue from her pocket and blew her nose.

'Phoebe has never heard you sing, Nishan. Why don't you show her how good you are? She winked at Phoebe and wandered back to the house leaving them alone once more.

Anastasia Stanis grabbed the silver cross around her neck and backed into the shrubbery bordering Villa Fabrini's drive. She couldn't believe her eyes. What she saw was her only granddaughter gazing longingly into the eyes of a huge black man who was serenading her with such passion in his voice. She blinked trying to expunge the image as questions flooded her mind. Who was this man? Where had he come from? Why was he alone with her granddaughter in the garden of Villa Fabrini?

Anastasia's heart stopped, her knees turned to jelly, her head spun in a vortex of anger and disbelief. She staggered back along the drive, her jacket snagging on the shrubbery, her mind in turmoil. This had not been part of her plan.

In a daze she retraced her footsteps, her vision blurred. It was hot, and getting hotter. She wiped her forehead with the edge of her sleeve doggedly moving on, trying to make sense of what she had witnessed. She stumbled down the old uneven track back towards her home, the stones jarring her shoes, her hair becoming tangled in the low branches of the trees. She needed to rest and think.

Anastasia had slept only intermittently since her argument with Phoebe, tortured by jealous rage, rejection and loss. A lack of food and hours on her knees in Ayios Lefteris praying for guidance had befuddled her brain and Marta Romano had turned into the devil incarnate. Father Voulgaris had tried to counsel her but she was adamant that her only course of action was to face her enemy head on, and as she wouldn't say who her enemy was, the priest was at a loss to know how to respond.

'I'll go to Villa Fabrini and confront Marta Romano head on,' Anastasia had muttered as she crossed to the taxi rank from her house. 'That woman's influence over Panayiotis and Phoebe has got to stop or I'll lose my family for ever.'

The taxi had dropped her above Ayia Katerina chapel, six kilometres from the Chorio. The driver was quite used to Symi's elderly ladies visiting the many monasteries and churches around the island to pay homage to the saints and light a candle for a loved one. 'What time do you want me to pick you up?'

'In an hour,' said Anastasia, and waited while he turned in the road and returned to the village, his car radio blasting out bouzouki music.

Ayia Katerina sat below the Panormitis road on a hillside overlooking the Vassilios Gorge. Anastasia had descended the steep steps to the chapel nestling in the trees but this was not her destination. Leaving the chapel on her left she continued along a stone path curving around the head of the gorge.

Villa Fabrini was difficult to see, screened by extensive gardens and a dry stone wall, but Anastasia had known from listening to Panayiotis waxing lyrical that Marta Romano's home stood hidden in a copse of trees surrounded by well-tended terraces.

You can't hide from me, she thought as the villa's wrought-iron gates came into view. Gritting her teeth, she raised her chin, thrust her shoulders back and had pressed on up the gravel drive. That was when she saw Phoebe.

Coming out of the trees by a bend in the main road she stared down at the Chorio far below, the landscape shimmering in the heat of the morning sun, the black-metalled road surface meandering round the hillside and disappearing below her feet. Anastasia's head was throbbing as she trudged along desperate for water and shade.

Meanwhile, Father Voulgaris was on his way south in his car. As he rounded the bend he saw Anastasia swaying towards him. He pulled up alongside her and jumped out.

'Anastasia Stanis, whatever are you doing walking around in the heat of the day without a hat?'

'Never mind my hat,' replied Anastasia, pushing past him to get into his car. 'Take me to the police station.'

'But, I'm on my way to Panormitis to finalise our visit on Sunday with the Abbot.'

'That can wait, this is more important.' Father Voulgaris's shoulders dropped and he walked round to the driver's door just as a taxi motored up the hill.

184

Anastasia jumped out into the middle of the road and stuck up her hand. The taxi driver's emergency stop came to rest just inches from her feet as Father Voulgaris clutched his crucifix.

'You're late,' she loudly chided as she climbed into the passenger seat, ignoring the priest. 'I need to get to the police station immediately.' Father Voulgaris was apparently now surplus to requirements.

The driver looked at his watch and frowned but didn't argue. He had known Anastasia Stanis for many years and found her formidable. While he concentrated on driving her safely to her destination, she muttered under her breath, irritatingly tapping her right foot against the floor mat. She now knew who the black man was. She had seen him once before in Kambos Square with other illegal immigrants when she was shopping in Yialos.

On arrival, she rummaged in her pocket and pulled out some drachmas placing them on the dash-board and was out of her seat, across the road and mounting the police station steps before the taxi driver had switched off his engine.

'I want to speak to the Police Chief,' Anastasia demanded as she appeared in the door of the office.

'Excuse me,' said Christos Nicolaides to a German skipper he was dealing with at the time. 'He's in Kos at the moment. If you would like to take a seat I will be with you shortly.'

'When is he back?'

Christos raised his eyebrows. 'Tomorrow.'

'That can't be right,' said Anastasia, pushing the German to one side. 'We don't have a ferry arriving from Kos tomorrow.'

'No, dear.' Christos was now getting rattled. 'Chief Kakos is with the Coastguard in their patrol boat. Be assured, he'll be back tomorrow.'

Anastasia stretched across the counter and dug her forefinger into Christos's chest. 'Then make sure he comes to see me as soon as he arrives. It's urgent.' With that she turned on her heels and left.

Marta couldn't keep still. One minute she was sitting by the bar, the next out on the Kali Strata steps constantly getting under Philippe's feet.

'Would you do something useful, Marta. All this pacing is making me nervous.'

'Sorry, Philippe. I'm waiting for Phoebe but she seems to have been delayed.'

'No, I haven't,' said Phoebe, breezing into the bar, the package still under her arm.

Marta waltzed her Goddaughter upstairs and closed the apartment door behind them. 'Where have you been? I've been waiting for ages.'

'Where do you think I've been?' Phoebe handed over the DNA test kit and flopped into a chair. 'Rushing around Symi doing your bidding, that's where I've been, and a thank you wouldn't go amiss.'

Marta grunted and walked over to the bureau. 'I must get this back to the courier's office before they close for lunch. With luck the samples will be back in Ireland by Monday. How was Nishan?'

'In fine voice,' said Phoebe, pulling herself up. 'You're right, Aunt Marta, he's very talented.' She paused at the top of the stairs. 'I think I'm in love.'

Marta's jaw dropped open as her Goddaughter's head disappeared below the top step.

Down at Kambos Square Danielle and Evadne were sitting in the secretary's studio flat, a small black ledger open on Evadne's lap. As she examined the contents Danielle sat by her computer quietly observing the expression on Evadne's face. It was as if a very bad smell hovered under the older woman's nose, revulsion clinging to every pore. Columns of dates, ships names, quantities and type of cargo and ports of departure and arrival were all chronologically listed, dating back to the early nineties, the whole written in her husband's wiry scrawl.

She tracked down the list of cargo recognising some like LSD and Crack. Others were a mystery. 'What's China White?' she asked, looking up.

Danielle tapped the words into her search engine, the deep lines etched into her sallow face reflected in the back light from her computer screen.

'Heroin,' read Danielle aloud.

'And Black Tar?'

'The same.'

Evadne closed the book and sat forward resting her head in her hands. Under our very noses, she thought, my husband has been clearing shipments of drugs through Symi and on into Greece and, no doubt, taking a cut from the wholesale value of the cargo. 'The question is, who is he working for?' She didn't realise she had spoken aloud.

'Fabio Grigio' suggested Danielle, recalling the man's fleshy fingers between her legs. She shuddered.

Evadne looked up. 'A possibility. Krios certainly knew Grigio in Athens when he was a captain in the Narcotics Division. Intermezzo has been based at Zea Marina in Piraeus for years. Fabio Grigio may be Italian but his crew are all Greek which I've always found strange. It's not a big leap to imagine that he's running a drug cartel. Perhaps the purchase of *Intermezzo* was one way of laundering the drug money.'

'Well, he certainly has contacts in Turkey through Krios. The power-boat that met us in Thessalona Bay was definitely from there even though it was flying an American flag. My father once told me that most Turkish boats and gulets are registered in Wilmington, Delaware for tax purposes.'

Evadne thought about that for some seconds before commenting. 'So, drugs out of Afghanistan could easily be moved across Turkey by road to one of their Mediterranean ports. All the criminals would have to do is clear their vessels into a Greek port like Symi . . .'

'and, bingo,' interrupted Danielle, 'their illegal cargo is in Europe.' She spread her hands. 'Who better to supervise that part of the operation than Symi's Police Chief? No one would have the nerve to question him.' Danielle could feel revenge as a warm glow in the pit of her stomach. 'If we could get sight of the police-log I'm sure we'd find that your husband met every one of those shipments personally.' She nodded towards the ledger.

'Unless your father and the others are in on the scam.' Evadne looked straight at Danielle.

'Oh, my God, I never thought of that.' Danielle's warm glow turned to ice. 'Surely dad would not be stupid enough to involve himself in this.'

Evadne sat back and rubbed her neck. 'Can you get access to this police-log without raising suspicion?'

'I don't know. It's kept in dad's desk at the police station and I don't have any reason to ask to see it.'

'Danielle,' said Evadne, leaning forward once more. 'I have no hesitation in placing my husband in the frame for this, but I have no intention of ruining anyone else's life in the process. We have to be sure Krios is working alone.'

Danielle bit her thumbnail as she considered her options. 'Dad doesn't normally work Saturday afternoons. If you could get me to the police station after lunch, I could pretend that Krios had asked me to check the duty log. Alex or Galen would assume Krios was checking up on his sergeant behind his back.'

'Be careful, Danielle, you could get your fingers burnt.'

'Maybe, but I need to know that my father is not part of this. If it wasn't for these blasted stitches I'd be off there right now.'

'OK. I'll come here and have lunch with you at one o'clock tomorrow then drop you at the steps of the station at two and park along from the Nireus Hotel. Can you make it back to me if you take it slowly?'

Danielle nodded. 'With luck, there'll be so many tourists milling about no one will notice me in the crowd.'

'Let's hope so,' said Evadne, running her finger down the ledger. 'Do you have a pen and paper so we can list the dates which need cross-referencing.'

They quickly compiled the list and realised that the last shipment hadn't yet arrived.

'This one is for next Monday at eleven o'clock,' said Evadne, reading aloud. 'The Sea Pearl. A fifty-foot motor-cruiser registered in Delaware.'

'See, I told you. I bet it's based in Turkey.'

'I would like to keep this,' said Evadne, holding up the ledger. 'If we can prove your father or the other officers are not involved I intend to go to Athens on Sunday and I want you to come with me. My brother-in-law is the new Colonel of the Hellenic Police Department and he will want to talk to you about your night on *Intermezzo*. As for this shipment,' she pointed to the last entry, 'it could be intercepted by the Coastguard after it leaves here.'

'But if I leave Symi, Krios will become suspicious.'

'I don't think so. You can report in sick and he will think nothing of it. Better still, tell him you are taking a week's leave. He will probably think you are going on a spending spree with the money that was given to you by Fabio Grigio.'

'I'm not sure my parents will be so easily fooled.'

Evadne needed Danielle to stay positive. 'Then we will have to think up a suitable reason for your absence. Do you know anyone in Athens?'

'No. I do have a school friend who now lives in Cephalonia. She's always asking me to visit.'

'Then that will have to do. Tell your parents that you have been invited to stay with your girlfriend and you have decided to take some well-earned leave. Hopefully, your parents will accept this as the truth. Do you have Krios's desk keys?'

Danielle eased herself from the chair and pulled the bunch of keys from her skirt pocket.

Evadne put them in her bag. 'I'll make sure they are back in Krios's bedside table tonight.'

'Do you think he will suspect anything?' asked Danielle, leaning forward to pull a buff coloured file from beneath some papers on the coffee table.

'No, why should he? I imagine the police conference in Kos will keep him occupied for a couple of days writing up his report.'

'Well, I won't be the one to type it,' said Danielle, imagining herself in Athens. She passed Evadne the file. 'I think you should see this too,' she continued, 'I found it in the drawer with the ledger.'

Evadne opened it, sifted through the contents then stared into Danielle's eyes. 'My God, will this never end.'

Chapter Twenty Six

Friday (evening)

Marta stood outside Danielle's studio flat and rang the bell. Like Evadne Kakos, she couldn't believe the change in Krios's secretary when she opened the door.

'Danielle, you look terrible.'

Danielle walked back into the flat. 'I looked worse on Tuesday.' Marta watched as she gingerly lowered herself into a chair. 'If you'd like a cold drink, please help yourself.' She pointed to the kitchenette.

Marta cut through the niceties realising that the visit was not a social call. 'What's happened, Danielle? Why did you want to see me?'

Danielle leant forward and lifted the buff file off the coffee table. 'I found this in Chief Kakos's desk drawer yesterday. Evadne Kakos and I both agree that you should have it.'

'I don't understand.' Marta took the file, sat down and placed it on her lap. She was about to open it when Danielle interrupted her.

'Miss Fabrini, you gave me some good advice last weekend. To my cost, I failed to take it. Perhaps you should hear what I have to say before you open that file.' Her finger hovered in mid-air. 'It is not a pretty story.'

Marta returned the file to the coffee table and sat back. 'Only if you're sure, Danielle.'

Krios's secretary squeezed her lips together, paused, then repeated everything she had told Evadne at the Nireus Hotel and what she had found out subsequently.

Marta listened in silence, inwardly weeping for Danielle's loss of innocence at the hands of Kakos and Grigio.

191

'Since I've discovered the ledger,' concluded Danielle, 'Kyría Kakos has insisted on taking me to Athens to report it all to the police. She seems very determined and has told me that if I stay here I may be in danger.'

Marta, leant forward and gently clasped the young woman's hands between her own. 'I think she's right, Danielle. What you went through is vile and what you've found out, shocking. The men responsible must be punished.'

'I know, but I have to prove that my father isn't involved. Kyría Kakos will only act if Chief Kakos is working alone.'

Evadne Kakos is no one's fool, thought Marta, running the scenarios through her brain. 'Can I do anything to help?'

'I don't think so, thank you . . .' Danielle pressed her hands against the arms of the chair and carefully readjusted her position. A short intake of breath accompanied her action. '. . . It was when I was searching through Krios's desk that I came across this file. Kyría Kakos wanted to be the one to give it to you but I insisted on doing it myself. I hope I'm doing the right thing.'

Marta opened her mouth but Danielle hadn't finished. 'She also asked me to give you this.' She pulled a Dictaphone tape out of her pocket. 'I believe it's yours.'

Marta took the tape and clenched it in her fist. 'Do you know if she's taken a copy?'

'No, but she did say she was going to report it to the police in Athens while we're there.'

Marta nodded and was about to open the file when Danielle placed her hand on the cover. 'Miss Fabrini, I think you should wait until you get home. What you decide to do after that can only be your decision but I want you to promise me that you'll tell no one about my night on *Intermezzo*. If my parents found out it would break their hearts.'

192

It was past midnight when Marta arrived back at Villa Fabrini. The house and garage were in darkness, Nishan and Rosa both asleep. Rather than disturb them, she crossed to the music-room and spread the contents of the file out on top of the piano. She stared at numbers of press cuttings from newspapers and magazines dating back to 1992 in disbelief.

As she read through the articles one by one her blood ran cold. She imagined Krios cutting them out from the pages of Italy's Corriere della Sera, La Repubblica, and La Stampa and others from the Athens News, USA Today and the Times. Antonio's photograph appeared above copy covering Carlo Cantotti's trial; while others were about herself, the headlines always in the same vein –

Italian soprano widowed by a terrorist bomb
or

Marta Fabrini buries her dead as the world looks on.

None of it made sense. She questioned whether Krios's interest in her was more than a passing infatuation and wondered why he kept the press cuttings in the first place? It was macabre, she thought, and what had any of this to do with him?

As she tried to gather the pages together with shaking hands, the pile slipped through her fingers and fell to the floor, a small brown envelope landing by her feet. She plucked it from the carpet thinking it was irrelevant but viewed the contents anyway. The room began to spin as she held a scrappy invoice, typed on an old typewriter, from some company in Izmir, Turkey.

Her heart pounded, her stomach muscles spasmed and sweat broke out on her forehead. Was this something to do with the Romano murders? Was it a vital piece of evidence in the search for Antonio's and Paolo's killers? Would Interpol trace the receipt to where a copy of Paolo's rucksack had been made?

Marta was now in the grip of a major panic-attack, her breathing short and rasping, blood pumping through her temples as Antonio's voice suddenly filled her head. *'The policeman has it, Paolo, now hurry up.'* Her hand went to her face where Paolo's last kiss had brushed her cheek as he rushed away from her for the last time; she smelt again the perfume of the multitude of flowers surrounding the grave as the two coffins sank into the earth and felt Panayiotis's strong hands grabbing her around the waist as she tried to follow her loved ones into eternity. The trauma was back and in force.

Clutching her stomach to stem the tide of nausea threatening to overcome her she walked over to the window and looked out into the night, her voice racked with sobs. 'Antonio, for God's sake help me.' As if in answer, the moon sailed from behind a cloud and high above the Vassilios Gorge the chapel of Ayia Katerina emerged from the darkness, glowing with diffused light.

Marta didn't hesitate. Grabbing a torch and a rusty key she left Villa Fabrini behind and took the rocky path across the hillside. The wrought-iron gate squeaked on opening but she didn't notice, intent only on reaching the sanctuary of the small church. She unlocked the door and stepped inside, allowing the deep shadows to slowly dissipate as her eyes adjusted to the dark.

With shaking hands she lit two candles and placed them in the sand box, their sputtering flames casting a warm glow over the chapel ceiling, then moving towards the iconostasis, Marta dropped to her knees and gave in to her remorse. A beam of moonlight pierced the tiny stained glass window surrounding her in a kaleidoscope of colour, the peace and tranquillity of the chapel easing her torment.

After a while, she moved to a wooden bench and laid her head against the chapel wall, the same question nagging at her repeatedly. What was the connection between Carlo Cantotti's court case and Krios Kakos? Marta was sure there was one but she couldn't identify it. The Madonna and child looked down on her from the opposite wall as Marta battled with her dilemma.

The answer finally came like a zephyr of wind on a calm sea. 'Thank you,' she whispered as she closed the chapel door and made her way back to the music-room. Searching through the press cuttings her fingers lifted a sheet from amongst the pile and placed it close to the reading lamp. Below a headline which read – 'CARLO CANTOTTI WALKS FREE' – a paparazzi photograph showed the Government Minister smiling at a crew member as he boarded a large motor-yacht.

Marta pulled a magnifying glass from the shelf and studied the photograph closely. The crew member's face was horrifyingly familiar and, at the top of the picture, slightly out of focus on the right, was a short, thick set man wearing dark sunglasses talking on a mobile phone. Marta lowered her magnifying glass and closed her eyes. The man was Fabio Grigio, the motor-yacht, *INTERMEZZO* and the last time she had seen the crewman, he was wearing an Italian police uniform.

Chapter Twenty Seven

Saturday (before dawn)

Phoebe rested her hand lightly on the tiller of her namesake and brought the bow thirty degrees to port. She whispered a thank you to Phillipe for giving her some free time to enjoy a night's fishing with her father after the debacle with her grandmother and she now felt a whole lot better.

Phoebe II had done well. The trammel nets had entangled grouper, red mullet, sea bream and snapper while the long-lines with their baited hooks had snared umpteen mackerel, so the fish boxes were full to overflowing.

Phoebe had worked happily alongside her father and between hauls they had chatted long into the night, one subject dominating all others - Anastasia. They were now heading home and the stars seemed so close that Phoebe thought she could pluck them from the sky.

Panayiotis sat at the bow mulling over their earlier conversation, his body outlined against the boat by the moon glow. Phoebe had chosen her words carefully as she recounted her argument with his mother, omitting the more insulting comments. However, she wasn't able to hide the fact that the situation between them was now dire.

She tied the tiller amidships and walked forward, sitting on the gunwhale close to her father as the fishing boat carried them north. 'What are we going to do about gran, dad?'

Panayiotis tilted his head towards her. 'I really don't know, Phoebe. How do you cross a generation gap that's the width of the Mediterranean?'

'I don't know, but there must be something we can do? Wouldn't Aunt Marta help? She could talk to gran, explain that she was not trying to usurp her position in the family.'

'I would imagine any comment from your Godmother would only rub salt into the wound.'

'You don't know that. Gran might end up liking Aunt Marta. Love thy neighbour as it says in the bible.'

'I thought you knew your grandmother better than that, Phoebe. Once she takes a dislike to someone nothing will shift her. Look how she is over your mother. She never liked Leonora from the moment I first brought her home and when she left me for your stepfather your gran wouldn't have her name mentioned in the house. She's stubborn, Phoebe, like all my women. It seems to be embedded in their female genes.' He paused.

Phoebe knew he was expecting a quick retort but for once she didn't rise to the challenge. 'It just seems so sad for gran to spend her failing years pushing us away when she really wants to keep us close.' She turned and looked out to sea. 'I miss the nanna I had when I was a child. She was so huggable then.'

Panayiotis tapped the deck with the palm of his hand and Phoebe moved from the gunwale, sitting between her father's legs as she had when she was a little girl, snuggling into his warm body and hugging her knees. He wrapped his protective arms around her slim waist and rested his cheek against hers.

'Do you remember when we used to go fishing, years ago? You were no higher than that gunwhale, stomping about in those pink rubber boots covered in daisy transfers, trying to catch the fish as they leapt about the deck.'

Phoebe giggled. 'Whatever happened to those rubber boots? They're all the rage again in Athens.' She fell silent. Panayiotis waited. 'What I remember most is swimming with the dolphins in Thessalona Bay at dawn. It was so magical. Sometimes at night when I'm alone in my room in Athens surrounded by revision papers and city noise, I close my eyes and think of my dolphins playing with the bow wave as *Phoebe II* motors back to

Yialos, you at the helm, the fish flapping in their wooden crates and me sitting on the cuddy roof under a starry sky. I miss it all.'

'We miss you too, Phoebe.' She could feel his whiskers brush her skin as he gently kissed her temple. 'Don't misunderstand me, I know your future is on the mainland and I would never try and hold you back, but on nights like this I long to have you share it with me, just like tonight.' He hugged her tight.

'We're a pathetically romantic pair, aren't we?' said Phoebe, leaning her head back on his shoulder.

'Maybe, but what do I do when you give some younger chap permission to take my place. Do I end up bitter and twisted like your grandmother?'

Phoebe squeezed her father's arms holding her close. 'That will never happen, dad. No one could ever replace you.'

Panayiotis sighed, his relief palpable.

His daughter turned and looked up into his eyes. 'Well, not unless he promises to buy me a new scooter!'

The morning was well advanced and Krios in a foul mood as the Coastguard patrol boat closed on the quay and made fast. The conference in Kos had proved to be a complete and utter waste of time as Krios had suspected.

Some bright spark in the corridors of power back in Athens had suggested a 'think tank' meeting of all the relevant services to try and come up with a plan to stop the tide of illegal immigrants from the Middle East and North Africa crossing into Europe via Greece. How any of his contemporaries expected to halt this ever increasing wave of humanity without the means to constantly patrol the borders on land and at sea was beyond him. To Krios, tinkering around the edges in a political fudge was never going to solve the problem, the lucrative trade in human trafficking would see to that.

He jumped ashore at the clock-tower and stormed across to the police station convinced that the only way to solve the problem was for Europe to provide a solid shield of manpower and equipment, positioned at the interface, patrolling the area night and day, paid for out of EU funds and with orders to shoot to kill. A few shattered bodies littering the border crossings or floating off the Turkish coastline would soon put a stop to the problem, he thought, but as usual the lily-livered MEP's in Brussels were not prepared to stand-up and be counted. They were too interested in benefitting from the EU gravy train and hid behind the stupid laws passed down by the International Court of Human Rights, shrugging their shoulders and passing the buck.

The police station was bulging at the seams and Christos was trying to keep order as skippers and crews all jostled for his attention, unaware that his boss had arrived back in Symi. Young Galen noticed Krios and nudged his Sergeant in the ribs. Christos looked over the top of his spectacles noting the thunderous expression on the Police Chief's face and returned to the job at hand.

Krios beckoned Galen over to his side, the young police officer squeezing between the counter and the wall, forcing his way through the crowd. Seconds later Krios was gone and Galen retraced his steps.

'What did he want?' muttered Christos under his breath.

'He wanted to know if there had been any problems during his absence. When I said, no, he told me to tell you that he will be at home all afternoon writing a report.'

Christos looked at the mass of seething bodies, wishing he had the opportunity to slope off home instead of spending his Saturday morning dealing with Symi's influx of visitors. 'Allright, allright,' he complained, 'who's next?'

Phoebe jumped as she turned around and found Krios Kakos staring at her from the other side of the bar. She hadn't even heard him come into the Jazz Café and remembered that the last time she'd seen him, he was being asked to leave. 'Yes, Chief Kakos, do you want something?'

'Where's your boss this morning?' Krios pulled out a stool and sat down.

'I have absolutely no idea.'

'I doubt that for one minute.' Phoebe clenched her jaw in defiance. 'Perhaps you would pass on a message when you next see her.'

She moved away from the counter with a tray of drinks and walked out of the bar, head held high and deliberately took her time with the customers hoping Krios Kakos would get bored and leave. He was still there when she returned.

'As I was saying, would you tell Marta Romano that I'm writing a report to Brussels on my experiences with illegal immigrants here in Symi? It will include a recommendation by me that any help given to these miscreants by members of the public, without permission, will be viewed as a criminal offence. She might like to remember that the next time she decides to act like Mother Teresa . . .'

Phoebe's blood ran cold. Was he referring to Marta's help at Kambos Square or did he have some inkling of Nishan's existence?

'. . . I've decided to overlook the recent incident in Kambos Square,' he continued, 'but, in the future, I suggest she stays out of police business.'

Chief Kakos,' said Phoebe, relieved and feeling argumentative, 'if this message is so important I suggest you tell her yourself. She will be interested to learn of your intention to ignore the rules laid down by the International Court of Human Rights in The Hague.'

Krios banged the counter top with his clenched fist making Phoebe flinch. 'Don't you bandy words with me, young lady? What you know about international law on illegal immigrants can probably be written on the back of a postage stamp.'

Phoebe smiled sweetly. 'Actually, Chief, you may be interested to know that I have just completed a three-thousand-word essay on the subject for my degree at Athens University. It happens to be a pet subject of mine. Now, do you want anything else or will you be leaving?'

Krios rose from the stool and placed his Raybans over his eyes. 'Don't fly too high, little bird; you might get your wings burned.'

His barbed words remained with Phoebe long after he had departed and like her Godmother, Phoebe now needed to tread very carefully.

The door to the kitchen was open at the Kakos villa and the cook could hear an argument going on in the morning room.

'Of course I'm going to Athens, Krios. My mother is far from well and I feel it's my duty to be by her side. You've certainly made it clear you don't need me here.'

Krios dropped into a chair. 'How long do you propose to be away?'

'As long as it takes. I'll ring you when I've talked to her consultant and found out how bad her angina is.'

Krios grunted and picked up the newspaper.

Evadne counted to ten. 'While we're on the subject of doctors and heart conditions, I've made you an appointment at the clinic for eleven o'clock on Monday for your INR test.' She went to open the window turning her back on Krios, waiting to see what response she would get. There was a pregnant pause.

'Well, you'll just have to cancel it. I have an important meeting at eleven on Monday and frankly INR tests are not on my priority list.'

I bet they're not, thought Evadne pushing the window ajar. She turned. 'Krios, you haven't had an INR test for months. You are supposed to have them every eight weeks and as heart failure runs in your family I strongly suggest you treat your arrhythmia will more respect. I assume you are taking your Warfarin tablets.'

'For God sake, Evadne, stop treating me like a child. It's my heart and I'm quite capable of looking after it.'

'Be it on your own head, Krios.' Evadne looked at her watch. It was time to go to Danielle. She picked up her sunglasses and handbag. 'I'm off to the hairdressers. I'll see you later.'

'I'll be in the study all afternoon writing a report on illegal immigrants and my views on dealing with them so I would appreciate not being disturbed when you get back.'

Evadne turned at the door. 'I can't imagine your opinion will hold much sway with the politicians in Athens, Krios. Genocide is not one of their options.' Her slight was ignored. 'Don't forget to cancel your clinic appointment first thing Monday morning. They are now closed for the weekend and I shall have my hands full with my mother.'

Danielle pulled her straw hat low over her eyes and climbed out of Evadne's car, cautiously moving amongst the mass of people, trying not to be jostled. The police station was quiet and Galen was alone, standing by the electric fan trying to keep cool.

'Hi, Danielle. You've just missed your father; he went off duty ten minutes ago. We were so rushed in here this morning he was late getting away.'

Danielle was thankful she hadn't arrived any earlier. 'Oh, well, I'm sure you can help me, Galen. Chief Kakos wants me to check the police-log. Some statistics he needs by Monday. I've not been feeling too well recently, food poisoning, so I thought I would catch up over the weekend.'

'Chief Kakos mentioned he had a report to do when he was in here earlier this morning.' Galen pulled out a chair. 'Help yourself, it's over here on your dad's desk.'

Another skipper arrived at that moment keeping Galen busy while Danielle pulled the log towards her and systematically checked the entries against her own list, turning the pages one by one and noting the details of the relevant vessels, skippers and flags in a notebook she had brought with her. She closed the log and put it back where she'd found it.

'Thanks, Galen. I'll tell dad I've been in here when I see him tonight.'

She arrived back at the car moments later, sweat pouring off her face, her straw hat wilting in the heat. She lowered herself onto the passenger seat and took the bottle of ice-cold water from Evadne's hand as the car engine coughed into life.

'Did you get it?' asked Evadne, easing the car through the crowds.

Danielle nodded. 'It's all here.' She raised the notebook in the air then lay back in the seat and closed her eyes, pain coursing through her groin.

Back at the flat she and Evadne settled down to analyse what they had.

'Is Krios working alone?' asked Evadne, her fingers crossed in her lap.

'Yes. In each case it was your husband's signature by the log's entry.' She handed the notebook to Evadne who studied it carefully.

'Right, that settles it. We need to get you packed and you must phone your parents to let them know you're leaving for a few days.'

When Danielle came off the phone Evadne was still examining the notebook. 'Were they surprised?'

'No, Mum thought it was an excellent idea. I nearly had kittens though when she suggested seeing me off at the ferry, but then she remembered she was going on the annual pilgrimage to Panormitis Monastery with the congregation from Ayios Lefteris church so wouldn't be around.'

'What about your father?'

'I doubt he would bother coming to see me off. He goes fishing every Sunday, rain or shine. It drives my mother wild, particularly when he hardly ever catches anything worth eating.'

'Still, to be on the safe side we should board the ferry separately.' She opened her bag and dropped a ferry ticket to Rhodes on the bed.'

'What time's the flight to Athens?' Danielle examined the ticket.

'Three-thirty. What are you going to do about telling Krios?'

'I've left a message for the Mayor's secretary. She'll tell him when he gets in on Monday morning.'

'Good. Have you thought anymore about counselling?'

Danielle nodded. 'I think what we are about to do is the best therapy I can have. I just wish I could do the same to Fabio Grigio.'

Alex was on duty in the early evening when the phone rang on the sergeant's desk.

'Symi police station.'

'Who's that?'

Alex looked at the hand set in surprise. 'Pardon?'

'I said, who's that?'

204

'It's Officer Laskaris.'

'Are you the lanky one or the one with spots?'

'Who am I speaking to?' demanded Alex, not amused.

'This is Anastasia Stanis and I want to know why Chief Kakos hasn't been to see me yet?'

'Kyría Stanis, I have no idea what you're talking about.'

'Well, that's not a surprise. None of you down there seem to know what day it is most of the time.'

'Now, just a minute.'

'No, young man, I haven't got a minute. I've been waiting for Krios Kakos to call here all day. Sergeant Nicolaides promised to tell his boss that I wanted to see him the minute he arrived back from Kos. Now, where is he?'

Alex was getting fed up with Anastasia's demands and wanted her off the phone. 'I imagine he's at home. Why don't you ring him there?'

The phone went dead. 'Silly old biddy,' he muttered under his breath and placed the handset back on its cradle.

Anastasia was livid. She grabbed her coat off the hook by the front door and crossed Syllogos Square. Arriving at the Kakos villa she mounted the steps and banged the knocker with great force.

The cook answered the door, surprised to see her friend on the other side.

'Hello, Anastasia. Can I help you?'

'Yes, Sybil, you can. I've come to see Chief Kakos, it's urgent.'

'I'm afraid he's not to be disturbed at the moment.'

'He'll agree to be disturbed when he hears what I have to say,' said Anastasia pushing passed. Which room is he in?'

'I'm sorry,' said Sybil, rushing around her and blocking her way. 'I can't let you see him right now; it would be more than my job's worth.'

'Sybil. I've been waiting at home all day to see Krios Kakos and I don't intend to wait any . . .'

'What the devil is going on out here?' boomed Krios from the study door. 'I thought I made it clear, Sybil, I didn't want to be disturbed.'

'You did, Chief, but . . .'

'Oh, for goodness sake, anybody would think you were the Pope,' said Anastasia, elbowing Sybil out of the way and crossing the hall. 'Chief Kakos, you and I need to talk and we're going to talk right now.'

Krios looked down at the little woman in her black coat, her collar littered with wispy grey hairs, and curled his lip. 'If you want to talk to me, Madam, you can make an appointment with my secretary at the Town Hall in normal business hours. Now, if you'll excuse me I have a report to finish.'

'If you had bothered to come to my house as I requested yesterday we wouldn't be standing here arguing now. So, do you want to know what I have to say or do I go over your head?'

Krios looked across to Sybil who raised her shoulders. He turned back to Anastasia. 'You'd better come in.' He closed the door on the cook and walked to his desk.

Anastasia sat on a hard-backed chair and waited for the Police Chief to settle. His face was a blank page but his knee drumming the underside of the desk showed his irritation. 'Now what is this all about?'

'Chief Kakos. I want to report that an illegal immigrant is living at Villa Fabrini with Marta Romano.'

Krios dropped his pen.

Marta wore a hole in her lounge carpet waiting for Captain Silvano to return her call. He finally phoned back on Saturday evening and apologised profusely. He had been investigating a bank robbery and had only received her message when he'd returned to the station later that afternoon.

'Is it safe to talk on the phone?' asked Marta.

'Yes,' confirmed Silvano, 'I'm ringing you on a protected line and I'm taping every word you say for our records.'

Marta divulged all she knew from the moment she received Danielle's phone call to finding the paparazzi picture amongst Krios's press cuttings. After a lengthy discussion the Inspector agreed that Krios Kakos's involvement in Antonio's murder plot was a strong possibility.

'Marta, can you fax me a copy of the picture and the invoice straight away. I will notify Interpol of the address in Izmir and get the newspaper to reproduce the actual photograph so that we can circulate it to all concerned.'

'Am I in danger, Captain Silvano?'

'I don't think so. Fabio Grigio will have no idea that we have linked him to Kakos or the police guard, so when Kakos is arrested for drug smuggling the only one in the frame will be this young girl, Danielle. She can place both men on Grigio's boat and witnessed a vessel from Turkish waters meeting it under suspicious circumstances. She will need round the clock protection. Fabio Grigio is not a nice man.'

Marta grabbed her knees trying to still them. 'Hopefully Evadne Kakos will make sure the Hellenic Police Force keeps her safe.'

Her implied criticism was not lost on Captain Silvano. He had promised to keep Antonio Romano safe but had failed with disastrous consequences. He paused. 'Marta, I don't want you anywhere near Krios Kakos, do you understand.'

Marta agreed, the thought of being near the Police Chief making her feel sick. She also had Nishan to worry about and didn't want anything to stop her getting him safely away from Symi.

'What have you done with the evidence?'

'It's here at the house, why?'

'If Kakos finds out that you have any incriminating evidence against him, he'll come looking for it. Can you bring it to Milan, immediately?'

Marta knew she couldn't leave while-ever Nishan was still at Villa Fabrini. 'No, I can't, but I will find a safe place which is not on his radar.'

'Make sure you do, Marta. That evidence is critical to our case.'

She smiled. 'Don't worry, Captain, I have the perfect answer. Now, what is the connection between Fabio Grigio and the murders?'

'He's Carlo Cantotti's cousin, Marta.' Icy fingers rippled across her vertebrae.

After dinner Marta packed the evidence into a plastic wallet and returned to Ayia Katerina. The large painting of the Madonna and child was ideal for her purposes. She had bought it in Rome years before and donated it to the chapel when she came to live in Symi. Lifting it off its hooks, she laid it face down on the tiled floor. Easing the pins from the plywood back, she placed the file and invoice behind the painting, pushing the small Dictaphone tape to the bottom left hand corner behind the mount. Pinning the plywood in place she hung the painting on the wall and stood back. The Madonna returned her gaze, the suggestion of a smile on her lips.

'Keep it safe,' Marta whispered, then locked the chapel door and returned to the villa, her mind at ease for the first time in days.

Krios put down his pen, leant back in his chair and placed his hands behind his head, his mood much improved. He now had power over Marta and he was going to use it to maximum effect.

Anastasia Stanis had insisted on nothing less than deportation for the Italian widow but Krios had other plans. He smiled, exposing his set of perfectly aligned teeth. By Sunday night Marta would be putty in his hands and he would enjoy watching her squirm.

He gathered his report together and put it in his briefcase before switching off the desk lamp and moving into the sitting room. Evadne was reclining on the settee reading a book. She looked up as the door opened but said nothing.

'I'm off to bed, Evadne. I didn't sleep at all well in the hotel in Kos, the room was like a prison cell and the mattress not fit for an animal.'

'Really,' said Evadne, her response full of innuendo. 'I'll be a while yet, Krios, I want to finish this before leaving tomorrow.' She held up the novel and waved it in the air.

Krios didn't bother to respond. All he could think of as he climbed the stairs was how he was going to make Marta perform, his mind superimposing her face onto that of women in the acts of erotic sex stored on his computer.

Evadne heard the bedroom door close and exhaled, the tension, which had been building all day, fragmenting. Her case was packed, the ledger and notebook safely hidden in the lining of the lid. Instructions had been left in the kitchen for Sybil and the roll of film taken in the clinic was inside her makeup bag ready for processing as soon as she arrived in Athens. All she had to do now was get through the next twelve hours and she would be able to begin her new life.

Chapter Twenty Eight

Sunday (a.m.)

Sunday dawned bright and clear with a fresh breeze from the northwest. Marta had not slept and dark shadows below her eyes divulged her inner torment. She was loading a picnic hamper into the boot of her car when Phoebe arrived in the drive sporting a pair of cut-off white slacks, a sleeveless pink gingham blouse and her hair tied back in a ponytail. She looked like a young Audrey Hepburn, and Marta thought again how attractive she was.

'Hi, Aunt Marta. Dad's already on *Arabesque* checking for last minute glitches. He said to remember to bring plenty of sun tan lotion, your passports and not to forget your sailing gloves.'

They entered the kitchen together and met Rosa coming the other way. 'I'm ready when you are,' she said, her pale blue baggy trousers, matelot top and cream loafers giving her a rather nautical air. 'Nishan is in the music-room, Phoebe. I've made some coffee and your lunch is in the fridge.'

Phoebe took Rosa in her arms and gave her a big hug. 'You're a wiz, Rosa. Now, disappear, both of you. Nishan and I will be fine. Have a super day out on the water and give my love to *Arabesque*.'

'I think we've been given our marching orders, Rosa,' said Marta, her smile masking fatigue.

'Sounds like it to me.'

Phoebe watched the car pull out onto the main road and went to find Nishan.

In the Chorio, Father Voulgaris was doing a good impression of a package holiday representative, chivvying his flock into the Panormitis bus and looking at his watch anxiously as he counted heads for the third time that morning. He was without one member of the congregation and was about to ask who was missing when Anastasia came around the corner, her head held high and beaming from ear to ear.

'Ah, there you are, Anastasia.'

'Isn't it a wonderful day, Father?'

'It certainly is, dear, and I'm pleased to see that you are looking more like your old self this morning.'

'I feel on top of the world, Father, on top of the world.' Anastasia boarded the bus and sat next to Sybil, leaving Father Voulgaris standing at the bottom of the steps catching flies.

'Right, ladies,' he shouted, trying to be heard over the din, it should take about twenty minutes to get to Panormitis, so sit back and enjoy the drive.'

Anastasia chuckled and leant into Sybil. 'If I didn't know better I would say Father Voulgaris had missed his vocation!'

The bus drove away from the village, passing Villa Fabrini minutes later. Anastasia looked down at the terraced gardens visible from the road and mumbled under her breath.

'Did you say something, Anastasia?' asked Sybil.

'Oh, I was just thanking the Lord for small mercies,' she said and turned to face the front.

Arabesque looked so peaceful resting alongside the dock in Pedi, her mast and sails in place, a Greek courtesy flag at the starboard spreader and her large Italian ensign fluttering from a flagpole at the stern.

Panayiotis jumped ashore and took the hamper from Marta then helped Rosa aboard.

'Are you OK, Marta?' Panayiotis looked at her sideways.

'Yes,' she mumbled and quickly changed the subject. 'I hadn't realised that the yacht was still registered in Italy, Panayiotis. When are you going to change it?'

'Oh, I'll get round to it, eventually.' He never took his eyes from her face. 'If anyone bothers to ask, I'll say you own it and I'm your skipper.'

'Fine, but why do we need our passports?' Marta shook her head not wishing to make a big deal of her night's nightmares.

'I thought we'd sail over to North Passage and the Kiseli Adasi anchorage for lunch.'

It was now Rosa's turn to frown.

'We're off to Turkey, Rosa,' explained Marta, pointing across the channel. 'Let's hope the Turkish Coastguard don't make an appearance.'

'If they do,' said Panayiotis, pulling a Turkish courtesy flag from inside a locker, 'I'll tell them we'll be checking into Bozburun later today.'

Rosa shrugged her shoulders, her mouth puckered.

'Tell Rosa not to worry. *Arabesque* has been to this anchorage many times and we have never had a problem. Flying an Italian ensign also helps. They think we're tourists.'

'If that's the case, captain, I think it's high time you took us to sea.'

The Westerbeke diesel engine coughed into life, cooling water spurted from the exhaust pipe and a fine mist of white smoke appeared, pleasing the skipper. With Marta on the bow and Rosa on the stern they cast off the ropes holding them to the dock and the Hinckley Bermuda 40 drifted away from the wall helped along by the breeze. Once clear, Panayiotis motored out into Pedi Bay, the sun reflecting off his sunglasses as his firm hands gripped the wheel, feeling the rudder's resistance through the helm.

He turned the Hinckley into wind and with Marta's help hoisted the mainsail before turning back onto a heading of seventy-five degrees and unfurled the genoa on its forestay. As the wind billowed the sails, *Arabesque* picked up her skirts, leant to starboard and creamed out of the bay at a steady six knots, the engine silent and Rosa hanging onto her straw hat as if her life depended on it.

For a little under two hours they sailed close-hauled across the Symi Channel in a steady Force 4 with the Aegean rippling along their hull and occasional flying fish rising from the surface and gliding across the waves beyond their bow before disappearing once more into the sea. Marta caught sight of the Rhodes ferry as it moved out of Symi Bay and thought of Evadne and Danielle on board. She crossed her fingers, praying that Danielle would be kept safe from Fabio Grigio's wrath.

As *Arabesque* crossed into Turkish waters on a north-easterly heading, gulets and charter yachts crossed their path all heading for the Hisonaru Korfesi, further north, while *Arabesque* headed towards a narrow gap of water between the Turkish mainland and a small islet. Panayiotis started the engine, turned the yacht once more into wind and stowed the sails.

Rosa sat mesmerised as the water under *Arabesque's* keel began to turn from deep blue to a vivid aquamarine, the colour and clarity of the water more commonly seen in photographs of some Caribbean island paradise.

Back at the helm Panayiotis asked Marta to go forward. She was on the bow in seconds, hanging off the forestay checking for underlying rocks while Panayiotis watched the depth sounder drop to three metres as the keel crossed the bar before rising again once inside Kiseli Adasi anchorage.

They dropped the hook and settled back on *Arabesque's* anchor chain, the only sound, that of the warm water lapping at the waterline.

'This is wonderful, Marta. Bella. Bella!' insisted Rosa.

Panayiotis and Marta looked at each other and smiled. No other words were necessary. *Arabesque's* crew were about to enjoy lunch in a stunning location far away from the stresses of Symi.

At Villa Fabrini, Phoebe and Nishan sat in the kitchen in companionable silence enjoying a pizza Fiorentina and green salad both made by Rosa earlier, with strict instructions left for Phoebe on how to cook the pizza.

They had spent the morning in Marta's office, Phoebe slowly explaining to Nishan why his DNA was so necessary and trying to find a way to describe what it was, with limited success. Finally, Nishan called a halt to the lesson and asked Phoebe about her life. Over coffee she told him what it was like to grow up in Symi as a child, why she was now living in Athens and why she wanted to be a journalist and third world activist.

He was fascinated, comparing her world to the one he had known as a child and had now left far behind. He thought of his mother and became silent. Phoebe sensed his thoughts were a long way off and asked what he was thinking.

'My mother, she think I'm blessed.' He looked around the kitchen. 'Her water, it not come from tap, she wash our clothes in stream. Many times I ask of my father. She say he was strong like an ox and cunning like a tiger. Now they are together with God.' He looked across at Phoebe. 'I think my mother, she like you.' He watched Phoebe's complexion ripen like a blushed peach.

'What would you have done if you hadn't met Marta?' asked Phoebe as she took the pizza out of the oven.

215

Nishan thought about the question and tried to take himself back to the derelict buildings on Yialos hillside just two weeks earlier. 'The police, they find me and send me away.' He stopped and looked down the valley to the sea. 'But, I never give up, Phoebe. I find my grandfather one day. I promise my grandmother and I fight to keep it.'

Phoebe pulled her scooter's keys from her trouser pocket and took a medallion off the key ring. 'Take this, Nishan, until you meet your grandfather, it will keep you safe on your journey.' She pointed to the Saint's image embossed on the metal tag. 'This is St. Christopher, the patron saint of all travellers.' She passed it across the table.

'*Grazie*, Phoebe, you are kind like Marta and Rosa.' Nishan took the medallion, squeezing it in his palm. 'When can I leave, Phoebe? I here too long. Marta, she is in danger.'

'I don't know, Nishan. She should have the DNA test results in a few days and then my dad can make arrangements to take you off the island.' She placed her hand over his. 'Don't worry, Aunt Marta knows what she's doing.'

Krios stepped onto the balcony of his villa and watched Poseidon arrive back in Yialos harbour on its return journey to Iskenderun from Athens. He was not concerned. The motor-boat wouldn't be carrying any illegal cargo going east so any one of his police officers could deal with Captain Kostas and the vessel's paperwork. His thoughts turned back to the arrest of the illegal immigrant at Villa Fabrini and his pursuit of Marta Romano.

Anastasia Stanis had been quite specific about Marta's movements for the day, stating that she would be out sailing with the old lady's son and his daughter on *Arabesque*. Marta's absence from Villa Fabrini gave Krios the opportunity to arrest the immigrant and have him locked in a cell at the police station long before she returned home. He enjoyed imagining her reaction when she found him missing.

Krios was also revelling in the knowledge that he now had a reason to get rid of his police sergeant by holding him personally responsible for failing to remove all the immigrants from Symi on the day they arrived. In his opinion, the man needed pensioning off. Not only was he incompetent, he was far too lenient with the younger officers and couldn't be trusted to carry out Krios's orders as had been shown in Kambos Square two weeks earlier. Christos Nicolaides needed to be replaced. Krios looked at his watch, picked up the phone and dialled the police station.

'Officer Laskaris, Chief Kakos here. I need the police car outside my house in one hour and a police officer in attendance. We have an arrest to make.'

The picnic hamper was resting on *Arabesque's* coach roof as the three occupants sat in the cockpit enjoying their lunch. Marta leant back against the varnished coaming, resting her elbows on the edge, and closed her eyes. It had been a terrible twenty-four hours and she felt exhausted. She sighed deeply. 'Antonio would be pleased to know that you've finally launched *Arabesque*, Panayiotis. Leaving her sitting in the boathouse gathering dust and depreciating in value was crazy.'

'I know, Marta, but I couldn't bring myself to sail his yacht without him.' He hesitated. 'Nishan's arrival has changed all that.'

Marta's eyes snapped open. 'Why? What's going through your mind?'

'I've been trying to decide how to get Nishan to Italy. We still have an Italian pilot book on board and I think our best option is to sail straight to the Italian mainland and make landfall at Crotone on the south coast. From there it's only

217

ninety kilometres to Cosenza where Luigi Amato lives and I figure the old chap and his daughter could easily drive down to meet us, assuming they knew when we were arriving. So, today is a bit of a shakedown cruise.'

Marta translated for Rosa. 'How long a passage would it be?' she asked.

'A rough estimate would be five days, although that's weather dependent.'

'But, it's summer, Marta,' pointed out Rosa clearing away the dishes, 'surely there wouldn't be bad weather now?'

'Unfortunately, Rosa, the Aegean is a strange mistress and can throw a Meltemi wind of Force 8 or more at us out of a clear blue sky, that's why I'm suggesting Italy rather than Greece,' explained Panayiotis waiting for Marta to translate. 'If we head for the Italian Embassy in Athens and a Meltemi blows up we would be punching into wind in very rough seas. By moving due west we would get a better angle on the wind and would hopefully leave the Meltemi behind as we approached the Peloponnese.'

'But, surely, the wind would then be out of the west as we went around the bottom of Greece and into the south Ionian?' Marta was not so sure this plan would work.

'True, but the westerlies should be lighter and with luck we might get enough of an angle to sail it.'

'What happens if you don't?' asked Rosa, reappearing in the companion way.

'We would have to motor to Crotone.'

'What about fuel?' Marta was not convinced.

'*Arabesque* already has a full tank. I changed the fuel last week as I commissioned the yacht. I couldn't rely on the old diesel; it had been sitting in the tank far too long.'

Marta pulled her diary out of her beach bag. 'If I get the fax from Ireland on Wednesday there's nothing to stop us leaving straight away. The Italian Immigration Department can deal with Nishan's temporary visa while we're at sea and when we land, Luigi can have Nishan's Italian passport sent to Cosenza.'

'I assume, Marta, you agree with my plan?' Panayiotis sipped his beer.

'Well, it could be worse and we do need to get Nishan away from Symi and Krios Kakos's clutches as soon as possible.'

'That's settled then, we plan to leave for Crotone on Wednesday afternoon. Now let's get *Arabesque* back home.' He squashed his beer can between his fingers and dropped it in the hamper. 'The yacht needs some fine tuning and a whole load of victuals.'

The anchor dripped saltwater as it settled on the bow roller. Marta made it fast and remained on the foredeck as the Hinckley crossed the shallows once more and turned towards Pedi. She wrapped her arm around the forestay and breathed in the fresh afternoon air. Soon, she thought, Nishan would be safe with his new family, and the law would take care of Krios Kakos and Fabio Grigio. A warm glow spread through her body. She felt good for the first time in a long time.

Phoebe sat at the piano in the music-room listening to the sound of Nishan's voice as it charmed her senses. He stood by the window, his eyes closed, his mind winging across the Ethiopian hills, the melody calling to his goats, their bells tinkling on the air as they caught the refrain and moved, as one, towards its source.

Movement on the road caught Phoebe's eye as Nishan stopped mid-stanza and hit the floor, grabbing Phoebe by the leg and dragging her off the piano stool.

'Someone coming,' whispered Nishan in her ear.

She crawled to the south window and peeped out. Her next words to him were a hammer blow. 'It's the police.'

Nishan pulled her round and grabbed her by the shoulders. 'Phoebe, you stay here. I go to garage, alone.'

'No, Nishan, I'm coming with you.' Her eyes searched his face for approval.

'NO!' He increased his grip, digging his fingers into her soft skin. 'If I caught, you need tell Marta. You stay here. Don't argue, Phoebe. I do this alone. It is my fight.'

'But, Nishan . . .'

He was gone, limping away from the summerhouse in a crablike run, his sticks in one hand, skirting the back of the house as an old Fiat approached down the drive. Phoebe hid behind the settee, biting her knuckles and praying to anything that came to mind. If the police found Nishan, what would she do? She had to think but her brain refused to respond. She heard voices, car doors slamming and a dog barking. Her mind whirled in horror. Oh, no, not dogs. 'Nishan', she silently wailed, 'Nishan, don't leave me.'

Squeezing between the trees Nishan threw himself into the garage and locked the door, cowering in the rear corner his pulse racing wildly. Every sinew in his body was on high alert, adrenalin coursing through his veins. He heard voices near the house, a dog barking and men shouting. He curled into a ball, his hands over his head and waited. Minutes later a dog sniffed at the door then scratched the ground. Footsteps pounded the gravel.

'This is the police,' yelled a male voice. 'Come out with your hands above your head. We know you're in there.'

Nishan shook, the demands obvious. He was terrified of dogs. He imagined being mauled by a vicious set of canine teeth, his flesh ripped open as the fangs dug to the bone, images of corpses in the desert attacked by jackals violating his mind. He began to sweat.

'OK,' he yelled in Italian. 'OK, I come.'

He heard the dog's strangled cry, a man shouting commands, a scuffle beyond the door, then silence. Nishan crossed himself, then rising, picked up his sticks and hopped to the door.

A key ground in a lock then the wooden door slowly parted from its frame. Krios held the dog firmly by its collar, saliva dribbling from the corners of its mouth, and signalled Alex to move forward with his free hand.

Alex hesitated, eyes downcast.

'Officer Laskaris, get on with it.' The tone of the Chief's voice brooked no argument.

Alex clenched his teeth and ran to the door, pulled it fully open and stopped dead in his tracks. Standing, feet away, stood a tall man with ebony skin and deep brown eyes, forehead beaded in sweat, jeans and T-shirt freshly laundered, left foot heavily bandaged, right encased in a new leather sandal, the whole resting on two sticks for support. Alex stepped back and slowly turned to his boss. 'You can lock the dog in the truck, this man isn't going anywhere.'

A local farmer, hovering at the rear, stepped forward, took the dog from Krios's grip and moved away down the drive. The Chief advanced, elbowing Alex out of the way and scanned the fugitive from head to toe, his vicious smirk only visible to Nishan as he was grabbed by the arm and pulled towards the police car, his right stick spilling from his hand and bouncing off the gravel.

Phoebe could hear an engine start, wheels crunching on gravel, a dog's constant barking growing fainter, then, nothing but silence. She crawled from the safety of the settee and moved

221

to the window. Peeping through, she checked for signs of activity. All was still.

'Come on, Phoebe, show some guts,' she said aloud as she opened the music-room door and ran across the garden, her fingers crossed, praying that Nishan was safe. The garage door was wide open, the interior empty. Her cry of pain shattered the silence.

She dropped to her knees and buried her head in her arms, questions coming thick and fast. How did the police know Nishan was here? Who told them Nishan existed? When was he seen? Her anger against the traitor began to bubble to the surface demanding revenge. She knew she had to get to Marta and her father. They would know what to do. They would take control.

Ten minutes later, the house and music-room were locked, the garage closed and Phoebe was driving like a maniac down the main road to Pedi. She screamed along the waterfront, dumped the scooter on its side by the house and shot inside.

The VHF hand set was sitting in its charger on the kitchen dresser. Pulling it out of its stowage she returned to the scooter, pulled it upright and gunned the engine. She needed to go high and retraced her route up to the Chorio then onto the track leading to the chapel high above Pedi. She stopped as the track rounded a ninety-degree bend, parked the bike and walked to the edge, turning on the VHF set and selected Channel 16.

Panayiotis was in the middle of telling Marta and Rosa one of his tall fishing stories when his VHF set sprang to life.

'*Arabesque. Arabesque. Arabesque.* This is *Phoebe II* mobile. Do you read. Over.'

He shot round the helm and dived for the companionway hatch as Marta grabbed the wheel.

'*Phoebe II* mobile, this is *Arabesque*. Go Channel 8.'
Panayiotis changed channel with practised ease. '*Phoebe II*
mobile, do you read?' His hand was drumming the chart-table.
Something was dreadfully wrong and he felt impotent stuck on
Arabesque in the middle of the Symi Channel.

'Dad, where are you? Can you hear me?' Phoebe sounded
hysterical.

'Phoebe, calm down. I can hear you perfectly. Now, tell me
what's happened and take it slowly. Over.'

Marta was sitting on the top companionway step, the yacht
on autopilot.

'It's Nishan. He's been arrested.' Marta stopped breathing.
'Krios Kakos came to the villa with dogs. They took him, papa.
I don't know what to do.' Phoebe began to cry.

Panayiotis threw the handset at Marta and squeezed past her
on the steps. 'Tell her we're on our way,' he shouted as he took
control of *Arabesque,* every sinew straining to move the yacht
through the water at breakneck speed.

'Phoebe, its Marta. Can you hear me? Over.'

A few seconds of silence was followed by a small pitiful
voice. 'I'm sorry, Aunt Marta. I'm so sorry.'

Marta felt her world crack apart. 'We're on our way back,
Phoebe. Where are you?'

'I'm on the hillside above Pedi.'

'Fine. You should be able to see us any time soon. Now take
a deep breath and tell me exactly what happened.'

Krios manhandled Nishan out of the Fiat and frog-marched him
up the police station steps, Nishan dragging his bad foot behind
him. The Police Chief was like a man possessed, pushing the
immigrant across the balcony, never pausing until his prisoner
was safely locked in a cell.

Alex watched with disgust, angry at the use of such unnecessary force. He followed with both sticks and made his way into the office, leaning them in a corner by the filing cabinet.

Krios appeared with the cell keys in his hand, picked up the phone on the sergeant's desk and dialled a number. 'Kyría Nicolaides, this is Chief Kakos,' he said. 'Please put your husband on the phone.'

Alex couldn't hear the reply but his boss's jaw went rigid, a thin white line describing his mouth.

'I don't give a damn if Sergeant Nicolaides is shark fishing with Jacques Cousteau; I want him in my office immediately. Is that clear?' Krios slammed the phone down with such force the desk shook on its frame.

Alex was convinced his boss was either high on acid or had been watching too many cheap American gangster movies. He stood by the counter waiting for instructions, his anger beginning to get the better of him.

'The prisoner is to be guarded at all times and no one is to be allowed to see him. Is that clear?' Krios's look could have frozen alcohol. 'I'm going to my office. If Nicolaides turns up here tell him I'm waiting for an explanation as to how he managed to allow that vermin,' he pointed towards the cells, 'to remain cosseted in Villa Fabrini for two weeks when he had strict instructions to make sure all the illegal immigrants were shipped over to Rhodes on the day they arrived here.' He shook his head in disgust. 'You lot couldn't round up a herd of goats.'

Alex had had enough. Normally he was very placid but once he lost his temper all reason abandoned him. At that moment he couldn't care less whether he lost his job or not, no one was going to treat him like an imbecile. 'Why don't you just calm down? The man in that cell is an asylum seeker not some dangerous terrorist, and Sergeant Nicolaides could never have guaranteed that all the immigrants were found on the first day as we didn't have a clue how many had landed. Throwing your weight about like some damned control freak is not going to change anything around here and frankly I've had enough of being the butt of your bad temper.'

Testosterone levels soared as the two men faced each other. The air was heavy with menace. Alex waited, ready to continue the verbal challenge.

'Your opinion is of no concern to me, Laskaris.' Krios turned on his heels and left, leaving Alex alone and completely mystified.

Picking up the sticks and the cell keys he went to check on the prisoner and found Nishan slumped on the concrete slab unravelling the bandage around his ankle. His expression as he looked up at his jailer was one of defiance and hatred. Alex Laskaris felt ashamed at the way the immigrant had been manhandled and handed over the walking sticks without saying a word.

Marta sat in the saloon; the shock of Phoebe's revelation having been total. From feeling in complete control she was now a pawn in the Police Chief's game and she knew exactly what game he would be playing. Marta had no idea who had informed Kakos of Nishan's existence but, whoever it was had dealt him a royal flush and she had no way of countering it. Nevertheless, she had to think of something. Krios Kakos had ruined too many lives and she would not allow him to do it again.

She informed Panayiotis and Rosa that she was going to confront the Police Chief immediately *Arabesque* came alongside in Pedi. Panayiotis thought Marta was mad and said so. When she insisted he lost his temper.

'Don't be a bloody fool, Marta, he'll arrest you on the spot for aiding and abetting an illegal immigrant. Are you insane?'

225

Marta knew that Panayiotis's anger was born out of a need to protect her and hated causing him so much pain.

'Take Rosa home,' he demanded. 'I'll go to the police station and try and sort this out. Once Christos Nicolaides knows Nishan has relatives in Italy I'm sure he will put pressure on the Chief to rethink his arrest.'

'Now who's being a bloody fool?' insisted Marta. 'Christos Nicolaides has about as much influence on Krios Kakos as the United Nations has over Robert Mugabe. No, Panayiotis, I got myself into this mess and I'll get myself out. Kakos may think he has the upper hand but, I assure you, I have information on that bastard which will turn the tables on him once and for all.' She had conveniently forgotten Captain Silvano's warning.

'Don't risk it,' countered Panayiotis. 'Kakos is hell bent on controlling you and will do anything to get his own way.' He thumped the helm. 'I told you this would happen, ten days ago, but you wouldn't listen. Now you face a jail term and Nishan has been allowed to taste a life he can never have, all on a gamble that had little chance of success.'

'It had every chance of success,' yelled Marta.

'Then perhaps you'd tell me why he's now locked in a police station cell facing deportation and your name is about to be dragged through the dirt for being a stupid middle-aged woman with her head in the clouds.'

'How dare you. If everyone acted like you, Panayiotis Stanis, we would all be back in the Dark Ages. I've taken risky decisions all my life, sometimes I've won, sometimes I've lost but at least I've had the guts to try. Nishan found me remember, I didn't go looking for him, but I'm mighty glad he did and no matter what the consequences I'd do it all again, with you or without you.' She stormed back down into the saloon, anger, frustration and hatred for Krios Kakos fighting for supremacy.

Rosa didn't have a clue what was happening, all she knew was that Marta and Panayiotis were at each other's throats and Nishan had been arrested. Panayiotis was too riled to even attempt to explain, even if he could speak Italian, and she knew from experience that when Marta was angry it didn't pay to ask questions. She walked to the bow and sat watching the boathouse increase in size as *Arabesque* edged ever closer to her destination.

Panayiotis tried to calm down. He knew he couldn't stop Marta doing anything she wanted and could feel her slipping away from him. He had no idea what information she had on Krios Kakos, but, whatever it was would only make the situation worse. He gripped the wheel making sharp indents in the suede cover with his fingernails, praying it would not all end in tears. Reducing speed, he eased *Arabesque* alongside the dock as Rosa threw the bow line to Phoebe, then cut the engine. Thank God, he thought, as he grabbed the stern-line and threw it ashore, at least my daughter hasn't been arrested in the process. She made fast then climbed aboard and buried her head in her father's chest.

Marta appeared in the cockpit breathing fire. 'If it isn't too much trouble, perhaps you'd arrange to get Rosa back to Villa Fabrini.'

Panayiotis turned, aching to take her in his arms and make the whole mess go away. 'I'll get *Arabesque* ready to sail to Crotone while you're in Yialos,' he said. 'Please take great care and bring Nishan back as soon as you can.' His words hung in the air where she had been standing and he watched her drive off, thinking, not for the first time, how much he loved her.

Christos stood outside the Police Chief's office, his pulse racing. He'd rushed from home to the Town Hall immediately his wife told him of Krios's phone call, and had naturally assumed that there was some major emergency. He was therefore totally unprepared for the verbal onslaught that met him as he came face to face with his boss.

'Correct me if I'm wrong, sergeant, but didn't I instruct you to remove all the illegal immigrants from Symi two weeks ago?'

Christos puckered his eyebrows. 'Yes, and I did.'

'No, sergeant, you didn't. While you've been out fishing, I've arrested an illegal immigrant hiding at Villa Fabrini for the past two weeks who is now locked in one of our police cells.'

Christos was lost for words. 'I . . . I don't understand.'

'But, I do, sergeant. This is not the first time you have failed to carry out my instructions and I now question whether you are up to the job.' He lowered his head and began writing on a pad.

Christos rocked on his feet. 'With all due respect, Chief, I fail to see how . . .'

Krios ignored him. 'Arrangements will be made to deport the immigrant as soon as possible. In the meantime, you are to suspend Officer Laskaris for insubordination to a superior officer this afternoon and I expect to see your written resignation on my desk by the morning. Is that clear?' Krios raised his eyes and glared at Christos.

The sergeant turned white. Krios Kakos appeared to be hell bent on getting rid of him and by resigning Christos knew he would be making his boss's job easier and put his police pension in jeopardy. His fear turned to rage. Stretching across the desk he grabbed Krios by his shirt and breathed into his face. 'If you want to fire me, Krios, go ahead. I'll be interested to see what the police union makes of your trumped-up charges. I joined this force when you were still wet behind the ears and I'll be buggered if I'm going to resign.'

Krios peeled the sergeant's hand from his chest and sat back, the smirk on his face one that Christos would never forget. 'On the contrary, sergeant, you don't seem to have any choice in the matter.' He pulled a set of black and white photographs from beneath his pad and pushed them across the desk, the images graphically capturing Danielle engaged in pornographic acts with several men. 'You will resign, sergeant, unless you want to see your daughter exposed as a whore.'

Christos physically shook at the repulsive images before his eyes, respect for his daughter instantly expunged. All he could think about was what the shame would do to his wife. He staggered backwards never doubting that the Chief's threat was real, and bounced off the door frame as he exited, his clenched fist pressed against his mouth. Dragging himself along the landing, he staggered down the Town Hall stairs and vomited into some bushes by the entrance, his whole life fragmented.

Marta drove the short distance between Pedi and Yialos reliving the past hour and her argument with Panayiotis, their first cross words ever. As she rounded Kambos Square she nearly ran over Christos Nicolaides blindly crossing her path. Skid marks painted the road as she cut the engine and jumped out of the car.

'Sergeant!'

Christos didn't respond even though he was only yards away. Marta made a five-yard dash and pulled him round by his jumper. 'Christos, where's Chief Kakos?'

The pain in the sergeant's eyes needed morphine. He looked through Marta, hatred, despair and loathing blurring his vision, a man carrying the world on his shoulders.

Marta punched him in the chest. 'Christos, where's Chief Kakos?'

He registered the impact of her fist and turned to look back towards the Town Hall. She didn't need telling twice.

Flinging open the Town Hall entrance door, she threw herself up the two flights of stairs, running into Krios walking the other way.

'Where the hell do you think you're going, Chief Kakos?'

'Ah, Marta. What a pleasant surprise.'

He turned and Marta followed him into his office and closed the door. 'Who told you about Nishan Amato?'

'Do you mean that piece of filth camped out in your garage?' Krios sat at his desk oozing self-confidence.

Marta placed her hands on the desk. 'Allow me to wipe that supercilious grin off your face. Nishan Amato is an Italian citizen in my care and I demand his release immediately.'

Krios seemed unfazed by the revelation. 'Then, no doubt, you have his passport to prove it.'

'His passport is with the Italian Immigration Department as we speak.'

'Oh, come, come, Marta. You expect me to believe that an Italian citizen was dumped on Ayia Marina beach two weeks ago with fifty-eight illegal immigrants. Surely, if he had nothing to hide he would have arrived by ferry like every other legal visitor.'

'Believe me, stranger things have happened.' Marta began pacing the floor.

'Good try, Marta, but not good enough. The prisoner sitting in one of my cells is obviously African scum who crawled onto Symi looking for the promised land and found a frustrated middle-aged female who, it would appear, enjoys black ham.'

Marta swung round, fire in her eyes, wanting to wrap her hands around his neck and squeeze the life out of him but her inner voice reminded her that Nishan's release was paramount. 'What you think of me is irrelevant, Chief Kakos, however, what you do to Nishan Amato will have serious consequences, that I can promise.'

'Your threats are wasted on me, Miss Fabrini. May I remind you that aiding and abetting an illegal immigrant is a criminal offence, or had you conveniently forgotten that fact?'

Marta's arms came out in front of her, her hands clasped together. 'Go ahead, arrest me. I'll be released within twenty-four hours when my lawyers get involved. I doubt our Hellenic Police Colonel will be amused to learn that his brother has arrested an innocent woman on some trumped-up charge before checking his facts.'

Krios's retort faulted, and Marta knew her words had ripped through his ego. He walked around the desk and Marta's skin crawled as his hot breath parted the hairs at the nape of her neck. 'Within twenty-four hours, Madam, your lodger could be on his way back to Africa and there isn't a damn' thing you can do about it, lawyer or no lawyer.' His words chilled the air. 'Symi is a long way from Athens and I make the rules around here.'

Marta's defiance hit a virtual brick wall. It was imperative to keep Nishan in Symi until the DNA results came through but this was only possible with the Police Chief's agreement. She remained silent waiting for the inevitable proposition.

'Of course, I could be persuaded to change my mind.'

Marta could hear Panayiotis's words ringing in her ears. *"He'll do anything to get his own way."* 'You mean you would release Nishan from custody if I offered you my body?'

'Exactly.' Krios ran his hands down her arms and eased her back against his chest.

Marta's skin crawled at the thought of sex with this man but Nishan had embedded himself in her heart and she wanted to fight like a lioness to keep him safe. 'How do I know you'll keep your side of the bargain?'

His lips sucked on her earlobe as he rotated her small pearl earring around on his tongue. 'How do I know you'll keep to yours?'

It took all of Marta's control not to tear herself away from him. 'Where do you suggest our assignation takes place, Krios?' She felt his hand slide around her ribcage and cup her right breast. Adrenaline coursed through her veins as her brain prepared for flight but she gritted her teeth and remained where she was.

'The choice is entirely yours, my dear.'

In that second she recalled everything she knew about the man caressing her body and felt revenge like a powerful aphrodisiac. Her words, when them came seemed from a distance, the tone conciliatory. 'What about your villa?'

'What time can I expect you?' replied Krios, his mind wrapped around carnal pursuits, never questioning how Marta knew Evadne was away.

Christos Nicolaides stood on the police station balcony looking out at the clock tower trying to find some composure. The meeting with Krios Kakos had shattered everything he held dear. He was a simple man with simple values and totally unequipped to handle the situation he now found himself in. Rubbing his fingers on the bridge of his nose he decided to deal with one thing at a time and moved in robotic fashion towards the office, his conscience placed on hold.

Alex sat in his chair, arms spread wide as the sergeant made an appearance. He turned and stared into the eyes of a man who looked as if he'd been to hell and back.

'You're suspended,' was the sum total of the sergeant's words.

Alex rose from his chair and moved away from the desk. 'Says who?'

'Says Chief Kakos.' Christos moved into the vacated chair and began to rearrange the pencils on the desk top.

Alex looked down at Christos, distaste written across his features then leant across the desk invading the sergeant's personal space. 'If you had any guts, Christos, you would stand up to that bastard.' He straightened and dropped the cell keys into his boss's hand and walked out, his departure lost on his superior who was battling with his own inner demons.

Panayiotis and Rosa collected food, drink, blankets and warm clothing from Villa Fabrini, piling it all into the back of his truck before returning to Pedi. He had tried to persuade her in broken Italian to stay put in case Marta rang but Rosa refused, determined not to be left on her own.

Back at the dock Panayiotis began unloading his supplies as dusk settled over Pedi Bay, *Arabesque's* hull visible only from the bloom of the arc light over the boathouse door. He climbed aboard and checked his watch, concerned that Marta was taking her time. He stowed everything away then sat at the chart-table committing the voyage to memory but his attention span was short, concern for what was happening in Yialos taking precedence.

'Concentrate,' he demanded to no one in particular. Looking down his list he came to his next job. Check pyrotechnics. The last thing he needed was to be in an emergency situation in the middle of the Aegean and have no working flares. He pulled the grab bags out of the locker by the companionway steps and was about to remove the lids when his eye caught sight of two empty metal clips deep inside the locker on the rear bulkhead.

'Shit!' He grabbed his truck keys, flicked off the battery switch and locked the washboards into place. Leaping over the stanchions he climbed into the truck and drove like a maniac towards the exit for the Chorio.

Phoebe watched him flash by the house and stood on the terrace, waving, hoping to attract his attention but Panayiotis didn't even see her. He had only one thing on his mind. Marta and what she had planned.

Chapter Twenty Nine

Sunday (early evening)

A light was burning above the porch as Marta climbed the steps
of the Kakos villa and stood before the entrance door. Her anger
of the afternoon had mutated into something darker, more
menacing and premeditated. Hatred of Krios had spawned a
resolve within her which chilled her heart and obliterated her
fear. 'You think you're getting my body, Krios,' she whispered
as she gripped the brass door knob. 'Well, think again.'

The door slowly opened exposing a darkened hall, a shaft of
light appearing below the crack of a door at the far end, casting
a wedge of light across the ceramic tiles. Soft music permeated
the air.

Marta moved in silence, her linen bag over her shoulder, her
soft gold pumps brushing the polished surface, her eyes fixed on
her destination. She pushed the door gently with her foot. It slid
open as if on runners.

Krios was standing by the desk, casually dressed in black
slacks and a silver grey polo shirt, the colour accentuating his
eyes and contrasting with his dark hair and tanned complexion.
He's a handsome bastard, Marta thought; handsome and corrupt.

She scanned the room taking in every detail. A room
designed for a man. The dark oak furniture was antique and
solid, the Persian rug, a rich mix of blood reds and aubergine,
the heavy damask drapes in matching hues. A heavy onyx
reading lamp stood on an occasional table beside a bronze shot-
silk wing-backed chair, the green marbled fireplace dominating
the internal wall. She felt daunted by the power of the décor and
clenched her jaw.

Krios's eyes slowly looked her up and down. He then lifted a
bottle of Dom Perignon champagne from an ice bucket standing

on the leathered desk top and poured the fizzing liquid into two frosted crystal flutes. 'Well, Marta, you came. Champagne?' His hand extended into fresh air holding her drink, his chin held high.

Marta left her linen bag by the chair and crossed to where he stood. 'You have style, Krios. This room could have stepped straight out of Vogue for Men.'

'I'm glad you like it, Marta.'

She took the glass from his hand and walked around the desk to the window, looking out into the night. She hadn't eaten since her lunch on *Arabesque* and felt her stomach rumble. 'Oh, I do, Krios, though I admit, I find it hard to believe that a captain's pay can stretch to such opulence.'

She watched him come close through the window's reflection and tensioned her stomach muscles. His ice-cold fingers caressed the nape of her neck chilling her vertebrae. 'Unfortunately, the Hellenic Police Department is not renowned for its generosity, Marta. I have my wife's family money to thank for providing such grandeur.'

An image of a black ledger filled Marta's mind countering his reply as bubbles tickle her nose and the sensual sound of a saxophone embellished the room's atmosphere. 'Giorgos Katsaros, I assume.' She nodded to the mini music-stack in an alcove by the fireplace.

'Mmm,' replied Krios, pressing his lips against her shoulder. 'One of Greece's finest. You seem to know your Jazz, Marta.'

'I should do, Krios, I *own* the Jazz Café.' Her stress on the word "own" was deliberate and appeared to reach its mark. Krios raised his head, drained half the contents of his glass in one go and moved towards the fireplace. 'Why don't we make ourselves comfortable and get acquainted?'

Marta watched his reflection sink into the wing-backed chair, his legs spread wide, his fingers tapping the cushion below his groin inviting company. She slowly turned and peered at him over the rim of her glass, remaining where she was. 'Not so fast, Krios. There's the small matter of Nishan Amato's release first.'

'Ah, Nishan Amato.' His smile was pure reptile. He tilted his head to one side, his eyes locking onto hers. 'Do you want something in writing, Marta or will a phone call suffice?' His hand moved towards the telephone as he raised an eyebrow.

The mention of Nishan's name concentrated Marta's mind. She could imagine him sitting in a locked police cell, alone and scared and felt loathing as a black void deep inside her for his captor. How dare you sit here bartering your libido for Nishan's freedom, she thought, tension grating her teeth together. 'Just ring the police station, Krios, and tell your staff to release the immigrant immediately.' She leant against the window frame, the thump of her heart against her ribs making her diaphragm pulsate.

'And, what reason shall I give?'

'Do you need a reason, Krios?' Marta touched her forehead which was beaded with perspiration and brushed the hair away from her eyes. She ran the tip of her wet finger around the rim of her glass making it hum and tried to steady her nerves. 'Why not tell the truth? The Ethiopian has Italian relatives living in Calabria, but your informant failed to mention this fact . . .' Her sentence hovered as she wondered again who that informant was, '. . . however, I can prove that this is the case so you have no grounds on which to hold him.'

Krios didn't seem to notice the tremor in her voice as he lifted the telephone handset off its base. Marta was having trouble breathing. Needing to do something she lifted the champagne bottle from the ice bucket and went to replenish Krios's glass and heard the line connect.

'Sergeant Nicolaides, Chief Kakos here. There has been a misunderstanding in regard to the African arrested today. I am reliably informed that he is not an illegal immigrant and therefore I want you to release him to Kyría Romano's care.'

There was silence on the other end of the line. Marta held out her hand, determined to check that Krios was speaking to Christos Nicolaides. He shrugged and handed her the phone.

'Is this Christos Nicolaides?'

'Yes, Miss Fabrini, but I don't understand . . .'

'There's no need to understand, sergeant. I will explain everything when I come down to the station in about . . .' she poured Krios more champagne, '. . . well, later. Please inform Nishan Amato that he's a free man.' Marta felt relief like a cool rain shower on a hot day.

Before the sergeant could respond Krios took back the handset. 'That is all, sergeant.' He placed it back in its cradle and looked up. 'Does that satisfy you, Marta?'

She nodded and returned to the desk, amazed at how easy it had been to get her own way. As she placed the bottle in the ice bucket Captain Silvano's warning filled her mind and her hand began to shake. *"Stay well away from Krios Kakos."* She closed her eyes and prayed. Keep me safe, Antonio. Taking a deep breath she turned to face Krios intent on only one thing, revenge.

'Aren't you worried that your wife will walk through the door?' she asked as she skirted the chair. Krios's hand gripped her arm, her elbow ending over his shoulder as she used the chair back as a barrier.

'Not at all, Marta. Right now my wife is in Athens with her ailing mother. I can assure you, we have the house to ourselves.' He lifted her hand to his lips and she felt saliva cover her index finger.

'So,' she whispered into his ear, 'we have all night.' He bit the base of her thumb sending a shaft of pain through her wrist. She squeezed her lips together hoping his libido was now clouding his judgement.

Easing her hand away from his teeth she began running her fingers through his hair and kept her voice low and husky. 'I'm intrigued, Krios. When did your infatuation for me actually begin?'

He leant back into the chair, his head moving from side to side, demanding more. 'Since I first saw you at the Jazz Café.'

Her heart skipped a beat but before she could argue, Krios turned his head and covered her mouth with his in a sensual kiss. Champagne and residue tobacco invaded her taste buds as his tongue flicked across her teeth and down into her throat. She nearly gagged, pulling her head back against his grip.

'Come here,' he groaned, drawing her around the arm of the chair, strength overpowering her resistance.

She could smell his lust like an animal smelling danger. You're playing with fire, Marta, cautioned her brain. She ignored it and dropped to her knees as his hand slid across her right breast. She looked into his eyes and pictured him cutting out newspaper articles as she buried her dead, the image of little Paolo waving to her from the back seat of the Maserati superimposed on his pupils and something inside her snapped. 'That's not true though, is it Krios?' She felt his fingers fumbling with the buttons of her blouse, his mind distracted.

'I don't know what you mean.'

Marta could now smell her own fear. Keeping Paolo's face firmly in her mind she went on the attack. 'Don't lie to me, Krios, your interest in me goes back a lot further than Symi. It started around the time my husband was murdered didn't it?'

'Why do you say that?' Marta felt her blouse slip from her shoulders, her naked flesh exposed to Krios's intense scrutiny.

'Because I've seen your file of press cuttings and the invoice from Izmir for my son's replacement rucksack.'

'You can't have,' he countered without thinking. 'They're locked in my desk . . .' Suddenly his head snapped up, murder in his eyes. She braced herself against the chair as his strong hands gripped her neck, thumbs squeezing her windpipe. 'That was very stupid of you, Marta.' She grabbed his arms trying to pull him away but the more she struggled the more determined he became. Blood began pounding in her ears as she watched Krios's face twist into strange shapes, his teeth bared, his expression one minute perfectly clear, the next through a haze of flashing lights.

'Where is it, your bitch?' he shouted. 'What have you done with it?'

Red lines crossed and re-crossed Marta's retina, her brain screaming for oxygen, blood vessels bursting around her corneas as her hands dropped to the floor. She could feel herself losing consciousness, her world turning black and she knew she only had seconds left. She allowed her head to drop forwards, her body going limp as her dead weight fell into Krios's chest pushing him back into the chair. As his fingers loosened around her throat her right hand shot from her bag on the floor, her body flexed away from his body and she thrust a live Taser deep into his groin. Krios arched backwards as 500,000 volts seared through his guts, then fell back into the chair clutching his chest.

Marta stood over him, the stun-gun still in her right hand and gulped air, hatred like venom coursing through her veins. 'That was for Antonio, you bastard,' she whispered through cracked vocal cords, 'and this is for Paolo.' With premeditated precision she thrust the Taser into his groin once more and watched as his eyes rolled into the back of their sockets, his head dropped to one side and his body sagged, all control gone.

She was trembling from head to toe but some inner strength made her go on. Keeping her eyes on Krios's prostrate body she slowly picked up her bag from the floor and backed towards the study door pulling her blouse back into place. Her revenge was complete, now all she wanted was to rescue Nishan from the clutches of the Greek police, get him aboard *Arabesque* and escape to Italy.

Chapter Thirty

Sunday (late evening)

Marta walked into the police station minutes later. Christos rose to meet her, his skin the colour of tripe.

'I've come to collect Nishan,' she croaked, looking around the office.

'But, Miss Fabrini, he's not here, I tried to tell you that on the phone.'

Marta felt a steel band encase her ribcage, recalling Kakos pulling the handset out of her hand before she could listen to the sergeant's words. 'What do you mean, he's not here?' Her voice sounded hollow.

'Chief Kakos took him away earlier.'

'Took him?' Marta was having difficulty functioning. 'Took him. Took him where?'

'That's classified information,' argued Christos without conviction.

She pushed the sergeant into his chair and picked up the paper-knife lying on the desk, pointing it at his throat. 'Then declassify it, sergeant,' she screamed. 'Nishan Amato is an innocent man and if you want to see tomorrow you'll tell me where he's gone.'

'I can't tell you.' Christos screamed back. 'I can't. Don't you understand? Krios Kakos has sworn me to secrecy. I daren't tell you.' He squirmed beneath Marta's shaking hand as Panayiotis walked through the door.

With two strides he grabbed her arm and pulled the paper-knife from her grasp, quietly placing it back on the desk. 'Why daren't you tell her, Christos?' He gripped Marta by her neck as spittle ran down Christos's chin.

A light flashed on in Marta's brain as she recalled all that Danielle had told her about *Intermezzo*. 'Because, if you do, Christos, Danielle will be exposed as a whore. Isn't that right?'

Any remaining blood drained from the sergeant's face.

'That's right, isn't it, Christos?'

He dropped to his knees and wrapped his arms around her legs. 'Please Miss Fabrini, if you have an ounce of compassion in you, please don't tell my wife. It would kill her.'

Marta knelt and took his face in her hands. 'Christos, listen to me. Whatever Krios Kakos told you was a lie. Danielle is not a whore, she's a very damaged young lady who was gang-raped by eight vile men on a motor-yacht called *Intermezzo* in Thessalona Bay last Monday evening. Kakos deliberately invited her on board for that very purpose. She was drugged, Christos, her drinks were spiked. Her only crime was to believe that wealthy people have more fun and she wanted a slice of it. What she got were eight stitches, vicious bruising and mental trauma which will take years of counselling to put right. If you don't believe me, ring Evadne Kakos at the Hotel Grand Bretagne in Athens where she and Danielle are staying tonight and she will confirm everything I've said.'

Christos looked into her eyes desperately wanting to believe her then shook his head. 'No, that can't be right. Chief Kakos told me she charged two-hundred-thousand drachmas for her services.' He could hardly get the words out.

'That is also a lie, sergeant. If she was a whore, she would have been charging a great deal more than that for the services rendered, believe me.'

Panayiotis stared at Marta, shocked at her apparent knowledge.

'The truth, Christos, is that Danielle was dumped at the Nireus Hotel in the middle of the night, in violent pain. When she came round the next morning Fabio Grigio's pay-off was lying in an envelope on her mat and *Intermezzo* was long gone.'

'That's right, Boss.' They all turned to find Alex standing in the doorway dressed in civilian clothes holding a packed sports bag. 'I heard it from the night porter. He watched *Intermezzo 's* crew carry her to the room and assumed she was drunk. It would seem from what Marta's just said that Danielle was too damaged to walk. The envelope was slipped under her bedroom door as they left. You and your wife thought she had suffered from food poisoning and I didn't think Danielle would thank me for interfering.'

The cry that left Christos's throat was that of a man having his guts ripped out.

Marta watched the sergeant descend into hell. She placed her hands on his shoulders, her face turned to stone. 'Krios Kakos can't blackmail you anymore, Christos. Believe me, he won't be blackmailing anyone ever again.'

Panayiotis shuddered.

'Now, where is Nishan Amato?'

Panayiotis elbowed Marta out of the way and grabbed Christos by his armpits, throwing him into the chair. 'Where is Nishan Amato, Christos?'

There was no answer. Christos's brain seemed to have crashed. Panayiotis shook him violently. 'For Christ's sake, man, where has he been taken? What has Kakos done with him?'

The words when they came were buried in saliva. 'He's on *Poseidon,* with instructions to Captain Kostas to dump him at sea.'

Panayiotis felt Marta sway and only just had time to catch her as she fainted.

Chapter Thirty One

Nishan lay in the stern of *Poseidon* his pupils dilated, hands tied behind his back, ankle pulsating as a second electrical tie held his feet firmly together. Krios Kakos and the Captain Costas had marched him from his cell and dumped him on board as the crew weighed anchor and the ship moved away from the quay, the Police Chief jumping ashore at the last moment. Now the lights of Yialos Harbour were fading from view.

Nishan watched Symi's coastline passing by and knew he had to find a way to escape before the island was lost to him forever. He couldn't swim, he had no life-jacket and he was immobilised but his survival instinct was strong and his mind crystal clear. He had come so far and no one was going to stop him now.

He shuffled to the guardrail out of sight of the saloon and turned onto his stomach, bent his knees and grabbed his left ankle with his hands. The pain was excruciating. His fingers searched for something hidden deep inside the crepe bandage. A small penknife had been in the garage at Villa Fabrini and he'd stashed it inside the bandaging while cowering below the work bench listening to the high-pitched bark of the police dog.

He unwound the crepe and grabbed the knife before it fell to the deck. The blade was rusty from years of neglect and it took some time to pull it out of its casing but when he heard it lock into position he attacked the strap around his ankles. It was blunt but the rusted edge made light work of the plastic and within seconds his legs were free.

He could hear laughter in the saloon, flickering lights from the interior reflecting off the polished chrome stern-rail. Nishan stopped what he was doing and turned to look behind. Symi continued to fade into the night, the Plough constellation shining brightly in the heavens above, the only marker to the island's location.

He sat up and rotated the knife plunging the blade between the palms of his hands and began to saw. Blood dripped off his fingers where the rusty blade cut into his wrist but he ignored it and kept sawing. Seconds passed, his shoulders ached, his mind focused on every thrust until suddenly the tie gave way and his hands parted.

He sucked at his wrist as he crawled to the edge of the saloon door and peered inside. The crew members were sitting, legs sprawled across the coffee table, watching a movie on the big screen, their heads turned away from the stern. Nishan didn't hang around. He slithered to the stairs leading to the swimming platform where the inflatable dinghy sat on its chocks. Once there he moved around the tender checking the restraining straps trying to feel in the darkness how these unclipped.

He counted four in total. One at the bow and two at the stern attached to 'D' rings in the deck and one running across the width of the dinghy, all using carbine hooks and tensioning buckles. He tried to release the bow strap but his fingers felt numb from a lack of circulation and he had to massage each finger to get feeling back to the tips. He heard the crew laugh again and prayed the skipper stayed in the wheelhouse long enough for him to make his escape.

Pushing hard on the first buckle with his thumbs he loosened the webbing at the bow and undid the hook. He repeated this at the stern then leant across the pontoon to tackle the last strap. It wouldn't budge. He pulled the penknife out of his jeans and tried to cut the webbing but the blade made as much impression as a feather on glass. He crouched below the dinghy trying to think of another alternative then realised that he could release the hooks if he straddled the rubber pontoon and pushed down hard with the full weight of his body. It worked and the dinghy was free of its restraints.

Launching the tender was one problem, he thought, but getting himself inside it was another. He could easily lose the dinghy in the stern wash before being able to jump aboard. He examined the rope attached to the tender's bow for use when tying it to a dinghy dock and then at his penknife. He knelt in the dark and began to cut through the rope close to the bow leaving only two strands intact then tied the other end of the rope to a cleat on the swimming platform. He now had to lift the dinghy off its chocks and slide it into the water without attracting the attention of the crew. What he needed was a diversion.

The engine room door behind him was unlocked. He quietly slid it aside, the engine decibels rising from the two Caterpillar diesel engines within. In the dark he could just see the outline of a fuel canister sitting by the door and unscrewed the cap. He shot back, his head reeling. Nishan had no idea why the canister was there but knew the contents would be ideal for his purposes if only he had some way to ignite it.

Poseidon continued east at a steady ten knots, ploughing through the water taking him further and further away from his guarantee of a better life. He screwed up his eyes, gritted his teeth and clenched his fists. 'Come on, Nishan, think.'

An image of the first mate lighting a cigarette on the stern gave him the answer. The crew member had thrown the cigarette packet and lighter onto the table when the captain, shouting from the wheelhouse, told him to get on and stow the ropes and fenders. With luck, they were still there. He mounted the stairs like a predator and inched towards the table on his stomach, stretching his arm over the slatted teak surface until his fingers made contact with the cheap plastic gas lighter.

Back in the engine room he checked to see if the lighter worked. The flame illuminated the two large engines and a mass of pipework, all separated by an aisle. He pushed the canister to the far end then rammed his crepe bandage through the neck and soaked the entire mass in petrol. Leaving one end floating, he pulled the wet strip down the canister side and along the aisle to the entrance. It wasn't a real fuse, he thought, but it was a good compromise under the circumstances. His eyes were streaming from the astringent smell of the fuel, his stomach churning as he back-tracked to the engine room door, wiping his hands on his torn T shirt. Praying to St. Christopher, he flicked the lighter, touched the crepe, watched it flame and closed the door.

Nishan knew he only had seconds left. He was a powerful man and his muscles were well toned from years of manual labour. Throwing his weight against the dinghy's stern, his arms wrapped around the transom, he lifted the dinghy off its chock and pushed it towards the water. He ran to the bow and pushed with all his might, jumping in at the last moment, his penknife at the ready. The dinghy leapt about in the turbulent water, Nishan hanging on for dear life with one hand as he slashed at the rope like a madman with the other. As the two strands of the umbilical cord parted a loud explosion shattered the night.

Chapter Thirty Two

Monday (04.00 hrs.)

The throb of *Phoebe II's* single cylinder diesel engine punctured the air as the fishing boat doggedly criss-crossed the Rhodes Channel south-east of Symi.

Panayiotis stood at the tiller watching Marta arcing the beam from his powerful torch across the water, any hope of finding Nishan dying as night gave way to dawn. They had been at it for hours but neither wanted to be the one to give in. If Nishan was out there they had to keep trying.

Earlier he had carried Marta to the boat in a fireman's lift, Alex running alongside taking instructions.

'Drive over to Pedi and tell Phoebe what has happened,' he had ordered. 'Rosa is with her and could have a heart-attack when she hears the news, so be prepared for anything. I'll need someone on the ridge with the VHF handheld in case I need to communicate with the shore. Phoebe knows what to do.'

Alex had nodded. 'What about Marta?'

'Leave Marta to me. She'll come round in a minute and I need another pair of hands to deal with Nishan if we find him.' His voice didn't sound optimistic. He'd stepped across the gunwhale and laid Marta on the pile of fishing nets. 'It's going to be a long night, Alex, and the chances of finding him are remote but we have to try.'

Alex helped to cast off the lines and *Phoebe II* turned towards the harbour mouth. 'Stay positive, Alex,' was Panayiotis's last instruction as they moved ahead.

Christos sat in his chair at the police station trying to make sense of Marta Fabrini's words. Did he believe her? He wasn't sure;

the shadow of Krios Kakos hovered over his head, poised to shatter his family forever.

'If you don't believe me, phone Evadne Kakos at the Grand Bretagne Hotel in Athens.'

Marta's words kept repeating inside his head and Christos couldn't understand what Evadne Kakos had to do with it or why Danielle was in Athens when she was supposed to be in Cephalonia. His jumbled thoughts went round and round, an image of the immigrant floating face down in the Mediterranean Sea lying heavily on his conscience. Finally, he picked up the phone and asked for the operator. It took seconds to get the number of the Grand Bretagne Hotel. He dialled and waited in silence.

A well-educated voice answered. 'Grand Bretagne Hotel, can I help you?'

'My name is Sergeant Nicolaides of the Symi police. I would like to speak to Kyría Kakos who I believe is staying at the hotel tonight. It's urgent.'

'Just one moment, sir, I'll try to connect you.'

In Pedi the night dragged on with no respite. Rosa and Phoebe sat at the kitchen table staring into space, each with their own thoughts, Rosa clutching her rosary beads and praying for Nishan's life. She didn't know what she would do if he died.

Alex had insisted on taking the VHF handheld onto high ground with a flask of coffee and a blanket. He needed to do something constructive to help assuage his feeling of guilt for being complicit in Danielle's deceit. Phoebe and Rosa had no idea what had happened at the police station and he needed time and space to put Marta's revelation into perspective. Time alone on a hillside would give him that opportunity.

He parked above Marathouda Bay and searched for *Phoebe II* out in the channel. Nothing was moving so he sat on the ground and recalled the events of the previous Monday night.

Intermezzo's stewardess had given him the night of his life on Nimborio beach, their gentle love making in stark contrast to Danielle's abuse by Fabio Grigio and his guests. He shuddered at the thought of Christos Nicolaides's daughter in an orgy of drugs and pornographic gluttony, and wondered where it would all end. Was Miriam part of the sham? If so, he had also been duped and the thought made him sick.

Marta had been kneeling in the bow for hours, condensation glistening on her hair. She had gone through two heavy-duty batteries and her fingers were numb but she refused to admit defeat. Periodically she would call out, her powerful voice meeting a wall of silence until her vocal cords gave up completely. 'Even in death, Krios has managed to have the last word,' she sobbed. 'He never had any intention of releasing Nishan, it was all a charade.' She sat and stared into a void of despair.

Panayiotis gently pulled her away from the prow and wrapped her in the warmth of his body. Neither spoke, no words were adequate. He eased the lamp from her fingers and trained the beam on the sea but he knew it was hopeless. Nishan would be another tragedy to add to all the others that had gone before and if Marta had killed Krios, as he suspected, then she would be lost to him too.

His conscience was clear, Krios Kakos had deserved to die, but it should have been at his hands, not at the hands of this brave, beautiful and talented woman. He loved her more than words could say and would fight to his last breath to protect her from a charge of murder. 'Marta.'

She remained silent enclosed in his arms shaking violently, like a small bird with a broken wing. 'Where is it? Marta. What have you done with the Taser?'

Alex was dozing when the VHF sprang into life.

'*Phoebe II* mobile. *Phoebe II* mobile. This is *Phoebe II*, come in please.'

Alex grabbed the hand set and pressed the PTT button. *Phoebe II*, this is *Phoebe II* mobile. Go.' He looked east and saw the sun edge the mountain peaks beyond the Symi Channel.

'Alex, we're on our way home.'

'Positive or negative?' asked Alex, crossing his fingers.

There was a slight pause. 'Negative.'

He had trouble continuing, the hollow feeling of failure creeping through his guts. 'What's your ETA?' he asked, his police training kicking in.

'06.00.' Panayiotis sounded exhausted. 'Alex?'

'Yes.'

'Thanks for being there. *Phoebe II* - out.'

Chapter Thirty Three

Monday (05.30 hrs)

The Monastery's small boat bobbed up and down by the jetty in
Panormitis Bay pulling on its mooring lines. A monk walked
down the steps and climbed aboard, jerking the outboard-motor
into life.

Thirty minutes later he lashed the tiller amidships, cut the
engine and allowed the bow to glide towards the beach, the
chines gently grinding into the sand. He walked across the
mound of hay in the bow and jumped ashore with the mooring
line in his hand and tied it securely to a ring embedded in a rock
above the waterline. He whistled and tiny bells rang out from all
directions as goats heard the call and came running to find their
breakfast.

This was a morning ritual. Seskli, an island at the south-
eastern tip of Symi belonged to Panormitis Monastery and had
been used by the monks for years to graze their goats and to
grow vegetables at the farm near Ayios Pavlos, a tiny chapel
which had been in existence for many centuries. It was said that
St. Paul had stayed on the island to sit out bad weather during
his travels around the Mediterranean and the chapel had been
dedicated to him.

It was a glorious Mediterranean dawn and the monk
transported the hay from the boat to the shore with a contented
heart. When his task was complete he climbed the rise and
walked towards the chapel, intending to pray before collecting
produce from the farm. Looking to his right he noticed a
mangled grey mass floating in the shallows and went to
investigate.

The remains of a tender was impaled on the rocks, the
pontoons punctured and the interior full of water. Droplets of

blood stained the rocks leading from the sea and tracked inland towards the chapel.

It wasn't the collapsed and battered dinghy that disturbed the monk's serenity that morning. It was a body, arms outstretched, head lying to one side covered in blood, sea kelp entangled around the ankles. The monk crossed himself three times, lifted his cassock and ran to the prostrate figure.

Gently turning the body onto its back he searched for signs of life. Three things were immediately apparent. The body was male, he was black and he was a Christian.

Evadne hadn't slept since the phone call from Christos Nicolaides the night before. He had needed her to confirm everything that Marta Romano had said regarding Danielle and *Intermezzo*. Evadne had hesitated, unsure if his daughter was ready to have her innermost secrets broadcast to her parents, but the desperation in his voice convinced her that he had to know the truth. Evadne asked him to repeat exactly what Marta Romano had said, one sentence turning her blood to ice.

"Krios Kakos can't blackmail you anymore, Christos. Believe me, he won't be blackmailing anyone ever again."

She walked to the curtains and pulled them apart exposing Constitution Square in the morning light, the imposing pale yellow Government Building sitting above the wide steps on the opposite side of the main thoroughfare. All was quiet, the odd street cleaner moving between the trees sweeping up the previous night's detritus and the garbage collectors emptying the bins. A local café owner washed the street in front of his premises with a water hose. It looked like any other normal day in Athens.

She felt empty, devoid of emotion. She stood for a long time, letting the daylight seep into her bones, conscious that this day would impact on the lives of everyone she knew, even some she didn't.

The spacious bedroom had an adjoining door. Evadne quietly knocked on it and waited, hearing a rustle of sheets. Danielle was not asleep either.

'Come in.' Danielle's voice was thin and splintered.

Evadne opened the door and crossed to Danielle's bed. 'I have something to tell you, Danielle. Let me finish what I have to say before you speak, then you can tell me what you want me to do.'

Danielle rubbed her eyes and nodded, too physically and mentally exhausted to care.

Phoebe II pulled in behind *Arabesque* and came to rest by the dock. Marta sat on the gunwhale staring into space, her life lacking any meaning. Phoebe took the stern rope from her father and wrapped it around the bollard, working automatically as Alex stretched for the bow line coiled around the forward Samson post.

Rosa stepped aboard and took Marta into her open arms. No one spoke. It was as if time had stood still and no one was capable of winding the clock. Minutes passed. Panayiotis began moving about the fishing boat putting things in order as Alex and Phoebe looked on. When he had finished, the solemn group left the dock and walked in silence along the waterfront towards his empty house.

Once inside, Panayiotis took control.

'Alex, I'm going to drive Rosa and Marta to Villa Fabrini. I would like you to stay here. Phoebe, find some bedding for Alex, he can sleep on the couch. You both need to get some sleep, we all do. On my way back here I'll call into the Jazz Café and leave a message for Phillipe telling him he will have to manage on his own for a few days.'

'You can't drive to the villa, Panayiotis,' said Alex, 'both your cars are in Yialos.'

Panayiotis turned, touching his temple with his hand. 'Of course they are. Right, let's think this through again. Marta, you can use my room and Rosa can take Phoebe's bed, with Phoebe sleeping on the sofa. Alex, run me to Yialos on your scooter. We can collect the vehicles and drive them back here, then we'll both sleep on *Arabesque*.'

No one argued. Panayiotis took Marta to one side speaking softly. 'I'll need the Jazz Café keys.'

Marta nodded and dragged them from her trouser pocket, slipping them into his hand before climbing the stairs, her face a mask of despair.

Panayiotis watched her go then walked onto the front porch and waited for the young police officer to follow when, from somewhere in the background, he heard a phone ring. He wondered who could be calling so early in the day and when he heard Alex refer to Father Voulgaris by name he closed his eyes and leant against the porch wall anticipating more bad news. he last thing he needed at that moment was to be called to his mother's deathbed. His eyes were still closed when Alex put his head around the door and whispered in Panayiotis's ear.

'They've found him. He's at Panormitis Monastery.' The older man didn't react. Alex shook his arm. 'Did you hear me, Panayiotis? The monks, they've got Nishan!'

Panayiotis thought he was crazy. 'How?'

'He had Phoebe's St. Christopher around his neck. It has her name and the word Symi engraved on the back so the Abbott rang Father Voulgaris hoping he would know who she was. Father Voulgaris doesn't have any other details except that Nishan was found dying on Seskli Island by one of the monks.'

Panayiotis suddenly sprang to life and grabbed the phone from Alex's hand. 'Father, Panayiotis Stanis here. Please repeat what you have just told Officer Laskaris.'

Panormitis Monastery was quiet as the Abbott greeted Father Voulgaris and his passengers at the entrance gate. Marta wanted answers to so many questions but the Abbott remained strangely silent as he gently shepherded the party up the steps in front of the Monastery's bell tower and through the arch into the black and white pebbled courtyard beyond. Within the hour it would be crawling with tourists but at that moment it was empty.

Something is wrong thought Marta as a premonition of death gripped her by the throat. Her pulse rate doubled and her stomach spasmed as a panic attack began to take hold. She clamped her jaws together determined not to lose control.

At the door of the Katholikon the Abbott paused and allowed Marta to continue alone. Her knees were buckling as she stood on the threshold, her body choked with premature sorrow convinced she was about to witness Nishan's body lying in a simple wooden casket.

The interior was dark as Marta stepped inside. Three large brass chandeliers hung from the roof above a wide expanse of marble floor. Garlands of large and small silver lamps filled the space between, all strung diagonally across the ceiling, their polished bowls reflecting the pale candlelight. High above, curving around the perimeter of the church, a freeze of saints, painted in muted colours and faded with age, looked down on her.

As Marta's eyes adjusted to the dimness she could see the miracle-working icon of Panormitis, Archangel Michael, mounted behind glass, his wings carved in solid silver, halo and armour interspersed with gold, left arm stretching out beckoning her forward towards the famous two-hundred-year-old wooden iconostasis. There, in front of the sanctuary gate, a lonely figure sat in a wheelchair, his heavily bandaged head bowed in supplication. Marta moved as if in a dream, her trembling hands locked at her breast, her feet silently closing the gap between herself and the praying silhouette.

She saw his head come up, his nose sniffing the air, her perfume filling his senses, and felt her heart fill with joy. He was alive. Her arms enveloped him, her cheek resting against his right ear and she knew their prayers had been answered.

'I thought I'd lost you, Nishan.'

'Marta?'

She took his hands in hers. 'Thank God, you're alive.' Her vocal cords were shredded, her voice ruptured. 'I slew your dragon, Nishan, but I couldn't find a way to bring you home.'

'I find the way, Marta?' he whispered.

'Yes, Nishan, you found the way. I should have had more faith.'

She turned the wheelchair around and pushed him towards two very familiar faces. Rosa and Phoebe traced his progress through liquid eyes and showered him in kisses once close. He lifted the medallion lying on his collar bone and looked up at Phoebe.

'St. Christopher, he keep me safe, Phoebe, like you say.'

Chapter Thirty Four

Monday (09.00 hrs)

Alex stood by the clock-tower in Yialos holding Marta's car keys in his hand and called over to Panayiotis. 'What are you going to do now?'

'I need to leave a note for Phillipe at the Jazz Café and then I'm taking *Arabesque* down to Panormitis Bay.' He opened the truck door and got in.

'Why?'

'If he's still alive, I'm taking Nishan to Italy and by sailing to Panormitis I'll save precious time.'

'But you're out on your feet, Panayiotis. Don't even think about making that journey on your own. Admit it man, you're knackered and you need another pair of hands on board. I've been suspended from my job and I've sailed dinghies all my life. *Arabesque* is just a big dinghy and I could be really useful.'

Panayiotis screwed up his eyes trying to focus on the wheel. He hadn't slept for hours and he now faced a five-day passage with Marta who was in no fit state to help. His priority was to get her out of Greece as soon as possible before anyone started asking questions but he needed to sleep and he couldn't do both. 'OK. Meet me in Pedi in fifteen minutes. We'll sail her round to the Monastery together and then we'll talk about it.'

Alex waved and climbed into the driving seat of Marta's car.

Panayiotis screamed up the hill and left his truck blocking an old gateway, covering the rest of the ground to the Jazz Café on foot. Once inside he made for the apartment and Marta's wardrobe. Pulling the Taser from the bottom drawer, he jettisoned the batteries and placed them in his pocket. He stuffed the weapon inside his trouser waistband, hiding it below his shirt, closed the drawer and left, placing a note on the bar counter. The message was short and to the point:

Phillipe, ring Phoebe at home later today. Marta has gone
away for a few days.
Phoebe will explain all.
Panayiotis.

When he turned onto the waterfront in Pedi, Alex was waiting. 'Park Marta's car in my garage, Alex. I'll leave the truck on the road. Your scooter's in the back.'

'Here.' Alex threw Marta's linen bag to Panayiotis as he opened the car door. 'This was on the front seat.'

Panayiotis lowered it between his knees and slipped the Taser inside, watching the VW Golf reverse off the road.

Thirty minutes later they were motoring out of Pedi Bay and turning onto a southerly heading. Alex took the helm and told Panayiotis to go into the cabin and rest. He didn't argue. In the shadow of the saloon he opened the locker and silently clipped the Taser back into its mounts. He would deal with it later, he thought. Climbing onto the sea berth he lowered his head onto a cushion and immediately fell into a deep sleep.

Nishan lay in one of the Monastery cells watched over by Rosa. Symi's doctor had arrived and examined him thoroughly, confirming that he was suffering from severe concussion and had lost a lot of blood but his injuries didn't appear to be life-threatening.

'Can he travel?' asked Marta, coming through the door.

'I wouldn't recommend it,' replied the doctor, placing the last steri-strip across the gash on Nishan's temple. 'It would be risky for him to be moved for the next few days. What he needs is peace and quiet and complete bed rest.'

Marta was unfazed. She knew that Nishan was made of stern stuff and what they both needed was to get to Italy without delay. 'Would you examine his left ankle, Doctor, Nishan damaged it two weeks ago and I'm not sure if it's broken.'

'I already have, Marta. It isn't, but there is considerable ligament damage. From what I can see it is healing normally and gradually any remaining pain and swelling will go. However, as soon as possible he should have a course of physiotherapy.'

Marta was thankful that his injuries were not as bad as she had feared. He was alive and in Symi, and the passage to Italy was now possible. She left the cell and went in search of help. She needed lots of padding if her patient was to survive a five-day crossing of the Aegean and Ionian Seas and she knew just where she would find it. Walking towards the stairs leading to the first floor balcony she saw a monk strolling through the colonnades and called out. On hearing her request he acted immediately, gathering spare pillows and cushions from the vacant guest rooms and piling them down by the wharf awaiting *Arabesque's* arrival.

Walking back Marta noticed Phoebe and Father Voulgaris sitting in a cloister deep in conversation. She decided not to disturb them and returned to Nishan's cell wondering what the future held. If she was arrested for murder Panayiotis and Phoebe would have to arrange to get Rosa back to Milan and something would need to be done with the Jazz Café. It was all too much for her brain to handle so she clung to the one thing that would keep her sane; delivering Nishan to Luigi Amato.

Arabesque motored into Panormitis Bay around mid-morning and Panayiotis brought her alongside the dock while Alex threw the mooring lines to the monks. He still looked washed out but a couple of hours sleep had partly replenished his energy levels. He nodded to Marta standing by the wall, his silent message passed and understood. What they needed to do now was get away from Symi and out into international waters. What happened after that would be dealt with as it arose.

Phoebe and the priest appeared at *Arabesque's* side. 'Dad, Father Voulgaris and I need to talk to you in private.'

Panayiotis looked from his daughter to the priest trying to read their expressions then jumped ashore and held his daughter by her shoulders. 'Phoebe, please don't tell me that Nishan has died?'

His daughter smiled a watery smile. 'No, dad, he's alive but he's lost a lot of blood and has suffered concussion.'

'Thank the Lord.' Panayiotis turned to Alex waiting in the cockpit. 'Alex, can you help Marta prepare a berth for Nishan in the saloon, and make sure the lee-cloth is pulled free from under the mattress. If it gets rough out there he's going to need it.' Panayiotis took his daughter's arm and walked along the pier, Father Voulgaris by his side. They sat at a table under a tamarisk tree surrounded by tourists drinking iced coffees and soft drinks bought from the Monastery café on the waterfront. Panayiotis dragged his hands through his matted hair. 'Now, what's this all about?'

'It's about gran, dad. Father Voulgaris found her walking towards the Chorio from the Panormitis Road in the heat of the day last Saturday, not wearing a hat. She seemed very agitated and demanded a lift. Her taxi suddenly appeared round the corner and she nearly killed herself jumping out into the road to stop him. Father Voulgaris questioned the driver sometime later and learned that gran had been dropped at Ayia Katerina that morning and, on the return journey, demanded to be taken straight to the police station.'

Panayiotis placed his head into his hands and closed his eyes.

Sybil walked into the kitchen and placed the groceries on the table. She had no need to rush. Evadne Kakos was away in Athens and the Police Chief was at work. It was Monday, wash day, so she packed away the food for dinner and headed upstairs to change the beds before loading the washing machine. She was happy in her work, singing away to herself as she dropped the dirty laundry into a basket and went to the linen cupboard for fresh sheets. The church outing to the Monastery the previous day had been wonderful and the drive to Panormitis Bay a delight, the sun shining off the sea as they passed farms and churches along their route. Sybil smiled as she set the programme on the washing machine and switched it on. Anastasia Stanis had been effervescent all through Sunday, chatting with the monks, waiting at table and leaving a large donation on the collection plate. After weeks of depression this sudden lightening of the humours could only have been the result of one thing, thought Sybil, as she made the double bed. Anastasia must have won the lottery!

She breezed into the morning room and threw open the windows. It was a glorious day and the room needed airing from the smell of the Police Chief's cigarettes. She looked at her watch. Ten past ten. She just had time to air the study, marinate the lamb for the evening meal and hang out one load of washing before returning home in time to put her feet up and watch her favourite midday soap on the TV. Checking for dust on the hall dresser as she passed, she opened the study door and entered. Her scream could have been heard in Pedi.

Evadne and Danielle were sitting in the Police Colonel's office at the Hellenic Police Headquarters on Kanellopoulou Street when the call came through. Marias Kakos replaced the handset and lowered his eyes.

'What is it, Marias?' Evadne instinctively knew something was wrong.

'Miss Nicolaides, would you be good enough to step outside for one moment,' asked the colonel, 'I need to speak to my sister-in-law in private.'

Evadne walked Danielle to the door and handed her into the care of a female police officer then returned to her seat. 'What is it, Marias?'

'It's Krios, Evadne. I'm sorry to be the one to tell you, but Krios is dead.'

Evadne dropped into the chair and gripped the arms, Marta Romano's words to Christos ringing in her ears. 'What? How?'

'Your cook found him an hour ago slumped in a chair in the study. The local police aren't able to confirm the cause of death yet because Symi's doctor is at the Monastery in Panormitis but Sergeant Nicolaides suspects he's had a heart attack. They have secured the scene and he has asked that you return as soon as possible.'

Evadne was now convinced that Marta had had something to do with it. She cleared her throat before looking directly at her brother-in-law. 'Marias,' she swivelled her Cartier watch around on her wrist and checked the time; 'the *Sea Pearl* is due into Symi in fifteen minutes. May I suggest you instruct Sergeant Nicolaides to impound it straight away and have it searched? We can discuss Krios's death on the way to Symi.'

The Police Colonel nodded. 'I'll get a police helicopter organised immediately.' He pointed to the ledger and notebook on his desk. 'These will just have to wait.' He watched his sister-in-law as she tried to maintain a semblance of control. 'I'm so sorry, Evadne. Whatever Krios has done, he's still your husband and my brother.'

Evadne nodded thinking back over the years of misery and heartache. She rose on unsteady legs. 'I need some time with Danielle. Is there somewhere we can talk alone?'

The female police officer showed them into a conference room and quietly closed the door. Danielle ran her finger over the black-topped table waiting for Evadne to speak.

'Danielle, I have just received news from Symi that Krios has suffered a massive heart attack.' Evadne's legs shook and she pulled a chair from beside the table and slumped into it.

Danielle looked across the table in horror. 'Is he . . .is he dead?'

Evadne nodded her head.

'Did he know the ledger was missing, is that what killed him?' Guilt spread across Danielle's face.

'We don't know that, Danielle. Krios had a heart condition and heart attacks run through the male line of the Kakos family. His father died of the same thing some months ago. If it was shock that brought on the attack then, maybe, he'd found out what we were doing. However, I don't think so . . .' Evadne couldn't get Christos's words out of her mind, '. . . either way I won't know anymore until I get back to Symi. My brother-in-law is arranging for a helicopter to take me there immediately.' She looked at Danielle trying to read her thoughts.

'I'm . . . very sorry, Kyría Kakos. I wanted vengeance for what Krios did to me, but I thought he would get a prison sentence not death.' She bit her lower lip. 'Now, all of this,' she passed her upturned palm across empty air, 'has been for nothing.'

Evadne blinked back tears. 'No, Danielle. It was not for nothing. My husband maybe beyond prosecution but Fabio Grigio isn't. You have to go on. Justice has to be done and I will support you to the very end.'

Silence blanketed them both. All Evadne could feel was relief. With Krios's death all the future months of stress and media attention had evaporated like fog on a summer morning. I'm a widow, she thought. A widow, not the wife of a disgraced Police Chief. She pushed her wedding ring up and down her finger. Stop thinking about yourself, Evadne Kakos. Danielle still has a mountain to climb and as for Marta Romano? She didn't allow her mind to even dwell on that subject. 'Danielle, do you want to return to Symi with me?'

The younger woman's sharp intake of breath was not unexpected.

'You will have to return to Athens with Colonel Kakos afterwards, but this is your opportunity to start building fences with your father.'

Danielle collapsed into a chair alongside Evadne and gripped her hands together. 'I don't think I can face him.'

Evadne placed her hand over Danielle's. 'Yes you can, Danielle. There is no better time than now, believe me.'

Nishan was moved into his sea berth on *Arabesque* with great care, arms supporting him as he descended the companionway steps, the doctor hovering in the background. Once his patient was settled to his satisfaction he handed Marta a medical pack.

'You have everything you should need in here. Whatever happens, keep his head and shoulders up and make sure he is immobilised, any violent movement could tear his wound. Get plenty of fluids down him; dehydration is a major concern so I've included rehydration sachets in the pack. Monitor his pulse rate every hour until you think it's stable. When he is awake try and get him to eat to build up his strength and let's hope he doesn't suffer from sea sickness as vomiting is the last thing he needs.' The doctor climbed into the cockpit, wished Marta luck and went ashore, shaking his head, convinced that the voyage was a terrible idea.

Panayiotis was getting impatient to leave, desperate to get Marta away from Symi but she insisted on speaking to his daughter first. He watched them walk away together and wondered what Marta was up to.

Marta pulled Phoebe around the corner of the mole and looked into her Goddaughter's eyes still unsure if this eighteen-year- old student journalist had the ability to do what she had in mind.

'What is it, Aunt Marta? Do you want me to do something for you?' Phoebe searched her Godmother's face for clues.

'Phoebe, do you think you could write a press release about Nishan's story and our voyage to Crotone?'

Phoebe's eyes were on stalks. 'Oh, I . . . I don't know, Aunt Marta.'

Marta sighed. 'It doesn't matter, Phoebe, forget I ever mentioned it.'

Phoebe's chin came up in true Stanis style and she suddenly looked very like her grandmother. 'No, I won't forget it. Of course I can write Nishan's story. But why as a press release?'

'Let me explain. If the DNA test result is positive, I need you to fax a press release to every newspaper and magazine editor in Italy. You must keep it concise and to the point and emphasise my role in the whole thing. If I know the Italian press they will jump at the story and will create so much fuss that the Italian Immigration Department will have no alternative but to issue Nishan's visa before we arrive on Italian soil. Does that make sense?'

Phoebe's smile reached both ears. 'Yes it does. You're so clever, Aunt Marta, and you can rely on me. I won't let you and Nishan down. It will be the best thing I've ever written.'

''Good girl,' said Marta, thankful for the Stanis genes. 'Right, now, we'd better get back to *Arabesque* before your father has a heart-attack.'

Phoebe giggled and began to run down the mole, her hair flying out behind. Half-way along she stopped in her tracks and turned. 'Aunt Marta, why aren't you my mother?'

I don't know, thought Marta, a heavy weight suddenly pressing down on her shoulders. 'Life just isn't that simple, Phoebe. I wish it was.'

Panayiotis was pacing the quay as Marta and Phoebe reappeared. He was finally able to hug his daughter, shake hands with Father Voulgaris and wave a farewell to Rosa. Minutes later *Arabesque* pulled away from the pier and pointed to the west heading for the Aegean. The sun was at its zenith as the yacht motored passed the windmill at the entrance to the bay and turned northwest towards the island of Nisiros.

Marta remained below tending to Nishan's every need like Florence Nightingale amongst the war torn soldiers of the Crimea. Her patient was awake but drowsy.

'Where am I, Marta?'

'You're safe on *Arabesque*, Nishan. Panayiotis, Officer Laskaris and I are taking you to Italy to meet your grandfather.'

He sighed. 'Will he know me?' The question was ridiculous.

'No, Nishan,' said Marta, looking at his bandaged head and wrists. Even your mother wouldn't know you right now.'

He smiled, his lips barely parting then closed his eyes and drifted into a shallow sleep.

Marta touched the St. Christopher hanging round his neck. 'Keep him safe, St. Christopher,' she whispered. 'Keep us all safe.'

While *Arabesque* rode the waves close-hauled in a stiff breeze, a Hellenic police helicopter crossed the Greek coast at Sounion, high above the Temple of Poseidon, and headed out into the Aegean. Danielle sat by the pilot leaving Evadne and the Police Colonel alone with their thoughts in the back. It would take another hour to reach Symi, plenty of time for thought.

Evadne tried to formulate a timeline since leaving Yialos on the ferry the previous morning. She hadn't known then that Marta Romano had been hiding an illegal immigrant at Villa Fabrini, nor that Krios was planning to use that knowledge to snare her and discredit Danielle's father.

The late night phone call from Christos Nicolaides at the hotel had been something she would never forget. His voice had sounded hollow, like a man on death row who had learnt that his final appeal had failed. He hadn't known how to begin, but once he started he couldn't stop. All the events of the day had come pouring out in a confession of tumultuous proportions. She had listened in horror to the lengths Krios had gone to get what he wanted and when she confirmed to Christos that Marta Romano had been telling the truth, her words had left him in a state of utter remorse.

The noise from the helicopter rotor-blades curtailed any private conversation between herself and her brother-in-law so she rested her head against the padded bulkhead and looked down on a group of islands far below, conurbations of white flat-roofed houses dotted across their barren landscapes. What she had to tell him, she concluded, would just have to wait until they reached Symi and closed her eyes, the freedom of knowing that she was single making her lightheaded.

Christos stood by the old police Fiat on the perimeter of the helipad above Yialos and watched the helicopter descend. He held onto his hat as the rotor-blades battered the ground with their strong propeller wash, kicking up a cloud of dust until the engine died and the blades slowly came to a stop. A door opened in the side of the helicopter and a tall man in full uniform stepped out and walked towards him.

'Sergeant Nicolaides. It is Sergeant Nicolaides, isn't it?'

'Yes, sir.'

'Is the *Sea Pearl* secure?'

'It is, Colonel. We found forty kilos of heroin stashed behind the forward cabin bulkhead. The crew are in custody as we speak.'

'Excellent, sergeant. I'll make sure your decisive action in this matter is highlighted in my report. Now, I understand from my sister-in-law that you need time with your daughter.'

Christos looked across to the helicopter and watched Danielle being helped to the ground by the pilot.

'Come along man, show some pride. Danielle has been instrumental in exposing a drug-cartel that we have been investigating for years. Greek society is in her debt and I can personally assure you and your wife that the Hellenic Police Force will be placing a protective cordon around her until the criminals involved are all safely imprisoned. You do know that she must return to Athens with me tomorrow?'

Christos nodded as Evadne walked up behind her brother-in-law. Their eyes locked, recognition passing between them of trauma and loss.

'My husband's sudden death is a shock to all of us, Sergeant Nicolaides, and I am in your debt for containing the situation so well, particularly under such difficult circumstances.'

Christos was struggling to retain his self-composure, but his admiration for Evadne Kakos knew no bounds and he would do anything to make her next few hours bearable. 'My condolences for your loss, Kyría Kakos. A taxi is waiting to take you to the Nireus Hotel. I assumed you would prefer to stay there rather

269

than the villa so I reserved a room for yourself and one for Colonel Kakos.'

'Thank you. I'm very grateful.' She shook his hand and walked towards a taxi waiting on the access road. The pilot followed carrying two suitcases.

'You are a credit to the Hellenic Police Force, Sergeant Nicolaides, and I'm proud to have you as a colleague. Perhaps we could meet at the Town Hall later and you can brief me on all the details of today's events.' Marias turned and saw Danielle leaning against the fuselage. 'Take your time, sergeant. Ring me at the hotel when you are free.' He walked away, leaving Christos and Danielle alone.

They both wore the scars of Krios Kakos's manipulation on their faces, neither capable of understanding the enormity of what he had done to them or how they were to move ahead. Evadne had made it clear to Christos on the phone that his daughter was never to be judged for her actions. She had paid in full for her lack of experience and it was now up to her father to shield her from local gossip and innuendo if Danielle was to return to Symi and continue to live amongst her neighbours and friends without shame.

Christos stepped towards the helicopter, his love for his daughter overcoming any revulsion he felt for what she had been through. Danielle was visibly shaking, her guilt casting a strong shadow between them. Christos would have moved mountains to return his daughter to the young woman she had been only days before but he knew that this was now impossible. He pushed the shadow aside and took her in his arms, raising his head to the heavens.

'Dear Lord, have pity on us. Make Danielle whole again and forgive me for ever doubting her in her time of need.'

Chapter Thirty Five

Panayiotis sat in the cockpit with the island of Nisiros growing ever larger on the horizon. The yacht skimmed across the water, the sails winched tight, and Panayiotis began to relax for the first time in hours. He was back in his element and alive to the sounds of the wind in the rigging, the ripple of the water along the hull and the gentle snores of his passengers and crew below.

At the clinic in Symi the doctor stood back and allowed Evadne Kakos to pass by. He waited for the grief to overtake her but she appeared to have her emotions firmly under control.

She moved into the room where Krios lay on a gurney under a white sheet and analysed her reaction as she stepped towards the body of the man who had controlled her life for over twenty-three years. She felt empty as she lifted the edge of the sheet and stared at her dead husband's face. Krios's body was nothing more than a cadaver, she thought, something that had once been a human being who could no longer harm her. Any trauma he may have felt in the last moments of his life were now masked by his closed eyelids and his pasty china doll skin. She lowered the sheet and stepped away.

'What, in your opinion, was the cause of my husband's premature death, Doctor?'

'Kyría Kakos, your husband was diagnosed with ventricular arrhythmia some years ago and should have been taking Warfarin daily. However, we haven't seen him in the clinic for months and have no recent record of his INR readings. Unless the dosage of Warfarin is monitored regularly there is the probability of the blood viscosity becoming either overly thick, causing a possible stroke or coronary heart-attack, or being too thin leading to internal bleeding . . .'

Evadne cut in. 'Yes, Doctor, I know. So did my husband even though he appeared to ignore it, but what do you think happened in this instance?'

The doctor ran his hand through his hair. 'My professional opinion is that Chief Kakos suffered a severe heart attack, probably brought on by stress or a sudden shock.'

'And the death certificate will reflect this, Doctor?'

'Yes, but . . .' He paused and lifted the sheet exposing Krios's left thigh. '. . . I've noticed four red marks on your husband's inner thigh. Have you any idea what might have caused them?'

Evadne coughed to hide a short intact of breath, Marta Romano's words yet again ringing in her ears. She examined the marks, running her fingers over the reddened skin. 'Yes I can.' She paused then looked directly at the doctor. 'My husband burned himself on the outboard motor of the police tender last week.' The doctor looked surprised. 'I am not an expert, of course, but I think you have to lean over the hot engine to check the oil level.' Evadne checked the time on the wall clock. 'When would be a good time to collect the death certificate?'

The doctor dropped the sheet, his brow furrowed. 'I can bring it to you tomorrow morning. Where will you be staying?'

'I have a room at the Nireus Hotel; you can leave it with reception. Can I make arrangements for my husband's body to be returned to Athens for the funeral?'

'Certainly, Kyría Kakos. Your husband's death will need to be registered with the appropriate authorities but I'm sure Sergeant Nicolaides can deal with any outstanding paperwork on your behalf once he receives a copy of the death certificate.'

'Very well. Thank you, Doctor.' They shook hands and Evadne walked out of the clinic without a backward glance, her husband's body of no further interest.

The wind instrument had been steady at fifteen knots out of the north when it suddenly shot to over thirty-five knots. *Arabesque* heeled violently throwing Alex across the cockpit as the mast angled at fifty degrees and the genoa foot dipped into the sea.

'Panayiotis,' screamed Alex as he grabbed the main sheet, eased it around the winch and dumped air. With less pressure on the main the yacht righted itself but they needed to reef both sails and do it fast before the wind built further. Panayiotis leapt into the cockpit half naked and started the engine as Alex repeated the exercise with the genoa sheet. It was pitch black and the sails were whipping back and forth, flogging in the force of the wind as the men rolled away the foresail.

It continued to strengthen blasting out of the North Aegean like an explosion, tearing up the sea and ripping into any resistance. They turned their attention to the mainsail and motored dead into wind to avoid placing too much strain on the inmast furling gear. Panayiotis hit the autohelm button as the wind came onto his face, the pitching effect of the waves and the noise of the wind lashing the boom making the whole procedure seem chaotic as Panayiotis yelled instructions to Alex.

They worked in perfect accord. Panayiotis wound the sail into the mast reducing the sail area by a third. Water gushed along the scuppers and waves bounced off the coach roof shooting stinging saltwater into their eyes and drenching them as they battled against the sudden Meltemi.

Below, Marta jumped from her bunk and leant over Nishan's lee-cloth, her feet jammed hard against the centre table and hung on with gritted teeth trying to keep him stable as the saloon bucked and reared, the bulkheads vibrating from the continuous crash of the sea on the hull. Nishan stared at Marta in horror.

Once the mainsail was heavily reefed, Panayiotis grabbed the wheel, disabled the autohelm and steered the bow back on course instructing Alex to let out a postage stamp area of genoa. The Hinckley heeled, gathered speed and drove forward on the northerly blow, riding the mounting waves like a true thoroughbred.

This was not the first time Marta had experienced the full force of a Meltemi and instinctively knew when *Arabesque* was back under control. She smiled at Nishan then staggered to the galley and put a light under the kettle swaying on the gimballed cooker as the yacht yawed from side to side. Panayiotis and Alex would need a hot drink and some dry clothes, she thought, so she grabbed her wet weather gear from the locker and, once dressed, donned her life jacket and clipped her lifeline to the buckle. At a twenty degree angle she pulled herself up the companionway steps and poked her head into the chaos of the night.

'Everything allright down there?' asked Panayiotis, standing in his drenched underpants, saltwater dripping off his nose.

'A walk in the park,' answer Marta trying not to laugh. 'A hot drink is on its way. Alex do you want a towel for your neck?'

Alex was saturated and beginning to tremble. 'No thanks, Marta. With luck the skipper will send me off watch sometime soon and I can dry out below.'

'Not until I've put some warm clothes on, you can't.'

'Then I'll stand watch with Alex while you get dressed. He can then make the coffee before crashing out.'

They both looked at Marta as she hooked onto the nearest 'D' ring and stepped into the cockpit, brooking no argument. Panayiotis could have hugged her and moved towards the hatch wondering if she had any idea how he felt. Seconds later a rogue wave smashed into the side of *Arabesque* tipping Panayiotis down the stairwell, his right shoulder smashing against the edge of the chart-table as he crashed to the floor. His scream of agony tore through the yacht splitting Nishan's eardrums. Marta unclipped her strop and leapt into the saloon her feet barely touching the stairs and knelt by his side, hanging onto her sanity by the skin of her teeth.

'Jesus!' shouted Panayiotis trying to move his arm.

'For Christ's sake, stay still,' demanded Marta as she peeled a cushion off the pilot berth and placed it behind his shoulder blade. 'It looks as though you've dislocated your shoulder.'

The blood drained from Panayiotis's face.

'Alex,' shouted Marta. 'I need to strap Panayiotis's shoulder. I think it's dislocated. Can you cope alone?'

Alex locked the yacht onto autopilot and shouted down the hatch. 'If it's a dislocation, I know how to put it back. Can you take over up here?'

Marta nodded. Panayiotis shook his head; the fear of Alex manipulating his shoulder terrifying him. 'Forget it, I'll put up with the pain,' he insisted as a hundred knives tore down his arm.

'Don't be pathetic, Panayiotis, anybody would think you were giving birth.' She turned to Nishan who had been watching all this from the safety of his berth. 'How are you doing, Nishan?'

'I want to pee.'

Marta's eyes rolled to the cabin roof. 'Don't move, Panayiotis,' she ordered and pulled an empty plastic water bottle from the rubbish bin.

'Where the hell do you think I'm going?' Panayiotis countered irritably.

'Shut up.' She fumbled for the kitchen scissors and cut the plastic top away, handing the open ended bottle to Nishan. Can you manage alone?'

Nishan nodded, dragging the duvet from around his legs, leaving Marta free to go on watch while Panayiotis continued to groan by the chart-table.

Alex didn't hang around. 'Drop your arm by your side, Panayiotis.'

'Do you know what you're doing?'

'Just do as I say.' Taking Panayiotis's right arm in a firm grip he raised the lower half until it was at a ninety-degree angle across his patient's chest then instructed his skipper to close his eyes and count to ten.

Panayiotis crossed himself, gritted his teeth and began to count. 'One, two, three, four . . .'

Alex slowly arced the lower part of the arm away from Panayiotis's chest, keeping the upper arm rigid and adding pressure at the shoulder.

'Five, six, seven . . .' Panayiotis thought his arm was being ripped off.

'Eight, nine . . . Oooowww!' The joint clicked back into position, killing the pain, at which point Panayiotis passed out.

'Where did you learn how to do that?' asked Marta watching from above.

'My older brother's a doctor. When he was a medical student he used to practise on me.'

'I'm sure Panayiotis will be delighted to know that. What do we do with him now?'

'We strap up the arm while he's still out for the count, then bring him round and administer pain killers and anti-inflammatories. He'll be fine but he needs to rest.'

'I finish,' shouted Nishan holding up the plastic bottle, steam rising from the open end.

'What did he say?' asked Alex rummaging through the medical kit and pulling out a triangular bandage.

'He wants you to take his bottle.'

Alex turned, registered what the steaming yellow liquid was and stood up.

'Pass it up to me, Alex. Nishan, go to sleep.' Marta poured the contents into the scuppers and let the sea water carry it away then settled down to begin her night watch leaving Alex to deal with Panayiotis and make him comfortable.

The kettle chose that moment to boil, whistling like a banshee. 'Coffee, Marta?' shouted Alex turning off the gas.

'I thought you'd never ask,' came the muffled reply from behind the helm.

The wind continued to howl and *Arabesque* drove fast but comfortably through the waves. Nishan and Panayiotis slept, both cushioned against the erratic rolling of the hull with pillows and cushions while Marta and Alex rotated on a 'one hour on, one hour off' watch pattern throughout the rest of the night, passing the island of Astipalaia and the spit of rock named Anidhros, lost in the gloom some way off on the starboard side.

At ten o'clock on Tuesday morning Panayiotis eased himself upright and disappeared into the head. Various expletives could be heard in the saloon as he attempted to empty his bladder without knocking his shoulder, finally reappearing demanding more pills. Marta sat at the chart-table fixing their position using the callipers.

'How are you feeling?' she asked without looking up.

'Bloody awful.'

'Can you stand a watch? Alex and I are both out on our feet.'

'Where are we?' Panayiotis leant over her and looked at the chart.

277

'I think we're southwest of Ios on our way to Folegandros. We lost the Yeoman plotter during the night along with our GPS signal. Since then I've been plotting our position every hour by dead reckoning.' She rubbed her eyes, fatigue closing in on her like a wet blanket. Her voice lacked enthusiasm. 'Using our heading, I've assumed an average speed of 6 knots and allowed ten percent for drift due to the strength of the wind and waves. If I'm right, we should be somewhere here.' She pointed the callipers at a dot on the chart.

Panayiotis studied the chart then lifted her chin with his left hand and kissed her on the mouth. 'Marta Romano, I love you.' He climbed the stairs leaving his words echoing in her ears, the taste of salt on her lips, then seemed to hesitate on the top step. 'Don't let it go to your head,' he shouted through the hatch, 'I'd kiss Alex if he was awake.'

Anastasia sat by her front door drinking a mug of hot chocolate watching the comings and goings on Syllogos Square. The news of the Police Chief's death had swept through the Chorio leaving the locals bemused and nervous. Her friend Sybil had spent most of the previous day locked in her own house, refusing to see anyone. Neither the police nor Father Voulgaris would be drawn on the subject. Anastasia understood from her neighbour that Evadne Kakos and the Athens Police Colonel had both arrived on Symi by helicopter and had visited the villa during the afternoon.

She was desperate to know if the illegal immigrant from Villa Fabrini had been arrested before Krios Kakos died, but could not ask the officer standing outside the Kakos villa without appearing heartless.

Perhaps, she thought, Sergeant Nicolaides's wife will know what's going on and decided to ring her. She was about to rise from her chair when Phoebe appeared on the square, her face grim. Anastasia puffed out her chest and remained seated, chewing on her bottom lip as she waited for the gate to open.

Phoebe stepped onto the terrace. At first neither spoke then Phoebe opened the conversation.

'Did you visit Ayia Katerina last Saturday, gran?'

'What if I did, Phoebe, it's none of your concern.'

'Oh, I think it is, gran. Did you happen to visit Villa Fabrini at the same time?' Phoebe glared down at her grandmother.

Anastasia began chewing the inside of her cheek. 'Don't be ridiculous, child. What would I be doing at Villa Fabrini?'

'I don't know, gran, that's why I'm asking you.'

Anastasia disappeared into the house, Phoebe close on her heels. 'You seem to have your wires crossed, dear. I never visited Ayia Katerina or Villa Fabrini last Saturday, and I don't like the tone of your voice, young lady.'

'And I don't like being lied to, gran. That's not what the taxi driver told me, nor Father Voulgaris who saw you walking back down the main road from that direction last Saturday.'

Anastasia huffed, waving Phoebe's words away as if insignificant and began wiping an already spotless draining board.

'I was sitting outside Aunt Marta's music-room with Nishan Amato at that time, gran.' She paused. 'You saw us there didn't you? You saw us and reported it to Police Chief Kakos.' Phoebe stood over Anastasia, her chest heaving. 'Didn't you, gran?'

'What if I did?' Anastasia spun round in defiance. 'I went to have it out with Marta Romano once and for all and found you there instead, staring up at some huge black man looking all gooey-eyed. What did you think you were doing, Phoebe? Have you any idea what the neighbours would say if they knew? My granddaughter fraternising with black filth who should be in prison, not enjoying the high-life at Villa Fabrini and not,' she shouted, 'with a member of my family!'

Phoebe stepped back in disgust, unable to believe what she had just heard. 'Perhaps you should have asked me who he was first?'

Anastasia shrugged. 'I didn't need to. I'd seen him in Kambos Square with the other illegal immigrants on the day they arrived. You couldn't miss him he was so tall.'

'For your information, gran, this black filth as you call him is an Ethiopian refugee who lost his father to a guerrilla's bullet and his mother to consumption because there were no drugs to make her better. He was trying the only way he knew how to reach his grandfather in Italy, who he's never met. Aunt Marta found out and was doing all she could to track down Luigi Amato and to bring his grandson home. As for me being gooey-eyed, Nishan Amato happens to have a fine baritone voice and had been singing me an Italian lullaby which his father sang to him when he was a baby.' She paused for breath. 'Why didn't you find out the truth before you went running to Chief Kakos stating that a suspected fugitive was staying at Villa Fabrini? What did you think was going to happen, gran? What was it that you demanded from our notorious Police Chief?'

'I did what any reasonable Symiot would do. I informed him that Marta Romano was harbouring an illegal immigrant. Krios Kakos was delighted to learn of this and assured me he would arrest them both and have them both deported.'

'Well, gran, your scheming little plan backfired. Nishan Amato was arrested, but he wasn't deported. He was shipped out of Symi under the cover of darkness with instructions from Krios Kakos to the ship's captain to dump him overboard and let him drown.' Phoebe paused to let her words sink in. 'I was also at the villa when Chief Kakos came to arrest him. He brought a dog to hunt him down, gran. It could have ripped him to pieces if Nishan hadn't given himself up. How does that make you feel? You have instigated the attempted murder of an Italian

280

citizen who was staying at Villa Fabrini while his Italian immigration papers were being finalised, and if he hadn't insisted on making me hide, you would have caused the arrest of your own granddaughter too. What would the neighbours have said then, gran?'

Anastasia went white.

'I have no doubt the police will want to ask you some questions very shortly as you were one of the last people to see Krios Kakos alive. I assume you know he's dead?'

Anastasia held onto the kitchen sink for support. 'How was I to know what would happen? You can't blame me for the Police Chief's actions and I can assure you he was alive and well when I left him in his study on Saturday night, so don't try suggesting I had something to do with his death.'

'If you had left well alone none of this would have happened. If you had not been such an interfering old busybody, my father and Aunt Marta would not have spent all of Sunday night scouring the Rhodes Channel for a drowning man without success. You're not a Christian, gran, you're a lonely old lady with a vindictive streak to your nature. You're a Judas, gran, and I hate you. I hope you go to hell.' Phoebe crossed to the passage.

'PHOEBE! PHOEBE! Don't leave me.' Anastasia sank to her knees screwing her handkerchief around her fingers, tears flooding down her cheeks. 'I didn't know. I didn't understand. Please, Phoebe. I can't live knowing that you hate me.'

Phoebe stopped by the door, her grandmother's pleas pulling at her heart strings.

'Please, Phoebe. Please understand,' sobbed Anastasia. 'I thought I had lost you. I thought Marta Romano had taken you from me and I couldn't stand it. I didn't mean to hurt anybody. Please believe me. I was missing you. I was missing your father and I didn't know what else to do to get you back.' She sank to the floor, saliva dribbling from her mouth.

Phoebe slowly returned to her side and wiped her grandmothers chin on her sleeve. 'You were never going to lose us, gran. It was all in your imagination. We love you, we always have; we just don't know how to make you see it.' She took Anastasia in her arms and rocked her like a baby as the old lady trembled. 'Don't cry, gran. Nishan managed to reach Seskli where a monk found him; he had lost a lot of blood but he was still alive. He's with Aunt Marta and dad right now on *Arabesque.* They're taking him to Italy. It could have been a disaster, gran, but it wasn't. I wasn't arrested and Nishan wasn't murdered. Do you understand me, gran? It's turned out allright in the end.'

Anastasia stopped trembling and became a dead weight in Phoebe's arms. 'Gran.' She shook her grandmother. 'Gran, please say something.'

'We're going to heave-to,' announced Panayiotis as he appeared from *Arabesque's* saloon, his right arm encased in a triangular bandage. 'We're all dead beat and eight hours' unbroken sleep and a solid meal are the only way we'll get to Crotone without any more serious accidents.'

His crew were too exhausted to comment, taking orders like battle weary troops on a long march.

They were south of Folegandros, sheltered by the island from the heavy seas. With the sails well reefed there was little to do so Panayiotis instructed Alex to tack *Arabesque* leaving the genoa sheeted in on the port side and allow the yacht to settle at sixty degrees off the wind where it would bob up and down in the swell going nowhere.

'OK, Marta, you deal with Nishan and I'll work out our revised arrival time in Crotone.' He locked the wheel and looked at his watch. 'It's now two o'clock. I suggest we crash out as soon as possible and then have a good meal before setting off again around midnight.'

Nishan was awake when they went below. 'Marta.' She placed her fingers on his wrist and checked his pulse.

'Yes, Nishan, what is it?'

He looked sheepish. 'I want toilet.'

Marta was about to fetch the plastic bottle from the cockpit when she realised what he meant. 'Right. Can you stand?' She lowered the lee-cloth and threw the duvet to one side. 'Put your arms around my neck and raise yourself off the bed slowly.'

Nishan felt dizzy as he sat upright and needed a few minutes on the edge of the berth to stop the cabin spinning. He was about to lift himself off the mattress when Alex appeared.

'Leave Nishan to me, Marta. Go and make him something to eat. We could be a while.'

Panayiotis watched the scene from his position at the chart-table as he set his watch to wake him at dusk to switch on the navigation lights and thanked his lucky stars that Alex had insisted on joining *Arabesque*. He had no idea how he and Marta would have coped alone and was eternally grateful for the young officer's help.

Within the hour they were all fast asleep, Marta in the forepeak, Alex on the pilot berth and Panayiotis opposite Nishan in the saloon. *Arabesque* drifted at half-a-knot in a south easterly direction as the sun set in the west and the tricolour lit up the sky above her mast. They were in the middle of the Aegean in a Meltemi with no one on watch but they were too mentally and physically spent to care. The radar alarm would sound if a vessel came anywhere close and as they were outside the main shipping channels Panayiotis judged the risk to be small.

Symi's doctor finished his examination of Anastasia Stanis and placed his stethoscope back into his medical bag. He was beginning to believe his practise was jinxed. He had accepted the post assuming that semi-retirement in a pleasant Dodecanese island would entail overseeing the occasional birth or death and prescribing the odd pill or potion to the elderly. A gang rape, a half-drowned African, a dead Police Chief, a cook with severe shock and now an old lady losing her mind were not part of his plan. He walked out of Anastasia's bedroom and faced her granddaughter sitting at the kitchen table. Phoebe looked washed out, her hair in disarray and her eyes red raw; her happy world in fractured pieces at her feet.

'Will she live?' Phoebe feared the doctor's response.

'My dear, your grandmother is as strong as an ox. Physically there is nothing wrong with her. Her heart is in excellent condition for a woman of her age, her blood pressure is normal and she doesn't have any medical history of dementia or Alzheimer's. I can only conclude that she has had some sort of mental breakdown. One moment she is lucid, the next in a world of her own. I have given her a sedative and recommend that she is not left alone.'

Phoebe nodded.

The doctor wrote out a prescription. 'She will need to take one of these every four hours.' He passed the prescription to Phoebe. 'I will call again tomorrow morning.' He patted Phoebe gently on her shoulder. 'Don't look so worried, Phoebe. Your grandmother can make a complete recovery providing she is kept quiet and without further stress.'

'Thank you, Doctor. I wish dad was here. He would know what to do.' She slid her hands into her trouser pockets and stretched her legs under the kitchen table.'

The doctor paused as he closed his case. 'Can you get a message to him?'

Phoebe shook her head. Not until he reaches Italy. I don't think I can cope on my own.'

'You don't have to, Phoebe. I will get the clinic to arrange for someone to stand in whenever you need it.' He squeezed her shoulder once more then departed.

Phoebe walked into the bedroom and stroked her grandmother's hand. 'Please, gran. Get better. Dad and I would be lost without you.'

Chapter Thirty Six

Marta's spaghetti carbonara tasted superb and the crew demolished it in seconds as the wind continued to howl in the rigging. They were now refreshed and ready to continue their journey.

While Panayiotis swallowed more anti-inflammatory tablets, Alex headed for the cockpit. 'What length of watch are we doing?'

'Three on, three off,' replied Panayiotis placing the blister of Ibuprofen in his pocket and rearranging his sling. 'Hang on; I'll need to help you tack the yacht round onto a south-westerly course.'

'How do I unlock the wheel?' called out Alex, placing his head torch over his hair and moving towards the helm.

'The knob on the side of the wheel pedestal. Turn it anticlockwise.'

'What's our heading?'

'Two-six-four degrees.' Panayiotis turned to Marta. 'Is Nishan well padded, this Meltemi could blow for another two days? All we can hope is that the wind angle veers and we can sail more freely as we approach the eastern end of the Peloponnese giving us less problem rounding Capes Maleas and Tainaron. If we keep up our average speed we should be in Crotone by early on Saturday.'

'We need to arrive in daylight,' pointed out Marta, hoping Phoebe had done as she asked, and stuffed pillows around Nishan's body.

'Then we'll just have to slow down as we close the Italian coast.'

Nishan began to fidget as Marta secured his lee-cloth. 'I want up.'

'What you want and what you're going to get are two very different things. If you're bored, you can always practise your scales. In fact, why don't you sing to us, it would be a damn' sight more pleasant than hearing this constant howling wind?'

Nishan took some deep breaths while Marta crossed to the galley intent on washing up the dinner plates. Softly at first then getting louder, the familiar refrain of '*O Solé Mio*' filled the cabin and escaped through the companionway hatch, the rich velvet tones drowning out the sounds of the Meltemi battering *Arabesque's* mast and sails. Marta glanced across at Panayiotis recalling his declaration of love. He looked up from the chart-table and winked, giving her a warm glow inside. Suddenly, like waking from a long sleep, Marta picked up the song's refrain, her clear operatic voice harmonising with Nishan's perfectly, the familiar song unlocking the chains that had, for so long, bound her in grief.

Out in the elements Alex leant against the coaming and gazed up at the Milky Way, the wind tearing at his hair. He closed his eyes, the glorious sound of two powerful voices rising as one on the crest of a wave flooded *Arabesque's* cockpit as she ploughed on through the night.

Phoebe sat on the pergola terrace at Villa Fabrini wondering where *Arabesque* was and praying that her crew were all safe. Father Voulgaris had insisted on staying by Anastasia's side that morning and told Phoebe to take some time to herself. She leant her head against the wall of the villa and closed her eyes. Minutes later she was in a deep sleep.

'Phoebe,' called Rosa from the kitchen window, 'Phoebe, the fax machine.'

She was out of her chair in seconds, sliding to a stop at the study door as the fax machine spew out its message onto the catchment tray. Crossing her fingers she lifted the sheet. There it was. The DNA results were through. Nishan and Luigi Amato were related. She twirled Rosa around and around in the hall, giggling like a child with a new toy, her face alight with joy.

Rosa grabbed the edge of the chaise-longue to steady herself, her head spinning. 'I take it they're related?'

Phoebe handed the fax sheet to Rosa and opened the front door. 'Yes, Rosa, they are, isn't it wonderful? Now I must do my part.' She ran from the house, heading for the music-room intent on one objective, to leak the news to the Italian press as Marta had asked her to down at the dock in Panormitis.

They would be told in a press release that Marta Fabrini, famous soprano and wife of the murdered Milan Prosecutor, Antonio Romano, was sailing to Crotone with an Ethiopian immigrant who she had rescued from the clutches of the Hellenic police in Symi because he had Italian blood in his veins. Risking life and limb on the high seas she intended to reunite him with his aging Italian grandfather, Luigi Amato who had been a soldier in Addis Ababa during the Second World War. To add spice to the story, Phoebe would mention that Nishan Amato had a wonderful baritone voice which Miss Fabrini intended to have trained at the Conservatorio di Verona where she had once been a student.

Phoebe grabbed her press release from the piano top, bubbling over with excitement and pride and kissed the page knowing that within minutes a facsimile copy would be received by every newspaper editor in Italy.

In Milan, Private Detective Alberto Zappa took his faxed copy of the DNA report across to his desk and sank into a chair. Shaking his head he picked up his phone and dialled the Italian

Immigration Department in Rome, thinking that life seemed stranger than fiction. As the phone rang in some civil servant's office he chuckled. 'You couldn't make it up!'

Cape Maleas on the southeast corner of the Peloponnese lived up to its foul reputation, the seas short and confused, the current strong, the wind bearing down on Arabesque from the high land whipping up the Aegean's surface in a fine spray. Marta remained below while Panayiotis and Alex kept watch, huddled together under the cockpit spray-hood feeling *Arabesque's* classic hull ride the waves as if competing in an ocean race, showing her stern to the rest of the pack and proving to other yacht designers just what a Hinckley Bermuda 40 was capable of. The two men were in their elements. This was boys' own stuff with a hint of danger.

The yacht had continued west cutting through the gap between Cape Maleas and Kithera Island, forty knot gusts trying to strip the yacht of her rigging. Periodically Marta would stick her head through the hatch delivering hot drinks or a sandwich then pop below again like a retreating Jack-in-a-box.

By seven that evening they were off Cape Tainaron and, just as suddenly as it came, the Meltemi blew out like a candle, the wind instrument shooting around the clock and settling in the west at a steady ten knots, leaving *Arabesque* nose into wind, her heavily reefed sails flapping like dying fish.

'The timing couldn't be better,' announced Panayiotis opening the hatch and going below. 'We need to head northwest from here to Crotone. If this wind holds it should give us a gentle passage up the Ionian and a chance to become human again.' He slumped onto the chart-table seat rubbing his right shoulder. 'Nishan, do you fancy some fresh air?'

While Marta turned some tinned chickpeas, a slab of paprika sausage, some chopped tomatoes, onion and garlic and a glug of white wine into a delicious Iberica stew, *Arabesque's* salt encrusted sails were fully unfurled on the starboard side, the autohelm given a new course and Nishan was eased into the cockpit. The wind was being kind, backing further into the southwest giving them a good angle to sail on a close-reach. Everyone breathed a sigh of relief.

'It feels good to be on an even keel,' said Alex as he made short work of his beer, washing the saltwater from his sore throat, his senses picking up the enticing smells emerging from the galley as the sun dropped towards the horizon.

'Have you ever seen a green flash, Alex?' asked Panayiotis.

'I can't say I've even heard of it.'

'Some people think it's all poppycock, but it's real enough. What you need is a clear horizon with no haze and no land. At the split second the last of the sun disappears below the sea there will be a green flash and looking at tonight's horizon I think we'll prove all those sceptics wrong. You'll need your sunglasses, of course, to protect your eyes.'

Marta was summoned to the cockpit to translate for Nishan then rummaged in the chart-table to find him an old pair of Antonio's sunglasses. They sat in silence as the Iberica stew bubbled away on the cooker, their eyes concentrating on the setting sun. Slowly, then with increasing speed, the large orange ball melted into the Ionian Sea until only a sliver remained.

'Anytime now,' whispered Panayiotis.

They all held their breath. Suddenly the sun's rim disappeared in a bright green flash and the sky turned from aquamarine to a soft amber hue. They sat spellbound.

'Wow!' declared Alex breaking the silence, holding up his can of beer. 'That'll give me something to impress the girls with back home. Cheers folks!'

Chapter Thirty Seven

It was just before dawn when Marta came on watch carrying two mugs of steaming coffee in one hand, the other gripping the handrail. She passed a mug to Panayiotis and sat opposite him.

'We're off Marathoupolis Head,' murmured Panayiotis pointed below the genoa. 'You can see the lighthouse flashing three times every twenty seconds.'

Marta waited for the sailor's friend to reappear and counted the flashes. 'We should be out of Greek waters fairly soon then?'

'In about four hours. Did you sleep?'

'Not really. The others are out for the count.' Marta leant back against the coaming and rested her head on the spray hood. Her bottom lip quivered as she looked at Panayiotis, his every feature as familiar to her as her own. He had been her strength for so long, her life-line when she had felt herself drowning in sorrow, and he had never once complained. She sighed realising that he was everything she could ever want but had been too traumatised to recognise it and couldn't believe the irony of discovering now that the man she desired was lost to her because of one moment of vengeance. 'Panayiotis, I need to tell you something.'

Panayiotis raised his hand, palm out, refusing to allow her to speak. 'Marta, I know what you're going to say and I'm sorry. I didn't mean to burden you with my affection; I was just tired, hurting and lonely. Please forgive me, I can't help the way I feel about you but I know I could never compete with Antonio's memory, nor would I want to.'

His remorse only added to Marta's agony. She had taken him for granted for years, too interested in her own grief to worry about what he must have been going through. She desperately wanted to refute his argument but realised that giving him false hope would be cruel. He deserved better than to be trapped by some pointless declaration of love. He needed to be free to meet someone who could return his affection and care for him into old age, and Marta was determined not to stand in his way. 'Panayiotis, don't apologise. I know how you feel about me, and you will always hold a very special place in my heart whatever happens. I treasure our friendship above all else and would never want to lose that.' Her words, said so innocently, burned her like tempered steel.

'Come here,' he whispered and beckoned her over onto his side of the cockpit and wrapped his good arm around her shoulders, a friend in need once more. 'When are you going to tell me what happened on Sunday night?'

Marta wanted to curl up in his embrace and never leave. 'There's not much to tell,' she said, 'he wanted my body and I wanted him dead.'

'Maybe, but did you kill him?'

'I think so. He certainly looked dead when I left.'

'So, what made you do it?'

'I learnt that he was involved in the murders.' Panayiotis's arm went rigid. 'He'd had a copy of Paolo's rucksack made in Izmir on Fabio Grigio's behalf. It was then stuffed with explosives, exchanged for the real rucksack sometime between Antonio and Paolo leaving the apartment that morning and getting into the car, and was then detonated by remote control killing them both. At least, that's what Captain Silvano now believes.' She looked at Panayiotis sideways. 'An eye for an eye, Panayiotis. I killed Kakos in revenge for both that and Nishan's attempted murder, and I don't regret it whatever the consequences.'

Panayiotis stared at the cockpit instruments in a daze. 'Marta, how did you get all this information and why didn't you tell me? I would have dealt with Kakos and you wouldn't now be facing a murder charge.'

Marta settled deeper into Panayiotis's arm, drew breath and began the long sordid tale beginning with the meeting about the Jazz Café's licence and ending with walking into the police station to collect Nishan.

'So, what you're telling me is that my best friend and my Godson were blown to pieces with the help of Symi's corrupt Police Chief and then he died at your hands before his brother-in-law could arrest him.' Marta was too choked to respond. 'Where does Fabio Grigio fit into all this?'

'He's Carlo Cantotti's cousin,' murmured Marta. 'His company built the block of flats which collapsed like a pack of cards killing forty-five people and injuring many more. He used cheap, sub-standard materials instead of those specified in the tender which Carlo Cantotti rubber stamped knowing what Fabio Grigio intended to do. Large amounts of EU money were then siphoned off from the Housing Ministry's budget to their private off-shore bank accounts. When the ground under the flats gave way in torrential rains, the whole scam came to light. We believe Fabio Grigio masterminded Antonio's murder to stop him getting to the truth but, until now, we had no way of proving it.'

'That's why you've hidden the evidence in Ayia Katerina?'

Marta nodded. 'Interpol are now searching for *Intermezzo's* crew member who I saw outside the apartment disguised as an Italian police officer.'

Panayiotis sipped his coffee. 'Did you leave any incriminating evidence at the Kakos villa, Marta?'

Two crystal glasses and a champagne bottle burned her retina as her conversation with Sergeant Nicolaides rang in her ears. 'Yes.'

Panayiotis's heart sank. 'But, surely a good lawyer could claim self-defence?'

'With a Taser?' The idea seemed preposterous. 'We're not in France, Panayiotis. Greece doesn't recognise crimes of passion.'

'There must be some defence your lawyer can use?'

Marta could tell he was grasping at straws. She had had hours to think over every angle of that night and already knew she had no defence. She had murdered Krios Kakos in cold blood and there was no mitigation on earth that would counter premeditated murder. She saw her future in horrific detail. 'I doubt anyone can help me now, Panayiotis, and I'm terrified of what will happen to me in prison. I'm not stupid. If being the wife of Milan's senior prosecutor and a well-known opera singer doesn't precede me, the media hype of the trial certainly will. I'm told prison inmates love a celebrity, particularly a lifer.' She waited for the implication of her words to sink in.

'Stop it, Marta. Stop it, NOW. I can't bear thinking of you in some jail being attacked by violent inmates. I've spent years loving you, caring for you, just being there for you and Antonio would never forgive me for breaking my promise to protect you.'

His passionate outburst compounded Marta's sense of loss and anguish. 'I've made Krios Kakos pay for what he did, Panayiotis, and, God willing, Interpol's investigations, Danielle's testimony and the evidence at Ayia Katerina chapel will put Fabio Grigio away for life. However, the law will prosecute me for murder whatever the circumstances, and there is nothing either of us can do to change that. You have been my rock over the years and I'll treasure our friendship forever.'

The finality of Marta's words had little effect on Panayiotis. 'I refuse to allow Krios Kakos to ruin your life from beyond the grave. Without a weapon, proving anything beyond reasonable doubt will be difficult.' He left Marta crumpled on the cockpit seat and crept below. Moments later, he reappeared with the Taser in his hand and climbed onto the stern.

Marta watched as he stared out beyond *Arabesques's* wake, his right hand raised. 'Please, God,' he shouted above the wind then hurled the weapon into the sea. 'Please, give us a miracle.'

In Italy, the media were buzzing with the story of Marta Fabrini and the Ethiopian immigrant. Archive footage of Marta burying her husband and child were repeated on every TV channel as newspaper editors screamed for copy on the Italian occupation of Ethiopia and the plight of children fathered by foreign soldiers. One Ethiopian correspondent was filmed interviewing the local nuns near to Nishan's village, asking all about his childhood and hearing from Sister Francis how the child had been blessed with a wonderful voice and regularly sang in the choir. A national newspaper tried to get a scoop on the grandfather but Alberto Zappa had closed off any link to Luigi Amato's whereabouts.

All of Italy was talking about the African who wanted to find his grandfather and the famous widowed soprano who had taken him under her wing. Everyone wanted to be present to see Nishan Amato arrive on Italian soil and the Italian Immigration Department knew they could not be found wanting. Nishan's temporary visa was already prepared, his passport only awaiting his photograph.

Luigi and his daughter sat watching developments on TV from the splendour of their secret hotel in the Calabrian hills. Luigi felt excited at the thought of seeing his grandson for the first time and daunted by all the media attention.

Letters of support, offers of marriage and pleas for help from other illegal immigrants poured into Alberto Zappa's home, couriered from newspaper, radio and TV stations across Italy. Sales of Marta's records soared and all leave was cancelled for the Crotone Police Force.

Arabesque covered the remaining two-hundred-and-fifty nautical miles far too quickly for Marta, the hours racing by as the yacht carried her passengers ever closer to their personal destinies. She was now constantly tormented with cruel dreams. Prison staff and inmates persecuting and abusing her as she screamed for Panayiotis from inside a prison cell; Panayiotis happily married to someone else, oblivious to her cries for help as he sailed *Arabesque* into the sunset with some new wife; Krios collapsed in a wing-backed chair, the whites of his eyes showing.

She was exhausted as she wrestled with the enormity of her situation while the yacht continued along her north-westerly course, only the occasional fishing trawler or commercial vessel crossing her path.

Nishan and Alex were not immune to worry either. In Nishan's case he had no idea what life would be like in Italy. His mother had never prepared him for what would happen after he found his grandfather and he didn't know if he would adapt without Marta constantly there by his side. Alex didn't know what his future would hold either. If he could not be a police officer in the Hellenic Police Force he had no idea what else there was for him. As for Panayiotis, he just felt numb.

They all desperately wanted the voyage to go on forever.

Chapter Thirty Eight

Saturday (midday)

Crotone docks were awash with cameras, journalists, anchor men and women, a whole raft of mobile TV units in large vehicles peppered with satellite dishes, and most of Crotone's population, all anxious to see *Arabesque* enter the harbour. Helicopters hovered overhead and vessels of all size and description bobbed up a down on the Mediterranean swell.

Captain Silvano sat in the Port Police office on the dock listening to the VHF radio. So far there had been frequent ship-to-shore traffic but nothing from *Arabesque*. He rubbed his eyes. He'd been up all night going over the facts that were now available.

The identity of the anonymous informant was still not known but Interpol had now visited the shop in Izmir and taken a written statement from the owner about the rucksack. The Turk even produced a photograph of the original with the dimensions written on the back. If the evidence in Symi was safe, Fabio Grigio could now be arrested.

Twelve miles out to sea *Arabesque* was closing the Italian coastline and the crew were all in the cockpit under a warm cloudless sky, each lost in thought.

An hour earlier, Marta had explained what she hoped would be the situation when they arrived in Crotone docks. 'Hopefully, if Phoebe has done her job properly, the press will be there as we step ashore.' She turned to Nishan. 'I want you dressed in clean clothes and clean dressings on your head and wrists. You are going to meet your grandfather in full view of the media and I want you looking your best. Alex, do you have your police uniform in your bag?'

'Yes, but Krios Kakos suspended me from duty. I can hardly appear in Italian newspapers as a Hellenic police officer, now can I?'

Marta looked at Panayiotis across the cockpit. 'Yes, you can, Alex, Chief Kakos is not around to argue. Let's arrive with you as Nishan's official escort. I doubt the Hellenic Police Force will argue with the kudos that they will get from sending one of their own to accompany this particular immigrant to the land of his fathers.'

Panayiotis shook his head. 'You should have been a politician, Marta. You can put spin onto anything.'

Her smile was half-hearted but she made an attempt at levity. 'Panayiotis, I think you should look every inch *Arabesque's* owner. The Stanis good name has to be upheld or Anastasia will never forgive us, so how about getting rid of that stubble and maybe changing into something that doesn't look as if you've been off fishing for five days?'

'What about you, Miss Fabrini?' came Panayiotis's retort. 'You look as if you've been dragged through a hedge backwards. What about the Romano name?'

She had to admit, he had a point. 'How much water do we have left in the tank?'

'Enough.'

'Then, if you'll excuse me, gentlemen, I'm off to have a shower and wash my hair.'

'Shout if you need help,' joked Alex, winking at Panayiotis.

So there they sat, all spruced up with not a trace of the gruelling voyage on any of them. Only *Arabesque* showed evidence of the passage, her dark blue gelcoat, spray hood and chrome work caked in salt as she cut through the waves, fifty degrees off the wind, at a steady six knots.

Panayiotis picked up the VHF and turned to Marta. 'Are you ready?'

Marta had said her goodbyes to Panayiotis in the quiet of the dogwatch when they had had some privacy, her tears drying on the wind. It had been a painful farewell but they were both determined to stay positive. 'Yes, Panayiotis, I'm ready.'

'Crotone Port Authority, Crotone Port Authority, Crotone Port Authority, this is the sailing yacht *Arabesque, Arabesque*. Do you read. Over?'

'*Arabesque*, this is Crotone Port Authority. Good afternoon, Captain, we have been expecting you. Please give your estimated time of arrival and call again on this frequency when you are one mile off the harbour entrance. Over.'

'Crotone Port Authority, affirmative. We expect to arrive in two hours, at sixteen hundred local time. This is *Arabesque* returning to Channel Sixteen – Out.'

Captain Silvano walked over to the phone and rang the hotel. 'Alberto, they'll be here at four o'clock. I'll meet you at the helipad here in the dock area.'

The helicopter rose above the manicured lawns of the hotel grounds and headed south-east arriving over Crotone town at three-thirty. Someone in the crowd shouted, pointing to the black dot in the sky and all heads turned, watching it descend and drop onto the concrete quayside specially cleared for the occasion. TV cameras were focused on Luigi and Teresa Amato as they disembarked and disappeared into the Port Authority office. Excitement was building as hundreds of Italian flags flapped in the breeze.

Nishan's Italian family were introduced to the Port Captain, Captain Silvano and his assistant police officer, then they all settled down to wait for the big moment.

When it came it was in a blaze of glory. *Arabesque* was surrounded by yachts and power boats, many dressed overall as she negotiated the crowded waters at the entrance to the harbour while helicopters buzzed overhead with cameramen hanging out of side doors filming their arrival for immediate television transmission. Nishan and Marta waved furiously, Marta's hidden turmoil masked by her smiles as Alex tied fenders to the guardrails and Panayiotis tried desperately not to run into anybody. A brass band struck up and played the national anthem as *Arabesque's* bow rounded the mole and two Italian Coastguard vessels escorted them to their berth to raucous cheers from the crowds packing the dockside. Uniformed police made a human barrier to stop the crowd pushing forward, one having his hat knocked off in the melee.

Panayiotis eased *Arabesque* alongside the dock and they were made fast by experienced dock workers all eager to do their part. From the Port Authority office five people emerged and walked towards the yacht, the Port Captain and Captain Silvano in front, Alberto Zappa and Teresa either side of Luigi at the rear.

The Amato family stopped fifty yards from the yacht leaving the two uniformed men to proceed alone. Luigi's legs began to shake, Teresa and Alberto holding him firmly by the arm.

'*Buon pomeriggio*, Captain, Miss Fabrini. Welcome to Crotone. May we please come aboard?' said the Port Captain.

The crew stepped aside as the two men entered the cockpit and shook hands firstly with Panayiotis, then Marta and then Alex, leaving Nishan to the last.

Nishan placed his hand over his heart and spoke in rehearsed Italian. 'Good afternoon. My name is Nishan Amato and I'm here to meet my grandfather.'

'Welcome to Italy, Nishan Amato. I have the honour to present you with your temporary Italian visa.' The Port Captain pulled the visa from his jacket pocket and handed it to Nishan. 'Your Italian passport will be ready once we have your photograph.'

Marta watched the formal procedure with tortured delight as Panayiotis stood behind her holding the ship's papers and passports of himself and his crew.

'Miss Fabrini.' Marta turned to face Captain Silvano who was looking grave. 'I must ask you to accompany me to the Port Authority office without delay.'

She shuddered and felt Panayiotis's hand on her arm.

'Certainly, Captain Silvano. May I first hand my charge over to his grandfather?'

'Of course.' He stepped ashore and waited while Alex and Panayiotis helped Nishan onto dry land. Marta was by his side immediately.

'Head up, Nishan. I'm told that your grandfather is the tall gentleman in the grey suit with white hair. Do you have his possessions?'

Nishan nodded.

'And have you remembered the Italian sentence I taught you?'

He nodded again.

'Right, let's go.'

They moved forward, bulbs popping, video cameras whirring, helicopters buzzing, Nishan limping across the open ground towards Luigi. Marta gently pushed him into the empty arena alone where he waited patiently.

Luigi, head held high, walked across the gap, placed his hand over his heart and looked up into his grandson's eyes. '*Selam neh way*, Nishan.'

'*Grazie*, grandfather. It has been a long journey.'

301

Luigi kissed his grandson on both cheeks then clasped him in an embrace as people cheered and waved flags in a collective show of approval.

When they parted Nishan placed his hand in his pocket and extracted a small well-worn brown leather pouch and handed it over to Luigi. In perfect Italian his words were broadcast to every TV and radio station across Italy. 'You left these in Ethiopia with my grandmother. She hoped that one day they would be returned to you.'

Luigi's hands were shaking so much he couldn't open it. Nishan smiled and loosened the leather thong. Luigi slipped his hand inside and brought out a metal dog tag, a small silver locket and a sepia photograph of a young Italian soldier standing against a building in Addis Ababa, his hat at a jaunty angle. He was too emotional to speak, nodding as he turned the photograph over and read the inscription on the back, written so long ago in his own hand.

To the most beautiful woman in Ethiopia
with all my love
Luigi

xx

He placed the dog tag and silver locket over his head and placed the photograph in his breast pocket. 'Thank you, Nishan. Your grandmother would have been so proud of you. She was a wonderful woman.'

Tissues dabbed at eyes across the dock as Teresa stepped forward and took Nishan in her arms. 'Welcome home, Nishan,' she whispered. 'Welcome home.'

The party was ushered into the Port Authority office where they could be alone before the press conference which would take place within the hour. Marta knew she would not attend that or any other press conference and shivered in the day's heat. Captain Silvano's hand on her arm felt like a shackle. Fear gripped her stomach as he escorted her to a separate building, her feet dragging, every cell of her body wanting to take flight.

'Alex, stay close to Nishan,' ordered Panayiotis as he followed in Marta's footsteps, away from the crowds and into the silence of an austere dockside building.

The captain pulled out a metal chair for Marta and looked surprised at Panayiotis's presence.

'It's allright, Captain Silvano. Panayiotis Stanis was my husband's greatest friend and knows everything that has happened. I would like him to be present right now.' She stretched out her hand to Panayiotis who took it in his.'

Captain Silvano frowned but nodded his agreement. 'Marta, I have some bad news for you. Krios Kakos is dead.'

Marta struggled to remain upright.

'I have to ask you one question.'

Her knuckles turned white as she dug her fingers into Panayiotis's palm. Her blood pressure pounded the valves in her heart and for a split second she thought she was going to faint.

'Where did you hide the evidence?'

With lips crushed between her teeth she tried to search for an appropriate response, picturing the Taser lying at the bottom of the Ionian Sea.

'What evidence?' she whispered.

Blood drained from Captain Silvano's face, his voice growing louder as he spoke. 'What do you mean what evidence? The invoice for the rucksack and the newspaper cuttings. For God sake, Marta, you did put them somewhere safe, didn't you?

Marta could feel the captain's anger and frustration across the desk. What had the evidence got to do with Krios Kakos's death? she thought, her brain working on overdrive. 'Yes . . . Yes, of course I hid them. I told you I would. They're inside a picture frame of the Madonna and Child in the chapel of Ayia Katerina above the Vassilios Gorge. Why?'

Captain Silvano's colour returned. 'Because the Greek police won't arrest Fabio Grigio unless they know I have the evidence in my possession, Marta. I'm prepared to bend the truth to make sure we get Grigio into custody, but I refuse to go out on a limb without being sure the evidence isn't compromised.'

'What is it, Marta?' Panayiotis sounded desperate, her nails drawing blood from his palm.

Marta shook her head. She had completely lost the plot and her panic attack was now threatening to cripple her. She held onto her stomach with her free hand, her breathing ragged. 'What has this got to do with Krios Kakos?' she gasped.

'Nothing,' said Captain Silvano, equally confused. 'He died of a heart attack in his home on Sunday night, probably brought on by severe stress. The Greek police think he found out that the ledger and file were missing and the shock killed him. His cook found him on Monday morning slumped in a chair in his study.'

Marta began to shake uncontrollably. Panayiotis grabbed hold of her and held her tight, repeating his question. 'What is it, Marta? Tell me. What's happened?'

Alex was standing outside the Port Authority office when Captain Silvano appeared around the corner and stood aside to let him pass. As he turned he saw *Intermezzo's* stewardess walking towards him dressed in Italian police fatigues.

'Are, there you are, Miriam,' said Captain Silvano. 'Allow me to introduce Sergeant Laskaris from the Hellenic Police Force.'

Miriam locked eyes with Alex and smiled. 'We've already met, Sir. *Kalispera,* Officer Laskaris.'

Alex's mouth gaped open.

Miriam coughed and addressed her boss. 'Sir, Officer Laskaris doesn't speak Italian. Perhaps I should fill him in on what has happened while he's been at sea.'

304

'Yes, of course, but be quick about it. We need to get back to Milan as soon as I've phoned Police Colonel Kakos in Athens and confirmed everything. I'll meet you by the helipad in fifteen minutes.' He opened the office door and paused. 'I promised Acting Police Chief Nicolaides in Symi that his sergeant would ring him immediately on arrival.' With that, he disappeared inside the building leaving Miriam and Alex alone.

When Alex got through to Symi police station, Christos confirmed that there had been no mistake in the Italian captain's words. Marias Kakos had promoted Christos to acting Police Chief in Symi, to be confirmed within the month, and on Christos's recommendation, had also promoted Officer Alex Laskaris to the rank of sergeant, his suspension never even mentioned.

Alex burst out laughing. One minute he was facing disciplinary action for insubordination, the next, promoted prematurely to sergeant on a higher salary and greater benefits.

'I need you back here now, sergeant,' concluded Christos. 'We have the little matter of one impounded drug vessel and five suspected drug dealers to process, plus the usual array of tourists and yachtsmen and I can't do it alone.'

'You can fly back to Milan with us then get a connecting flight to Rhodes,' said Miriam, leaning against the office wall. 'You'll be back in Yialos by the morning.'

The two officers walked towards the helipad, each wrapped in their own thoughts. Finally Alex stopped and pulled Miriam round to face him. 'OK, I get it. Your mother's Greek, your father's Italian and you've been working as an undercover agent for the Italian Police Department to obtain evidence against Fabio Grigio, but, what about me? Was I also part of your little scam?'

Miriam walked on, anxious to get to the helicopter. 'No, Alex,' she called over her shoulder, 'you were not, and if I find out that you've taken any other female to Nimborio beach instead of me I'll report you to your superiors for indecent behaviour not befitting an officer. Now, are you coming or not?'

Panayiotis sat alone in the Port Authority office with the telephone handset to his ear listening to the ringing tone. So much had happened since leaving Symi. He had been granted his miracle, Marta was not suspected of murder and was now free of Kakos for good. Nishan had reached his destination and Alex had been promoted, not sacked. So, why am I feeling so low, he thought.

'Phoebe Stanis.'

'Phoebe, it's dad.' Panayiotis could hear her intake of breath at the other end of the line.

'Dad, where are you? What's happening?'

'It's OK, *Koreetsi mou*, we're in Crotone and Nishan is with his grandfather and aunt as we speak.'

'Oh, dad, tell me everything, every little detail. How's Aunt Marta? What is Luigi Amato like? When are you coming home?'

Panayiotis felt a lump in his throat. 'One thing at a time, Phoebe. I'll tell you all about it, but first I have a message for you from Marta. She is over the moon with the media response here in Italy and is so proud of you. We both are. Now, tell me how things are in Symi and what happened when you went to see your gran?'

Pheobe didn't reply. '*Koreetsi mou*, are you there?'

'Yes, dad, I'm here. I'm afraid gran isn't very well. The doctor thinks she's had a nervous breakdown.'

Panayiotis gripped the side of the desk, a sharp pain attacking his chest. 'Tell me what happened, Phoebe.'

As Phoebe told him everything since his departure from Panormitis Bay her father sat in stony silence, riddled with guilt. 'How is she now?' he asked, his fingers crossed.

'It's hard to say, dad. One minute she is lucid, the next in a world of her own. The doctor is convinced she will make a full recovery but it will take time and she needs lots of help and understanding.'

'Phoebe, please tell your gran I love her very much and I'll be home as soon as I can to look after her.' He thought back to his plea to the Almighty as he stood on the stern of *Arabesque* believing he was about to lose Marta forever and realised what his mother must have been going through over the past months and years. 'From now on we will all go to church together and thank the Lord for giving us a second chance.'

'Oh, dad, do you mean it?'

'Yes, Phoebe, I do.'

'Gran will be so happy. The news is bound to help her recovery.'

Phoebe's voice cracked and Panayiotis longed to wipe away the tears that he imagined were running down her cheeks. 'Don't cry, *Koreetsi mou*, everything will be allright, I promise. Now, let me tell you about our passage to Crotone . . .'

Marta arrived at the press conference in a daze, desperate for answers. If Krios Kakos had died of natural causes, who did the police think had drunk the champagne; what about her telephone conversation with Christos Nicolaides from the Kakos villa and how did they explain the marks on Krios's groin? It was all beyond her comprehension but she didn't have time to dwell on it, the media were waiting.

She settled into a chair between Nishan and Luigi with Teresa further along the table and looked over the heads of the press to where Panayiotis was leaning against the back wall, his face etched in despair. Marta had been told about Anastasia and wanted to leap across the sea of faces to hold him tight, the way he had always held her when life was unbearable, but, as always, something else got in the way.

The room fell silent as the press conference got underway.

'Carlo Monteforte, RAI News. Miss Fabrini, can you tell us how you first met Nishan Amato?'

Marta leant towards the microphones. 'He appeared at the door of the Jazz Café in Symi, late one Saturday night, dehydrated, very hungry and injured.'

'Angelina Riccardo, La Stampa. How did you communicate?'

'With difficulty.' The audience laughed. 'We began by drawing pictures and using my old atlas but Nishan overheard a telephone conversation I was having with Captain Silvano in Milan and understood what I was saying. He asked me why I was speaking Italian. I nearly fell off my chair!' More laughter.

'Lorenzo Volpe, Internazionale. This is a question for Luigi.' The old man looked at the speaker. 'When you learnt you had an Ethiopian grandson, what went through your mind?'

Luigi paused then turned to his grandson. 'I couldn't believe it at first. When I left Ethiopia in 1942, Nishan, I had no idea your grandmother was pregnant. Having now learnt that she had to bring up our son alone, I will never forgive myself for failing to return to Ethiopia, but please believe me, I loved her very much and would do anything today to turn back the clock. Sadly, that is not possible, but your grit and determination to carry out your grandmother's greatest wish makes me very proud, and I feel blessed to have the opportunity to make amends for my past mistakes by spending my remaining years doing whatever I can to make your life secure and happy.'

Marta had a lump in her throat as her eyes found Panayiotis. His limp smile acknowledged her unspoken sentence. She had risked everything to get Nishan to Italy and it had finally paid off.

'Serena Franchino, Corriere della Sera. Miss Fabrini, we understand from the press release that Nishan hopes to become a student at the Conservatorio di Verona, where you trained. What are his chances?'

'His chances are excellent,' replied Marta. 'He has a remarkable voice. For the last three weeks I have been putting him through his paces and remembering my own days as a student.' She smiled at Nishan.

'Does this mean you will be returning to the operatic stage again, Miss Fabrini?'

Marta could hear a pin drop. A ripple of excitement travelled through her body at the thought of the Milan Opera House, the cast of musicians, the applause and knew she missed it all. She looked to the back of the room wanting to gauge Panayiotis's reaction and found an empty wall. 'I have no plans to return to my career at the moment,' she said. 'Meeting Nishan and hearing his story has made me realise that life must go on, no matter what, so we will see.'

'Vincenzo Zocchi, Radio 24 . . .'

Panayiotis walked across the dock shrouded in loneliness and sorrow, hands in his pockets; head bent, oblivious to the stevedores going about their nightly routine. He had watched Marta handle the press like a consummate professional and realised that her three years in Symi had been a mere pause in her amazing life. She belonged in Italy amongst her own people, he thought, and knew he had to learn to live without her.

Arabesque waited patiently alongside the quay. He stepped aboard and stood by the helm staring into the night. 'I've done everything you asked of me, Antonio. Now, release me and let me get on with my life.'

Moving into the cabin, he took a bottle of brandy and a glass from the locker and sat at the chart-table. The amber liquid glowed in the soft cabin lighting as his eyes took in the beautiful marquetry of the saloon woodwork. Paolo looked back at him from the bulkhead. 'Your Mum's going to be allright, Paolo. Rest in peace, little boy.'

He raised his glass and drank the contents in one go then picked up his dividers and looked at the Italian chart lying below his arms. Well, old girl,' he said, thinking of his long, lonely journey home, 'it's just you and me from now.' He idly twisted the dividers along his reciprocal track and sighed. 'I guess another miracle today is more than I deserve.'

Marta basked in all the attention, massaging the egos of the great and the good of Crotone as she worked the room, before saying farewell to Nishan and his new family who were being helicoptered back to their secret hotel in the hills to have a few days' privacy in which to get to know each other. Nishan had held onto her as if his life depended on it.

'Don't worry, Nishan. I'll be back before you know it. We have an appointment in Verona which we mustn't miss. Make sure you train that voice of yours every day.' She shook Luigi's hand. 'It has been a pleasure finally to meet you, Luigi. Take care of my special boy and bring the family to Symi very soon. We have a lot of catching up to do.'

They had flown off into the sunset as Marta stood waving, Phoebe's St. Christopher clasped in her hand, given to her by Nishan as he climbed aboard the helicopter.

'Give back to Phoebe,' he'd said. 'I now safe.'

The film crews were packed up and rolling out of the docks when Alberto Zappa finally found her, standing alone, looking pensive.

'When are you returning to Milan, Marta?'

'I don't know, Alberto. So much has happened to me I can't even think straight right now. I need some time on my own. Time to put everything into perspective.'

'Well, you have my number, and if you find any more African waifs and strays, all you have to do is call.'

She watched him walk away. 'Alberto.' He turned. 'I haven't said thank you.'

'All in a day's work, Marta. All in a day's work.'

She slumped onto a capstan and stared out to sea. The buzz of the press conference had been like a drug, giving her a high she hadn't felt in years. But the audience had now gone and reality struck like a hammer blow.

'Did I kill him?' she asked the night. The evening breeze lifted her hair from her shoulders, the question hovering amongst the midges circling above her head. She closed her eyes wanting to feel euphoric again but was too numb to feel anything. She sat in silence and allowed her mind to wander aimlessly. For three long years, she felt as if she had been cast adrift in a cruel sea, tossed around in the storms of life with no idea where she was heading. Then, from nowhere, Nishan had become her compass and Panayiotis her guiding light and with only dead reckoning to keep her on course she had come home with her sanity intact.

She looked across at *Arabesque* and recalled the words of her bereavement counsellor.

"You'll know when you're well again, Marta. In your mind's eye you'll be able to walk out of the room where your loved ones are resting and into the room beyond. You need never worry, the door between will always be open and you can look back whenever you wish." Sometime during the voyage to Crotone she had walked into that other room. She had finally found closure and was now able to move on. The question was, in which direction?

Panayiotis was slumped over the chart-table, glass in hand, when *Arabesque* gently rocked with the weight of someone climbing aboard. Marta stood on the companionway steps looking down at the tumble of greying curls spread across the chart-plotter and breathed in alcohol fumes.

Carefully removing the glass from Panayiotis's clutches she reached for a cushion and gently slid it under his head and damaged shoulder. 'You're going to have one hell of a hangover in the morning, Panayiotis,' she whispered, running her fingers softly through his hair.

Panayiotis sighed in his sleep, oblivious to her caress. She knelt at his side and kissed his cheek. 'I love you,' she said, 'and my life would be pointless without you to share it.'

Silently closing the companionway hatch she lay on Nishan's berth and dragged the duvet over her legs, exhaustion overcoming all other emotion. This is where I belong, she thought, and this is where I intend to stay, growing old with my Symiot fisherman.

She reached up and doused the cabin lights and drifted into a fitful sleep, her nightmares banished for ever.

Chapter Thirty Nine

Sunday (morning)

The sea was like glass, the contours of Symi's hills mirrored perfectly in the still water. Christos Nicolaides sat in his fishing boat, a baited line over the side and a broad-brimmed hat on his head to keep the sun from his eyes. He'd been out west of the Nemos Channel for three hours and, as usual, hadn't caught a thing. Anyone looking at him in his threadbare shirt and stained shorts would never have believed that this was the island's acting Police Chief, but Christos had been fishing dressed like that every Sunday for years and he didn't see the need to change a habit of a lifetime.

He reached below his seat and pulled out a worn fishing bag, the zip rusty from constant sea spray. Undoing the bag, he slipped his arm inside and pulled out an empty Dom Perignon champagne bottle, two crystal glasses and a set of black and white photographs tied to a paper weight. One by one they slid into the water, sinking into the depths of the Aegean.

Christos knew he would take his secret to the grave.

On the previous Sunday evening, after his phone-call to Evadne Kakos in Athens, he had left the police station and driven to the Kakos villa determined to face Krios with his crime. He found him slumped in a chair in the study clutching his chest, his lips turning blue. Christos stood over the man who had wrecked so many lives, and let his pleas fall on deaf ears.

'Help me, Christos, help me, please.'

Ignoring his boss, and without a shred of remorse Christos pocketed the evidence that could incriminate Marta Fabrini and secreted the black and white photographs of Danielle aboard *Intermezzo* inside his uniform jacket. As he watched Krios take his last rasping breath he nonchalantly dropped the report on illegal immigration into the Police Chief's lap and backed away.

Only four words left the his lips as he closed the study door. 'Go to hell, Krios!'

Epilogue

May 1996

On a balmy Athens night, the Odeon of Herodes Atticus on the south slope of the Acropolis was packed. Tickets had been changing hands at record prices, everyone wanting to be a part of a very special concert.

Famous artists and musicians from around the world had gathered in the unique venue, all appearing without charge, the proceeds of the night going to the Marta Fabrini Foundation for talented Third World children.

The concert was drawing to a close when Evadne Kakos walked out onto the ancient stage and stood by the microphone, the evening breeze playing with her newly cropped blonde hair.

'Ladies and Gentlemen, it now gives me great pleasure to introduce a young man whose lonely journey from Ethiopia to Europe highlighted the plight of talented youngsters around the world and who set the precedent for the Marta Fabrini Foundation. His story is the stuff of legends and his voice is already bringing pleasure to thousands around the world. Ladies and Gentlemen, I give you, Nishan Amato.'

The stage went dark, then a single beam slowly expanded between two Doric pillars. Nishan, dressed simply in a white jellaba, stood at its centre, hands by his side. The Italian conductor raised his baton, waiting for the applause to die down then nodded to his musicians. The opening bars of Andrea Bocelli's famous song, '*Con te Partiro*', filled the auditorium.

Nishan walked forward, breathed in, relaxed his throat and began to sing. His powerful voice reached out across the amphitheatre to every listener, the melody tugging at heart strings as it ascended to the illuminated columns of the temple of Athena, standing majestically above on the summit of the Acropolis.

When he hit the final note the audience were on their feet stamping and clapping, demanding more. Nishan bowed and, once the applause subsided, looked down at the conductor and nodded. The audience settled and the baton was raised once more.

Nishan began again and on reaching the refrain, a pure soprano voice flooded the auditorium. He turned to the source of the sound as the audience spontaneously rose as one and Marta Fabrini appeared through the arch to his right, her crystal clear voice harmonising with his, her long royal-blue gown shimmering in the lights. She stretched out her hands and walked towards her protégé. They both turned to the audience who were cheering with delight, and allowed the melody to build and build across the applause until it carried them both to a crescendo of sound which echoed across the hillside and out into the night.

When the last note finally fell away the audience went wild. Roses skimmed across the footlights landing at their feet, the string section tapping their instruments with their bows, five thousand feet stamping against the Hellenic marble slabs, their cries for more repeated over and over again.

Nishan plucked a rose from the stage, walked forward and handed it to a young woman in the front row then returned to Marta's side and kissed her hand. Phoebe turned to her father and smiled as she breathed in the perfume of the flower. This was the most exciting night of her life. The sky exploded with fireworks in starbursts above their heads as the applause grew ever louder.

Marta scanned the front row. So many familiar faces returned her gaze. Christos and his wife either side of a Danielle, Anastasia between Phoebe and Panayiotis, Luigi, Teresa, Rosa and Alberto Zappa beside Alex, Miriam and Captain Silvano, each clapping for all they were worth.

She looked to the side of the stage and smiled at Evadne. Krios's widow nodded, so proud to be a part of this special night as one of Marta's closest friends.

Nishan leant in to Marta and whispered in her ear as he bowed. 'A man, he call from Dream Work. He want to make me into a film.'

'What did you say?' asked Marta, curtseying to the ecstatic crowd.

'I tell him he need to speak to you.'

Marta met Panayiotis's eyes across the footlights and blew him a kiss. I wonder who they'll get to play the Greek fisherman, she thought.

Acknowledgements

Symi is a Greek Island very close to my heart. Over the years I have sailed into Yialos Harbour, Pedi Bay, Thessalona Bay and Panormitis with my husband on our yacht, Kookaburra, and always found the Symiots to be welcoming, cheerful and generous of their time and advice. For anyone wishing to follow in my footsteps, information and links on visiting Symi can be found on the following pages.

Amongst the many Symiot people who I have met, a special thank you must go to Dina and Ioannis Manolakis from the Platia Café in Yialos Harbour, who helped in my research for DEAD RECKONING as did Dina's father, Hristos, whose many memories have been woven into this story. I am grateful for their enthusiasm for the project and for providing so much background information about island life. What would I have done without you?

Yolanda López Segura from DCD Productions in Menorca also gets my sincere gratitude for her talented, patient and creative input as my graphics designer and Lynn Curtis, who professionally edited the first draft of the novel and whose critique helped move the story along.

To all my close friends and family who supported me in the months and years leading up to publication, I say, 'well done', you believed in me and that means a great deal. As for my husband, David, who never failed to keep me buoyant during those periods of self-doubt and argued his point of view with vigour and sound common sense I can only say, 'Without you, this novel would never have seen the light of day!'

Finally, it is to Symi that I reserve my greatest appreciation. DEAD RECKONING owes its creation to the many experiences I had in and around her shores and from where the kernel of an idea for this novel first materialised. Thank you, Symi, I dedicate DEAD RECKONING to you!

About the Author

Su García was born in Nottingham, England in 1948 and spent her early years dreaming of a career in the theatre, following in the footsteps of her late grandfather, Harry Cassidy (Moss García) whose contemporaries in Variety included such famous names as Stan Laurel, Charlie Chaplin and Vesta Tilley.

One of the author's first professional child appearances was as young Estelle in the Nottingham Playhouse production of Charles Dickens, GREAT EXPECTATIONS, under the direction of John Neville and starring a young Donald Sutherland as Abel Magwitch.

Leaving school at sixteen, she joined the Sadlers Wells Opera Company in London and toured the UK appearing in such operas as Tosca, La Traviata and The Bartered Bride before leaving the stage for a career in aviation.

Her passion for sailing became a lifestyle when, in her fifties she retired and became a live-aboard sailor covering over 50,000 nautical miles and crossing the Atlantic Ocean four times with her husband, David, on their private yacht. Professional articles for the sailing press and regular blogs for family and friends back home followed and, with a backlog of personal experiences to draw on, Su began to write fiction. DEAD RECKONING is her debut novel.

Su continues sailing the Mediterranean from her summer home in Menorca and uses her wealth of experiences to weave intricate plots for her many and varied characters.

facebook.com/Su-Garcia
twitter.com/sugarcia_author
www.baggatellepublishers.com

Other Publications by this Author

Novels
RUM PUNCH

Published by Baggatelle Publishers Ltd
www.baggetellepublishers.com

Nautical Articles

HOOKED ON SYMI
IS BLING YOUR THING
WE SHOULD HAVE USED AN AGENT
STEERING TROUBLE

Published by Baggatelle Publishers Ltd
www.baggatellepublishers.com

Information about Symi

Symi is a member of the Dodecanese group of islands in the Aegean Sea and lies 24 nautical miles to the north east of Rhodes, 3.75 miles from the Asia Minor coast and 255 miles from Athens.

Its climate is dry and temperate, the contours mountainous, its inhabitants engaged in boat-building, tourism, commerce and fishing. Symiots are a very proud people whose island has its own position in Greek Mythology. According to Stephanus of Byzantium, Strabo and Eustathius of Thessalonica, some of its ancient names were Cariki, Aegil, and Metapontis. Its first inhabitants were the Carians, the Leleges and the Phoenicians, and Symi is considered to be the birthplace of the Three Graces, daughters of the nymph Aigle and God Apollo.

For over three hundred years, the Symiots lived under Turkish rule and prospered from sponge fishing, low taxes and enviable health care and education, but the Greek War of Independence in 1821 created a period of instability for the islanders, made much worse when Italy conquered the island in 1912 and the harshest period of occupation began.

Torture, persecution, expatriation and financial decay led to many Symiots abandoning their island home and migrating to far flung countries such as Egypt, America and Australia where their descendants still live today.

In WWII Germany undertook an aerial bombardment of the Chorio and Yialos Harbour destroying many beautiful villas on the Kali Strata and blowing up the ancient castle. Finally, the island was liberated by the Allied Forces in 1945 and, after more years of persecution, Symi finally gained its independence under the flag of Greece on March 7th 1948.

It took many years for the island's economy to recover, the main road between the centres of Yialos Harbour and Panormitis only completed in the 1980's. Even today, Symi does not have an airport, visitors arriving daily by ferry or hydrofoil from either Rhodes or Kos or by private yacht.

Retaining its historical charm and beauty, Symi is an unspoilt jewel of the Aegean where visitors can relax, away from the pressures of city life, amongst the splendid architecture, unspoilt beaches, Symiot culture and Greek mythology.

The following pages provide information on how to get to Symi and links to travel companies, ferry timetables and accommodation sites.

Symi awaits you!

Travel Information to Symi

There is no airport on Symi which is partly why it is so peaceful. Unless you are arriving by private vessel, getting to the island involves a ferry trip either from Greece's main ferry port at Piraeus near Athens or from one of the neighbouring islands.

The following links will give you current information on ferry services to Symi, hotels and apartments in Symi and excursions in and around the island. The tourist season is generally between April and October but the mainland and island ferries operate all year, subject to weather.

Links to Symi
Symi Best
www.symibest.gr
Symi Dream
www.symidream.com
ANES Ferries
www.anes.gr
Dodekanisos Seaways
www.12ne.gr
Symi Visitor Accommodation
www.symivisitor-accommodation.com

Rum Punch

by

Su García

Copyright

'The man who would be fully employed should procure a ship or a woman, for no two things produce more trouble'
Titus Maccus Plautus
(254 – 184 BC)

Chapter One

Terri

It is said that life is stranger than fiction, so when an exciting opportunity to cruise the Caribbean came out of the blue, Terri Gillingham closed her eyes, grabbed it with both hands, and let fate take its course.

Two months later, sitting in a rubber dinghy in the pitch black somewhere on the Caribbean Sea with what could only be described as a miner's lamp on her forehead, Terri decided that fate wasn't all it was cracked up to be.

It all started on a drab May morning. Terri was at a publication meeting on the eighth floor of the British Electricity Board building in Paternoster Square, London, when her mobile vibrated in her pocket. Checking that her boss, Harold Crompton, Head of Marketing, was locked in conversation with the CEO, she eased the phone from her jacket and read the incoming text.

'Congratulations, Terri Gillingham, you are the lucky winner of this month's True Life Movie competition. We are going to whisk you and your family off to the Caribbean for a two-week cruise. All you have to do is contact Adrian Falks at Global Adventure Holidays on 0798532664 and quote this reference number – A56395. Don't delay, he's waiting for your call!

'Terri, how many brochures have we actually printed?' Terri's head shot up as six pairs of male eyes bored into her.

'Uh. . . ten thousand,' She replied, ramming her mobile back into her pocket as, in her mind, she lingered on the stern-deck of a cruise liner sipping champagne.

'Did we know that the Chairman was unhappy with our new BIE logo before we went to press?' Harold's expression resembled that of a recently spayed bull mastiff.

'Logo?' Terri replied, her teeth now leaving their imprint on the inside of her lower lip. 'Er . . . you mean the elliptical world map with the letters BIE across the middle?' Obviously, Terri was playing for time.

Harold's eyes disappeared into his eyebrows as his finger stabbed at the logo on the front cover of his copy of the new, forty-six-page, full-colour brochure promoting the services of the British International Engineering Division. 'The very same, Terri.'

'Well . . . no . . . actually.' A collective intake of breath instantly depleted the oxygen level in the room. She scanned the furrowed brows around the table and felt a Damoclean sword hover over her head at the thought of ten thousand brochures being fed into the shredding machine in the basement. 'A-As far as I know,' she stammered, 'th-the logo was approved at board level last month.'

All thoughts of the Caribbean were now buried beneath a raft of implausible excuses and possible buck passing rotating around in her head. If the Chairman had not been copied into the memo requesting approval of the said logo then she was for the chop. Sweat broke out on her forehead and she wanted the ground to swallow her whole.

Back in her office she grabbed the BIE file from the filing cabinet and extracted the memo, her shaking hands hindering progress. Terri scanned the list of names at the top of the page. Her stomach flipped. Cyril Trowbridge's name was nowhere to be seen. She had completely ignored the Chairman in her haste to get the logo listed in the previous month's Directors' Meeting and no amount of wishing otherwise was going to change that.

Terri picked up the phone and dialled the CEO's PA, hoping to find a way out of her dilemma.

'Chief Executive's Office,' said Anne Blakemore in her crisp, efficient manner.

'Mrs Blakemore, it's Terri Gillingham here in Marketing. I wonder if you could tell me if the Chairman attended the Directors' Board Meeting last month?' She had her legs crossed, incontinence threatening.

'Just one moment, Terri, I'll check.' The line went dead and Terri's lungs stopped functioning. 'Hello, are you there?'

'I'm here,' she choked, her face resembling a beetroot.

'Yes, Lord Trowbridge attended,' the rush of air from her lungs sounded like a Boeing 737 in reverse thrust, 'but he had to leave early for a BBC interview on the Daily Politics Show.'

Terri collapsed into a chair. She knew if she asked the obvious question, Anne Blakemore would become suspicious. Be devious, Terri, she thought. 'I believe the board approved the BIE logo but I seem to have lost my copy of it. Could you let me have a further copy for my file?'

The pregnant pause went on forever. 'Looking through the minutes, Terri, there doesn't seem to be any reference to the logo. Maybe they ran out of time. It often happens with "Any other business".'

Terri could practically feel the sharp whack of cold steel on her neck and pictured her head rolling onto the desk. Bloody hell, she thought, rubbing the skin above her spinal column, her head still firmly in place, how do I explain this to Harold?

The Head of Marketing had already left the building by the time Terri plucked up enough courage to admit to her mistake, which put the whole matter on hold until after the weekend. She walked towards St Paul's tube station, feeling like a rugby player on his way to the sin bin and wondering how she was going to get through the next two days without having a nervous breakdown.

She stepped off the train at Ealing Broadway, reliving the conversation with Anne Blakemore for the hundredth time, willing the outcome to be different and toying with the unlikely notion that the Chairman would have changed his mind by Monday morning and she would be in the clear. Fat chance, she decided, a vivid image of bailiffs repossessing her house upstaging all else. More likely my P45 will be in the post come Tuesday morning and I will be signing on at the Job Centre. The situation didn't bear thinking about so she made a determined effort to forget all about it, stepped out into the road without looking and caused a local cab-driver to practise his emergency stop technique, nose-diving his rear-seat passengers into the glass partition.

Number 45, Deloitte Villas looked forlorn in the evening drizzle as Terri crossed the intersection and walked up the path to her door. She had bought the Victorian semi back in the eighties with a small inheritance from her grandmother and a hefty mortgage with the Woolwich. At the time she had assumed she would be moving on to some exotic residence in Surrey with the inevitable Prince Charming and would keep Deloitte Villas as an investment, renting it out, but, twenty years on she was still single and still there. A number of frogs had passed under the Victorian portal over the years but, sadly, none had turned into anything resembling a prince.

Dropping her bag on the hall table she wandered into the kitchen and checked her answer-phone messages.

'Hi, Terri. Sam here. Are you going to the reunion tomorrow? If so, do you want a lift? Ring me soonest. Bye.'

Terri stared out of the kitchen window onto a border choked with weeds and a lawn full of dents from the impact of numerous dirty footballs kicked over the fence by the two young hooligans next door. She felt depression slide over her like a moth-eaten fox fur.

'Oh, for goodness' sake, Terri, get a grip.' Her words fogged the window in front of her. She shrugged off her mood, opened a bottle of Cabernet Sauvignon and lifted a large wine glass from the wall cupboard.

Terri's ancient, blue Dralon-covered Chesterfield groaned under her weight as she settled in for the evening to consider her options. Can I be bothered to go to the bi-annual reunion for over-the-hill Beagle Air crew? What is the point? she thought. The last time Terri had pushed a trolley up and down the aisle of a BAC 1-11, dispensing duty-free booze to package holiday makers, was 1975. Twenty-five years later it was becoming a tad embarrassing as she struggled to recognise the others beneath a surfeit of excess flesh and dental implants. The old jokes, which had had them rolling around the galley in fits of laughter in their twenties, now seemed immature and gauche nudging fifty, while a litany of various medical complaints merely emphasised their ages and, frankly, she thought, she could do without the saga of the Chief Stewardess's varicose veins again.

'Maybe I'm getting old,' she mumbled as she felt the cushion below her posterior fold around her hips and disappear between two webbing straps.

Draining the last of the wine from her glass, she changed her mind. She didn't have anything else worth doing on Saturday night, so, she concluded, why not? At least it would take her mind off Lord Trowbridge and the BIE logo. She made a mental note to ring Sam within the hour then promptly forgot as her Indian take-away arrived from the local curry house and more cheap red wine accompanied it.

Terri awoke with a rick in her neck as the ten o'clock news was finishing and decided to call it a day. She undressed and stood naked in front of the full-length bedroom mirror, examining her body. It was not a pretty sight. The bags under her eyes were playing a duet with her puffy eyelids, providing little room for her blood-shot orbs to take in her reflection. Wrinkles weaved their way across her neck and upper arms, which, toned in her youth, now flopped about her armpits, probably making it possible for her to sky dive without a parachute. Her boobs were hell-bent on reaching her stomach which, in turn, amply masked where her pelvic bones used to jut out and remained stubbornly inflated even when she tensed her stomach muscles. Grey hairs peppered her brown bush where her thighs joined forces, and the dimples in her backside looked more like a Waitrose crumpet than cheeky dimples.

Directing her eyes to the stretch marks running like tram lines down the outside of her legs, Terri felt depressed. No, she thought, I feel suicidal. Her grannie used to say that she wasn't overweight, she was just built for comfort, not speed; but then her grannie was biased. Terri knew that no amount of exercise, dieting or spa pummelling was going to halt her descent into middle age and pined for the Terri of yesteryear.

'Stop being pathetic,' she told the mirror, running her hand through the bird's nest travesty of her hairstyle. 'Be grateful for wrinkle cream and remember to stay in subdued lighting whenever you're out.'

She picked up her dressing gown and carried it into the bathroom. 'Anyway,' she concluded, 'middle-aged men don't have six packs either. In fact, most can't even see their penis, so why should I worry?' This logic didn't seem to help her mood.

She flopped into bed and flicked out the light. 'Damn',' she muttered into the duvet. 'I forgot to ring Sam.'

334

Chapter Two

Sam

Brompton Road was awash with traffic as Sam stood opposite Harrods in a gale, waiting to cross to her apartment in Pont Street. She was running late and knew that CJ would have arrived before her. He hated being kept waiting, but then he had a chauffeur-driven Bentley to transport him between Knightsbridge and the City while Sam had to struggle with local transport.

Her security card flashed green at the entrance to Beauchamp Villas and she entered the lift alongside a portly lady of the hooked nose and blue rinse variety who was shackled to a brush-on-a-lead, known to its owner as Twinkle, her Yorkshire terrier.

'Excuse me,' groaned Sam as the brush-on-a-lead tried to copulate with her right calf. 'Could you keep your dog under control?' She was not in the best of moods.

The blue rinse sniffed the air and rearranged her ample chest inside her overcoat, refusing to comment. As the lift door opened at the fourth floor the women went their separate ways, a cold stare boring into Sam's back.

Beethoven's Fifth blasted Sam's eardrums as she opened the apartment door, and her heart sank. CJ always played Beethoven's Fifth after a good day at the office and it followed that she was now in for an athletic night.

'Hi,' she called above the strains of the LSO as she dropped her bag on the hall table and walked through to the bedroom, kicking off her shoes by the bed and moving into her dressing room. Minutes later she reappeared in the lounge.

'You're late,' commented CJ, seated on the cream leather settee reading the Evening Standard, a glass of whisky in one hand.

'Umm,' replied Sam, not bothering to elaborate. She poured herself a Campari and Soda from the drinks cabinet and flopped into a chair, wrapping her feet under her left hip. She knew she looked good. A personal trainer, some help with Botox and a diet of salad leaves had delayed her ageing process. Samantha Hutchins was six foot in her stockinged feet and looked ten years younger than forty-nine. Clad nonchalantly in a black silk jumpsuit with matching ballerina pumps on her feet, her long blonde hair piled on top of her head and anchored in place with an amber clasp, she could have given Angelina Jolie a run for her money.

'Do you want to eat in or out tonight?' asked CJ.

'In, I think. It's been a bitch of a day and I really don't feel like going out again.'

'Right, I'll ring down to L'Escargot and order something to be brought up. Any preferences?'

'No,' said Sam, sipping her drink, 'just keep it light.' She never could perform on a full stomach.

CJ picked up the phone by his elbow and began to dial.

'I assume your day went well.' Sam flicked through Elle magazine.

'What makes you say that?' He looked up, his amber eyes below bushy ginger eyebrows undressing her from head to toe.

'Beethoven's Fifth,' she replied, meeting his gaze and trying to raise the energy and inclination for sex. It wasn't easy after twenty-five years. CJ had become as familiar to her as an old shoe over the decades, their long-standing affair feeling more like George and Mildred than Dirty Dancing.

They ate in silence, the scallops cooked to perfection. Sam toyed with her rocket and balsamic salad, a general malaise dulling her appetite. 'Where are we holidaying this year?' Her question hung in the air for ten seconds. She waited, fork hovering between plate and mouth.

CJ seemed to be closely examining the condiment set. 'I'm taking the family to Alaska, whale watching.' He refused to meet her stare.

'Nice,' said Sam, returning her fork to the plate. 'Where will I be . . . in the bilge?' Normally CJ rented a villa for his mistress twenty minutes from the family's exotic holiday resort so that she could placate his libido whenever the need arose. His fingers drummed the table and female intuition told her something was not right.

'I, umm . . . that's something we need to talk about.' Sam's forehead creased as she watched him shift position, his chair legs scraping across the oak floor. 'I'm going to be cruising for most of the time, so . . .' He wafted his palms in the air.

Sam sensed her annual holiday was about to go down the plughole. 'And what about me? Have I become surplus to requirements?'

'No, of course not.' He stuck his fork in a scallop, pinning it to the plate.

Sam's eyes followed his every move, anger bristling just below the surface. The silence was palpable. She knew she was being irrational in picking a fight like this, but there was nothing rational about their relationship.

CJ was a happily married man with two children and five grandchildren and, when not in London, lived in rural splendour somewhere in leafy Berkshire with a Country Casuals wife who showed little interest in his business activities, or where he was during the week. It had never been his wish to leave her and Sam had accepted that fact years ago.

Equally, he had been very good to Sam. As his mistress, she had a generous monthly allowance paid for from his company's coffers, the apartment on Pont Street was in her name and she had a corporate credit card with no limit. Whenever he went abroad on business she went with him, flying first class, staying in five-star hotels and socialising with the world's finest. In return, she was at CJ's beck and call at any time of day or night, 24/7, and had long since forfeited other male company, her lover's possessive nature having seen to that.

However, Sam didn't like change, and losing out on her all-expenses-paid annual holiday in some exclusive location did not go down well. CJ's holiday plans were now messing with her head and her jealous streak was surfacing with a vengeance. Staring through a yellow mist, she felt CJ's hand caress hers as he eased her out of her chair and led her towards the bedroom. It was time to pay her dues.

Lying on her back in the super-king-sized bed, Sam heard the answer phone spring into life as CJ climaxed, his groans masking what her caller was saying. He slid off her naked body and rolled onto his back. Within seconds his snores were bouncing off the bedroom walls, nasal contortions producing a sound like a cracked trombone. Sam watched his nostrils flare and wondered what she would do if ever he croaked while visiting Pont Street. He was in his late sixties and at least two stone overweight having spent a lifetime over-indulging in expensive wines and exotic foods, and taking little exercise other than sex. A sudden coronary at the height of ejaculation was not out of the question and Sam had no idea what she would tell the paramedics if they asked who she was. She eased her leg from under his thigh and decided that the last thing she needed was a media scrum outside Beauchamp Villas and a distraught wife vying for her blood, while her deceased Captain of Industry was wheeled into an ambulance in a body bag. The horrifying image doused any hope of sleep so Sam turned on her side and began to count sheep. Half an hour later she was still counting.

Over breakfast she was still fizzing about missing out on her holiday. 'I thought you hated water?'

CJ continued to butter his toast, head deep in The Times. 'Sorry?'

Sam knew that tone of voice. Apprentices heard it when they were about to be fired by Alan Sugar. 'Nothing.' She poured more coffee. 'What dates are you away?'

'Last two weeks of July, first week of August.' He folded his newspaper, any further conversation on the subject at an end.

'Right,' said Sam, watching CJ glance at his watch, leave his seat and pick up his briefcase.

'I'll see you Monday.' He kissed her on the neck and stroked her left breast. 'Great sex last night, by the way.' The front door clicked shut and Sam was left alone.

She was still analysing their one-sided conversation as she rewound the answer-phone tape from the night before.

'Hi, Sam, Terri here. Sorry, have I called at an inappropriate moment. Whoops, I didn't mean to say that, I meant . . . Oh, hell.' Pause. 'Just give me a ring when you have a mo' regarding the Reun . . . er, thingy. 'Bye.'

Sam walked into the bathroom and poured Jo Malone foaming oil into the bath. Fortunately, CJ would not have heard Terri's garbled message, being otherwise engaged at the time, she thought as warm water frothed and the aroma of gardenias soothed her senses. The Beagle Air reunion was a secret Sam had always kept very close to her chest, as Terri well knew. His mistress fraternising with ex-airline pilots would not have gone down well with CJ and Sam certainly didn't want to rock the boat at this juncture. The reference to boats challenged her equilibrium so she eased herself into the bubbles and concentrated on the positives. While CJ was off whale-watching with his wife, she mused, she would have three weeks in which to do what the hell she liked. The water caressed her nipples as she leant back against the porcelain. 'Mmmmm,' she murmured as she sank below the bubbles. 'Mmmmm, indeed.'

Chapter Three

Terri

John Humphrys was questioning some female Labour MP as Terri's radio alarm clock sprang into life. She opened one eye to stare at the clock. Mistake. Lights flashed across her eyeball and her eyelid clamped shut as her head buried itself below the duvet like a rock crab in sand. The two bottles of cheap red wine with the Madras curry seemed to be gripping her body in a vice. Is it me who's groaning? she thought. Guessing it was, she promised herself for the umpteenth time that she would never do that again.

The power shower didn't help, the needle-sharp jets of hot water shot-blasting Terri's head, giving her a headache. She staggered into the kitchen wrapped in her faded pink track suit, desperately in need of some strong black coffee. Then the phone rang.

'Terri, Sam. Have I woken you?'

'Yes . . .No . . . Well, let's put it this way, my body is downstairs but the rest of me is still prostrate.'

'Too much cheap red wine?' said Sam, annoyingly.

'I will treat that remark with the contempt it deserves.'

'Fine, have it your own way, but I have known you for thirty years, Teresa Gillingham.'

Terri stuck a china mug under the Dolce Gusto coffee machine and pressed the espresso button. 'OK, OK! Yes, I'm a bit hungover. Why?'

'Because, you rang me at eleven-thirty last night. Not a good time as you well know.'

Terri imagined CJ leaping off the wardrobe in Beauchamp Villas and groaned once more. 'Oh, hell, Sam. I'm sorry.'

'So you said, last night. Anyway are you going to the Beagle Air reunion or not?'

Terri watched black liquid splutter into the cup, trying to remember what decision she'd settled on. Needless to say she couldn't. 'Yes I . . . think so . . . how about you?'

'Terri, I'm the one who'll be driving us down to Crawley, remember?'

'Oh, yes.' Total recall was becoming a problem. 'Um . . . sorry, Sam, I'm having trouble with the old grey matter this morning. Just tell me where and when and I'll be there.'

'Right. Six-thirty at Pont Street, and don't be late.' With that, Sam cut the line and Terri felt hot coffee slide down her throat. It was bliss! She was on her second cup when her mobile rang.

'Hello, is that Teresa Gillingham?' asked a male voice with a strong Yorkshire accent.

'Who's this?'

'Adrian Falks.'

Terri was none the wiser. 'Ugh?'

'Adrian Falks from Global Adventure Holidays in Leeds. Am I speaking to Teresa Gillingham?'

'Yes, but . . .'

'Congratulations, Mrs Gillingham. All you have to do is answer the following question and . . .'

'Look, I'm sorry to butt in, but are you trying to sell me something because I've had one hell of a week, it's my day off and I want to be left in peace?'

'Far from it.' His Yorkshire accent was grating on Terri's nerves. 'I'm ringing about the True Life Movies competition. The one you entered by giving the correct answer to the question, "Where is the island of St Lucia?"'

'Did I?'

'Yeeeesss.' Adrian was sounding unsure.

'I don't wish to be rude, Andy . . . '

'. . . Adrian.'

'Adrian, but I think you have the wrong Teresa Gillingham.'

'This is 0798 521 3476, isn't it?'

'Yes, but . . .'

'And you did use this number to text the True Life Movies competition line last Sunday night, didn't you?'

'Did I?' She was beginning to sound like a cracked record. All Terri could remember was waking up on Monday morning with a mouth as dry as a burnt crisp, bags under her eyes which she could have used as barrage balloons and a resolve never to drink on an empty stomach again.

'Yes, you did, and you're the lucky winner. What do you say to that?'

Her mouth opened but nothing came out.

'Hello, are you there?'

Terri hit the espresso button once more and tried to concentrate. 'Yes, sorry. What were you saying?'

'All you have to do is answer the following question correctly and the prize is yours.' He sounded like Chris Tarrant in Who Wants to Be a Millionaire. 'Now, you will have received a text with a reference number. Can you tell me what it is?'

An image of the dreaded publication meeting flashed across Terri's retina, her mobile vibrating in her pocket. 'Right . . . um . . . hold on.' She scrolled through her messages. Flicking a few buttons, she tapped on the relevant text. 'Hi, Alan . . .'

'Adrian.'

'Adrian.' She'd never been good with names. 'The reference number's A56395.'

'Well done, dear.' He now sounded like Michael Winner. 'All you have to do is decide on a departure date and we can get things moving.'

The espresso was finally reaching the parts other beverages couldn't reach and Terri was on the case, mentally packing her bikini and lying in a cruise liner's steamer chair, browning nicely as the Caribbean Sea drifted past.

'How old are your children?'

'I'm sorry?' She felt as if a brick wall had smacked into her forehead.

'Your children. How old are they?' He waited in vain for a response. 'Your prize is for a family of four, Miss Gillingham.'

Oh, hell, thought Terri, and parried, thinking on her feet. 'When do we have to take this holiday, Ala . . . Adrian?'

'Anytime between June and September this year.'

'Isn't that the hurricane season?'

'Nooooooo.' He was now imitating a Highland cow giving birth. 'Well, not that you'd notice in the Grenadines anyway.'

'But St Lucia isn't in the Grenadines,' she countered.

'True, but Grenada is.' This was all as clear as mud and twice as thick to Terri.

'You start in St Lucia and end in Grenada. You'll spend the majority of your holiday below the hurricane belt.'

'Sounds painful,' she quipped.

Adrian's guffaw rattled Terri's molars and exacerbated her headache. 'I'll get back to you after the weekend,' she said moving the conversation along. 'Must speak to those indoors. You know, check on the cricket fixtures and the kids swimming events.'

'Oh.' The silence was riddle with question marks. 'Right.'

Obviously Adrian didn't do kiddies' activities, thought Terri. He's probably still at the binge drinking stage, she decided, and cut him off with a brisk: 'I'll ring you on Monday. Bye.'

She wandered into the lounge determined to find a way around the problem. This was the first time in her life that she had won anything, if one didn't count the goldfish in a plastic bag that she'd won at the Kursaal in Southend when she was six, and she was not going to let the little matter of a missing husband and kids foul it up.

'Is there such a thing as "rent a family"?' she muttered, as she stretched across the coffee table to pick up her iPad. She didn't have a clue and, sadly, Google didn't either. . .

Rum Punch is published by Baggatelle Publishers Ltd and can be purchased from:
Amazon Kindle
Goodreads
Smashwords
Barnes & Noble
Kobo
Nook
(www.baggatellepublishers.com)

Printed in Great Britain
by Amazon